Contents

For my mother. For my father.

so you go you see
to a city
suspended somewhere
between prayer
and the hanging rope

where most men
have
the faith
but few
have hope

—Barry Callaghan,
excerpt from "On The Abu Gosh Road,"
The Hogg Poems

Introduction
By Dara Horn

You are holding in your hands a rare thing: an act of literary courage.

What is courage in American literature—a culture where either anything goes, or nothing goes anywhere? Too often we are led to believe that the courageous writer is the provocative one. But in a world where there are no more sacred cows, the provocative has become cowardly, obvious. Today, literary courage is something quite different: not a writer's willingness to attack the sacred but to create it.

It would be enough to tell you that Papernick brilliantly captures the Israel of recent years, down to the pictures certain bartenders tape to the mirrors behind them, with an accuracy and depth that few other American writers have shown before or since. It would be enough to tell you that Papernick is provocative in the way that is often shallowly praised—his writing is honest, blunt, sometimes even graphic. But the stories you are about to read offer far more than history, far more than travelogue, far more than provocation. He has built something entirely new here, and also entirely ancient. Readers who have been conditioned by contemporary American short stories—whose moral centers are often predetermined either by history or by the groupthink of the politically correct—should prepare to be stunned.

In "An Unwelcome Guest," the masterstroke of this brilliant collection, Papernick at first lulls us into thinking that we are reading an anti-Zionist allegory. A Jewish man from New York gets out of bed in his Jerusalem apartment in the middle of the night to make himself a cup of tea, only to find an elderly Arab man sitting at his kitchen table, claiming that this apartment was once his home and now he has come to take it back. It's a scenario that feels easy and reductive, almost cheap. But by the end of the next page, when the unwelcome guest pulls out a backgammon board and offers to play the Jewish man for the right to speak—and when the apartment's owner, sensing a trap, feels compelled to accept—the situation shifts, first subtly and then less so, from the allegorical to the unbearably surreal. You are not sure where the story stands until the end, at which point you feel as though you've been flimflammed in the most ingenious way—not by Papernick exactly, but by everything you have been told your whole life that this story was going to be. This is not a story about the Israeli-Arab conflict like any you've read before; in fact, it isn't really a story about the Israeli-Arab conflict at all, except as an example of a much larger problem. It is a story about a historical and psychological illness that has long afflicted the Jewish people and many other people around the world: the deep disease of assuming others to be rational, of accepting someone else's terms for one's own existence, and of forfeiting one's destiny by choosing to live by the rules of someone else's game.

Papernick loves to play this game of three-card monte with the reader, and he lures us in again and again as we keep trying to figure out what he might do next. "The Ascent of Eli Israel," a novella of sorts, fools us as well. Eli Haller, a formerly successful television producer spiraling deep into personal and psychological ruin, receives a prophetic "call" telling him to "Go to the house of Israel"—an apparently divine message received while Eli is astoundingly drunk. Heeding this call, Eli goes to Israel and moves in with his last friend in the world, a newly-religious ex-convict who lives in what he calls the "Wild, Wild West Bank" . . . and a wreck of a man is inexorably drawn into a full-blown psychosis. In the age of Yitzhak

Rabin's assassination by an extremist rabbinical student, this sort of narrative would have been enough.

But not for someone of Papernick's caliber. The tale of the newly-religious nutcase is only the outermost layer of Papernick's work. The story's depth and darkness come from the ancient figures Papernick places in the shadows behind his characters: Ezekiel heeding a beautifully bizarre and divine call, David unapologetically hurling a stone at his thoughtless opponent's head, Abraham armed on a mountaintop, ready to sacrifice a precious child to an unfathomable God. As Eli becomes a shepherd and literally sacrifices animals to the God of his own delusions, Papernick tells us, "He thought of the binding of Isaac, the ultimate act of faith. . . . He could not imagine tying up his son, prepared to slash his throat. What if God did not stop him?" The wife and child whom Eli viciously abandoned stand silently behind this question, but so do thousands of other wives and children over thousands of years. When the story concludes with the words "God forgives you for what you do," one can hear the obvious and terrible irony of a man who confuses divine forgiveness with his own weakness. That much many writers might have given us. But because this is Papernick's story, one also hears the echo of an earlier scene, when a thirteen-year-old Eli attacked a taunting anti-Semitic classmate and his own father "crossed his arms to cover his tattoo, and said in his thick accent, 'Apolochize.'" Papernick's architectural storytelling forces us at every moment to confront both the divine and human limits of forgiveness

Papernick has every opportunity to do things easily—that is, to thoughtlessly satisfy the reader's expectations. He never does. In "For As Long as the Lamp is Burning," about an elderly, demented Holocaust survivor and her son, Papernick could have exploited the tired trope of the victim, or the equally tired trope of the victim who victimizes others. Instead he surprises us with an utterly unsentimental ending that exposes the light of the story's title—not the expected admonition to "never forget," but a revelation of a flame of compassion that exists and persists independent of history. In the hilarious "King of the King of Falafel," a less talented writer would have derived the humor from stereotypes; the title character is a Yemenite falafel stand owner, a Jerusalem type as familiar as a South Asian cab driver in New York. Instead, the story is told from the point of view of *another* Yemenite falafel stand owner—and instead of exploiting these characters, Papernick invites us into their minds, with candor. The hijinks that inevitably ensue are earned, and the story's broad messianic overtones are not a skewering of sacred cows, except in the most literal sense. Instead, they are reminders of the many forms redemption can take here on earth. In "Lucky Eighteen," when a secular photographer takes a scantily-clad girl into the religious neighborhood of Mea Shearim in order to provoke the locals, his equally secular escort tells us what he cannot tell his photographer friend: "At that moment, Kravetz hated Shawn, as he had hated him a thousand times before. . . . [Shawn] really didn't understand, he hadn't seen the anger in the eyes of those men." The moment of seeing that anger—and the delicate interplay between two secular men, one who can see it and one who can't, even when he captures it on camera—is far more than an awkward moment between friends. It is also far more than the centuries-old tension between the secular and the religious. It is an encapsulation, in a single and deceptively simple paragraph, of the eternal pull of human dignity, of how some people will always feel that pull while others never will, of how the feel of that tug on the soul, no matter who feels it, is itself the sensation of the holy.

When Papernick first published this collection nearly ten years ago, these stories were contemporary. Today, they are prophetic. Readers familiar with Israel can see the minor points where the world of the book differs from the reality a decade later, but they can also see how astonishingly similar it is, how events have proceeded exactly along the trajectory that Papernick so incisively foresaw and described ten years earlier. The limits of human and divine forgiveness have been drawn in the sand, as they have been for thousands of years. In the space within them, in this artist's vision, one discovers the sacred.

Malchyk

*On the Fifth Day of Iyar, in the Jewish Year of 5709 (May 4th, 1949,
by our calendar), which was the first anniversary of Israel's Declaration of Independence and attainment of statehood, a rabbi in Jerusalem
suggested that women who bore children . . . should name their infants
Teshua (Redemption) if they were girls, and Herut (Freedom) if they
were boys. . . . Later on the semantics of maturity may cast a shadow
across the word(s), but on the Fifth Day of Iyar, 5709, it meant only
one thing to every man, woman and child in Israel, and they thronged the
roads, filled the cities, shot fireworks into the air, paraded, applauded,
cheered and sang in freedom's honor.*

Irwin Shaw, *Report on Israel*

Pirkl slept an uneasy sleep and dreamed again of his father's death.

A dark legionnaire appeared at the head of his mattress, whispering in his ear between machine-gun fire and the incessant boom of the big guns sounding off throughout the city. "The Grand Mufti himself sent me." Flares and tracers from the sky flashed across the stranger's beard, his black eyes burned electric green. "The quarter has been sacked," the Arab said.

Pirkl closed his eyes tight, *go a-way, go a-way, don't come back 'til Judgment Day.*

"Beautiful boy," the stranger said, stroking Pirkl's cheek with an empty shell casing. There was blood on the legionnaire's chest, and Pirkl touched a deep stain on his uniform shaped like the Shield of David. "His brave blood," the stranger answered and a tear rolled from his cheek. Pirkl drank the tears down as they poured from the stranger's face and the Ras el 'Ain pipeline was flowing again with cool springwater.

He awoke to his mother stroking his hair. "Shhh," she said, mopping sweat from his brow. Only a small kerosene lamp burned against the early morning darkness. Her eyes were ringed in black. She was as gaunt as a baby bird and wore a blue bandanna around her neck. A soldier with a bandaged head groaned from a stretcher not five feet away. "Shhh," she repeated, holding a small tin cup to Pirkl's lips. "Drink."

He sat up in bed as a whistling shell fired from the Katamon neighborhood crashed in a nearby street. "I'm going to find Abba," Pirkl said.

When the Jewish state was declared two weeks earlier, Pirkl had followed his mother to the sixth floor of their apartment house, where an Arab Legion shell had crashed through the roof of a neighbor's flat. The shell did not explode but had smashed a large jagged hole in the ceiling. White moonlight poured in through the opening, lighting the room with a silvery glow. Pirkl watched his mother step through the shattered glass and plaster and thought she looked like an angel. The air was thick and hot and smelled of crushed stone as Pirkl kicked up the white dust into clouds, imagining heaven.

Someone's wireless set crackled loudly from a lower floor and echoed through the darkened stairwell and the now-abandoned apartment. "This is *Kol Hamagen HaIvri,* the broadcasting service of the Haganah, calling on a wavelength of thirty-five to thirty-eight meters or seven to seven-point-five megacycles. Here is our English transmission. . . ." His mother pulled a bookshelf up to the hole and climbed the shelves, disappearing a moment later through the twisted steel into the hot night air. "Come, Malchyk," she called. Pirkl bristled at the childish nickname that had been his since he was six years old, and began to climb, careful not to step on the leather-bound commentaries. The broadcaster read from David Ben-Gurion's Declaration of Independence, his voice catching on the words, ". . . by virtue of the natural and historic right of the Jewish people and on the strength of the resolution of the General Assembly of the United Nations, hereby declares the establishment of the Jewish state in Palestine, to be called Israel. . . ." Pirkl repeated the word "Israel" as he pulled himself out onto the rooftop.

His mother took his hand, and he wanted to pull away and say, *I don't need to hold your hand anymore,* but realized for the first time as she squeezed him tightly that *she* needed his hand. The bombing that had gone on nightly for weeks continued; incandescent blood streaks across the sky, the east flickering like an undecided sunrise, gray plumes of smoke climbing into the night. "Do you think we will have a king at last?"

"I don't know," she said wearily.

"Father is there?" Pirkl asked, pointing to the smoke seething from within the besieged Old City. Only the Arab Legion's artillery answered.

He had not seen his father since the *hamsiin* began, when the hot sirocco wind blew from the desert at the start of May draining the life and color out of everything.

"How can they fight during the *hamsiin*?" Pirkl had asked his mother.

"Yihye tov," his mother answered, "It will be all right."

Pirkl knew his father was there within the twisting rabbit warren streets defending the ancient Jewish Quarter. He had heard rumors of a Haganah unit disguised as an Arab Legion marching band who arrived at Damascus Gate blasting their trumpets. When the gates opened Pirkl imagined his father's kaffiyeh dropping to the ground, his trumpet magically transformed into a Sten gun, his voice raised singing, "Rifle on rifle our guns will salute / Bullet on bullet our guns will shoot." His father had taught Pirkl the "Song of the Barricades," how to hurl stones at the British, and how to fashion a grenade out of an empty jam tin with bits of broken glass, shrapnel, matches, and gunpowder. It seemed like years since Pirkl had helped his father to sandbag windows on Gaza Road.

"Father is there," Pirkl said, "I know he is there."

A half-dozen smoke rockets blasted up into the sky from the Old City just two kilometers away. His mother turned her back on the distress signals and did not answer.

The wireless continued to echo throughout the dark stairwell, "All laws enacted under the Palestine White Paper of the British government, and all laws deriving from it are declared null and void. . . ." Pirkl felt his way down the stairs, following his mother's breathing. And then someone was jamming the wireless transmission and a voice cut in laughing, "We will drink blood from your skulls. Into the sea, Jews!"

That night Pirkl began to dream about his father's death.

Pirkl slipped into his dirty overalls, which hadn't been cleaned since water-rationing began. He placed his knitted cap onto his head and tied his shoes. The morning sun was coming up blue through the slats of the iron shutters. His mother took the tin cup from his side and tried to smile, touching his cheek. The soldier with the bandaged head sighed deeply in his sleep. Tsrili had been injured defending Ramat Rahel and was anxious to return to the battle but fell down dizzy and confused every time he stood up. Pirkl enjoyed singing Palmach marching songs with the injured soldier but was tired of hanging around the iodine-smelling apartment plugging wounds and beating away buzzing clouds of flies.

Just the night before Pirkl had stood showing off with his girlfriend Hannah, wearing an oversized helmet on his head in the middle of the living room. He declared in his most official-sounding baritone, "Pirkl of Rehavia you are conscripted in the name of Zion."

"What are your duties, brave one?" Hannah said, batting her eyelashes dramatically.

"To save Jerusalem!" Tsrili shouted from his stretcher before losing consciousness.

Now his grandmother entered with a crust of bread in one hand, a satchel thrown over her right shoulder. She handed him the bread, which was thinly covered with bitter chocolate spread. Pirkl gobbled it down.

"Good morning," she said.

"The reinforcements are ready," he answered.

"You make a handsome soldier."

His mother interrupted, "Pirkl is not a soldier. He's too young."

"I'm older than David when he killed Goliath."

"Don't talk nonsense."

"What is he, a worthless *shmatte,* a worthless old rag?" his grandmother said. "Let him go. Every man must fight for Jerusalem. He will soon be bar mitzvah. He smells like a man," she said, pinching her sharp nose.

"You belong at home . . ." his mother began.

"But what about the brave Trumpeldor?" Pirkl shot back.

"He was killed at Tel Hai," his mother answered, shaking her head.

"Defending Tel Hai," his grandmother said. "He didn't die in vain."

"You're not going to look for your father. Promise me," his mother said.

Pirkl smiled, but didn't say anything. He thought of the Russian-born, one-armed Joseph Trumpeldor. His father's hero.

Pirkl's grandmother winked at him.

"All right," his mother said. "Come straight back, Malchyk! Just go to the barricade. Hold this above your head," she said, handing him a piece of white muslin cloth. "Hold it high so the snipers can see. Look for the Red Cross, leave the package, tell them it is for those trapped in the city. They will listen to a child."

"Let him go!" his grandmother said. Though he was just five feet tall, she still had to reach up to kiss his cheek. "Be strong and brave," she said.

His grandmother had packed a small satchel filled to the top with two loaves of stale bread, three cans of asparagus soup, a tin of chocolate spread, a package of dried fruit, some potatoes, a cup of dried beans, sweet halvah, candles, a blanket, week-old copies of *Ha'aretz* and some small dark jars which contained a liquid that must have been medicine.

His heart quickened, he could feel it boiling in his chest as he bounced down the stairs. The full weight of the *hamsiin* hit him as he stepped out into the magic pink light of morning. He walked around behind the apartment house and emptied the bag onto the ground next to a jagged bowl-shaped crater where a twenty-five-pounder had hit one night during heavy shelling, and dug in the dry earth where Tsrili, the soldier injured at Ramat Rahel, would later be buried.

When his mother was busy tending to the wounded, he had hidden a pair of three-inch Davidka mortar shells made out of old pipes, a few dozen Enfield rifle bullets, three bayonets, and the pièce de résistance, a round Thompson submachine gun magazine. He held the magazine to his chest, like a stack of precious 78 rpm records that his mother used to play on the phonograph. And for a moment, he saw his parents dancing and laughing in their living room, his mother's head thrown back with such joy, he could hardly recognize her now.

He pressed the bullets into the stale bread until they all disappeared into the now-heavy loaves; wrapped the bayonets thickly in the old newspapers, and swaddled the Thompson magazine in the blanket, piling dried fruit on top in case he was stopped and asked the contents of his bag. Pirkl imagined his two rockets, marked "Dear King Abdullah" and "For Haj Amin Mufti," hitting their targets squarely on top of their heads. Two shells can win the war, he thought, and pictured himself riding along King George V Avenue in an open car with Hannah at his side. His reverie was interrupted by the thump of shelling from the east.

Hannah lived in the next apartment house with her mother and stepfather who were Communists. She was the first girl his own age Pirkl had ever thought was pretty, with her long almond-shaped face, spinning green eyes, and brand-new breasts. He liked her for that, but he also liked the fact that her parents let her do as she wished. Sometimes in the evenings, during the bombing, she would throw rocks at Pirkl's window and he would meet her in the stairwell where they would kiss in the thick darkness. She promised soon that Pirkl could touch her *there.*

He gathered up the cans of soup, the potatoes and the beans, the chocolate spread, some dried fruit, and even the sweet halvah, and left them on the doorstep outside her flat. She had gotten so skinny, Pirkl thought, so light, he could have carried her on his back all the way to the Old City. He heard her stepfather behind the door glumly singing the "Internationale." Pirkl ran off to gather his satchel humming "Hatikvah," The Hope, the nation's anthem.

Skipping over shell craters and tangled telephone wires, counting broken windows and garbage piles, Pirkl continued humming as he went. He counted in Hebrew, and then English, then in Russian. Sometimes he mixed the three together.

Farther on down the road Pirkl could see the barricade, and behind that no-man's-land. A high nasal voice called to him from behind a low stone wall, "Hey, boy. Curlyhead! Come here." Pirkl stopped beneath an almond tree and adjusted the heavy bag on his back, about to move on.

"Boy, you are going to the Ancient City?"

"Who wants to know?" Pirkl asked.

"I know," the voice said. "I know."

And then, the oldest man Pirkl had ever seen stood up from behind the wall. He was barefoot and dressed entirely in black, with a black felt hat tilted back on his giant head. He had a wild white beard, wispy like dry grass, and his eyes were pale and glassy.

"Come here, boy," the holy man said, holding out his long bony hand.

Pirkl could see the veins in his hand so clearly they might have been above the skin. His back was hunched and he smelled of old books and damp soil. And then he spoke and his breath smelled of fish bones that had been almost picked clean.

"You are going to the Ancient City."

Pirkl put his bag down. "Do you live there?"

"Yes."

"But you ran?" Pirkl said.

The holy man laughed, but instead of a laugh it was a breath and not a breath, as if he had one of those fish bones caught in his throat. "I ran?"

"How long did you live there?"

"Five hundred years," the man answered, then wheezed and laughed again. "Your name, boy."

Pirkl told him. He could not stop looking into the man's glassy cataracted eyes, dreamy like cracked crystal balls.

"Your mother?"

He could hear heavy machine-gunning in the distance and the savage boom, boom, boom of the bigger guns.

"Rosa," Pirkl said.

"Take this," the holy man said, slipping a small silver amulet into Pirkl's hand. He gripped his arm tight and did not let go. Pirkl closed his eyes and began to sway. He thought he felt the old man reach into his overall pockets, but he ignored it, thinking the poor man was simply searching for hidden food. The old man's pink tongue rolled around in his toothless mouth trying to form words, his voice high-pitched and broken: "In the name of Shaddai who created heaven and earth and in the name of the angel . . ." He was shaking faster and Pirkl felt an ache in his groin and a vibration down his spine. "In the name of Pirkl son of Rosa, protect him in all of his two-hundred and forty-eight organs against danger and the two-edged sword. Help him, deliver him, save him . . ."

He felt the man's soft hand sliding against him and electricity buzzing down all the knuckles of his spine and out into his rib cage. "Vanquish and bring low those who rise against him. May all who seek his harm be destroyed, humbled, smashed so that not a limb remains whole . . ." He felt a fire in his legs and arms now, burning through his veins and arteries, a white fire cleansing his very soul. "Save him, deliver him from all sorcery, from wicked men, from sudden death. Grant him grace, and love and mercy before the throne of God and before all beings who behold him." The old man let go of Pirkl's arm, and his eyes snapped open. He continued to chant, his stinking pink mouth an open wound, "Yah Yah Yah Yau Yau Yau Yah Zebaot. Amen Amen Amen." And all at once the electricity was gone and Pirkl felt his body shiver as if he had exploded. The man again broke into a sepulchral laugh and Pirkl noticed the man had wet his pants. He felt damp in his own pants. He had been tricked by a madman.

"Pirkl, Pirkl, beautiful boy," the man cackled, taking the amulet back into his long bony hands. "Pirkl, Pirkl."

He walked away laughing, and Pirkl grabbed him by the shoulder not concerned anymore that the old man might crumble into dust.

"Why did you touch me?"

"For luck," the old man said. "For luck."

"I don't need luck," Pirkl said, sickened and angry.

"You want to die as a lamb?"

"I'm not going to die."

"Child, you exaggerate your own importance. Death is in the air." And with that, he raised his nose to the sky, sniffing, his nose hairs waving like tiny spider's legs.

"Come with me," he said, sliding a finger into his tooth-less mouth.

Then Pirkl said a word so foul that he had never said it aloud before. The old man's face dropped and he began to shuffle away.

"If you must go," he said, color rising to his pallid face, "enter through the small door, my little dung beetle."

When Pirkl reached the barricade, he removed the bayonets from his heavy satchel, throwing them on the ground in disgust. He was sticky and felt something dripping down his leg and wiped it up with the gauze his mother had given him to ward off sniper fire. Through a peephole, he could see a park where he once played, strewn with barbed wire and rough cement blocks. He didn't smell death in the air, only burned gunpowder and dust. His father, the best person in the whole world, was only a few hundred meters away, inside that stony prison. Pirkl felt tears surge up from his belly and he wanted to run to him as fast as his legs could carry him.

Though it was still early morning, a white sun made the whole world look like an overexposed photograph. Pirkl removed his wool cap, and standing on top of his own small shadow, peered through the peephole again. The Old City. "I can dribble a football that far," he thought. "Kick it right through Jaffa Gate."

Pirkl made a bet with himself as he walked along the barricade that he would not be spotted moving across no-man's-land. He was simply too small to be of any consideration, too much a part of the landscape to be noticed. With the satchel humped up on his back, covered with dust, he might be mistaken for a camel.

He found a breach in the barrier and slipped through,

scraping his arm on a bracelet of barbed wire, and began walking toward the flames and pounding shells. "This is easy," he thought, heading toward the well-fortified Jaffa Gate. He had just begun whistling "Song of the Barricades" when he heard a bullet ricochet past him, then another. Pirkl could not see where the marksman was shooting from, but dove face-first onto the ground and crawled behind a pile of stones, closing his eyes. His heart beat hard behind his eyelids.

With his face pressed into the dry earth, Pirkl thought of Hannah. He once told her he would die if he didn't touch her *there.* And now he was sure he would die.

"You won't die," she had said, her lips against his, her words disappearing into his mouth.

He spoke back into her mouth, "I will!"

"No you won't. If I let you touch it now, what is there to look forward to?"

"Lots of things," Pirkl said, kissing her dry lips.

"No," she said. "You will *have* to live. So you can touch it later."

"Please."

"Not now," she said, placing his hands on her behind and pulling him closer. She smelled of kerosene and sweat.

Pirkl wanted to tell Hannah that he loved her, he loved her so much, but said, "When do you think my father will come home?"

"I don't know," she said. "Stalin took my father when I was three. His father died in a pogrom in Dokszyce. But don't worry," she said. "You can get a new father."

.   .   .

What would happen if he died in no-man's-land? Would Hannah cry for him and call him brave and wish she had let him touch her, Pirkl wondered. Sweat poured down his neck, tickling him, the way Hannah's fingers did. His mouth was full of soot, he didn't dare raise his head. Would his mother know the moment a bullet ripped through his body? Would she feel his last breath fade away the way she felt his first breath when he came into the world?

Some dried apricots spilled out of the satchel onto the ground. "My last meal on earth, and I don't even like apricots." Then a horrifying thought crept into Pirkl's mind: If my father is dead, would I know? He is defending the Old City and bombs are falling. Can he walk between a million raindrops and not get wet?

The sniper must have thought he had hit his target, for the ricocheting bullets stopped, as did the bombing within the Old City. Only the odd report of machine-gun fire echoed from within the walls. Pirkl removed the awkward Thompson magazine from his bag and laid it beside the pile of rocks, pushed himself up off the ground and ran as fast as he could back toward the barricade and the breach he had slipped through. Not a shot was fired.

Down by the Yemin Moshe neighborhood he decided to try again. *Of course* Jaffa Gate, the main gate in the west, would be heavily guarded. It was stupid to try, Pirkl thought. And Zion Gate, too, was a fortress. But the little gate! He peered up at the city and he could see fires burning from within the Jewish Quarter. The bombing had stopped.

In the winter his father had taken him to Montefiore's Windmill at the top of Yemin Moshe, which offered a majestic view of the Old City and the valley below. To the south, his father pointed out the British High Commissioner's "Government House" on a gray hilltop. He chuckled at the irony that the seat of the mandatory government would be located on the Hill of Evil Counsel. They looked out on the walled city that seemed to be almost buried in the mountains, and down below, the Hinnom Valley, or Gehenna. His father told him that in ancient times, pagans had built a shrine to Moloch, an angry god hungry for human flesh. Children were sacrificed in that valley, and their blood flowed all the way to the Dead Sea. Pirkl asked his father if children were still sacrificed. He said, no, not if they were good.

Now he was in that valley, making his way across the burnished earth to the Old City, and the Union Jack was gone from that gray hill, replaced by mortars and cannons. He imagined walking over the bones of children burned in the bronze arms of Moloch. Down he went and he heard goats bleating in the distance and he heard the mournful clanging of their bells. Across the valley he counted ten white dots moving slowly among the twisted olive trees. Every once in a while he heard the rat-tat of gunfire from within the city.

He wanted to eat some of the dried fruit as he walked along, but was afraid he would not have enough when he reached his father. His bag was lighter now, and he cursed himself for leaving behind the Thompson magazine. He only had the two mortars for King Abdullah and the Grand Mufti, as well as the two loaves of bullet-loaded bread. Loose dried fruit tumbled around in his satchel. He could make out tiny figures on the ramparts as he passed Mount Zion and the mighty edifice of Dormition Abbey. "Moloch, come out wherever you are," Pirkl thought defiantly. "I'm walking through your valley."

Pirkl climbed the steep eastern slope of the valley on his way to the little gate of which the madman had spoken. Pirkl smiled. Dung Gate, the smallest and most insignificant entrance into the city, so small that a man on horseback would have to dismount to enter, a gate that once served as an open sewer in times of antiquity. Dung Gate, the closest gate to the Jewish Quarter and his father.

He stepped through the barbed wire and dust and rubble, sweating furiously. He was so thirsty his head began to buzz. Still not a sound from within the city, but the smell of smoke and death burned in his nose. He removed the thin blanket from within his satchel and wrapped it around his face like a kaffiyeh.

A solitary legionnaire sitting languidly in an opening above the gate waved and said, *"Marhaba."* Pirkl smiled and said the same.

The gate was even smaller than Pirkl remembered. He noticed the decorous Star of David carved above it and mumbled the Sheheheyanu, a prayer said on joyous occasions that he remembered hearing old men muttering.

Skirting the Arab Muhgrabi Quarter, he walked uphill toward the battered cupola of the Tiferet Israel Synagogue. The narrow streets were littered with rotting vegetables, twisted bed frames, scattered clothing, smashed crockery, books, photographs, broken furniture, rubble, and all the debris one might have acquired in a lifetime. A terrible sadness rose up from within Pirkl; he wanted to scream out and curse and stamp his feet.

He came to a small storefront where a young Arab sat at a round table.

"Hello," the Arab said in English.

Pirkl ignored him and continued to walk.

"'Hello,' I said. Come back or I will shout that there is a Jew still alive."

Pirkl froze.

"The Jews are surrendering today," the Arab said to him.

Pirkl shook his head and thought of his handsome father and him singing: "On the barricades we will meet at last / And lift freedom on high from the chains of the past."

"You're lying," Pirkl said.

"You have lost the Holy City."

"No," Pirkl said.

"An Arab flag flies over the Haram."

"It can't be," Pirkl said, and then thought, "We have taken Katamon and Bakaa and Talbiyeh. We've recaptured Ramat Rahel."

"You look thirsty. I have water and some dates."

Pirkl sat down, suddenly exhausted, deflated, and thirsty.

"This morning, two rabbis carried a white bedsheet between two broomsticks. They have surrendered."

"We would never give up Jerusalem," Pirkl said, trailing off, ". . . rather die."

"What is in the bag?'

Pirkl hesitated. "Some dried fruit."

"Good. We will share." The young Arab stood up and limped over to a stone counter. His leg was twisted so that the foot faced the wrong way. "I am the *mukhtar,* the mayor."

"I am the Messiah," Pirkl said.

There was a small fishbowl in the middle of the table. A single goldfish swam in a few inches of murky water.

"I am really the *mukhtar,*" he said, handing Pirkl a glass of water. He had a sparse mustache, and his eyes wandered lazily. The goldfish swam rapidly back and forth.

"A Jewish fish," he said. "A gefilte fish," he added, laughing.

Pirkl drank the water, thankful but annoyed by the young Arab.

"Can you keep a secret?" he said, spitting a date pit onto the ground. Pirkl nodded.

"This fish. He does not belong to me. It is the only gold I got from the houses. Who has ever seen a fish in the desert?"

Pirkl thanked him for the water and stood up to leave.

"Wait, wait," the young Arab said, his eyes looking past Pirkl. "I want to show you something." He stood up and clubbed his way over to a cabinet, returning with a pile of photographs. He smiled. "Look. Jews!"

Pirkl saw mutilated bodies, both male and female, their faces twisted, smashed, eyeless. Disemboweled bodies, here he saw an arm, there a leg, and wondered if he would recognize his father's hand among those bodies. A bare bootless foot, burned and bloody. Would he know?

Pirkl leaned over and heaved onto the ground. Only the water came out, clear and hot. He coughed and coughed and finally stood up. "I'm going."

"Wait, wait," the young Arab said. "Please. Take the fish. He does not belong to me."

Pirkl grabbed the tiny fishbowl in his arms and ran up

the cobbled street toward the once glorious Tiferet Israel Synagogue.

"Careful," the Arab called after him. "Don't spill."

On the next street a half-dozen fierce-looking irregulars from the Liberation Army ransacked a house. Pirkl hid behind a wall as the men cut open a mattress in search of treasure, laughing as the stuffing flew out. One man wearing a British-style helmet fired his rifle into the mattress.

Pirkl turned up a narrow alley, the blanket almost totally obscuring his face. The two mortar shells clinked together as he walked. Then he heard it, at first one voice, then hundreds, singing, he was sure he heard singing: the Shema. He ran toward the voices that seemed to be coming from out of the stones themselves. "Hear, O Israel: the Lord our God. The Lord is one!" He ran as fast as he could without spilling the goldfish onto the maze-like streets.

He arrived at Ashkenazi Square dazed, but exhilarated by the sound of the voices. Hundreds of people milled about; men with beards and sidecurls, wide-brimmed felt hats and long coats, carrying bundles in their arms; women wearing babushkas and long dresses stared blankly; boys in shorts and sandals and pigtailed girls huddled close to their parents, scratching at the earth with their feet.

The dome of Tiferet Israel seemed to have been erased, supplanted only by the blue sky. All the windows were blown out and bullet holes peppered the walls. Pirkl pulled the blanket off his head as he noticed kaffiyeh-wearing men, with bandoliers slung across their chests, standing close by with rifles in their arms. He wandered confused through the crowd with the goldfish bowl in his arms.

"It's over," a man in beige pants and shirt said in English, walking through the crowd. "It's all over. Your rabbis are in the Armenian Seminary now discussing the terms of the surrender." The letters "U.N." were painted in white on his helmet.

Surrender! Over! Pirkl thought. What is over? It can't be. We still have my two mortars. We're not done yet. I have bullets. I'll fight. It can't be over. The Old City is over?

Most of the men were Orthodox Jews who would not have picked up a gun to fight.

"Where are the fighters?" Pirkl asked a man swaying, lost in prayer. "Where is my father?" he asked another, who said something in Yiddish. "Why didn't you fight instead of pray?" he said to another, kicking dust up at him.

He saw a young girl standing alone on the edge of the crowd staring into the distance. She reminded him of Hannah the way her shoulder blades showed through the back of her dress, the way her hair was cut unevenly at the neck. He touched her arm softly and held out the goldfish to the girl.

"Does this fish belong to you?"

She looked through him as if he were not there and batted the fishbowl out of his hands. It shattered on the ground. Watching the fish struggle for a last breath of desert air, Pirkl wanted to cry, but he did not want his father to see him crying like a baby.

"You are looking for the *Portzim*?" a man asked Pirkl. "Go to Rothschild House."

Pirkl went. And there he found more refugees gathering baskets and bedding onto their shoulders. One woman carried a baby in her arms and a box of matzo. He saw a crowd of men standing beneath the arches of Rothschild House, soldiers in beige short-sleeved shirts, some wearing wool caps, others bareheaded, exhausted, weary, standing with their hands at their sides. There were no more than two dozen of them and Pirkl scanned their faces. And then he saw his father standing with a coat slung coolly over his shoulder. Pirkl ran to him, threw his arms around his father's waist.

"Malchyk! What are you doing here?" his father asked, disentangling Pirkl from his waist. "Where's your mother?"

"Look what I brought," Pirkl said, opening his satchel. "We're not beat yet!"

"Go back to the square. Get out of here."

The harshness of his father's voice broke Pirkl's heart. He had never heard him speak that way, and he burst into tears, throwing a bear hug around his father's waist.

"Look! I brought bullets."

"I want you to go back home," his father said.

"But, we still have my shells."

"Why didn't you stay with your mother?" his father said, shaking his head.

Pirkl knew he couldn't go home now, he wasn't a quitter. He stood in silence next to his father, writing his name in the dusty earth with his foot.

A few minutes later a smartly dressed Arab Legion officer addressed the group of assembled soldiers in both English and Arabic. "From this moment on, you are prisoners of His Majesty King Abdullah of Transjordan and you cannot be harmed."

. . .

The prisoners were marched along the Gate of Heaven Road toward the old Turkish prison near Jaffa Gate. Pirkl felt his legs were too short as he walked behind his father, who did not say a word, or look back. One of the fighters put his Haganah cap on Pirkl's head as they filed along Rehov Beit El, House of the Lord Street, and asked him his name. He said only his last name. The fighter tapped Pirkl's father on the shoulder and said, "The youth brigade has taken over." Before turning up Rehov Ha Yehudim, the Street of the Jews, Pirkl's father finally did look around and he saw his downcast young son and the Jewish Quarter burning at their backs.

From the prison window as he tried to sleep, Pirkl could see the Tower of David rising from the Citadel. He imagined climbing the stone walls of the tower, wrapping his arms around its neck and reaching out for the moon, hovering low over the blanched city; and there were no fires, and there was no bombing, only the scattered sky filled with stars and the lonely tooting of a single shepherd's flute. Pirkl did not know then that he would spend the next half year in a Jordanian prison camp where he would sleep in a tent beneath a cold moon and become bar mitzvah in the Iraqi desert. He did not know that he would not return to the Old City until another nineteen years and another war had passed, and that he would enter Lion's Gate as a soldier, only footsteps behind the future prime minister. He did not know as he knelt by the prison window that his mother searched hospitals and makeshift infirmaries for her only son. He imagined his mother standing on the rooftop of their apartment house in Rehavia sadly looking toward the walled city. And he called to her and waved his free arm and said, "Momma, I found him. I found him!"

An Unwelcome Guest

Yossi Bar-Yosef felt his young wife Devorah stir in sleep. He rolled over in bed, felt her warm breath against his face and lay watching her until she was still again. Then she slept quietly. A large round moon hung low over Jerusalem, its white light spilling into their Muslim Quarter apartment. He sat up in bed, reached for his *kippah* on the nightstand, and placed it on his head. The night was silent in contrast to the chaos of the day; Arab merchants hawking fruits and vegetables, pilgrims shouting prayers and curses, army patrols strolling through the narrow stone streets. Now he could only hear his wife's even breathing and the two soldiers joking quietly in Hebrew beneath their bedroom window. In a few hours the muezzin would call the Ishmaelites to prayer for the first time in the new day.

He got out of bed and made his way to the kitchen by moonlight, nearly skipping all the way in his bare feet. It was the month of Tishri and the stone floors were chilly even for early autumn. He filled a pot with water, lit the gas with a match, and stood by the stove for a moment thinking of his wife, his Devorah Bee: her soft olive skin, her curly brown hair, her green eyes, the way her body felt beneath his.

"You are welcome," the Arab man said, startling Yossi. "Welcome. Have a seat," he said gesturing to the empty chair at the kitchen table. "Welcome," the Arab man said again, smiling.

Yossi did not wonder how the old man had crept past

the soldiers in the street, nor did he wonder how he had found his way through the locked door. He had waited every Passover for Elijah the Prophet to arrive and drink his cup of wine, and he prayed daily for the coming of the Messiah. Yossi knew that many people wandered the dreamy moonlit paths between sleep and prayer in this golden city of light and stone.

The Arab may have been sixty-five or seventy years old. His face was cracked like a wadi in the heat of summer, his nose round, bulbous, and pocked like a Judean hilltop, his thin salt and pepper mustache ratty, careless, a goatherd's mustache. He wore a black and white checked kaffiyeh on his head and a filthy striped caftan that reached almost to his slippered feet.

"Sit," said the Arab man in English. "We will share some tea and nana."

"What do you want here?"

The Arab man said nothing.

"My wife. She's sleeping."

"She sleeps like a baby."

The thought of someone invading his new wife's privacy, someone even imagining Devorah asleep infuriated Yossi. He took a step forward and whispered through his teeth, "Get out! Why are you —"

"The water is ready," the Arab man said, cutting Yossi off.

Yossi turned his attention to the pot. The water bubbled over, hissing against the stove's flames.

"My name is Ziad."

"Who *are* you?" Yossi asked.

"I am Ziad Abu Youssif."

"You are in the wrong place. This is a private home," Yossi said, returning with the pot of water.

The old man only straightened his kaffiyeh on his head, smiled, and reached for a glass. He poured himself some water and said, "You are a rabbi?"

"No. No. I am studying. Near the Kotel."

The Arab man smiled a brown-toothed smile. "So you are a rabbi."

"I'm not a rabbi yet. I am studying," Yossi said, and then asked, "Why are you here?"

"This is my home, rabbi," the Arab man answered in an even tone. "A tea bag, please."

"Your home?" Yossi said, surprised. "This is *my* home."

"How long have you stayed here?" the Arab man asked.

"Eight months."

"You are just married?" the Arab asked, taking a tea bag from a tin on the table. "Where are you from?"

"New York," Yossi answered.

"I was born in that room, where you sleep. My first son, Youssif, the dark one, was born in the same room. My father was born where you are sitting. This was not always a kitchen."

"If this is your house what color are the tiles on the floor of my bedroom?"

"The Jews are always changing things."

They sat in silence while their tea brewed in front of them. Then they drank. After a moment Yossi bit his lip at the corner, about to ask, "Why did you leave?" but before he had a chance, the old man said, "There were wars."

Yossi knew that many Arabs had fled Israel in 1948 and again during the Six-Day War. He had seen the squalid refugee camps and the anguished faces on his TV set, but he also knew the names Chmelnicki, Babi-Yar, and Auschwitz like a mantra. After a moment he said, "Abraham is your father as well as mine."

The old man did not seem to hear as he bent over to pick something up off the floor. It was a small wooden box. The Arab carefully placed it on the table between them. Yossi swallowed hard and thought about calling to the soldiers outside the window, but knew it would be useless. The bomb would go off before they could make it halfway up the stairs.

It had only been eight months since he and Devorah had stood under the *huppa,* only eight months since he had first kissed her after stomping the traditional glass representing the fragility of life, eight months since he had first touched his virgin wife. That was supposed to be the beginning; a family, a Jewish family in the heart of Jerusalem, and now, they were about to be blown to bits like that bus he had seen smoldering in the spring rain on Jaffa Street.

The Arab man undid a small latch and folded open a backgammon board.

"You play *shesh besh*?" he asked.

Yossi looked out the window and could see the moon higher over the city now, its light so bright, the face of the moon almost pulsing.

"It's the middle of the night."

The Arab began setting up the board, the white stones first, then the black stone disks in their places.

The old man took the last sip of his tea. "I will play you for the house. If you lose, I will live here again. If I lose, I will return to the Street of Chains begging for baksheesh."

Yossi was not interested in hearing about a broken man begging for shekels. He said, "No," and then said, "no," again.

"I am joking, of course," the Arab man said. "We will play for the right to speak."

Yossi would not get back to sleep now. He could feel his blood boiling through his body, his hands shaking, the small hairs at the back of his neck standing on end. "Okay. I'll play. Just let me check on my wife."

"But, it's your turn to roll." The Arab man had already rolled the first die: a four.

Yossi imagined his Devorah Bee curled up in bed, wetting her lips in sleep, kicking her leg against a bad dream. He thought of her slightly rounded belly and the child swimming within it. He stood halfway up from his chair, then picked up the die and rolled a three.

"My move first," the Arab man said. "Some more tea."

The old man rolled a six and a one. He moved the black stone to his side of the outer board, covering it with the one. Yossi rolled a two and a one. Already, one of his stones was unprotected. The Arab picked up the dice in his large hands and rolled. Then Yossi rolled. Only the sound of the dice clicking against the wooden board could be heard above the old man's labored breathing.

"Do you speak Hebrew?" the Arab asked.

"To read the Torah," Yossi answered, head down.

"Tell me, Rabbi, how did you get here?"

Yossi tried to move his two white stones from the inner board but could not. His pieces were almost entirely blocked in.

"Why here?" the Arab said.

"'If I should forget thee, O Jerusalem, may my right hand forget its strength.' *Tehillim*. Psalm One thirty-seven," Yossi said.

"I do not forget," the Arab man said, holding out his right hand.

Yossi did not look up from the board and said matter-of-factly, "This land was given to Abraham by God. Abraham was the father of the Jews. We are here because we are Jewish. Because the land was promised to us by God."

The Arab rolled again, saying, "But we are both sons of Abraham."

Yossi rolled quickly and made his move. His mind was not on the game now. The Arab rolled the dice again.

"Abraham was the best of men," Yossi continued flatly, "but he contained some bad elements as we all do and those elements came out in his son Ishmael. He was the son of a slave girl. A wild man."

The old man's stones were all strongly in place on his side of the inner board. Yossi rolled but still could not move his two white stones trapped deep among the Arab's black stones. The Arab rolled and began removing his pieces from the board. "Beit 'Itab," he whispered. "Beit Mahsir," he said on his next roll. "Deir el Hawa," he said, removing two more pieces. "Jarash." "Lifta." "El Maliha." "Suba," he said, winning the game. Yossi cleared the board and began to set up another game.

"Deir Yassin!" the Arab said loudly. "Do you know Deir Yassin, Rabbi?"

Yossi motioned for the man to be quiet, he did not want to wake up his wife. The Arab lowered his voice.

"Do you know of Deir Yassin? No. It was a beautiful little village of orange and lemon trees, almond trees, and date palms on the outside of Jerusalem. Like the others, it is also erased from the face of the earth. Now it is called Givat Shaul. I'm sure you know Givat Shaul."

He did know Givat Shaul; his wife's aunt and uncle lived in an apartment not far from the mental institution. He had visited once or twice, but never saw a sign of Deir Yassin.

"You came to Deir Yassin one morning —"

Yossi interrupted, "I've never been —"

"It's my time to speak. I won the game. Now you must listen."

Yossi shifted uncomfortably in his chair.

"You came to Deir Yassin, a small quiet village at dawn. You were three hundred men with guns and mortars. You broke into homes, shot whole families, women and children, threw bombs into houses, machine-gunned us, butchered us, raped us. You took prisoners into the streets blindfolded and shot us dead. You left our bodies on the ground. You bound our hands, stripped us naked, put us in trucks, and drove us through the streets of Jerusalem. We were afraid and some of us ran."

Nonsense! Yossi thought. He had not even received his military training yet. He rolled the wooden die.

"You tried to scare the Arabs out of Jerusalem," the old man said and straightened his kaffiyeh. Then he rolled a three. It was Yossi's turn to roll first. The moon had moved behind some clouds, leaving them in almost complete darkness.

"Do you have a candle?" the old man asked.

Yossi stood up in silence, walked to the pantry, and returned with two Shabbat candles. He lit them.

"We'll play until the winner of three," the Arab said.

This time Yossi was determined not to get caught in the back of the board. He would rush his two white stones out from the very start and race the rest of his stones around to his side before the Arab could do the same. Yossi rolled, and then the old man, and then Yossi. They moved quickly, sliding their stones around the board, hypnotized by the rhythm of the rolling dice. He was so busy concentrating on the board that he did not notice the old man had been speaking in Arabic. Smelling tobacco smoke, Yossi looked up from the table to find three more Arab men sitting on the kitchen floor beside the old man. He grabbed the table, nearly knocking the board to the floor as he tried to stand up. But he was unable, paralyzed in his seat. Two men slightly younger than Ziad wore kaffiyehs and took turns smoking from a tall gold-plated water pipe, a third ancient man with a battered fez planted on his head awkwardly fingered a set of worry beads. Yossi could still hear the soldiers' radio crackling faintly outside his kitchen window.

"Do not worry," Ziad said. "We are old men. There is nothing to fear. They are only my brothers and our blind father. Do not worry. Please. Please play."

The four men continued to talk in Arabic. Yossi, not understanding Arabic, did not know what to do. He took a deep breath but still could not fill his lungs.

Ziad asked Yossi, "Do you smoke the nargilah?"

"No. No," Yossi said, coughing. Then he remembered his pregnant wife as smoke filled the kitchen. Yossi excused himself.

From the bedroom doorway he saw Devorah asleep as before, her long hair splashed out onto the pillow. Yossi sat on the bed for a moment looking at her. Moonlight shined through the window and lit up her face. He kissed his index finger and touched it to the end of her nose. "Sleep tight, my Bumblebee," he whispered and opened her night table drawer, removed his wife's mini 9 mm pistol, and placed it in his side pocket. Then he closed the bedroom door tight and hurried back to the kitchen half afraid of the encroaching Arabs, half determined to prove that he could win the game.

"She is sleeping?" Ziad asked.

Yossi nodded his head and sat down at the table.

"I shared that room with my brothers as a child," the old man said.

Yossi rolled the dice, ignoring him.

"There was a pomegranate tree at the window. My son Youssif liked to climb in it."

"It isn't there anymore," Yossi said, rolling a three and a one. He moved his first lone stone four spaces and said, "The tree is gone. There is no tree."

"I am just remembering," the old man said.

Yossi's white stone was open at the edge of the outer board one space short of safety. The old man paused a long time before rolling the dice again. With the moon high above the apartment the three Arabs sat cross-legged on the floor; two of them passing the water pipe back and forth between them, the older man continuing to fumble with his worry beads. It was only now with the moon out of the clouds that Yossi noticed the blind father's empty eye sockets.

"How would you feel if someone took that glass of tea from you?" Ziad asked.

"This glass?" Yossi said.

"Yes. That glass," the Arab said, rolling the dice.

"I would get another glass."

The old man rolled and promptly hit Yossi's single stone, removing it to the center bar. Yossi rolled, and entered in the fourth slot, moving his other lone piece from the first to third slot. His two stones were now open at the back end of the board. The Arab rolled again and Yossi found his stone back on the bar with the fourth and sixth slots occupied. He rolled a two and a three. His stone came off the center bar, but Yossi's stones were still hemmed in.

The Arab asked, "How old is your wife, Rabbi?"

"Nineteen," Yossi answered.

"And what is her name?" the Arab asked, rolling and knocking Yossi's stone to the bar again.

Yossi did not answer.

The game continued, and Yossi's stones were alternately knocked onto the center bar as the old man removed his pieces from the table two by two, whispering in Arabic. The Arab men on the floor clapped their hands on each other's shoulders — the blind old man mumbled something in Arabic that could have been a prayer.

"I've had enough of this. I'm going to sleep," Yossi said. He had not removed any of his stones from the table.

"But you can't. Nobody has won three games. Sit. Sit. I won the second game."

One of the Arab men got to his feet, a silver sheath shining among the folds of his caftan. Yossi fingered his wife's pistol in his pocket and said, "Okay. We'll play another game."

The old man picked up the stones in his hands and began chanting quietly the names he had just whispered: " 'Allar;

'Artuf; Beit Naqquba; Deir Aban; Ishwa'; El Jura; Kasla!" Do you know of the village of —"

"All right. It's time to play," Yossi said.

Yossi began setting up the board.

They played on, the dice rattling against the old wooden board. The men on the floor were anxious, groaning in discomfort with every move, shifting from one knee to the other. Yossi blocked the men from his mind, focusing only on the board. When he had established a lead he looked and flashed a confident wink at Ziad. The old man sat calmly, pondering his next move. Then he called out a question in Arabic and was answered by a woman's voice.

Four Arab women dressed in black stood over the kneeling men. One wore a *hijab* over her face, the other three sternly looked on. One of the women spoke loudly in guttural Arabic. The old man listened and turned to Yossi, who was beginning to remove his stones from the board.

"My wife, Zahira," Ziad said.

Yossi continued to play, ignoring her. His only interest now was to beat the old man, throw the Arabs from his home, and return to bed with his wife.

"These are my brothers' wives. And," he said, pointing to the tiny woman in the *hijab*, "this is our mother."

"It's your move," Yossi said.

The old man rolled. He had twelve stones left on the board. Yossi had six and rolled low but still removed two stones. The woman who had spoken to Ziad pushed her way forward and placed her hands on the table. Yossi saw the black under her fingernails, her eyes cold as the chipped stones on the board. Her face had the worn look of an old leather saddle. He rolled double four and won the game. The woman grabbed up the pieces and began to quickly reset the board. Yossi tried to place his hand on top of hers. She pulled away.

"Hevron!" he said, making eye contact with all the Arabs except the blind father. "We were neighbors in Hevron and you came to our homes," Yossi said, borrowing the tone of the old man, Ziad. "And you raped us, burned us, chopped off our hands."

"That is not true," the woman said.

"It is true," Yossi said.

"Liar!" the woman said louder.

"You were not born then," Ziad said.

"You came to our homes in the City of the Patriarchs —" Yossi said.

"Isra-ay-lee pig!" the woman yelled. "Liar!"

"— and tore us apart like fresh bread," he added.

"Arrogant Jew. Liar. Zionist," the woman shouted, and the men joined in shouting, knocking against the table. The woman stood face to face with Yossi and said, "You have no place here. Pig!" Then she spat in his face.

Yossi reached into his side pocket, pulled out his wife's pistol, and jammed it hard beneath the woman's ribs, doubling her over momentarily. He felt her soft stomach rebound against his hand.

"Quiet!"

The men moved back, but Zahira, the wife of the old man Ziad, stood her ground. "Put your toy away, *yeled*."

"It was a long time ago," the old man said.

"It was only sixty years ago," Yossi said.

"You were not born. You were not there," the old man said.

"Memory is in the blood," Yossi said. "I was there as I

was at Sinai to receive the commandments. I was exiled from Spain. I wandered. And I remember pogroms beyond the Pale and the killing. I remember. And the camps, I remember that, too. Jews have been in Hevron since the time of Abraham. You have only lived there since the thirteenth century."

He waved the pistol at the Arabs and tasted blood in his mouth, sour and metallic. He wanted to lay the Arabs face down on the floor with their hands behind their backs, and fire a bullet into the brain of each. He would clean the floor with the old man's kaffiyeh and return to bed with his wife.

Zahira stepped closer, her weathered face inches from his. "Okay, boy," she said. "Shoot me." She pulled his pistol closer to her stomach. Yossi's hand was compliant. "I am all used up," she said. "Make me a martyr of the great battle." The men looked on impassively, the women stood stone-faced. Ziad, too, stared expressionless. "I am the mother of generations. But now I am finished. I am the husk of a pome-granate, my seeds have been scattered and grown. Shoot me. I am only a husk." Yossi pushed his pistol into her stomach and then pulled it back.

"Sit. We're going to play again," Yossi said.

The men sat, and the women did too.

Zahira reached forward and touched Yossi's cheek and said, "You are weak and sad."

"We will play?" Ziad said.

"Do not fear us," Zahira said. "We are old and not to be feared. But fear our children. Fear my son Youssif. He will burn your crops, tear down your home, and eat the flesh of your children."

Yossi rolled the dice.

"He will eat the flesh of your children," she repeated.

They began to play again, the Arab leading two games to one. The sky was turning from deep black to dark bruised blue. The moon was gone. Yossi slipped the pistol back into his pocket.

"The tea. It is cold," the old man said.

Yossi stood up to boil another pot of water, then returned to his seat and rolled the dice. He opened with a solid four and two, occupying the four slot on the inner table.

"My sweet wife was beautiful as a flower," Ziad said. "We married when she was fifteen. Her lovely name means flowers."

The old man rolled and Yossi turned to the woman.

"I brought her to the place to take her gift, and my father and uncles waited outside the room with stones and knives — if she was not a virgin. But there was blood. . . ."

Yossi remembered his wife's red blood on the white bedsheet and the feeling that she was truly his.

"It hurt her and she cried and cried for days, did not stop."

Yossi rolled again.

"And we prayed that, *Inshallah,* we would have a strong boy who would not cry," Zahira, the old man's wife, said.

"And when he was born he cried," the old man said. "He cried for Palestine, and the bloodstained hilltops, and the weeping seashores. And I slapped his face and shook him and said, 'Do not be weak! You are an Arab!' And Youssif grew to be an angry barefoot boy."

The old man rolled and Yossi watched him slide the stones around the board with his rough fingers. The smell of hashish mixed with the smell of tobacco filled the room. Yossi was afraid to look up, feeling the weight of claustrophobia on him. He just stared at the board and at the old man's chipped black stones.

"It's your turn," the old man said.

The room was jammed with Arabs. The children had arrived. Eight young men with thick hair and mustaches crowded around the table with the others. Yossi could feel one of the newcomers breathing at his neck. Some drank beer from brown bottles, others smoked. They were all slim and strong and Yossi was afraid. The kitchen was so crowded that the Arabs pressed right up against the table and chairs.

"I need room," Yossi said and the woman called out, "Lebensraum?" and laughed. "I need room," Yossi said again, but the Arabs either could not or would not move. Then he thought of his wife alone in the bedroom and wanted to run to her.

"It's your turn," the old man said. Yossi stared blank-faced. "My sons," the old man said. "And my brothers' sons."

"I don't want to play."

"But you must. We are the majority," the Arab said.

Yossi wanted to call the soldiers down below, but couldn't raise his voice to speak. His wife's pistol in his pocket comforted him, but he knew he would never use it. He rolled again. Then the old man rolled. The young Arabs pressing in toward the table kept a running commentary of the game in Arabic. One imitated the sound of the clicking dice with his tongue. Yossi rolled again and he was leading. He removed his first stone from the board. The old man held up his empty cup and said, "Your pot is burning." Black smoke rose from the stove.

"Your house is on fire," the woman said.

Yossi pushed his chair back into one of the Arabs, stood

up and forced his way to the stove. The Arabs laughed, and as he waded through them and tried to pull his *kippah* from his head, one reached into his pocket. Someone had thrown a dish towel into the flame. Yossi dropped it into the sink with the blackened pot and turned on the water.

"Some more tea," the old man said in a cracking voice.

When Yossi returned to the table his white stone was on the bar and six or seven of the Arab's stones had been spirited away without even a single roll of the dice.

"Where is the tea?" the old man asked.

"There is no tea," Yossi said. "Put the stones back or I won't play."

"All right. I will put them back and you will play."

"Where is your toy?" the woman asked.

Yossi felt his side pocket. His wife's pistol was gone and had been replaced with a slab of olive wood. Yossi's head felt light and then heavy.

"You will play now," the old man said.

Yossi's stomach churned and his mouth tasted bitter, acidy. With the pieces back in place, he rolled again, more determined than ever to beat the Arabs. "When I win you'll give me back my gun," Yossi said.

"You still don't understand. We make the rules," the old man said.

Yossi bit his lip and rolled again — double four. A lucky roll. Five stones left. The room still smelled of hashish now mixed with body odor and Yossi's head felt too heavy for his neck. The Arabs rolled. Then Yossi — two more stones off the board.

"Which one is Youssif?" Yossi asked.

The young Arabs laughed and one called out, "Youssif no home."

"Youssif is not here yet," the old man said.

Yossi put his hand to his forehead and rolled again — two more stones.

"You have won," the old man said, picking the last stone off the board with his battered fingers. "Now tell me of the six million, or some other lies, Rabbi."

"Tell me, Jew," the woman said. "Tell me some more fairy stories."

Yossi remembered the burned-out carcass of the bus on Jaffa Street, the shattered glass, the body parts scattered in the street. The bomb blast had woken him and Devorah in their apartment within the walls of the Old City. He had rushed from their bedroom to see, arriving while the acrid smell of burning flesh was still thick in the air.

"Bus number eighteen. I was there when the second bus blew up."

"Good. We have a bomb-maker here," the woman said, pronouncing the second "b" as she pointed to the young Arabs.

"He's a terrorist and should be killed," Yossi said, remembering the *Hesed shel Emet* workers cleaning flesh from the statue of the winged lion who sat perched atop the Generali Building.

"That is not very humane. Does your Torah allow that, Rabbi?" the old man said, setting up the board.

"The Torah of Israel is not about being humane," Yossi said. "This is the land of Isaac and Jacob. This is the land of my fathers and the land of my children and it will be the land of their children. This is our land. The land of Israel. The land of the Jewish people. I don't give a damn about your orange trees and date palms and pomegranate trees. You do not belong here. You are Amalek. I should have poisoned your tea."

"You should have," the old man said. "But your right hand forgot its strength."

"What?" Yossi said, stunned.

"I have read your books, Rabbi. Does it not say, if someone is going to kill you, it is your duty to rise early and kill him first? Yes, I am Amalek and you are not welcome here. You have scattered my children, chopped down my trees, thrown me from my home," the Arab said. "I am a son of Ishmael and you are a son of Isaac. But for that, we are not enemies. We are enemies because you came to make a family in Al-Quds. The land of Palestine is an Islamic holy possession, given to future Muslims until Judgment Day. You are a cancer and you must be cut out." The Arab paused for a moment. "Now it is your turn to roll again."

Before Yossi had a chance to reply, he heard what sounded like a window smashing in his wife's room, the glass shattering onto the stone floor. Yossi's stomach turned. He tried to stand up but was forced down by his shoulders.

"Help!" he called, before the old man pulled off his checked kaffiyeh and stuffed it into Yossi's mouth with the help of his laughing nephews.

"If I forget thee, let my tongue cleave to the roof of my mouth," the old man said, shaking his head.

"Psalm One thirty-seven," Yossi thought, sickened.

Yossi could hear someone stepping through the broken glass. His wife, in a panic, would rise in search of her gun, pull open her night table drawer and find it empty. The taste of the dirty kaffiyeh in his mouth made Yossi want to throw up.

"*Hacol b'seder?*" a soldier called from beneath the kitchen window.

"*B'seder,*" one of the Arabs answered.

"*Lo b'seder,*" Yossi thought in Hebrew. "It's not okay. There are Arabs in my kitchen!"

"*Tov,*" the soldier said. Then there was silence.

The old man placed the dice in Yossi's hand. He dropped them onto the board.

"A good roll," the old man said, moving Yossi's pieces around the table. "Do you have *mazel* tonight?" the Arab man said mockingly.

The sky outside the window was turning quickly from a deep blue to a glowing purple. The bald old man reached into his caftan, removed Devorah Bee's mini 9 mm pistol and placed it on the table. Yossi struggled but could not move. He was held in place by three of the young Arabs. "My children studied at the revolutionary school. They drank anger and ate fury and threw stones. But they are not just bomb-makers and pickpockets. They will be the leaders of this land." The old man prodded the pistol with his index finger and spun it on the board. There was an inscription on the handle.

"What's this?" the old man said, " 'Darling Devorah: For a safe life in Jerusalem. Love Daddy.' A thoughtful gift, and practical, may it protect her from all harm. And a very pretty name. What does Devorah mean?"

Yossi blinked his eyes hard and fast as if he were trying to say, "Fuck you. Fuck your mother you filthy Arab."

The woman picked up the gun and held it against Yossi's

temple. Then she pulled his *kippah* from his head and dropped it to the floor. "It is almost time to pray," she said.

Yossi prayed to his God, wishing Moses had never led his people out of the wilderness, wishing that he had never come to this violent desert land, wishing that he and Devorah were safe in bed back in New York.

The old man looked on, his big eyes pitying, his pink peeling head almost glowing as the sun continued to rise.

Yossi looked at the woman, her face as hard as fire-forged steel. And then the muezzin cried, calling the Arabs to prayer. *"Ull-aaaaaw-hoo-Ak-bar! Ull-aaaaaw-hoo-Ak-bar!"* And the unwelcome guests, as surprisingly as they had arrived, began disappearing into the blue morning light. The blind father, the wives, the mother, the woman, the sons, and the nephews dropped to their knees, foreheads on the floor. And were gone. The old man, too, climbed from his chair and vanished. Yossi pulled the dirty kaffiyeh from his mouth and ran to the hallway, his heart breaking in his throat. The bedroom door opened and out stepped Youssif, a tall handsome Arab in a sweater and slacks. He held a broken bottle in his hand.

Youssif stepped past him, dropping the bloodied bottle to the floor.

"She is not dead," Youssif said. "She is only crying for the ghosts of her children and their children, too."

The sun continued to rise, the muezzin wailing in Arabic, "There is no God but Allah and Muhammad is the messenger of Allah."

The Art of
Correcting

One morning, Rabbi Israel Frummann could not rise from his bed to say his morning prayers. It was the first time in his entire sixty-three years that the great Dokszycer rebbe did not greet the new day with prayer on his lips.

"My back is aching," he said to his wife, Sarah. "I can't move."

"Get up. You must go and pray."

"Like the mortar of Egypt," he cried. "I am turning to stone."

She brought him a hot towel to lie on and some ointment for his neck. He waved it away and then winced.

"All right, my wife. Bring it here."

"Then you must go and pray. You are the rebbe."

With that, the Dokszycer rebbe pulled himself up on his elbows and then fell quickly back onto his pillows. "I cannot go," he said.

"But what about the minyan?" Sarah said, raising her voice.

The Dokszycer sect was a very small order, so small in fact that without the rebbe, only nine men could appear at the Western Wall to perform morning prayers.

"Don't worry, they can worship without me," the rebbe said. "They are all grown men."

"What do you mean?" Sarah said, horrified. "Man's prayers are only truly heard when he prays as part of a congregation. Get out of bed now!"

"All right, wife," the rebbe said and began resolutely to climb from his bed, but screamed out in pain, "The Angel of Death is killing me slowly."

"Are you going to pray?" Sarah said.

"His sword is wedged in my spine!"

"Then, rest," Sarah said, finally. "I will bring you some tea and honey."

"Bring me Luria!"

Lev Luria was a local kabbalist whose mastery of amulets, prayers, and spells was known outside Jerusalem as far as Bnei Brak. It was said he had once revived a dead yeshiva student who had been hit by a bus simply by breathing the word *chayim,* life, into his mouth.

Pale, long-faced Luria arrived sometime after noon and found the rebbe in bed with his window curtains pulled closed.

"The rebbitzin sent for me. What is the matter?" Luria said, stepping close to the rebbe's bed.

"I did not go to prayers this morning," the rebbe said in such a sad tone that he may have been lying on his death bed.

"Why me?" Luria asked, placing his hands in his pockets and stepping away.

"My back feels like it has been walked on by an elephant. My spine has been a ladder for a thousand monkeys. . . ."

Luria took a step closer to the bed. The rebbe was not dying. "How are your eyes?"

"My eyes?" the rebbe said, trying to lift his head from the flattened pillow. "They hurt sometimes."

"It is not your back," Luria said, and a thin smile formed on his face. "The Talmud says a heavy step detracts one five-hundredth from the light of your eyes. Rebbe, if I may be so bold, there is nothing wrong with your back. You must simply learn to take lighter steps or else" — and here Luria's voice fell to a whisper — "you will be blind before the year is over."

"What shall I do?" the rebbe asked.

"Tomorrow you will walk. But softly. Today we must take care of your precious eyes."

"Yes. Yes! We must. Without my eyes I cannot read the Torah."

Lev Luria concocted a potion of kiddush wine, sage, egg yolk, and a sprinkle of golden Jerusalem earth to bathe the eyes of the ailing rebbe. He also placed a fist-sized stone, purplish-blue in color, underneath the rebbe's mattress.

"This is the Stone of Issachar. It will help cure what ails you."

Sarah applied the concoction to the eyelids of her husband, and stroked his hair when she was done. Then, she placed two cucumber slices on his eyes and told him to rest.

The next day, the rebbe was in a rage. He had slept badly, tossing and turning from the pain, feeling every contour of the Stone of Issachar beneath his back. And now his eyes really did hurt. They were red and bloodshot, and he screamed at his wife Sarah to call the kabbalist to come to his bedside immediately.

"What's the matter?" Luria said, entering the dark room shortly afterwards. He leaned over and pulled back the rebbe's eyelids with his index fingers.

"Worse today," the rebbe moaned.

"Good, we have no time to waste. It is happening even faster than I thought. You must stand up now."

"But I can't," the rebbe said. "Termites are eating at me."

"Stand up," Luria said, and pulled the rebbe's arm.

The rebbe slid out of bed and fell onto the floor in a heap of bones. He felt as if he was going to burst into flames. "Pick me up," he screamed.

"The floor is hard. Today you will sleep on the floor."

The great Dokszycer rebbe cried out for his wife Sarah to throw the mad kabbalist from his house. "The Dokszycer rebbe does not sleep on the floor. My father slept on goose-down, and his father on swan feathers."

That evening, the rebbe's followers stood above him and performed the *Ma'ariv* services. From the floor the rebbe could easily see the nine smiling faces that completed the minyan. He slept better that evening, but in the morning, cried out in pain once again.

Sarah came to comfort him with a cold towel for his forehead, and though she was not much taller than his congregation's large Torah scroll, he believed she could cure any ill. "If I see that Luria again, I will beat him about the head," Sarah said, shaking her little fist like a dried-out citron. "He is as bad as the cut-and-slash doctors. I will fix you a warm bath with Epsom salts."

"Wife," the rebbe said, "how wonderful it would be to pray again at the Wall and to walk back and forth over the earth as I please. But I am afraid my spine is broken like a matchstick."

Sarah knelt down and he looked into her smooth, worn face and remembered her as a young girl when she still wore braids on either side of her head. Now she wore a blue snood adorned with gold stars that covered all of her still-brown hair. "You are a good wife. Bring me the bottle of wine."

Sarah brought an herbalist who concocted a mixture of valerian root, skullcap, and devil's claw to soothe the rebbe's pains, but the rebbe wouldn't touch the murky elixir and shouted the herbalist from his home. Sarah brought a Yemenite master of prayer who offered mud and salts from the Dead Sea to rub against his skin, and a rabbi who could read cures in the stars, but the rebbe would not see them, preferring the solitude of his dark room. Sarah only entered while he slept to remove the refuse bucket from beside the bed. When she brought him food and knocked, saying, "If you chew well with your teeth, your back will find its strength," he said he was not hungry. When she said, "You must drink," he called out, "More wine!"

Finally, the rebbe called Sarah to open the door. She entered, and the dark room smelled stale and musty like old books and bedsheets. The rebbe lay on the bed with pillows propped under his legs and back.

"How does one begin a conversation with God?" the rebbe began, his voice thin and strained. "How does one start such a conversation? What does one say?"

"You are tired," Sarah said.

"What does one say? And in what language?" the rebbe said.

"You know what to do," Sarah said.

"I have never had such a conversation."

The rebbe lived every day in the shadow of his great-great-grandfather, the first Dokszycer rebbe, peace be upon him, who had summoned God to protect his village from rampaging cossacks. It is said that he stood in the village square with his eyes closed as cossack hoofbeats pounded nearer and as they reached the square hooting and howling, a giant hand reached out of the sky to pluck the riders from the horses' backs.

"I have been in the dark. Alone. No angels met me. No voice answered my calls. *Elohim!*" the rebbe screamed. "*Elohim!* Master of the Universe."

"Oh, Israel," Sarah said. "The Lord tests the righteous. Rabbi Jonathan said the potter does not test cracked pots, because if he tapped it even once it would break. But he does test the good ones because no matter how many times he tests them they do not break. So God tests not the wicked but the righteous."

"You are saying that Rabbi Jonathan thinks I am like a clay pot?"

"Turn on the light," Sarah said, exasperated. "Yitzchak has been waiting to see you."

"In my distress I cried unto the Lord and he did *not* hear me," the rebbe said, misquoting the first line of Psalm 120.

Yitzchak was the rebbe's nephew and only heir to the leadership of the Dokszycer dynasty since the rebbe's son had left the closed walls of the community for the greener shores of New York's Long Island. The rebbe wore his shirt torn in the corner every day as if his only son had died.

Yitzchak was whip thin and as tall as Solomon the Wise was said to have been, though not nearly as sharp, the rebbe often observed. He entered the rebbe's room with an unusual spring in his step.

"How are you feeling today?" he asked. His suit was rumpled and the rebbe could see a soup stain on the front of his shirt.

The rebbe pulled himself up, so that he sat leaning against a couple of pillows. "How am I feeling?" he asked. "Has the Messiah arrived yet?"

"How is your back? And neck?"

The rebbe threw out his arm in a weak backhand and released from his lips a long agonized "Aaaaaaaach!"

"I have found someone," Yitzchak said, smiling and then covering his mouth with his hand. His teeth were as large as those of a horse and the rebbe often joked that he should pray with his mouth closed so he would not scare God from the world. "I have found someone who can help you, Rebbe."

"Only God can help me," the rebbe said, shaking his head slowly until he had to stop from the pain.

"I have found someone," Yitzchak repeated.

"I'm sure you have found someone," the rebbe said.

"I met him at Zion Square," Yitzchak said. "Demonstrating tricks concerning the back."

"No more tricks," the rebbe said.

"He is a healer," Yitzchak said, picking up the edge of the rebbe's bedside table with one shaking hand, spilling a half-full glass of water onto the floor. "Last week, I could not have lifted this."

An hour later Sarah entered, drew the curtains, turned on a small lamp, and led a tall pale man dressed all in white into the rebbe's room.

The rebbe sat propped against his pillows, wearing only his bedclothes and a black *kippah* on his head. He had never seen a grown man so clean shaven. He thought the man looked like a glass of milk. His hair was blond and cropped short and he wore round steel-rimmed spectacles tightly on his face.

"Hello," the man said. "I have come to help you. Doctor John J. McGraw. "

The rebbe had passed the war years as a child in England and spoke English fairly well.

"You have come to help me?" the rebbe said.

"Have you been in bed since you hurt your back?" Dr. John J. McGraw asked. The rebbe nodded. "Sit up on the edge of the bed."

"Why?" the rebbe said.

"Don't be an old goat," Sarah said. "He is trying to help you."

"I can't. I am broken," the rebbe said.

"Very slowly," the doctor said slowly. "You must get out of bed. There is nothing worse for a sore back than immobility."

"Nu?" Sarah said, leaning close to her husband.

"Wife. Leave us," the rebbe said, and then he slid to the edge of the bed.

"Remove your shirt and stand up," the doctor said with such authority that the rebbe didn't question, and stepped into a pair of slippers before pulling off his shirt. Nobody had spoken to him that way since he was a child. He felt small and naked and immediately wanted to cover himself. The doctor told him to drop his hands to his sides.

"Close your eyes," the doctor said.

"My eyes?" the rebbe said. "I'm sure it is not my eyes."

"Close your eyes," the doctor said, and reached under the rebbe's beard, placing his fingers beneath his chin to lift it straight. "Turn your head to the left."

"But it is hurting," the rebbe said.

"Turn your head to the left, and then to the right."

He could feel his nose grazing the doctor's hand on either side as he turned.

"Now, look straight ahead and open your eyes," the doctor said, flatly.

The rebbe was shocked to see that when he opened his eyes, he was not looking straight ahead but down and to the right, toward a pile of dirty laundry.

"I can help you," the doctor said, removing a small silver camera from his pocket.

"What are you doing?" the rebbe said.

"I am going to take a picture of your posture as it is now," the doctor said, aiming the camera. "Look at the curve in your back, and the way your shoulders —"

"No. No!" the rebbe said. "You can't do that. It is against the Second Commandment."

"Just to record your progress," the doctor said.

"No graven images," the rebbe said, turning away.

The doctor put his camera away and apologized to the rebbe. "I am sorry. I am very sorry."

The rebbe looked into the doctor's eyes for the first time, and they were blue and shining like the springtime pools of his youth. He wore some sort of silver charm around his neck that was shaped like the English letter "t." The rebbe shuddered and again thought back to his youth.

"McGraw," the rebbe said, pronouncing the name for the first time. "Where do you come from?"

"Saint Louis."

"I believe there really are Jews everywhere," the rebbe said, smiling.

"I'm not Jewish," the doctor said. "You can put your shirt on now."

"Well, why are you here?" the rebbe said, not quite understanding. He noticed that the doctor's breath smelled like peppermint. "Why did you come to me?"

"I practice the art of correcting," the doctor said. "I

locate spinal malfunction and fix it. Do you have frequent back and neck pain? Do you have pain in between your shoulder blades? Do you feel a numbing or tingling in the arms or hands?"

"Yes! Yes! Yes!" the rebbe screamed.

"Israel, are you all right?" Sarah called from outside the door.

"I am fine, wife." The rebbe pulled his shirt over his head, forgetting his beard inside his nightshirt. "How are you going to help me?"

The doctor explained how nerves connecting to the spine, when pinched or compressed, can cause pain or irritation in almost any part of the body, and how he simply, through controlled pressure, restores the spine to a more normal position, in turn reducing pain and irritation.

"Imagine a garden hose as a nerve and the water flowing through it as the nerve impulses —"

"A what?" the rebbe said.

"A garden hose," the doctor said.

"Do you see a garden around here?" the rebbe said. "In Jerusalem, everything is stone."

"But you are made of flesh and bone," the doctor said. "We must ease the pressure on the nerve. This will take some time. Maybe a week, maybe a few months. Your spine is curving like a question mark."

"A question mark, huh? I have a question for you," the rebbe said, reaching out toward the doctor. "Do you mean you can fix my back?"

"You must have faith."

The doctor walked around behind the rebbe, told him to place his arms across his chest in the form of an "x." He pressed himself close to him and reached around the rebbe. Placing one pale hand on top of the rebbe's and one between his shoulder blades, he pulled in and thrust forward at the exact same moment. There was a pop, pop, and the rebbe screamed out.

"That feels good," the rebbe said, after a moment.

"You should come to my office," the doctor said. "For a complete adjustment, to prevent it from being hurt again."

"But I feel fine," the rebbe said, kicking up his slippered feet, humming a joyous-sounding *nigun* under his breath. "The just among Gentiles are priests of God. Thank you, thank you," he said, "I am so grateful. How can I pay you?"

"You will find a way," the doctor said, removing his glasses to clean them with a handkerchief.

"But a physician who takes no fee is worth no fee."

"I am no physician," the doctor replied.

But the rebbe was so happy, he sang, "I feel so good, I feel so good," and called out for Sarah. "Wife, come look! I feel strong as an ox! Thank you, thank you," he said again to the doctor, who just stood silently, looking about the room.

"You have some very curious objects here," the doctor said, motioning to the rebbe's Galician spice box on the dressing table.

Sarah rushed in, still holding a wooden spoon in her hand. "Israel, I've never seen you so happy," she cried.

"I have found my youth again."

The doctor shook the rebbe's hand, and before walking out of the room, tapped him lightly on the back with his index finger. "Until next time," he said.

Within a few hours, not long after the sirens began wailing throughout the city to announce the sabbath, the rebbe was on his back again, moaning in pain. He had tried to pull himself into his Shabbat finery but fell back onto his bed, where he lay all of Saturday and Sunday. The clanging church bells of the Holy Sepulcher were like mosquitoes in his ears that day in bed, as he lay in the dark with one pillow arching his neck and another covering his face.

Several acres of the Jerusalem forest had caught fire in the dry heat, and the smell of smoke woke the rebbe early Monday morning. Dr. John J. McGraw knocked on the rebbe's door soon afterward. At first, Sarah would not let him pass, and raised her voice when he offered to adjust her and fix her dowager's hump. But finally she relented when the rebbe called, "Let him come."

The stubborn rebbe had piled two pillows onto a chair and sat on them, where he hunched over a small table covered with an open copy of the Talmud. The rebbe looked up and squinted at the doctor. The doctor was dressed in a white shirt with beige pants and looked like nobody the rebbe had ever known. He was thin and plain-looking, like a slice of his wife's challah waiting to be buttered.

"You?" the rebbe said. "I waited for you yesterday. But I couldn't wait," he said, pointing to the pillows beneath him.

"How do you feel?" the doctor said, stepping forward. And for a moment his glasses caught the overhead light and a glare flashed into the rebbe's eyes.

"I feel like I'm sitting on a cloud," the rebbe said. "Filled with fire."

The doctor stepped closer, reached into the rebbe's beard, and placed two fingers beneath the rebbe's chin, raising it. "Do you read like that all the time?"

"Yes, yes," the rebbe said. "I am in very close study."

"Stand up," the doctor said. "You should never read like that."

He led the rebbe to the center of the room. "Does it hurt to walk?"

"Only when I walk."

He placed the rebbe's arms across his chest as he had the first time, and pressed himself close enough that the rebbe noticed that the minty smell had been replaced by cinnamon. The doctor pulled in and thrust forward, and again there was a pop, pop. But this time, the rebbe did not scream out. He simply said, "*Baruch Hashem,* Praise God."

"And now we must walk."

Out in the streets of the shabbiest section of the Mea Shearim quarter, the rebbe walked beside Dr. John J. McGraw. He shuffled his feet at first and then took baby steps, before his feet stuck to the ground not a block from where he lived. A pink stretchy substance clung to the bottom of the rebbe's shoe. "That's mine," the doctor said apologetically, pulling the gum off the rebbe's shoe with a handkerchief. "I spit it out on my way over."

Before long, the rebbe strode like a young man at the side of the doctor. They passed gray stone walls plastered with Yiddish-language posters, walked beneath caged-in balconies where children cried from above, stepped over potholes in the road. They passed bearded men in striped caftans, a woman with a scarf on her head carrying grocery bags, a couple of young yeshiva students bent almost double from the weight of their books, and then a red-bearded Bratzlaver whom the rebbe knew from prayers at the Wall.

"They all do not see me," the rebbe said. "You would think the sun had gone out."

They walked as far as the Street of Prophets, and then turned around, walking back toward the sky blackened with smoke. When they reached a small synagogue not far from the rebbe's home, where the sound of prayers floated out the open windows and into the street, the rebbe stopped to catch his breath.

"My back feels okay. But my lungs, they're bursting."

The doctor peered into the window and began to laugh. "Like pecking chickens," he said under his breath. The rebbe joined him at the window. He had prayed there many times before and saw men bobbing and swaying as if their prayers were taking them very far away. Others sat hunched over large leather-bound books searching for hidden wisdom. The rebbe felt a pain in his heart.

"The Torah says, 'If you forsake me for a single day, I will forsake you for two days,'" the rebbe said. "It has now been six days."

The doctor wiped his brow with a handkerchief. "Look at them," he said, arching his neck to get a better view. Praying men moved like rusty engines and lifted piles of books as if they would collapse under their weight. The doctor turned to the rebbe. "They only need one book. I imagine they feel as much pain as you."

"But I feel pain *not* praying," the rebbe said.

"I will help you fix that," the doctor said, touching him lightly on the back. "But you mustn't shrug your shoulders like that."

The next morning when Dr. John J. McGraw arrived to treat the Dokszycer rebbe, Sarah told him to wait.

"The rebbe is not feeling well," she said. "His back is sore again."

Overhearing his wife in the hallway, the rebbe called, "Let him come."

The rebbe stood gingerly beside his bed wrapping the leather straps of his tefillin around his left arm.

"I don't mean to interrupt," the doctor said, as he entered the rebbe's room. "But what are you doing?"

The rebbe placed the second box of the tefillin onto his forehead and said, "I am putting on my tefillin. And then I am going to pray."

"How is your back today?"

"It hurts," the rebbe said, tightening the straps.

The doctor stepped forward and touched the rebbe's arm where the leather straps were wound tightly against his skin. He walked around behind the rebbe and tapped him between the shoulder blades. "Can you touch your toes?"

"I am trying to pray."

"I can see the tension in your shoulders," the doctor said. "Prayer should not mean pain."

The rebbe smelled cinnamon and felt a sickness in his stomach. "Don't you know there is pain in everything?"

"There doesn't have to be. Those straps are too tight. Look how your body is being pulled to the left, while you lean to the right. The vein in your neck is like a rope," the doctor said, starting to unwind the straps from the rebbe's arm. His nose was so small it looked like it belonged to a young child. "And when you bend over you must remember to bend your knees."

"Bend my knees?"

"Become flexible, and then pray. Like supple reeds on the banks of the Jordan."

He had finished unwrapping the straps of the tefillin

from the rebbe's head and laid the two boxes on the cluttered table beside them.

"But I must say the blessing," the rebbe said. "It is a mitzvah."

Dr. John J. McGraw hesitated and said, "Finish quickly then."

After the rebbe completed his prayers the doctor adjusted him, making tiny pops in his back and neck.

"Good," the doctor said. "When you are ready I will bring you to my office for a thorough adjustment."

"What will happen then?" the rebbe asked.

"Prayer," the doctor said. "Painless prayer."

The doctor showed the rebbe how to stretch his back simply by lying face down on the floor and pushing up with his hands. The rebbe hesitated at first, saying he felt like an animal, but relented when he felt the warm stretch in the muscles of his back. He learned to stretch his calves, neck, and pectorals, and wondered how he could not have known to do something so simple.

Afterward they walked under a hot June sun, through the cluttered streets of Mea Shearim, past the Street of Prophets as far as the British Council Library and the Ethiopian church.

The next morning, the rebbe rose early, wound himself in the leather straps of his tefillin, and muttered the prayers under his breath. As he lay on the floor stretching his back the rebbe wondered if the pinching pain he felt was guilt.

"Good. You've already stretched," the doctor said when he arrived. "We are going to walk a little bit farther today," he added, smiling.

It was already a blazing hot Wednesday morning, as the doctor and the rebbe stepped out of the dingy apartment and into the street. From the doorway Sarah waved a cup and called after the rebbe as he walked away, "Israel, drink some water first! The *hamsiin* has arrived." A dry wind had blown in out of the desert and carried with it a stifling heat that made the asphalt soft beneath their feet. The perfect blue sky was marred intermittently by thin wisps of smoke that rose into the sky like floating Hebrew letters. The sun was already high enough in the sky to bleach all of the stone buildings a harsh, luminous white. There was not a shadow in sight.

The streets of Mea Shearim bustled as usual, as bearded, hat-wearing men dressed in customary black hurried back and forth on their way to or from prayer. Their wives in kerchiefs and long dresses, some pregnant, some not, dragged strollers piled high with children and bags from the market.

The rebbe smiled at a pair of passing men whose noses were buried in prayer books. "Isn't it wonderful," the rebbe said. "Jews everywhere."

"It is wonderful," the doctor said, suddenly beaming.

"Tell me," the rebbe said. "How does a Gentile find himself living in Jerusalem."

"I came to be here for the millennium."

"The millennium?" the rebbe said, confused.

"The year two thousand," the doctor said, ushering the rebbe out of one of the neighborhood's many gates.

"Oh-ho," the rebbe said, laughing. "Two thousand years since . . . It is funny, it must be ten years since I have seen your calendar. For us, for Jews, it is the year fifty-seven sixty."

"And your Messiah has still not arrived."

"Today," the rebbe said. "I am absolutely sure he will arrive today. I have been absolutely sure of that every day for the last sixty-three years. If not today, then tomorrow, which when it arrives," the rebbe said in a singsong manner, "will be today."

"Tell me, what will happen when your Messiah comes?"

"Of course, the Temple will be rebuilt. And we will have a King of Israel at last, and the entire world will be full of the knowledge of the Lord," the rebbe said nonchalantly. "And yours?"

"Exactly the same," the doctor said. "It is written that the Lord Jesus Christ will return to a hill east of Jerusalem and redeem the world."

"And how will you know it is him?" the rebbe said.

"I will look at his hands and at his side, and see if the scars are there. And if there are scars —"

"Enough," the rebbe said, laughing. "Enough of this. Let's turn around. I'm tired of walking today."

They stopped just short of the walls of the Old City, near Damascus Gate, where the doctor offered him a sip of his water. The rebbe was sweating in streams, and gulped down most of the bottle. The sun was still directly above their heads, and felt to the rebbe as if a thousand-pound weight were on his shoulders. They began slowly walking back up the sloping hill.

"Do you know there is a way to walk all around Jerusalem without walking up a hill?" the rebbe said.

"And have you found that way?"

"No."

"Take off your coat and hat. It is too hot for you to wear wool on a day like this."

"But I always wear this," the rebbe said, refusing to remove his heavy wool coat. "I have worn it for hundreds of years."

The next morning, Sarah waited until the rebbe had finished his prayers.

"Israel," she said. "Nobody has seen Yitzchak for days. Do you know where he is?"

The rebbe was in a foul mood as he unwound the tefillin from his aching arm. Aside from his back still aching, now the muscles of his legs were sore. "What, am I Yitzchak's keeper? Do I know where he is every minute of the day? He is a young man, so he is out praying. Maybe he went to Shchem, maybe he went to Hevron. His cousin is living there."

"But nobody has seen him," Sarah said. "Nobody knows where he is. We must find him. Last week a yeshiva boy from Sanhedria was found stabbed in the street."

"All right, all right, wife, I will call Schmuelik, I will call Reuven, I'll call everybody. We will turn the world over, if that's what you want."

And that was when the doctor walked in, looking red and childlike, burned from the sun. The rebbe wanted to say, "Now you know why we wear the coats?"

"Your door was open," the doctor said. "Are you ready to go?"

"I'm not going anywhere today. Now besides my back hurting and my neck hurting and my arms hurting, my legs are hurting, and precious Yitzchak is missing and we must find him, because if we don't find him, my wife will never let me sleep."

"You shouldn't wave your arms like that," the doctor said, with his arms still at his sides. "It will throw your whole body out of alignment. We must continue to strengthen your back. You are doing so well. In a few more days, your back will be as strong as a tree, and the adjustments will hold."

"Ach, the forest is burning," the rebbe said. "Today my business is Yitzchak. Surely you can wait until tomorrow to make me better. If you want, you can make the popping in my back."

"It's important that we continue to build your strength. We have come so far."

The rebbe asked Sarah to leave the room, turned his back to the doctor, and crossed his arms over his chest.

"The rebbe is asking you to pop him quickly," the rebbe sang, "and tomorrow you will return to walk with him. But right now, he must find Yitzchak."

The doctor pressed himself close to the rebbe, took his crossed arms in his hands and thrust in with supernatural force. The rebbe screamed out in pain, and felt like he was being broken to pieces. He actually called out for his mother, and then fell to the floor. "What have you done to me?"

"Tomorrow, we will walk," the doctor said, and lifted the rebbe up. He placed a hot hand between his shoulder blades, pushed in slightly, and left the stunned rebbe alone in his room.

The Dokszycers searched synagogues and study halls from Pisgat Ze'ev to Efrat but did not find Yitzchak nor any sign of him that day. But the rebbe said not to worry, there are not many places Yitzchak could go.

Friday morning the doctor arrived as promised. The rebbe had not slept at all the night before. He had tossed and turned in his bed thinking of Yitzchak and the doctor and Sarah, who had yelled at him while he stretched on the floor, telling him to get up, he looked like a snake. She was angry that he would not spend another day searching for Yitzchak, who would have to spend Shabbat among strangers.

The rebbe appeared wearing a plain white shirt, buttoned to the top, and a pair of black suspenders. On his head he wore only a large black silken *kippah* pulled low over his brow covering his hairline. His heavy wool coat and large-brimmed black hat lay on top of the rebbe's bed like a sick or dying man.

"We are walking farther today?" the rebbe asked.

"If you are ready," the doctor said.

"Look," the rebbe said, pointing to a bottle hooked to his belt. "Water."

The doctor adjusted the rebbe's back, repeating, "Good, good," as he worked.

"Hurry back," Sarah called after the doctor and the rebbe, but they didn't hear, lost as they were in discussion.

"So you are saying that Jesus was the son of God and is the Messiah?" the rebbe said rhetorically as he mopped his forehead with a handkerchief.

The doctor nodded his head.

"So the Messiah has come?" the rebbe said.

"Yes."

They walked in silence for a few moments through the buzzing quarter of Mea Shearim, where men hurried off to pray before the sabbath and the women frantically rushed about buying food for their Shabbat tables.

"No," the rebbe said. "The Messiah has not come. Because if He had, the world would be a very different place. So your Messiah has not come. So you wait."

They arrived a while later at Damascus Gate. Even the cool-blooded doctor was sweating now, as they stepped down toward the massive entrance to the Old City. Young Arab men joked and pulled their kaffiyehs around their faces against the gray smoke that still swam through the city. Women sat on the ground along the entryway, selling fruits and vegetables on outspread headscarves. An Israeli soldier sat languidly in an opening above the entrance and picked his teeth with a telephone card. They entered the ornamented stone gate and were immediately swallowed up by pressing crowds and the tinny sounds of Arabic music. The air smelled to the rebbe like barbecued meat. It was the Muslim sabbath and thousands of men dressed in kaffiyehs inched their way toward the Dome of the Rock to pray to the mighty Allah. This was the way the rebbe always walked to the Western Wall, but had never been that way on a Friday morning. Bearded kaffiyeh-wearing men pressed forward, their ragged caftans flapping as they walked. An old man waved his arms, shouting loudly in Arabic. The rebbe looked over at the doctor and saw his milk-dish of a face contorted with fear. The rebbe, too, felt unease in the pit of his belly and reached out to take the doctor's hand in his, so as not to lose him.

They turned into a small street and the rebbe let go of the doctor's hand. Immediately the crowds and the smells of spice and Turkish coffee were gone. The street narrowed and then widened out again. A group of men and women dressed in white and beige, topped with gaudy sunhats, moved toward the rebbe and the smiling doctor. They were singing hymns and several dragged a large wooden cross. "That can't be good for the back," the rebbe thought, stopping to catch his breath. He stared around in wonder. These people, pale and plain as cotton balls, nodded their heads to the doctor as they passed. Who were they? One man wearing round glasses like the doctor pulled out a camera and shot a quick picture of the rebbe standing beside the Third Station of the Cross.

"What?" the rebbe screamed. "What are you doing?"

The man smiled and took another picture. The rebbe screamed again, a curse so ancient that even he did not know its meaning, and then he charged at the man, kicked at him, and jumped on his back. The doctor pulled the rebbe away, almost throwing him onto the ground as the group scattered.

"My back," the rebbe said, from the ground where he lay awkwardly on his side. "Ohhhhh! My broken back."

"Like the agony of Christ," the doctor said, smiling. "This is where Jesus fell for the first time."

"My back, my back! What are you, crazy? Take me home."

"Do you want to be saved?"

"Yes. Pop my back. Please pop it."

"God made his original covenant with a Jew," the doctor said. "And now it is time to renew that covenant."

"Pop my back!" the rebbe screamed. "Pop it. I must go home."

"Do you know that even from here on the Via Dolorosa, you can hear the Shabbat sirens sounding for the Jewish sabbath. I can leave you here," the doctor said. "Or, I can pop your back now and you will come to my office for a final adjustment. It is not far from here."

"What are you going to do?" the rebbe said, wincing in pain.

"I will fix you so you do not feel pain when you pray," the doctor said.

The rebbe paused for a moment and looked down at the stones beneath him. He stood up. "Okay. I will go. But I must be home by Shabbat. Now, please pop my back. I am broken in two."

The doctor moved in behind the rebbe and placed his hand between his shoulder blades and thrust forward as he pulled in from the front. "Now we will walk."

"Who were those people? Who was the man with the camera?" the rebbe asked, and took a long drink of his water.

"Pilgrims," the doctor answered. "Holy pilgrims."

As they passed the Condemnation Chapel and the Chapel of the Flagellation, the doctor excitedly explained the importance of the buildings. "And just over there is Our Lady of the Spasm."

"Spasm?" the rebbe thought. "What is this, sick? Flagellation, condemnation?"

Then they passed the Church of Saint Anne and left the walled city through Saint Stephen's Gate.

"There is the Garden of Gethsemane, and the Basilica of the Agony where Jesus was betrayed by a kiss. And of course across the valley, there is the Mount of Olives."

The rebbe knew the Mount of Olives well. He planned to be buried near his father on the western slope facing the Old City. His head began to buzz from thirst and the heat and he wanted to sit down, but he didn't dare, as they were passing through a Muslim cemetery. A shepherd and his flock were fast approaching through the tall, dry grass. "How much farther?"

"Not far. How is your back?" the doctor said, not waiting for an answer as the road sloped down into the valley. "When the Messiah returns, all who are buried here will be resurrected."

"Yes," the rebbe said. "I know that."

They walked in silence down among the cracked Hebrew gravestones. The rebbe read the names to himself and mumbled a silent kaddish for the dead. And though he knew they would one day be returned to the earth he felt a deep sadness for them as there was one thing the dead could not do. They could not perform God's mitzvah of prayer.

After noticing a grave marked with the name Ben David, the rebbe bent over and placed a stone on the grave. "Our Messiah must come from the house of David."

"The same as Jesus," the doctor said.

The rebbe turned around and faced the Old City. The sun was finally starting to move down the sky toward the west and he removed his *kippah* for a moment and mopped the sweat from his brow. "There. You see." He pointed vaguely toward the city. "The sealed gate. It is called the Gate of Mercy. That is the gate the Messiah will use when he at last enters Jerusalem."

"The same gate that Jesus last used when he entered Jerusalem," the doctor answered. "You see. We are just splitting hairs."

They walked farther up the mount, the rebbe close on the heels of the doctor as he drank the last of his water. The rebbe's beard felt as heavy as stone against his chest. When they crested the hill they could easily see the black smoke rising from the forest to the west as the fires moved slowly toward Tel Aviv.

"Blessed are the humble-minded, for they will possess the land," the doctor said, his voice rising. "Blessed are those who are hungry and thirsty for uprightness, for they will be satisfied. Blessed are the merciful, for they will be shown mercy. Blessed are the pure of heart, for they will see God."

"That is beautiful," the rebbe said.

The doctor smiled. "You have reached the top. Look!"

The rebbe looked out beyond the Valley of Kidron and saw the Old City and the shining gold of the Dome of the Rock and imagined a time before the walls and the city when Abraham, a simple man, answered a call from the wilderness and was tested.

The doctor put his arm around the rebbe and said, "We are very much alike." They began walking toward a white arched building at the end of a gravel road. "Prayer is the backbone of your life, and prayer is the heart of my life. Look to the west. It is burning. They are sinning in Tel Aviv, they are sinning in London, they are sinning in New York. But here in Jerusalem, in this prayer factory, there is goodness. It is us against them. Those who will live and those who will die."

They arrived outside of the new hastily constructed Resurrection Hotel that had been built to accommodate the thousands of expected pilgrims arriving to celebrate the millennium and await the Resurrection.

"You know, there is only one God," the doctor said. "It is just that you are praying in the wrong language, so to speak, in an awkward manner. Look at how these prayers have twisted your body. I know that terrible things have happened to the Jews. Terrible tragedies. Because your prayers simply went poof, into the sky. Nobody was listening."

"Many strayed from the path," the rebbe said, sadly. "But I am a good person. I perform all six hundred thirteen of God's commandments."

"But it is time for a new covenant," the doctor said, leading the rebbe under the archway into the Resurrection Hotel.

The hotel lobby was sparsely decorated and shabby. It looked as if the furniture had been borrowed from another hotel. Several plain-looking people dressed in drab colors and comfortable shoes lingered in the lobby, talking quietly.

"Vus nu?" the rebbe said, raising his voice to break the silence of the cool lobby. "What now?"

"My office is just down this corridor," the doctor said, leading the rebbe to a wooden door where a sign hung that said: Holy Mission Chiropractic.

The doctor opened the door and the rebbe followed, feeling faint. There was another closed door across the room, emblazoned with a golden crucifix. The rebbe stood stunned. He felt that he was in another land, far from home.

"Would you like some water?" the doctor said, pulling a paper cone from beside the water cooler.

"No, no," the rebbe said. "I will be okay."

"I know you will. I must apologize," the doctor said, gesturing toward the closed door. "It seems my colleague is in with a patient. He will not be long."

The rebbe began to sway back and forth and mumble under his breath as he moved. He felt a pain in his spine, but it was a good pain, a familiar pain, a pain that belonged to him.

The doctor smiled and said, "You are praying again," and dropped a cushion on the floor before them. "Let me show you how."

The doctor fell to his knees on the cushion and placed the palms of his hands together. He looked up at the rebbe. "It is easy. And it does not hurt."

"No," the rebbe said. "No!"

"It says in Revelations that the conversion of the Jews will herald the coming of Christ," the doctor said. "Please kneel."

The door opened, and out stepped the man who had photographed the rebbe on the Via Dolorosa. Behind him, in the center of the room, the rebbe could see tilted to an almost vertical position on the chiropractic table, Yitzchak, precious Yitzchak, smiling a horse-toothed smile, with his arms stretched out wide to meet the rebbe.

"He has been adjusted," the man said. "Is your patient ready, Doctor McGraw?"

"Yitzchak!" the rebbe called, and sang out the Shema, "Hear, O Israel: the Lord our God. The Lord is One," as loud as he could both forward and backward, as he had been told his great-great-grandfather, may his memory blessed, had done to vanquish the cossacks in the town square of Dok-szyce all those years ago.

The Ascent
of Eli Israel

Toward Jerusalem

Spring was in full flame again and Eli was a shepherd at Betar, south of Jerusalem, but up even higher in the sky. His friend Zev knew a man who had a flock of sheep out over the Green Line, who knew that Eli needed help. He asked if Eli could watch over his sheep. Most of the great leaders in the history of mankind have been shepherds, Eli thought: Abraham, Isaac, Jacob, Moses, David, Joseph. All the twelve tribes, all of Jacob's twelve sons, had been shepherds.

Eli recalled the words of Micah the prophet that said the Lord would come forth from his throne and tread upon the high places of the earth.

So he agreed to go.

"Just melt into the land," Zev had said to Eli. "And you're gone."

Eli fashioned a carpetbag out of an old red, black, and green riding blanket, and tied the heavy load to him with rope. And he herded sheep out there, protecting the Green Line between Israel and the West Bank, with just his wooden staff, an old .38 Special, and his lumpy carpetbag pressing into his back.

It was quiet. He had never heard quiet like this. Every once in a while, some broken-down fellahin would ride by on their donkeys and wave, or an F-15 would buzz the sky overhead, but Eli was alone out there, waiting for his next instruction.

Sometimes a gray wolf would saunter past and sit down. Even in broad daylight. And the wolf wasn't looking at his sheep at all. They would sit and stare at each other for hours, and Eli would ask him questions, questions about life and purity and goodness. He would fall asleep, and when he awoke the wolf would still be there, watching him.

With all the static of the world gone, a simple piece of grass became a thing of monumental beauty. He would hold a single blade in his hand for hours and feel its texture, as smooth as a satin dress then rough as sandpaper, causing his fingers to bleed. He discovered that all the elements of the universe existed inside of everything, and if he looked the right way he could turn a blade of grass into a meal filling enough for a week, or a sky full of stars into an intricate checkerboard that would entertain him until the sky turned blue with morning. He stretched his shadow across the land and ran after it laughing, or ran from it crying. Sometimes, he saw things that he would normally have heard and heard things that he should only have seen.

He could feel God moving throughout creation and would call out, "Do you hear me? Do you hear me?" and tell him how far he had been from him and ask him to bring him closer to his strength.

It had been more than a year since he had been called.

"Eli Haller, son of man. Go to the house of Israel."

He had jumped up off his mother's couch, spilling the scotch he was pouring into a tall glass, and said, "What? Who?"

From the darkness of his aging mother's Brooklyn apartment he heard a heavy silence. His mother's door was still closed, and only the flashing of the muted television lit the room. He lay flat against the floor, his heart beating against the carpet. Over the top of the couch he was able to see that the door was still triple bolted.

"Shit," he said, reaching for the bottle of Dewars on the low glass table beside him. The light and shadows cast upon the ceiling from the streetlights down below seemed to blur and distort before his eyes, like something melting.

The voice came again and he dropped the bottle.

"Who are you?"

The answer was more of a breath than a name. Eli felt it through all of the cells of his body.

"Who are you?" Eli screamed.

The room filled with fire, a black fire radiating darkness, a fire so dark he could only see inside himself, his ribcage heaving, blood racing through the veins, heart pumping, bubbling cells and microcells and the spaces between them. His bones ached, and it was inside him now, a winged pillar of black fire with four faces, looking to the east, west, north, and south. He could see them all at once. One face was a child, the other a man, the third was a lion, and the fourth face an eagle. Four voices joined as one and said, "I am the Lord and I have judged you."

"No," Eli screamed, and tore at his hair, banged his head against the floor. He saw the hurt faces of his wife and child, felt the soft touch of her hand against his cheek. He lifted his face from the carpet, and heard a distant crying that he knew belonged to Josh.

"You have known the dark path," the voice said. "I will

breathe a new spirit into you, remove your heart, and give you a new one. You will walk in my light and follow my laws, and others will, too. And I will be your God and their God."

A wind came and the wings whipped the dark fire into a pillar of burning orange flames. "Those who don't walk my path will know no God and will suffer famine and pestilence and the sword."

When God had gone Eli Haller lay still for hours afterward crying everything into the carpet.

In the City of the Patriarchs

On the bus from the airport, an old rabbi turned his face away from Eli and told him in heavily accented English, "You are dying, friend."

Just after nightfall, the bus dropped Eli off outside a barbed-wire compound at a place called Tel Romeida, which sat on a bluff overlooking downtown Hebron. His body shook beneath a crushing headache as he searched for the home of his only remaining friend in the world. Muezzins began to wail from their minarets under a tangle of faintly blinking stars. Eli forced a stiff-necked nod as he passed bored-looking Israeli soldiers who leaned against gray cement blocks spitting sunflower seed shells into the air.

Eli had managed to find his way to the city of Hebron from the address on an old postcard Zev had sent him in New York.

Zev lived in a caravan on the top of a hill, just above the Arab homes and vineyards clustered together down below. He hugged Eli close to him, saying with a smile, "Brother!

Just in time for the *simcha*." He took the bag from Eli's hand and dropped it to the floor.

"I knew you'd come someday," Zev said, stretching his arms expansively as he whooped: "Welcome to the wild, wild West Bank!"

Zev was still a big man, with giant shoulders and long hair, and could have been Eli's brother or a mirror image only five years older. Now he wore a *kippah* on his head and a long beard with sidecurls at his ears. They had met years back at a John Lennon memorial at Strawberry Fields in Central Park, had prowled the streets of New York, and flunked out of A.A. together. Zev had been at the hospital when Eli's son was born and they'd celebrated together on pills Zev had stolen from the E.R.

Eli covered his ears and said, absently, "You look great, Zev." He felt burning throughout his body, as if his veins were filled with something other than blood. His eyes felt as if they were swathed in cotton.

"I'm doing my best to be my best," Zev said, leading Eli into his home. "You look like shit."

"I do," Eli said, and he wanted to sit down before he fell down. He still heard the voice in his head, but it was in no language he had ever heard.

"What?" Zev said.

"I don't know," Eli said, and was silent for a moment as he looked around at the spartan interior of the caravan. "Is this the house of Israel?"

"This is the house of Zev, man. Come on, take a load off."

"Okay," Eli said, and Zev suddenly looked like some giant biblical Samson. "You look healthy. Really."

"It's the Torah, man," Zev said. "You have no idea." He led Eli to a red plastic chair, and watched him drop into it. "The shiksa?"

"Gone," Eli said.

"The kid?"

"Gone, too."

"Well, he's not Jewish anyway," Zev said, surprising Eli. "Thems the breaks, bubelah."

"What?" Eli said.

"One man's garbage is another man's treasure. I wish her luck," Zev said, ruffling Eli's hair. "Smile, man. You're part of the tribe of the Messiah. We're going to a party. *Sefer Torah,* man. A party for the new Torah scroll. Stick with me. I'll get you back on your feet."

"Let me lie down first."

"You just got here and you're crashing?" Zev said.

"I'm an 'elder statesman of American television,'" Eli said bitterly, quoting the *TV Guide* critic who pronounced his production company, Ellis Hall Home Entertainment, and his Cold War schlock "a dinosaur deader than Ed Sullivan."

"You're only forty-three, dude."

After Eli rested and drank some coffee, he felt somewhat renewed. His footsteps marched in synch with Zev's down the hill past dimly lit Arab homes. They heard children laughing and the sound of televisions blaring in Arabic. Zev pointed out, "This was a Jewish home. This was a Jewish home," as they walked.

The air smelled to Eli like nothing he had ever smelled before, clean and fresh and natural. He felt the cool spring air wash over him and felt healthy for the first time in a long time. He looked up in the sky and the stars seemed closer than they had ever been before.

The synagogue was crammed with black-clad yeshiva *bochers,* and full-bearded men wearing jeans and knitted *kippahs,* like Zev. It was the first time he had been in a synagogue since his bar mitzvah, not long before he left home for good. This was not the way Eli remembered synagogue.

Zev whispered in Eli's ear, "It's like we are actually standing at Sinai waiting for Moshe Rabeynu, our great rabbi of rabbis, Moses to bring us God's commandments. You have no idea how special it is when a Torah scroll is completed. They are not mass produced like some Gideon's Bible, they are written by hand on parchment the same way they have been written since the time of our prophets."

Eli noticed there were no women and thought of his life in New York. His wild days when his shows were doing well: *Spy, Berliner; Hotel Cadillac;* and *Walkabout Willie,* all top ten in the Nielsen ratings. Women constantly. He remembered going on a talk show and admitting he was a sex addict. Later he said he had become a Buddhist. He didn't come home for days at a time, found himself in orgies without even knowing how he got there. His wife was hysterical, threatened to throw him out. It was simple to drink. And then that last night with the prop from the set. Didn't she know he was only playing?

Eli saw a room full of praying men and was thankful that temptation had been removed. Had these men also been called by God? And where was God now, hiding in the parchment of the new Torah scroll? A whining clarinet started up and the men began to dance in spinning circles.

Zev squeezed his hand and pulled him closer to him. "This is great," he shouted. "I can see us together on Judgment Day, riding the lightning with Moshiach."

Eli stood still, trying to maintain his balance. The nap and the coffee had only provided a temporary respite. Zev invited him to join the circle, but he begged off, saying he wanted to watch first. He felt his eyes must have looked like swollen golfballs. His head began to spin again as the men whirled around and around.

"Am Yisrael Chai, Am Yisrael Chai, Am Yisrael, Am Yisrael, Am Yisrael Chai!" they all sang.

Zev pumped his fist from where he stood beside Eli and sang along. The room smelled of sweat and one of the dancers slipped on the floor, flying out of the circle.

"Have some vodka," the man said, gripping a bottle in his hands. Sweat poured down his face from underneath his large-brimmed hat. He looked like a gangster. This can't be what God intended, Eli thought.

"I'm okay," Eli said.

"Drink," he said, climbing to his feet.

"No," Eli said.

"Take a drink," Zev said, taking the bottle in his hands. "Just one."

He gulped at the bottle and a lightning bolt shot straight to his head. He felt adrenaline kick into his heart. The man plunked his hat onto Eli's head and pulled him into the circle. The Torah scroll appeared, carried by a tiny white-bearded man under a blue wedding *huppa,* and the men began to whirl even faster. Eli felt his legs melt beneath him, and then he saw feet blurring all around him.

"Am Yisrael Chai, Am Yisrael Chai, Am Yisrael, Am Yisrael, Am Yisrael Chai!"

Eli survived on olives, almonds, figs, sage, carob, mint leaves, anything he could find in the hilltops and wadis out there in the wilderness. He slept in caves when he could find them, bathed himself in fresh mountain water, and sometimes didn't speak a word aloud for weeks.

One day as he was grazing his sheep on the rough tangled bushes and grasses of the Judean hills, an army jeep pulled to the top of a rocky cliff above him. He could see an Israeli flag standing stiff in the wind. He knew there was no use in running, so he sat among his sheep, staring into the distance. They called and waved him to come up. And now the grass stopped singing to God and Eli's blood began to churn up again.

Zev had warned Eli before he left Hebron not to talk to anyone; Arabs, of course, but especially the army.

"That's my hill," Eli shouted and pointed with his staff to another bare hill. "And that belongs to King David." He had not spoken aloud in such a long time, he was not even sure his voice would carry far enough for them to hear.

He sat on his carpetbag and looked back toward his sheep. The sun was a giant copper disk, pressing down on his head, and he looked toward his .38 lying nearby.

A few minutes later a dark, Sephardi-looking soldier wearing a helmet two sizes too big sauntered down the hill lighting a cigarette. *"Nudnik. Boker tov,"* he called.

Eli called back good morning in English.

The soldier lit another cigarette then took off his helmet

and sat on it near him. He unstrapped his M–16 and laid it on the ground beside him.

Eli's heart began to pump faster than it had since he had come to the wilderness. He could feel his heart squeeze like a fist. He shifted on his pack. Eli thought, this punk is eighteen, nineteen at most. What does he know?

"Nize day. Cigariah?" He held the cigarette out to Eli, who didn't say anything. He noticed that the soldier had a terrible case of acne and a long feminine nose. Two soldiers laughed like camels at the top of the hill and danced to music blasting from Army wave radio.

"You don't smoke," the soldier said with a slow thick accent. "You can't to be here. It's not safe."

"I don't see any Arabs," Eli said. "Just me and my sheep."

"You are paralyzed to an army shooting range," the soldier said.

"You mean 'parallel'?"

"It's not safe," the soldier repeated.

"I'm okay," Eli said. He only wanted the soldiers to go away. But then he thought about his beard, and sidecurls, and the fringes of his *tzitzis* hanging from his pants and realized: these rock 'n' rollers think we all look the same.

"What is that stink?" the soldier said, pinching his nose.

Eli didn't even notice anymore that his bag smelled. He didn't answer.

"Come. Have some tea and nana in the jeep. Let me invite you," the soldier said, pointing up to the jeep.

"No."

"You must not to be here," he said, putting the second cigarette in his mouth. And then one of the other soldiers called to him from the hilltop. "Motti. *Yala! Imshi!*"

He waved him away and said, "You like young girls? Boys? Come to the base. You can't to be here. We have food and beds to sleep."

"What about my sheep?" Eli asked.

"You like fuck sheep?" The soldier laughed. "Okay. Sheep okay."

"Get out of here," Eli said. "My sheep don't eat in a mess hall, and I don't need a bed. The land will take care of us. I can go wherever I want, I'm a Jew on Jewish land."

"It's not safe," the soldier said.

"Safe, not safe. I don't gave a damn."

The soldier looked toward the red, black, and green bag again. Eli shifted uneasily. "That is the Palestine colors," the soldier said, moving closer. "I should take that from you."

"No!" Eli screamed in the upper register.

"I joke," the soldier said, laughing. "Let me help you carry your sack up the hill."

"No," Eli said forcefully.

"Homo," the soldier said, laughing, and ran back to meet his comrades. "You stink."

The jeep drove back toward the road, and Eli could still see them laughing. He picked up his .38 Special from the ground and pointed it toward the soldiers in the jeep as they got smaller and smaller in his sight. "Bang," he whispered. "Bang, bang, bang, bang, bang."

Eli's beard grew in thick and gray and he rested in Zev's bed for the next month. He was restless to answer his God when he first arrived, anxious to walk the land and drink in his wisdom, and he felt God's spirit burning through his veins, but was too weak to move. This must be a joke, Eli thought. I'm here and I can't even get out of bed. He threw up in the mornings and apologized to God: "I'm failing you. I'm sorry." Zev slept on a cot in his makeshift kitchen, cleaned up Eli's vomit, washed his urine-stained sheets, and nursed Eli back to health.

During the first week of his convalescence Eli awoke one night and thought he heard Josh calling, "Daddy!" He rolled over to tell his wife to check on him, but the bed was empty. He could see stars and a glowing moon pasted onto the ceiling, as mysterious as the real night sky, and he remembered he was with Zev in Hebron. It frightened him at first and he rolled over, sure that he smelled Kate on the sheets. He felt emptied out inside and thought out loud, "What do I do now? What do I do now?"

"It's okay, man," Zev called from the kitchen. "Trust in Hashem. God will take care of you."

"Has God ever whispered in your ear?" Eli said, thinking of the voice that sent him to Hebron, the voice that was silent now.

"Every day, brother. Every day," Zev said. "There is nowhere that a Jew can be alone, because wherever he goes, his God is with him."

Eli pulled his pillow close to him, remembering the words, "You will walk in my light and follow my laws, and others will too. And I will be your God and their God."

"Is God with me?" Eli said.

"You betcha."

It began to dawn on him that maybe Zev was one of God's angels, sent to watch over him, to lead him in the right direction.

The next morning Zev began to speak to him of the miracles of Torah study as he fed Eli yogurt and hard-boiled eggs for breakfast.

"The words of the Torah, man, are like golden vessels," Zev said, "and the more you scour them and polish them the more they shine and reflect the face of who looks at them."

Zev brought Eli a new hardcover translation of the Torah, with Hebrew on one side of the page and English on the other. Eli began to read, slowly, bit by bit, of the creation of man, the sacrifice of Abraham, Jacob's blessing of Isaac, the darkness of Egypt, and the Exodus.

He lay propped up against two pillows and thought of his studies as a child for his bar mitzvah. "Are these the same words?" he wondered.

Later, as his mind wandered to the slick bodies of his past, his hand slid down to stroke himself underneath the blanket.

"You're gonna want to save that."

Eli stopped.

The voice?

It was only Zev standing in the doorway. "You're not going to flush a nation down the toilet."

Zev lit candles for Shabbat and taught Eli the prayer inviting the sabbath bride.

Eli's fever began to break near the end of Shabbat and Zev brought in a spice box for him to smell.

"How are you feeling?" Zev asked, taking a sniff from the silver spice box.

"Better," Eli answered. "But awful."

"You're back in the world, man," Zev said, smiling. "Your eyes are starting to shine again. You know, Torah can do all sorts of miracles, fighting sickness and degradation, even the Angel of Death. Saved my life."

The last time Eli had seen Zev before he came to Hebron, Zev was drinking heavily and eating from restaurant Dumpsters. He was in and out of jail. Then one night, under the glow of a big autumn moon, he said, "Going to see the rebbe," and wandered off.

"Something inside me just told me it was time," Zev said. "I went to Brooklyn, man. Met the Lubavitcher rebbe and started studying Torah."

Eli learned that Hebron was the first Jewish city and that Abraham bought a field and a cave near Tel Romeida from Ephron the Hittite, and that later his wife and descendants down to Jacob were buried on that land. He learned there was a massacre in 1929 where Jews were torn to pieces by their Arab neighbors after living side by side with them for hundreds of years, and that the Israeli government did not want Jews to resettle and live in Hebron, the City of the Patriarchs.

If Jews were told that they couldn't live in one of the five boroughs of New York, Eli thought, if they were told that it was being reserved for blacks and Puerto Ricans and Jews couldn't live there, people would call it anti-Semitism, racism. So, why shouldn't I live here, he thought?

When Eli was well enough, Zev took him to the *mikvah* and he immersed himself in the cleansing waters of the bath, feeling a new energy flowing through his body. He passed his days studying the words of the Lord and his prophets and began to realize the profound mistakes he had made in his past life. In the book of Hosea he learned that since he had forgotten God and married a Gentile, God would forget his child. He learned in Isaiah that he had been arrogant in his wealth, supplanting God with material gains, and that for punishment he would be "brought down to the netherworld, to the uttermost parts of the pit." Eli remembered the darkest days after his wife threw him out and he thanked God for bringing him close to his breast. He sang psalms of praise with Zev and slept with the words of the Lord burned into his brain.

He wore his beard long and a *kippah* on his head, and prayed daily at the Tomb of Machpelah, the burial place for Abraham, Isaac, Jacob, and their wives. When he wasn't praying he walked the streets of Hebron. One day a man spat in his face, called him a "Zionist pig," and cursed at him in Arabic. Eli ran after him, but lost the man in a crowd. He felt proud to be wearing a *kippah*. He wandered into the Casbah and the merchants would not sell him their wares. He saw a camel hanging upside down from a hook with its intestines spilling from its sides like extension cords and felt nauseated. Children laughed like monkeys and shouted at him as he passed. Eli wondered what God had in mind when he made the Arabs.

Zev and Eli went for lunch with a rabbi and his wife who lived over at Shilo. The rabbi had planted a bomb that had blown the legs off of an Arab mayor in the eighties and had served thirty months in prison.

Eli could not imagine spending thirty minutes in prison. The walls would close in on him and he would be alone inside his head. Eli would never go to prison. Never.

"I don't want to be a fascist, but I have no choice," the

rabbi had said. "God gave this land to Abraham and the Jewish people, forever."

"Forever," Zev added, popping an olive in his mouth.

"Listen," the rabbi said, turning to Eli, "as long as we have this secular system, we are going to have chaos. The waters of Babylon are rising."

"This is the Holy Land, man," Zev said. "Put it back in God's hands and give him the respect. If you want to be secular, go to America."

"I'm done with that," Eli said. "Sodom and Gomorrah."

"You said it, brother," Zev said. "Hey, today's leaders, they haven't even gone to any kind of leadership school. They're just buying their way into politics and government."

"Amen," Eli said.

"Amen," the rabbi said, standing up from the table.

About a month before the prime minister was assassinated Eli and Zev went to a rally in Jerusalem where thousands of people crowded forward, fists raised in the air, as a man shouted from a podium before a placard that said: **Danger! All Hands to the Defense of Jerusalem!** Their voices all raised as one, cheering at intervals. Their cries rising and falling like waves. Eli smelled something burning and saw gray smoke snaking into the sky.

"They're saying the prime minister is the son of an Arab and a Nazi," Zev said to Eli, a cigarette burning between his lips. "You can't trade land that God gave Abraham for a piece of paper."

The smoke carried a terrible odor over the crowd and smelled like something rotten and foul.

The crowd let up a roar and Eli felt waves rolling throughout his body. They were burning the prime minister in effigy and the crowd rushed forward, smashing at the body with sticks until it was beaten to the ground.

Eli had never felt this connected to anything in his life before, even when the Yankees won the World Series in 1977. He raised his fist in the air and shouted out, "Rabin the traitor, Rabin the traitor."

During the curfew, Eli and Zev walked alone through the streets, sloping down to the Beit Hadassah compound where other Jews lived. Zev's Uzi submachine gun bounced against his back as he walked.

"Enjoy this," Zev said, "this quiet won't last. If you listen carefully, you can hear the violence sizzling in the air."

He felt proud, walking through the streets with Zev. This was not the Judaism he remembered.

Eli thought of the schoolyard in eighth grade when Connor Peters hit him in the head with a roll of pennies and pushed him to the ground shouting, "Pick 'em up, Jew," as a group of fifth and sixth graders laughed at him. *Is this what a Jew is?* Eli had thought. He picked up a stone, pulled himself off the ground, and slammed the stone into Connor's face. Eli remembered that the laughing stopped.

When his father came to get him from the principal's office, he saw the two boys; Connor holding a bloody rag to his face, and Eli sitting quietly on the bench. His father looked at Eli with his frozen blue eyes, crossed his arms to cover his tattoo, and said in his thick accent, "Apolochize."

At that moment, Eli hated his father. He felt his father had failed a mighty test and had revealed the true nature of the mystery of what it meant to be a Jew.

On al-Shuhada Street, "the street of the martyrs," Eli and Zev passed shuttered storefronts spray-painted with Stars of David, some had fists painted inside them. A donkey poked his head out over a low wire fence and brayed. They passed more graffiti in red: "Rabin is an Arab!" "Kahane lives!" "Deport, Kill Arabs!" and then sloppily written and partially crossed out, "With blood and fire, Jews out."

To their right, beyond a run-down cemetery, tiny lights flickered inside the bare-faced concrete pillboxes of Arab homes stacked up into the Hebron hills. The March air was cool and damp and Eli pulled his parka closed. He wondered if the inside of their homes looked as much like prisons as the outside.

They walked into the depths of the Arab casbah, their footsteps echoing on the empty streets. Vegetables rotted on their wagons and the air smelled foul. Eli leaped behind one of the wooden carts and began to bark out prices like one of the Arab merchants. "Special price," he laughed. "Special price for Jew," and he spat into a pile of rotting tomatoes.

Zev didn't laugh but kept on walking and lit a cigarette. A puff of smoke rose above his head. "Over fifty people killed on their way to work. Real holy," he said.

The curfew had been in place for more than a week now, since the two buses had been blown up in Jerusalem. A muezzin began to wail *"Ull-aaaaaaw-hoo-Ak-bar! Ull-aaaaaaw-hoo-Ak-bar!"*

It seemed that the volume on the minaret speakers had been turned up again.

"These kids are being brainwashed," Zev shouted. "Do you know what kind of gutter religion we are talking about? Do you know what they are being told? That their reward for killing Jews will be seventy-two virgins waiting for them in heaven."

"I didn't know there were any virgins left," Eli said, and they both laughed.

He thought of Josh back on Long Island and the time he had set fire to a pile of old newspapers in the garage. Eli had grounded him and taken away his allowance for a month, but he was on the streets playing again in a week.

"Listen up, and listen good, brother," Zev said. "Nobody ever screwed in heaven. It's all lies. Bubbe meysehs!"

Eli was far away now, even as they reached an army checkpoint and the high walls of the Tomb of Machpelah. Josh would be thirteen this week, and Eli didn't even know where he was.

"You've got to take away their keys to heaven," Zev continued, "you've got to get them while they're still in bed, or while they're preparing for their deaths."

He should have his bar mitzvah soon, Eli thought.

"You should bury the bombers inside pig skins," Zev continued. "Then they'll think twice about the glories of heaven."

Eli was silent for a moment and then said, "This doesn't sound like the 'undercover peace-and-lover' some of us used to know."

"Nah," Zev said, looking straight ahead. "This is real-politik. Hardcore."

The muezzin had stopped praying. They couldn't even hear the soldiers laughing at their checkpoints.

"Listen to the quiet," Zev said. "It's nuclear quiet. Real spooky. Take this," he said, reaching into his belt and pulling out a .38 Special.

"No way," Eli said. "I don't need this." Zev had offered Eli the gun before, but he had always been afraid to take it.

"You do," Zev said. "I mean you really need something with a cartridge out here. This is the OK Corral, man. Injun country."

Eli handed it back to Zev. The last time he had held a gun was the night *Spy, Berliner* was canceled. He was drunk and had taken it from the set and brought it home. He wore the long-nosed opera mask on his face and fired blanks at his wife as she ran screaming out the back door.

Zev pressed the .38 back into Eli's hands and slung his Uzi around into his own hands. He smiled. "God created the universe and this is the instrument of his will. Do you have earplugs?"

"No," Eli said. "I'm not taking this."

"Always carry earplugs, boychick," Zev said, ignoring Eli, brushing back his sidecurls, his graying peyot, as he slipped the plugs into his ears. He gave a pair to Eli, who did the same. "This is target practice," he said. "Do you see the water tanks on top of the houses?" He marched ahead up a steep potholed street as he cocked his gun. Water tanks, solar heaters, and TV antennas rose out of the rooftops in a chaotic mess. The air was just cold enough that Eli could see his breath moving ahead of him in the dark. He knew now that he would follow Zev anywhere.

Zev gave him the thumbs-up sign and said, "Let's kick out the jams."

And then pop, Pop, POP, from Zev's gun, as he ran, firing at rooftops and whooping like an Indian. Eli held the gun at his side and ran to keep up with Zev, who continued shooting at the tanks, the odd shot answered with a metallic ping.

They stopped for a breath at the crest of a hill where Zev coughed and spat phlegm on the ground. From the next street over they could hear Israeli soldiers barking Hebrew orders into a megaphone. Blue siren lights strafed across the run-down buildings, as army patrol jeeps squealed around the corner from both directions and a half-dozen soldiers jumped out, shouting at them in Hebrew. Eli tried to run, flinging his gun to the ground, but a short Russian soldier with a bullet-shaped head in a red beret jammed his gun into Eli's chest and pushed him against a wall. Another soldier did the same to Zev. They spoke quickly in Hebrew. Eli didn't understand a word.

"Just show them your ID," Zev said. "No big deal. You'll understand real fast that there are two laws in the wild West Bank: one for us and one for the Arabs."

The tallest soldier addressed them in English. He wore oval-shaped glasses and Eli thought he looked like an arrogant prick. "You come to Israel because you are a Jew and you act like a maniac. Tell me, why is it that all of the scum of the world comes to Israel? You have a home in Brooklyn or Miami, no? You are a Zionist? Good. Go to Jeruzalem," he said, pronouncing the "s" as a "z." "We don't want to fight for Hevron."

"We're just living on the land of the Jewish people," Eli said. The short Russian pressed himself hard against Eli's chest. He had a gold front tooth.

"You don't have to tell these assholes anything," Zev said, picking the .38 up off the ground and handing it to Eli.

"Where are you going with your girlfriend?" the soldier asked Zev.

"Can't a Jew walk down the street without being hassled?" Zev said.

"Trust me. The Messiah will not come any faster if you stay in Hevron," the soldier said, smiling. He lit a cigarette and offered one to each of them. "Since you did not shoot anyone, you can go. But be quiet. There is a curfew. Go straight home. And put your guns away. Leave the killing to the army."

The Russian soldier backhanded Eli in the face, bloodying his nose, before jumping into the jeep and driving off. The streets were quiet again. Zev spat onto the ground and whispered, "Fucking brownshirts."

Eli patted Zev on the shoulder as if to say, "It's okay." He still had the .38 in his hand. He aimed it down the empty street and cocked the trigger. The hammer fell and white fire burst from the barrel as the chamber emptied. It was as if Eli were underwater, the sound muffled by his earplugs. He fired his gun until it was empty, and then he and Zev hammered at windows, cars, and anything else in their path as they made their way back home.

Eli led his sheep down from the hills and into a dried-out wadi. He caught a glimpse at himself in the blade of his knife and he was wild-haired and dirty, and was ashamed in the presence of the gray wolf.

"I'm sorry," he said to the wolf. "You are so beautiful. I know God is in you. How can I get more of God in me?"

The wolf was silent.

Eli clipped his fingernails and toenails, cut his itching hair to the scalp, wrapped a white sheet around his body, fraying the corners, and wound a dirty shirt around his head like a turban, all the time repeating: "I believe with complete faith that the Creator blessed is his name knows all the deeds and thoughts of human beings. I believe with complete faith the Creator blessed is his name rewards with goodness all those that observe his commandments and punishes those who violate his commandments. I believe with complete faith in the coming of the Messiah and even though he may delay I anticipate every day that he will come."

When Eli prayed, he was talking to God. When he meditated he listened. And after a while if he listened carefully, his head would tighten and God would say, "You are doing all right," or "I will call for you when it is time."

A shepherd can't sit still, Eli figured, especially when he is seeking the Almighty. And the soldiers may return, he thought. So he hefted his load onto his shoulders and wandered. With the sun rising in his face, he wandered to the east with his sheep, crossing the main highway south of Beit Lechem. His pack seemed to lighten as he zigzagged back and forth between the villages and settlements, never stopping for hospitality, prodding his flock onward. East of Tekoa on the edge of the Judean wilderness, the blue sky turned dark with hundreds of black storks flying overhead, their red stomachs winking between their flapping wings.

The desert rolled like women before him, naked and round, lounging in the sun. He saw spread legs, bare breasts, and long arched necks. He even saw the hurt face of his wife but pushed it from his mind. It was like the very landscape before him was a relief map of his past. He huddled close to his sheep for warmth.

One morning, he awoke to find that the wolf had taken one of his sheep and torn it apart, leaving the carcass for him to find, slashed apart upon a large flat stone. A sign, Eli thought.

He knew it was time now to atone for his sins. He laid his bag on the ground and dug in the earth with his hands, pulled up rocks and boulders, and carried them to the highest spot he could find. He prepared an altar of stone, bound the healthiest sheep he could find on the altar, and cried out to God that he would never sin again. He thought of the binding of Isaac, the ultimate act of faith, and thought: If I were Abraham, I would not have had the faith to bring my son to Mount Moriah, the way Abraham had been told to do with Isaac. He could not imagine tying up his son, prepared to slash his throat. What if God did not stop him?

I am not a good father, Eli thought, I am not a good father. And then he thought of his own weak father who had survived the Holocaust, gone to synagogue on the sly, and put up Christmas lights every winter. His father used to say, "the Jews are the chosen people, chosen to suffer." He just didn't get it, Eli thought. His father hadn't understood what a gift it is to be a Jew.

Eli shouted out, "For the master race!" as he slashed the throat of the long-eared sheep. And it was so serene as he grabbed a handful of its beige coat in his fist and cut back across its throat with a penknife. He poured the blood on the altar and burned the flesh, and the smell was heavenly, like a divine barbecue. When the flesh was charred and hard, he ate it and felt closer to God, felt the burned offering become part of him.

Eli and Zev walked every night through the empty city during the curfew. The air was still cool and damp, and they splashed through puddles, laughing through the streets.

They reached a dark alley at the edge of town, then plunged down a slope into an Arab vineyard. Eli followed close behind Zev, heard his feet stick and unstick in the mud, his gun swaying as he moved.

"Rabbi Kahane goes to Heaven and meets God who invites him to dinner," Zev said, chopping his arm up and down for emphasis. "God introduces the rabbi to the other guests, 'This is Jesus Christ, this is Moses, this is Buddha.' Kahane shakes their hands and sits down."

Eli caught up to Zev, laughing. He had told this exact same joke to some yeshiva students the day before. "The soup comes and there's no spoon. 'God,' says the rabbi, 'I don't have a spoon.' God looks over his shoulder, snaps his fingers and calls . . ."

"Muhammad," Eli burst in, "you forgot the spoons!"

They reached the barbed-wire fence surrounding the Jewish settlement of Kiryat Arba, which was known throughout Israel as being a hotbed for Jewish extremism. But to Eli and Zev, it was just a suburb of Hebron, a bedroom community with neat rows of whitewashed villas, TV antennas, solar panels, and clean, quiet streets.

Zev worked part-time in the falafel stand by the city's entrance and knew the guard by name. "Shalom," Zev called to the guard.

"Zevic! *Ma nish ma?*"

"*Yala!* Open up, Yossi. There's Arabs out here."

The guard was one of those big-bellied Yemenite men one might see at soccer games, shouting and waving their thick arms. His *tzitzis* hung sloppily from his pants and his blue knitted *kippah* almost covered his bald spot. He tossed newspapers into an oil-drum bonfire as he spoke about the curfew in a slow guttural English.

"Vis-à-vis the closure. It is our only tactic," Yossi said.

"When they kill Jews, people on the street, what can you do? We are in a militantic struggle with the Arabs." Yossi paused while he closed the gate. "But Jews don't antagonate. Everything here is only about security."

"Baruch Hashem," Eli said. "Security. Then peace."

"This peace," Zev added, "is a peace of shit."

"You're here to see Doctor Goldstein?" Yossi asked.

Zev had been friends with Goldstein and had been his next-door neighbor for more than a year. Now he continued to visit him twice a week. Eli had been in a bar in the East Village when he heard about the massacre on the news: twenty-nine Palestinians killed during prayer at the Cave of the Patriarchs, almost two hundred injured. He had seen the sprawled bodies and hysterical widows and mothers on his television, but he didn't understand at the time that Baruch Goldstein was a hero, like Judah Maccabee, or Samson.

His resting place lay in a municipal park at the entrance of the city, not a mile away from where he was murdered by the angry mob. They walked in silence along the stone promenade until they reached the grave. Eli had not gone to his own father's funeral or visited the grave. And every time Eli made the stroll along the stone promenade, he could feel the blood slowing in his veins, his mouth dry, his head pulsing, as if a wire had been tightened around his skull.

They reached a giant block of polished stone engraved in Hebrew. There were benches on either side, a cabinet full of prayer books, and a sink for hand washing. Zev blew some smoke into the air with a deep breath, grabbed a prayer book, and began to sway in silent worship. Eli walked over to the cabinet and pulled out a leather-bound book. Just beyond, he could see the outlines of rough boulders and twisted weeds and plants, and farther beyond, the blue flashing light of an army patrol jeep driving along the Hebron Road.

A cold wind swirled around them out there on the edge of town unprotected by trees or buildings. Eli could barely hear Zev's prayer above the wind, which he was sure was God's breathing. But he joined in, repeating the words he had said so many times since he had come to Hebron:

> *Blessed are You, Adonai,*
> *our God and God of our fathers,*
> *God of Abraham, God of Isaac, God of Jacob,*
> *Great, mighty, and awesome God,*
> *Highest God and Doer of good, kind deeds,*
> *Master of all,*
> *Who remembers the love of the Patriarchs*
> *and brings a redeemer to their children's children*
> *for His name's sake with love.*
> *King, Helper, Rescuer, and Shield.*
> *Blessed are You, Adonai, Shield of Abraham*

Zev was wailing, crying out to the sky, sobbing, as he shook his fist at the starry sky.

"What's the matter?" Eli asked.

Tears poured down Zev's face into his beard.

Zev sniffled above his prayer book. "You know, man, we have these places everywhere where someone died, these little, like, shrines." He paused and closed his prayer book. "Do you know why I came to Israel?"

"Because you're a Jew," Eli said.

"Jerusalem," he said. "*Ye-ru-sha-lay-im*. City of Peace. Believe it or not, I thought that was so beautiful. I was into peace and I just got on a plane one day with my rucksack. But you can't be into peace here, people look at you like they want to put you away, they say 'what do you mean, "peace"?' Reality poisons you, you just look around and everywhere there is violence and hatred and brutality. On the buses, on the street, people will kill you if you take their parking spot. Forget about the Arabs, there's nowhere else in the world where Jews are hated so much by other Jews. Everybody's fighting here. Everybody's at war."

"Zev," Eli said. "Let's go home."

He took Zev's arm in his, but instead of him straightening up, Zev threw his arms around Eli and continued to sob. His hot breath tickled Eli's ear, the way his boy's breath had the last time he saw him.

I'm not strong enough for this, Eli thought. And he began to cry, too. His throat felt thick and his body trembled as he grabbed tighter hold of Zev.

"He was my friend," Zev said.

"I'm your friend, too," Eli said.

"I know, man. You don't have to cry."

"I can't help it," Eli said. "I was just thinking."

"It's okay," Zev said. "He's in a better place now."

Eli pulled away from Zev. The tears in his eyes made everything seem double. "I'm not crying about a killer."

"He wasn't a killer," Zev said, stiffening. "He was a doctor, a fine doctor. He didn't just go down there and say, 'It's time to kill Arabs.'"

"I'm sorry," Eli said. "I shouldn't have . . ."

"He saved people's lives, man." Zev paused, and shook his head in disgust. "I remember the day of the massacre, when I heard about the massacre at the Cave of Machpelah, I was so thankful that it wasn't Jews who were killed."

"I'm thinking about my family," Eli said.

"You're with your family," Zev said.

Eli could see the blue lights of an army jeep moving in the distance.

"Do you know, after that horrible last night at home," Eli said, "I went on a six-month bender, ended up lost in the subways without a wallet or shoes. I don't even know how I got to my mother's place. She wouldn't even look at me."

"Let's go home," Zev said, offering a tissue to Eli.

"No," Eli said. "Josh should have his bar mitzvah soon."

"He's not even Jewish," Zev said. "His mother's not a Jew."

"I don't know if they'll ever speak to me again."

"Forget it," Zev said. "Keep on keepin' on. We'll find you a real wife, a Jewish wife."

"But, I loved —" Eli started to say.

"You didn't love anyone. Now, listen and listen good. It's not the same. Not even close," Zev said. "That is your goyish little family. This man is a major player in Jewish history we're talking about."

Each day Eli's flock became smaller. He wandered back and forth, both against the sun and toward it, not bothering any longer to prepare an altar for each sacrifice. Sometimes he tore at the sheep with his bare hands and they screamed like crying infants. He ate the flesh raw and wore the skins on his back, or stuffed them into his bag. He prayed hard and waited for an answer. A nauseating hunger tore through his stomach and he thought, "The closer you get to God, the faster and harder you get smacked. But I am getting closer."

He stared at the full moon, at the curve of its edges pulsing against an endless night sky and it was as if he was gazing into the eye of God. He prayed with fury for hours, shaking and calling out to the sky, "I am dust, and there is nothing lower than dust." Sweat began to pour down his face and he cried out, "Don't you understand me?" He buried his face in the rough wool of his pack and wept.

Eli thought he heard a child's voice calling him and he woke up clinging to his pack. The moon was at the top of the sky now and lit the hillsides with a brilliant silvery glow. Then he heard it: "Eli Israel, son of man."

"Hello!" Eli called.

He heard thousands of wings flapping near him, and then closer still. He leaped to his feet and jumped up and down, batting at his head as if a swarm of bees had flown into his ears and were working their way into his brain. A flash of color filled his eyes, a prism of colors that he had never seen before. All the organs of his body began to tremble and he was sure he was going to die, as excrement and urine and vomit poured out of him.

"You are purified," a voice said at last. "Go to the mountain. Go to Jerusalem and speak my words."

"You need to find a wife," Zev said to Eli one day. "A Jewish wife."

He had been with Zev for nearly a year and had spent most of his time studying. Eli had not thought of women in a long time. "It says in the Torah you're only half a person if you're not married."

"But, you're not married," Eli said.

"I'm not ready yet. But you, my friend, have come so far."

It was true. Eli could quote the Torah, the Talmud, the Zohar, and other texts as if he had been studying for years.

"I know a rabbi in Jerusalem. Rabbi Lev, the Love Rabbi. I'm sure he can arrange a *shiduch.*"

"Why haven't you gone to see him?" Eli asked.

"I have, man. But it was a disaster," Zev said. "One was a Moroccan widow with six kids who could cook couscous with chicken that melted from the bone and knew Torah left to right and right to left, but I didn't want to get tangled up with someone else's children, if you know what I mean? Another wanted to move to Brooklyn to wait for a sign from the Lubavitcher rebbe, but I'm not going back to Babylon, man. Listen, some didn't even speak English. Could you imagine smearing the language of the Torah, to order McDonald's cheeseburgers, to buy toilet paper, to discuss the weather? It was a total disaster. That only proves that I'm not ready. But you," Zev said, embracing Eli in a warm bear hug, "you have achieved *tschuva,* redemption."

Eli felt his stomach drop and he thought of Kate and Josh and how things had fallen apart. "No. I'm not ready."

"Yeah, man, you are. You're, like, fucking clean. A clean slate."

"Do you remember when the show went off the air, *Spy, Berliner?* And I told you I got drunk and came home from the set wearing that long-nosed opera mask, with a pistol and fired blanks at Kate, just scared the hell out of her. And I really thought Josh was out on a sleepover. So the whole thing started as a joke."

Zev nodded his head and smiled. Eli could see him absently fingering the handle of his pistol.

"Well, I didn't tell you that after she ran out, I just started bawling. Like I knew that I was on the edge of a really deep pit, and I was crying and crying, I thought I was such a schmuck, you know I was messing around with every guest star on the show and Kate must have known. I was feeling sorry for myself, and she slipped in through the screen door and came over and put her arms around me." Eli wiped a tear from his eye with his finger and then slid the finger into his mouth. "She put her arms around me and said it'll be all right or something, and this is *after* I fired the gun at her. And then I just snapped, I was still wearing that ugly mask, I don't know what I was thinking, I just sort of threw her on the floor and started to, started to . . ."

Eli took a deep breath, but couldn't get enough air.

"I know, man," Zev said. "But she was your wife, that's part of the deal."

"No!" Eli shouted suddenly. "With the fucking nose. That's how I did it, maybe I thought it would be fun, or different, and I know now I was hurting her, it was like I was nodding my head, yes, yes, yes, into her as she was saying no, no, no. And then the kid walks in, and she starts screaming bloody murder, 'Get out! Get out of my house.' And that was it."

"Hey, man. Don't sweat it. God forgives you."

"It was awful. You should have seen his face. He didn't know what his father was doing with that mask. But he saw his mother curled up on the floor like a wounded kitten or something."

"Hey," Zev said. "It's over. You paid for it. God knows you did. That's what counts. You're even-steven, now."

A few days later Eli called to speak with Rabbi Lev.

"Eli," Rabbi Lev said, with his Brooklyn accent. "I found your *beshert*. A terrific girl. A regular Bess Myerson. Come to Jerusalem and meet her."

Beneath a steady rain, Eli Israel dug in the rocky earth with his penknife and then with his hands, until he had grooved out a shallow pit. His hands were raw and bloody and he lifted the bag he had fashioned from the old riding blanket and tossed it into the groove in the earth. He hastily covered it as he mumbled Kaddish.

He walked all afternoon before reaching a highway, and continued, warmed by his thoughts. He felt light and his groin pulsed. He allowed himself to think about having a woman again without fear, knowing that he was pure of mind and spirit. "Children," he thought. "Imagine, one for each tribe of Israel: Judah, Levi, Gad, Asher, Binyamin, Zevulun, Reuven, Naphtali, Simeon, Dan, Issachar, Joseph, all of them populating the land." Eli smiled. He thought of returning to Rabbi Lev, but knew he could find his own woman now.

When he finally reached Jerusalem, his feet were raw and bruised and he thought of what it says in the Talmud: that of the ten portions of beauty in the world, nine were deposited in Jerusalem. He arrived late that night and was stunned to see the city, as if seeing it for the first time. Across the darkness, buried in the mountains, floating in the sky, surrounded by hills were the walls of a city that was like a dream. Jerusalem was almost there, and almost not, more spirit than stone, a ghost against the sky, domes and towers climbing straight to heaven.

Eli thought of Zev back in Hebron and wondered if they would soon meet again. He smiled and took a deep breath, remembering what Zev had said about going up to Jerusalem: "You are going into the eye of the hurricane, man, the tip of the arrow, the top of the mountain. How can you not feel like one of God's angels?"

The first morning light seemed to rise out of the stones themselves. As he walked down into the Hinnom Valley he saw silhouettes of trees and bushes and heard bells peal across the gray sky, and voices from all around, wailing, echoing through the valley. Then, still silence. Nothing moved at all and a pink blush spread from the east into the full colors of morning, then a brilliant white sun, huge palm trees, and the vaulted entrance of Jaffa Gate.

Eli felt as if he was two thousand years old, three thousand even. He felt as if he had just been born. In the month of Nisan in the year 5756, Eli entered Jerusalem prepared to bring the Messiah at last to Israel and the Jewish people.

Eli borrowed Zev's car for the last time as he drove up to Jerusalem to meet his *beshert*. He had to drive through Halhul, a dusty Arab village, and always gunned his engine through to the main highway. He knew the Arab urchins along the road could pick out yellow Israeli plates from a mile away and sometimes threw stones at cars as they passed.

The radio was turned up loud, tuned to a pirate station that played American music. Eli had almost made it by the vegetable stands and the last cluster of houses at the edge of town when he saw a group of boys gathered at the side of the road. He pressed the gas harder, just as they started hurling stones at his car. One of the boys slingshotted a fist-sized stone that smashed his window, cracking a huge spiderweb on Eli's windshield. Eli tried to turn the car away as a second volley of stones flew at it, but the car skidded into a ditch, nearly spinning completely around. With the car stuck in the ditch, Eli suddenly realized how bright the sun was and how his eyes hurt. At first Eli began to pray, terrified now that with his car idle another kid might launch a Molotov cocktail at him. He'd seen Jewish cars burned up at the side of the road before, and he reached into the glove compartment and grabbed his .38. Eli jumped out of the car. Most of the kids had scattered into the narrow side streets, but Eli could see a young Arab boy riding away on a donkey, calling, *"Itbah al-Yahud,"* "kill the Jew."

Everything became quiet for a moment as he drew his pistol. The whole world seemed to be frozen in that blazing white light. All he could think was *never again, never again, never again, never again, never again.* Then, total clarity. The sort of locked-in feeling he had felt during prayer. No sound, smell, taste. Nothing. Just the visual, intense, superreal, a tunnel of light and colors from him to the boy.

Eli fired until the gun was empty and dropped the kid into the dirt at the side of the road. It seemed to take forever for the bullets to reach him and then the bright yellow dust came up all around him and Eli was back in the world. The boy's donkey skittered off as Eli reached into his utility vest pocket for more bullets. His hands shook and he could only press two bullets into the gun, dropping the rest onto the ground. The boy lay still at the side of the road. He was dead, Eli knew that right away. His ears rang with a high-pitched hum as he walked toward the boy with the gun still in his hand.

Lying there in the dirt the boy looked so young, no more than thirteen, Eli thought. He could have been his kid. He smelled of sweat and still wore a backward smile and the first hints of a mustache on his face. Eli brushed his hand through his brown hair and closed his own eyes. For a moment, he saw the darkness of his eyelids and wondered, *"Is this what death looks like?"*

One of the bullets had come out the boy's chest and another had gone in his shoulder. Eli pushed the body over with his foot so he wouldn't have to look at him anymore.

The boy's red, black, and green riding blanket lay crumpled on the ground not five feet from him. Eli picked it up and shook out the dust. He wrapped the thick blanket around the boy, who was bleeding furiously from the chest and mouth.

The boy wasn't very heavy, maybe eighty or ninety pounds, like a small deer. He could have lifted the boy's weight three times over. And for a moment, he remembered carrying Josh with a fever of a hundred and three, up the stairs to his room, and laying him on his bed.

The boy's bare feet dangled from the blanket, slapping together as Eli walked. There was no one around — no Arabs, no Jews, no one. Not even the sound of a distant car engine to break the silence. It seemed to Eli that even God had winked and turned his back at that moment. He felt nothing carrying the boy back to Zev's car, as if he weren't even there but only imagining the whole scene. Somewhere in the distance black smoke rose into the sky where the local Arabs burned garbage.

Eli opened the trunk and threw the boy in next to the spare tire. The blanket covered his face but his body was twisted in a strange way. Eli closed the trunk, and for a moment his head spun, like it was being ripped open from the inside. He opened the trunk again and placed the boy inside the blanket and wrapped it twice around him, covering him completely.

He got into the car and prayed, hoping the engine would start before anyone returned. And the car revved and pulled itself out of the ditch and back onto the road. The radio was blaring Presley's "Blue Moon of Kentucky." Eli turned the volume down and opened the glove compartment. He tossed in his pistol, and pulled out an old pair of Zev's mirrored sunglasses.

"God teaches you hard," Eli thought, putting the glasses on. "These things happen on the road to redemption, on the road to Jerusalem. But God forgives you for what you do and I love Him."

For as Long as the Lamp Is Burning

For Merilyn Papernick, 1944–2010

The week before, Avshalom Cohen and his aging mother, Miriam, sat drinking tea together in her Rehavia apartment. It was summer, and violin music played through the trees and gardens outside the open kitchen window. In the next building Mr. Herzog scratched out the music that had saved his life at Auschwitz with a deeper sadness than usual, his arthritic hands fumbling across the strings, the bow just missing the right note. Miriam Cohen told her son that Mr. Herzog had fallen on Azza Street on his way home from the *shuk* and had refused, as he had his whole life, to visit a doctor. He was finally ready to meet his wife again in the Great Beyond.

"Such nonsense," Miriam said. "I know my Hershel is not waiting for me. He has gone to dust and there he will stay."

"Momma," Avshalom said for the thousandth time. "Of course Poppa is waiting for you."

"That's why he has written my name across the stars," she said bitterly. "He has forgotten me, left me behind. I will never forget. Never forget."

Avshalom knew that another one of her crying fits was coming on — whenever she said she would never forget, she wept, tore at her hair, waved her tattooed left arm in her son's face, cursed at him.

"You were such a good boy, Avshi. As good, maybe, as your brother and sister. And then you left me, too, and moved to Mevaseret with the Sephardi school teacher."

"It is only a twenty-minute drive," he said, ignoring the jab at his wife.

"You never visit," she said. "The only visitors I have are the gestapo and their black dogs gnashing their teeth when I try and sleep."

"Momma, don't talk that way. Put it out of your mind."

"Never!" she said. "I don't sleep anymore. They are in my room. I can hear them whispering. Last night, I woke up and could not breathe and I went to the kitchen and someone had snuck in and turned on the gas. I could have died. I couldn't breathe."

"It was just bad dreams and your emphysema," Avshalom said.

"I have no such thing. I can't even pronounce the word. I'm telling you, the Nazi Arabs came to my home. They move things when I am not looking so I can't find them."

He placed his hand on her veined, shaking hand. "Momma, I'm going to leave now."

"Leave!" she said. And then, all at once, Mr. Herzog's lugubrious playing came to an abrupt end.

Avshalom's telephone rang sometime after midnight. He was in bed with his wife, Shira. She picked up the phone.

"Avshi, your mother."

"Hello, Momma," he said, taking up the telephone.

Her voice was thin and scared on the other end of the phone. "Where were you when I called?"

"We were only in Eilat with the boys for a couple of days."

"You must come over. The Nazis, they are here again."

"But Momma," he said.

"Did I give you the last milk of my breast?" she asked.

He hung up the phone and turned to Shira, softly kissing her cheek.

"Sad dreams?" Shira asked.

"Another one of her fits," he said.

When he arrived at his mother's home, Avshalom found her standing in the door of her apartment brandishing a worn slipper in her hand.

"Hurry, Avshi, hurry!" she called as he got out of his car.

"How are you feeling, Momma?"

"The Nazis," she cried. "They were here."

He climbed the stairs slowly, his tiny mother waving her slipper to speed him up.

"You heard Mr. Herzog died," she said.

"No," Avshalom said, taking his mother's soft hand. She wore a brown cardigan sweater over her cotton nightgown. She squeezed his hand tightly.

"He died and stayed in his home for three days before someone found him."

"He was a nice man," Avshalom said.

"And look where that got him," she said.

His mother's usually immaculate apartment was a mess: plates were piled in the sink; papers lay everywhere, on the floor, the table, the sofa; the curtains were pulled closed; the room smelled stale; even his father's study, a model of German order, was a testament to chaos — his large leather-bound books had been pulled from their shelves and strewn about; his ashtray that had lain full for the last eight years since his death had been turned over on his desk; his banker's lamp lay smashed and broken.

She had always been neat in the German tradition. She once joked with Avshalom as a child that if he went out to play after dinner without brushing his teeth and *has v'chalila* he died in an attack, she promised to pry open his coffin with her stirring ladle to clean his teeth for the journey.

"What happened, Momma?" Avshalom said, surveying the damage.

She threw the slipper at him, missing his head by a few feet. "I told you, the Nazis came and took things."

He pulled his mother close to him and held her in his arms, an embrace so warm he hoped it would chase away every phantasm until Judgment Day. She, too, carried an odd smell about her, a smell of age and neglect that he had never noticed before. She pulled herself violently from his arms.

"I made a prayer for him."

"Who?" Avshalom asked.

"Good-bye, Mr. Herzog. Good-bye."

"Momma. What happened?"

"Like *Kristallnacht*," she said. "They even took my mezuzah from the front doorpost."

She began to cry, quiet at first, her lip trembling, then from the depths of her body she burst out weeping. "My beautiful mezuzah!" She swung her arms and struck out at her son. "I will never forget."

Why would somebody steal his mother's mezuzah? Avshalom wondered. He went to the door and could see the outline, slanting inward at the top of the doorpost, where the mezuzah had been for more than forty years. It had been pried off, that much he could tell. And it was a beautiful piece, crafted in Weimar Germany, a time when Jews enjoyed a brief renaissance before the yellow stars and cattle cars.

Two portions of the Torah from Deuteronomy inside the silver case, gone. "Hear O Israel: The Lord Our God. The Lord Is One," he repeated to himself in Hebrew, running his fingers over the bare space on the door. "You shall write these words on the doorposts of your house." Why would someone steal an old woman's mezuzah? He remembered as a child being too short to reach it, kissing his fingertips and touching them to the doorpost beneath the shining silver. And later, when he had grown, he could finally see the intricate carving: flowers blooming at the top and the bottom, a jeweled crown, and tiny silver doors like a miniature ark, revealing on its parchment when opened the holy name *Shaddai*. What a mystical thrill he had felt, repeating that name as a youth, an all-powerful name that was older than any tree or building or person he knew.

"I know who took it," his mother said.

"Who?" Avshalom said, closing the door and leading his mother back into the living room.

"The man who plants the flowers and fixes the garden. He is a Nazi Arab. I have seen him. He took my mezuzah. The Nazi took it."

"Dudu took your mezuzah?"

"Yes. Yes. Dudu took it."

"Dudu is Jewish," Avshalom said. "Why would he take it?"

"No, no," she cried. "He is not Jewish. I have seen him riding his donkey and goose-stepping on the street. He is the one. He took it."

"Sit down, Momma."

"It hurts my bones to sit. I will stand."

"Sit down, Momma," he said, clearing a space on the couch.

She sat, and slid the sleeves of her brown cardigan up her arm, revealing the blue numbers burned into her skin.

"Momma, I am sure Dudu did not take the mezuzah."

"Oh, you are sure," she said. "The laborer from Meva-seret has all the answers now. Tell me, Rashi: Why is the grass blue? Why is the moon made of Limburger cheese?"

"Stop it, Momma."

"You are lucky you were not at the camps. You would not have survived like your father and I. You are too believing. Poor Avshi, if the Nazis had told you to go to the showers, you would have run there smiling with a towel and shampoo in your hands."

They sat in silence. Avshalom seethed. For a moment, he wanted to strike his mother, dash her broken to the floor like a rag doll.

"Momma?"

"Son of mine," she answered.

"What's wrong?"

"And to think you were the smart one. I told you, the Nazis took my mezuzah."

"Did you go to Mr. Herzog's funeral?"

"Achh!" she said. "Funerals. I have been to too many. After your father, I never went to another. What good is it?"

"To pay your respects."

"To the dead? You don't understand anything, do you? When your father died, I had to take everything from his life and carry it with me. Right here." She tapped her right temple with her forefinger. "And when Moses Solomon died, and when Esti Hertz died, all of them. Now I have to remember for Mr. Herzog, too."

"You miss Mr. Herzog."

"Never!" she said. "He scraped at that violin all day like a cat scratching on a pole. Miss him? No. But we are one less now. You don't understand. You live in Mevaseret with your family and you build things with your hands. You will forget me when I'm gone. Soon, there will be none of us left. Next door there are students living, and they play rock and roll music, bang, bang, bang, all the time. What do they know of anything? I am tired, Avshi. My mezuzah is gone. Your father's study is ruined."

"Momma, go to sleep."

"For what?"

"Let me tell you a story I remember from school."

"A story about car engines and grease monkeys I do not want to hear."

"There are two ships sailing on the seas."

"Ha! What do you know of that, you only know the Kinneret and the *Yam Ha Melach*."

"The ship that comes into the port is seen by the wise man as more of an object of joy than the ship about to leave the harbor."

"Not if the ship is going into Cyprus," she said. "I have been to Cyprus, you know . . ."

"Momma, listen, just because a ship is leaving the port does not mean you should be sad or afraid. Because, soon that ship will reach another harbor, a glorious harbor . . ."

"My smart boy," she said. "My smart, smart boy. You are speaking Greek." She let out a long loud yawn. "But you have found success. I will sleep now."

Avshalom stood up and helped his mother to her feet. He took her arm and led her to the bedroom. She sat on the bed and removed her brown cardigan and handed it to her son, and she got into bed.

"Do you remember what I said to you as a child when I put you to bed?"

"You said, 'goodnight.' "

"Oh, Avshi. Turn out the light. I will clean up the apartment tomorrow."

He clicked off the light, leaned over, and planted a soft kiss on her forehead. He walked out of the room with her sweater over his arm.

"Schlaf gut, mein Kind," she called after him sarcastically.

Alone in his mother's living room, Avshalom began to tidy up, gathering loose papers in his arms. He still had his mother's brown sweater draped over his left arm. He hung it over a chair and then noticed a weight, something in the pocket. He reached inside and found shining in his palm his mother's Weimar mezuzah. She must have taken it down to clean it, polished it to a fine shine, and then placed it in her pocket and forgotten it.

She had turned over pillows on the sofa, pulled chairs out from the living room table, emptied her china cabinet, breaking two plates. She had entered her husband's study, ransacked the bookshelves, torn papers from his drawers, then she had gone to the kitchen — and that is where Avshalom found the soup spoon, bent and twisted from the effort of prying, on the floor beneath the kitchen table. And in the bathroom, beside the sink among tubes and pills, he found a small jar of silver polish, her toothbrush lying on the floor, its bristles tarnished and black.

He held the mezuzah tight in his hand and thought of his wife and what she would say to him: "You want your impossible mother to live with us?"

Avshalom slowed his car at the edge of the city and pulled over at the top of a valley. He stepped out of his car and walked to the edge of a steep cliff. The abandoned village of Lifta lay below. Somewhere in the darkness, a solitary horse neighed. He pulled the mezuzah from his pocket, cradled it in his two hands, and shivered against a wind. He would never tell his mother about the mezuzah. He would let her think that her mind was a steel trap and would let her live with the mystery until she stepped off the planet to meet her husband. He would give the mezuzah to his twelve-year-old, David, and he would fasten it to his door when he had a home of his own.

Avshalom looked into the black sky splashed with yellow stars and the glowing horn of the moon.

"Of course we will not forget, Momma," he whispered to himself. "Look at the stars. There are six million of them. And the moon, it is so beautiful tonight."

The King of the
King of Falafel

Mordechai HaLevi was still very young — only seventeen years old — when his father, Boaz, the King of Falafel, tried to run over his chief competitor with his rusty Toyota truck and was sentenced to three years in prison in the outskirts of Jerusalem.

The King of the King of Falafel had opened business across the busy thoroughfare of King George Street only six months earlier, undercutting the King of Falafel, selling two falafels for the price of one. Boaz told his son that Benny Ovadiah, the newly crowned king, must have been scraping vegetables off the floor of the Mahane Yehuda market and selling them in his sandwiches for such a price.

"He's using rat meat to make his shwarmas. I know it," Mordechai's father said. "How else can a man sell falafels so cheap and still keep the rain off his head?"

"Maybe the angels," Mordechai said.

"The only angel I know is the Angel of Death," his father answered, turning his wedding ring on his thick finger.

The week before his father went berserk, Mordechai was sent across the street to plead with Benny Ovadiah, who was a war hero, saved by golden-winged angels at the Allenby Bridge. He was a religious man and would listen to reason.

Manufactured air blew into Mordechai's face as he entered the gleaming oasis of polished marble and glass where twisting rams horns, bronze water pipes, and wide-eyed *hamsas* hung decorously from the walls. Hungry patrons sat in plush chairs covered with richly embroidered swirling Yemenite stitchwork beneath a sky-blue domed ceiling. They ate from round marble tables that were smoother than ice and whiter than snow. Mordechai wiped his brow, leaving the heat of King George Street behind. Pictures of the great mystics — the Baba Sali, Ovadiah Yosef, and others — were taped on the glass beside the mandate-era cash register that ka-chinged with annoying regularity.

Benny Ovadiah stood behind the counter wearing a large black *kippah* pulled low onto his forehead.

"My father wants you to move away," Mordechai said. "He is the King of Falafel."

"But, I am the King of the King of Falafel," Benny Ovadiah said, throwing a falafel ball in the air and catching it in an open pita.

He was right. His prep men juggled their falafel balls in the air, tapped their tongs on the counter, and sang *Heenay Ma' Tov* as they made their sandwiches. The King of the King of Falafel offered thirty-two different toppings, including thick hummus, zesty tahini, tomatoes, cucumbers, pickled turnips, radishes, olives, eggplant, red peppers, onions, and chips.

"Give this to your father," Benny Ovadiah said, handing Mordechai the fully dressed falafel.

"But when will you leave?" Mordechai asked.

"When the Messiah comes."

When Mordechai returned to the falafel stand to tell his father, he had to shout above the noise of the ancient ceiling fan that clattered like battling swords. His father slammed Benny Ovadiah's falafel against the wall and said, "The fucking Messiah! I'll kill him!"

Mordechai did not love falafels, but he did love his father, so he agreed to run the business while his father was away. With the help of his friend Shuki he secretly planned to drive the King of the King of Falafel out of business to honor his departed father.

Shuki was a juvenile delinquent who did not want to serve in the army and did his best to convince society that he was unfit to die in Lebanon. He wore a T-shirt that said "Rage," smoked filterless cigarettes, and spat on the street as he walked. He whispered ideas in Mordechai's ear and laughed like a sick braying beast.

They paid a Russian farmer from the north to deliver pork to Benny Ovadiah's back door, but the King of the King of Falafel could smell *treif* a mile away and threw it in the street in front of Mordechai's falafel stand. The flies buzzed above the meat all afternoon until Benny Ovadiah approached Mordechai at the end of the day as he was sweeping the floor. Only an autographed team photograph of the *Betar Yerushalayim* football club hung on the wall next to a yellowing dog-eared kashrut certificate.

"Not many customers today," Benny Ovadiah said. "The smell is difficult, the flies are worse."

"It is not so bad," Mordechai said, wondering if Benny Ovadiah smelled of body odor or cumin powder.

"You are losing money. Come and work for me. You can buy cigarettes to send your father in prison."

"I want you to leave," Mordechai said. "Go to Katamonim. We don't want you here."

"You are a punk, but there is hope for you. You honor your father even though he is a maniac. It's a commandment of God."

"But I don't love my neighbor," Mordechai said, sure now that no cumin powder in the world could smell so rank as Benny Ovadiah.

"Leave!" Mordechai shouted.

"When the Messiah comes," Benny Ovadiah said, laughing.

"There cannot be two kings of falafel."

"Why don't you call yourself the King of Shwarma, or the King of *Fuul,* or," Benny Ovadiah said in English, "the King of Fools." He grabbed his rounded belly and laughed again. "Or, maybe, the son of the King of Fools," he said, opening the door to King George Street.

To gain leverage over his enemy, Mordechai stayed open on Shabbat to take advantage of hungry tourists wandering the empty streets of Jerusalem. For a while, he did a brisk business until the black-hatted ultraorthodox from Mea Shearim caught wind of it and pelted stones and bags of dung at his falafel stand.

"Go back to Germany and destroy the sabbath," they shouted.

Cars packed with families arrived from as far away as Nahariya, Afula, and Yeroham to savor the delights of Benny Ovadiah's King of the King of Falafel.

"What spell has he put on them?" Mordechai wondered. "What angel watches over him?"

Even his most loyal customer, Reuven the Watcher, walked away from the King of Falafel saying, "Your falafel tastes like sand. I wouldn't feed it to the dead."

Mordechai gave away free samples, concocted the fruit falafel, painted a new bright red sign, shouted down his adversary through a megaphone, and continued to lose business to Benny Ovadiah. He even considered calling himself the King of the King of the King of Falafel, but did not have enough space on his tiny storefront.

Shuki suggested they steal the pita bread that was delivered to Benny Ovadiah's front door hours before the King of the King of Falafel opened for business.

"Falafel without pita is like the Dead Sea without salt," Shuki said.

They were amazed to discover that without his pitas, the King of the King of Falafel did not fold up and blow away. He thrived, in fact. People lined up all along the street, jockeyed for position, and shouted across to Mordechai and his empty stand. Finally a policeman on horseback arrived to calm the crowd, but he too dismounted and joined the hungry line.

"What's going on?" Mordechai shouted to one of the patrons.

"It's amazing," a young girl called back. "He is serving falafel on manna from heaven."

When his father wrote him asking how business was, Mordechai lied; when he asked after the nudnik who called himself 'king,' Mordechai said the filthy dog was on the run: "He's in the *mikvah* now, preparing for the Messiah."

"He should drown," his father said.

One day Shuki drank a jar of olive oil and bit into a shwarma at Benny Ovadiah's restaurant. He threw up on the floor right in front of the King of the King of Falafel and screamed, "Bad lamb! Bad lamb!"

But Benny Ovadiah had seen Shuki hanging out with Mordechai and beat him with a broom.

"Don't break your teeth. I'm not leaving," Benny Ovadiah shouted as he brought the broom down onto Shuki's head.

"What about the Messiah?" Shuki said.

"Show me the Messiah."

Frustrated and tired of falafel, they ate hamburgers at the new McDonald's, where Shuki tried to lighten the mood, moving the buns of his burger like the mouth of a hand puppet. "I am the red heifer. I taste better with cheese." And he bit into the burger, laughing.

"I am the pink heifer," Mordechai said, holding his burger. "Cook me some more, please."

"Stupid!" Shuki said, hitting Mordechai on the forehead with the palm of his hand. "Don't you remember from religion class in school where God told the children of Israel to purify themselves?"

"Take a shower," Mordechai said, laughing. "With soap!"

"He told them to sacrifice a red heifer, a pure red heifer without blemish or spot, because only the ashes of a red heifer can purify Jews so they can rebuild the Temple." Shuki paused and beat a drum roll on the table. "And-bring-the-Messiah-the-King-of-Israel."

"But there hasn't been a red heifer in Israel in over two thousand years," Mordechai said, remembering the mysterious passage.

"Yes," Shuki said, "that is true. But now . . ." And he began to hum, and then Mordechai joined in and they were singing, "Moshiach, Moshiach, Moshiach!"

They drove out of the city under a starless sky toward the west and the coastal plain. The air became warmer as they descended. Shuki rolled down his window and lit a cigarette. Mordechai fiddled with the radio dial as they drove, finding Jordan Radio in English, then *Arutz Sheva,* the Jewish settlers' pirate station, and finally *Galei Tzahal,* Army wave radio. They sang along in English at the top of their lungs.

"Remember when we were young?" Mordechai asked Shuki as they turned off the highway.

Shuki knew the kibbutz guard by name, because he used to hitch down every week to make out in the banana fields with a girl he'd met on a school trip to the Holocaust museum. They waved and drove by him, but they didn't stop at the girl's room, they kept going along the dirt road past the bulls kicking up dust, and on to the dairy. The air smelled of fresh cow manure and trees.

"Cows are so dumb," Mordechai said. "All they do is shit. They live in shit, they sleep in shit. . . ."

"Quiet," Shuki said. "Operation Secret Messiah."

The frightened cows moved away from them as one, their hooves rumbling against the earth. Mordechai and Shuki followed them twice around the pen under the moon-less sky. The cows were brown and black and some were just brown.

"Okay," Shuki said, "let's get this one, she's stopped moving."

"She's too big," Mordechai said, laughing. "Even bigger than Tamar."

"My sister's having twins, idiot. Just grab one," Shuki answered. "Grab it by the tail."

But they couldn't catch the other cows, who kept circling around and around the pen in the darkness.

"Let's get this one before she wakes up," Mordechai said, slapping the fat sleepy cow on the rump. *"Yala!"*

It wasn't easy to get the giant brown cow into the truck. She wouldn't move after being prodded out of the pen.

When she finally did move she stepped on Mordechai's foot and then didn't move again.

"Ouch," Mordechai called. "She's on my foot."

"Punch her," Shuki said.

"What?"

"In the nose."

"No. You punch her."

"Tickle her, then," Shuki said, spitting onto the ground. "Like she's your girlfriend."

When they finally got her into the truck they covered her with a tarp and gunned the engine past the guard when his back was turned.

When they pulled back onto the highway, Mordechai and Shuki sang the song that they thought was so hilarious calling for the Messiah. "Moshiach, Moshiach, Moshiach! Ai, ai, ai, ai . . ."

"We should call her 'one million burgers,'" Mordechai said as they drove back up toward the holy city.

"She's the red heifer," Shuki said. "And I'm a blond."

In the alleyway behind the King of Falafel they slathered red paint onto the cow and worked it into her coat.

"The hairdresser at work," Mordechai said.

"If that will keep me from the army," Shuki said, kissing the cow dramatically on the forehead.

The cow stood still, big-eyed, oblivious.

It was nearly four o'clock in the morning when they led the red-painted cow across King George Street. Mordechai and Shuki were as red as the cow, their hands and faces smeared with paint. They were high from the paint fumes.

"Ai, ai ai, ai, wo-o, wo-o, wo-o . . ." Mordechai sang.

"Quiet," Shuki said.

"Jews are depending on you, big girl," Mordechai whispered. "In the morning they will wake to trumpets and flutes and harps. . . ."

"Shut up," Shuki said, leading the cow into the alleyway behind the King of the King of Falafel.

"At last the Messiah can come," Mordechai added, patting her on the head. "Isn't that right, Red?"

Not even a moo.

Shuki jimmied open the back door of Benny Ovadiah's King of the King of Falafel with a pocket knife he carried in his jeans. They had difficulty leading the beefy cow through the back door, her wet paint rubbing off against the door, but they forced her through, laughing as they went.

"Through the red door, destiny awaits," Mordechai said.

They left her standing alone in the dark, in the middle of the restaurant.

From across the street they could hear the red-painted cow rattling around in the darkness, a breaking of glass, battering against the steel shutter that said: King of the King of Falafel, and then the graffito, "Is the king of nothing." They heard hooves stamping and long, loud moos.

Mordechai imagined Benny Ovadiah's unblemished marble tables shattering on the floor, his tapestries trod upon, his bronze *tchotchkes* battered and stomped on. He imagined the Lubavitcher rebbe climbing out of the photo from beside the mandate-era register to sweep the cluttered floor muttering lamentations, and the frightened cow nuzzling close, dripping snot on the black-clad rabbi.

From the time they locked the cow inside, there was not

a moment of silence. Afraid that the paint fumes had made her crazy as a bull, they agonized all night under the moonless sky, without a star to wish on.

"You go see her," Mordechai said.

"No! You!"

"She's destroying the place."

"She's destroying the place," Shuki repeated, and they both broke out laughing.

Mordechai's insides heaved as he laughed and he felt a warm glow inside him. He laughed so hard he could not tell if sweat or tears poured down his face.

For a moment before the sun rose, the sky filled with stars and then morning burst out of the east to greet them.

Things were not so hilarious by the time Benny Ovadiah arrived to open the King of the King of Falafel. Both Mordechai and Shuki were exhausted and a little afraid.

"Caught with red hands," Shuki said, but he did not laugh.

The sun was out now, and there was nowhere for the two boys to hide. They stood by the side of the road and could hear Benny Ovadiah screaming and cursing, calling them sons of whores, sons of bitches, sons of shit. Mordechai turned to Shuki and offered a prayer for his soul. He was only half joking.

When Benny Ovadiah emerged from his battered restaurant, he was completely red, covered in paint or blood or both.

He carried a bloody butcher knife in his shaking hand. "You had better hope the Messiah comes now," Benny Ovadiah shouted, stepping into the street. "Then, the dead can rise again. And you will be the first."

"You can't kill us," Mordechai said.

"Why not? I can share a cell with your father."

He reached the sidewalk and grabbed Mordechai by the hair.

"It was just a joke," Mordechai said, almost in tears.

"I've slaughtered your joke," Benny Ovadiah boomed.

"But, we're neighbors," Mordechai said, the words almost swallowed. "Look," he said, pointing to the pathetic sight of Benny Ovadiah's ruined falafel restaurant across the street.

"No! Look!" Shuki cried, wide-eyed.

And, from behind an overturned table, Mordechai saw a little red calf stumble unsteadily out of the wreckage, its legs buckling like a drunk, as it mooed and stepped out to join the morning traffic.

Lucky Eighteen

Elijah's Cup

Very early on the morning of his twenty-third birthday, Stuart Kravetz and his friend Shawn Silver stepped out of a misty rain and through a rusty ornamented gate, into the subterranean gloom and smoke of Elijah's Cup. They stepped down three stone stairs, careful not to slip on splashes of beer or vomit as they ducked their heads below an iron pipe, Kravetz holding on for balance. Shawn smiled at every face he met. He wore a light meter and camera around his neck and carried a silver briefcase in his left hand and a suitcase in his right. He wore a stylish black linen suit and a small ponytail that seemed grossly out of place for both the Holy City and Elijah's Cup. But Kravetz remembered that Shawn always dressed to travel, whether it was a road trip to Boston or a plane flight across the world. The room was filled with barefoot English travelers, blond Swedish tourists, wayward rabbinical students, wild-eyed mystics, mustached Palestinian laborers, broad-shouldered U.N. troopers, Russian whores, and bullshitters of all political stripes pounding back cheap Israeli beer, hummus, and olives.

Kravetz had not seen Shawn since leaving for Israel six months earlier, and besides having grown a goatee that covered his cleft chin, he also seemed to have gained weight. Kravetz noticed that Shawn's face seemed somehow harder, and though he was only a year older than Kravetz, he looked dried out and bloated at the same time.

The prime minister had been buried on Mount Herzl that morning, and after a long day Kravetz had gone to bed early, with his radio tuned to *Galei Tzahal* playing mournful music from the darkness. The telephone woke him at midnight. "Happy birthday, kid," the familiar voice said. "How about a drink?"

Kravetz was silent and clicked on his bedside lamp.

"I'm at the airport, brother," his old friend, Shawn Silver, said, sounding more nasal than usual. "Meet me outside Elijah's Cup in an hour."

And now they were under the smoky dome of Elijah's Cup, passing old Ministry of Tourism posters for Tiberias, Eilat, and the Dead Sea tacked to the wall. A dustpan-sized ceramic *hamsa* hung behind the bar, the shape of a hand, a dreamy blue eye centered in its palm to ward off evil. Faded photos of rabbis — a hawk-nosed Baba Sali, a turbaned Ovadiah Yosef, and other Sephardi mystics — were taped to the mirror behind the bar. A stained and tattered petition sat on the bar; the bar's owner had been caught with drugs in the Sinai, and was currently serving twenty-five years in an Egyptian prison. A wooden barrel of black olives stood nearby; customers dipped their hands in and sometimes spat the pits back into the barrel.

Shawn found a table covered with graffiti and sat down beneath a television that mutely flashed CNN's *World Report*. Kravetz could see the Kings of Israel Square on the television screen as he sat down. He could see blood on the pavement where the prime minister had been shot, and his stomach tensed.

"What are you doing here?" Kravetz said, still buzzing from nerves. Shawn had a history of surprising Stuart, and it usually meant trouble. They had been friends since second grade in Hebrew school when Shawn had dropped his pen so he could catch a peek up Miss Makhlabani's skirt and was smacked on the head with a ruler. Shawn had been his best friend, but that was a long time ago.

"Two Goldstars, *Motek*." Shawn snapped a finger in the air to get the waitress's attention. "Shit. She's the bomb."

Kravetz nodded his head, and thought women were always bombs, or chicks, or puss to Shawn.

"What am I doing here?" Shawn said, returning to Stuart's question. "I told you I'd come. I'm good for my word. You must be lonely, anyway. The literary exile. Shit, your parents haven't heard from you in months."

It was Kravetz's parents who had sent him to Israel in the first place, and it had nothing to do with Zionism, or making the desert bloom, or becoming a light unto nations. Five years earlier he and Shawn played in a punk band called Bitefinger Baby, and their drummer had stabbed someone at one of the clubs they were playing. His parents figured something bad was bound to happen if he stayed in the city, and he was too old for summer camp. So Kravetz and Shawn went to Israel.

They had spent a wild summer drinking together after their senior year of high school, as they traveled from the Golan Heights in the north to Masada and Eilat in the south. They had promised one day, stuffing notes into the Wailing Wall, that they would return to Jerusalem together.

"I kind of like the quiet," Kravetz said. "Gives me time to think."

"The last thing you want to do is think, my friend. Can I stay?"

"How long?"

"I love you, too, buddy. Do you remember when those skinheads tried to steal your Doc Martens?" Shawn said. "They called you a Jew and I convinced them that you weren't Jewish." Shawn poked Kravetz in the ribs and crushed him in a headlock. Kravetz gagged from the smell of his friend's Drakkar Noir cologne.

"But I am Jewish," he started to say before Shawn's bicep muffled his words.

"I saved you," Shawn said, letting go after a moment.

"Yeah. Thanks," Kravetz said, remembering that he once felt that Shawn and he were as close as brothers. "How long?"

"I don't know. Until I strike gold."

Shawn always seemed to get his way, and was not afraid to point out an obligation to him. He called in his favors again and again as if the debt lasted a lifetime.

"You know," Shawn said. "Until I milk this place for enough pics for a show."

A man and a woman sat together at a small table in the corner. The woman was crying. Kravetz wondered if the woman was crying because she and her boyfriend were breaking up, or whether she was mourning the death of the prime minister.

"I placed the ad," Shawn said after a moment. He lifted his silver briefcase onto the table and opened it. Kravetz could see another camera with a flash attached to it and a long zoom lens strapped in against the foam bedding. A small Polaroid camera lay beside the lens. Film canisters were strung across the top half of the case like a bandolier.

Kravetz remembered Shawn's idea for a spread for the upstart Heart-Shaped Jeans Company. He thought it was a stupid idea at the time: a bunch of beautiful, naked models frolicking in a heart-shaped pool, with their clothes crumpled and scattered around the deck like sex-deflated bodies. But now that he pulled a folded magazine out of his silver case and showed him the glossy ad, with the heading "Good Jean Pool," he had to laugh.

"If you will it, it is no dream," Shawn said, quoting Herzl with a smirk. He lit a filterless Noblesse cigarette. "It's brilliant, isn't it?"

"Yeah, it is," Kravetz said, and paused as the beers arrived. "Have you heard from Jana?" His voice almost caught in his throat.

"Nah, haven't seen her," Shawn said, sipping from his Goldstar. "This tastes like chlorine."

Kravetz was silent, and he thought of Jana again, his Janushka, and felt sick in his stomach and somewhat amazed that he could ever have been close enough to her to call her something as childish as Janushka. He wondered how she could be so far away and yet seem as if she were still in the room with him. Whenever he smelled patchouli oil, he always turned around to see if Jana had come looking for him.

Three Russians at the next table began singing an off-key, operatic rendition of "Hotel California." Jana hated Russians and never failed to give the finger to anyone on the road who drove a Lada.

"This place hasn't changed a bit," Shawn said.

"It's the only place open tonight," Kravetz said, thinking of the long lines of mourners making their way up to Mount Herzl that morning. "You're lucky."

"Always have been, always will." Shawn picked up his camera and looked through it. There was seldom a time that Kravetz remembered seeing Shawn without a camera around his neck or pressed to his face, so he wasn't surprised when Shawn pointed his camera toward a bald giant with a cinder-block head and thin purple lips who sat alone with his head down at a table across the room. "What's the deal with that guy?"

"That's Asher," Kravetz said. "He's a survivor. Sobibor."

"Fucking golem," he said and turned his camera toward a bearded man with a cell phone pressed to his ear. Shawn played with the lens as if he were focusing for a shot.

"That's Shmuelik. He used to be a rabbi, now he sells guns," Kravetz said, taking the first sip of his beer. "One of the guys who helped liquidate the Warsaw or the Lódź ghetto is living in Canada. Shmuelik knows a man who will pay any-one fifty thousand dollars to kill him."

"Shit, who wants to go to Canada?" Shawn said and spun in his seat, aiming his camera at Kravetz. "You look good. Better. Really."

"I don't know," Kravetz said. "Sometimes I'm thinking about what I want to eat or something, and suddenly Jana pops into my head. You know, the way she stood. I see trees that remind me of her. And sometimes I see a woman hold-ing a baby on the bus or something, and she doesn't even look like Jana, but you know —"

"Fuck her," Shawn said, finishing his beer. "You've got to be part animal, part machine." Shawn always felt empow-ered by paraphrasing punk-rock lyrics. He raised his camera to his face again, blinding Kravetz with his flash. "A fuckin' hot animal machine," he said, expelling a mouth full of smoke.

A Marriage Made in Heaven

A few days later, Kravetz sat on his sixth-floor balcony with a volume of Amichai's poems open in front of him. He read, "You are beautiful, like prophecies / And sad, like those which come true." And he thought of the time when he and Jana walked through the shallows of the water at Brighton Beach after visiting her aunt and eating some lardy meat prepared in the style of the "old country." Her hair was wet and she smelled seaweedy in the last purple light of day and she came up close to him almost shouting, "Hey!" as she pulled a damp pack of cigarettes out of her shorts pocket. "So 'cause I'm not Jewish or anything, does that mean you would never marry me?"

"You could convert," Kravetz had said, not sure if he was serious or joking.

The sun burst through the hard gray sky, its rays refracted like spotlights throughout the city. Kravetz looked out beyond the slope of Independence Park and the remains of the Mamilla Cemetery toward the Old City; the city that Twain had called the knobbiest town in the world with its crooked streets and countless domes, a city where Melville had written in disgust about the Crusader church being a sickening cheat where all is glitter and nothing is gold. But, looking toward the golden Dome of the Rock, Kravetz thought of how far he was from New York and Jana. He knew he would never run into her in the winding streets and alleys, and he felt glad for a moment.

That week Kravetz and Shawn sat up late drinking Goldstars and talking. Shawn knew Kravetz better than anybody, except Jana, and he built him up, saying, "You're a handsome guy. Look at those deep poetic eyes of yours. You're the handsomest guy."

Kravetz recounted every detail of his relationship to Shawn, told him how she kissed with her eyes open, how the blonde hair on her arms held the sun in the morning, and her secret nickname for him. He felt somehow lighter, as if he had unburdened himself of a great weight, and was thankful Shawn never once asked, "How was she?"

Kravetz was still a virgin, a junior in high school, when Shawn Silver had woken him with a drunken phone call at two in the morning to announce, "Gentlemen, that's lucky eighteen."

Lucky eighteen had always been sort of a joke between Shawn and Kravetz, but it seemed somehow appropriate that Shawn would invoke it after his eighteenth lay, since his first came shortly after his bar mitzvah. It was always the cheapskates who didn't have the class to buy them bar mitzvah gifts that handed them crumpled handfuls of money that always added up to eighteen dollars. Eighteen signified *chai,* or life, and was supposed to bring good luck.

Shawn wore his hair in a mohawk at the time, something Kravetz couldn't get away with, having curly hair that would have looked like a strip of carpet. Girls curious about Shawn always wanted to touch his hair.

He told Kravetz how he had gotten redheaded Jenn Liska drunk on peppermint schnapps, how she had ridden him like a horse in her parents' bed, with her tights rolled down to her knees, and how her breath tasted like an ashtray.

"Wow," Kravetz had said, half excited, half disgusted by the blow-by-blow details that made him hard.

"You'll get there, my son. You'll get there," Shawn said.

When Kravetz finally did sleep with a Montreal cocktail waitress ten years his senior that New Year's Eve, Shawn burst into the bedroom as soon as they were done, snapping the two strangers in bed with his Nikon.

"My boy Kravetz's first time," he had told the horrified waitress, laughing as she disappeared under the wrinkled sheets like a ghost.

Kravetz closed the book of poetry and felt the weight of loneliness all around him. Jana, he thought, "You are beautiful like . . ."

Kravetz had not heard the hum of the noisy elevator and the slam of its heavy door.

"Honey, I'm home," Shawn called, opening the apartment door. He appeared on the balcony a few minutes later, with the waitress from Elijah's Cup at his side. "Stuart, this is Ravit." She extended her hand, and Kravetz shook it, realizing she was the one wearing patchouli in the bar that night. She was tall and had dark hair, was maybe a Yemenite or Moroccan. She had a bright smile, and wore a loose red shirt.

"Ravit wants to be a star," Shawn said.

"Shut up, stupid," she said, hitting him lightly on the shoulder. Shawn pulled away and said, "Ow."

Kravetz knew now that they had had sex, or would soon have sex. He knew Shawn's gambit well — baiting, antagonizing, then feigning hurt to gain the girl's sympathies.

"Come on, we're going for a walk," Shawn said, adjusting his camera at his neck. "You can't study all day."

"You aren't religious, are you?" Ravit said. "I *hate* the religious."

"It's poetry," Kravetz said lamely.

"She hates the army, too. She just turned eighteen," Shawn said, grabbing a handful of her hair. "You're a nice girl," he said, leaning in close to kiss her.

"Fuck the army," she said, pulling away. "And fuck the crazy religious of this city. I'm going to Thailand next week." She laughed a loud, mannish laugh as she pretended to take a drag from a joint.

Kravetz noticed that her eyes seemed to be almost spinning with energy and were a deep, piercing green, the color of liquor-soaked lime rinds. He put his book down and said, "I gotta be at work in an hour."

Shawn popped open the back of his camera, reached into his vest, slid in a roll of film, and snapped it shut again without even looking at what he was doing, like a gunslinger loading up in the wild west. "Come on. Call in. Kids are united," Shawn said and stuck out his fist as he had so many times during their youth. Kravetz hesitated and then punched it with his own, adding his lines, "Never be divided."

A half an hour later they arrived at an ultraorthodox neighborhood that looked like an eighteenth-century Jewish ghetto. It was built like a stone fortress, with Yiddish posters plastered everywhere to the blackened walls. The streets were gray and potholed, and black-garbed men with beards and side curls walked through the crowded streets speaking in Yiddish. Shawn wore an open motorcycle jacket with a T-shirt that had "Social Distortion" written across the front. Kravetz noticed that Ravit walked with supreme confidence, taking dramatic, modelesque strides, not unlike Jana when she had felt the world was hers. Ravit spoke in a tuneless yet musical way and laughed, sometimes touching Kravetz on the shoulder.

"So serious," she said, frowning. "You must to have fun." She smiled.

They stopped before a sign that said, "**ATTENTION! YOU ARE NOW ENTERING THE ULTRAORTHODOX NEIGHBORHOOD OF MEA SHEARIM. WOMEN ARE TO DRESS MODESTLY.**" The sign said that women should wear sleeves that reached at least to their elbow, and skirts that reached below their knees. Necklines were to be no lower than the collarbone.

Ravit undid the top two buttons of her cherry red shirt.

"Here we are," Shawn said as two men passed. "On your right you'll notice the latest ghetto fashions of the year of our Lord seventeen ninety-two. The bearded gentleman," and here Shawn laughed. Ravit hummed along to his commentary. "Oh, they're both bearded. The taller gentleman models a fur *streimel,* made out of the finest rat fur, trapped in the kitchens of Schmuel the baker."

Kravetz felt his stomach turn. "Shawn, what are you doing?"

Two more men passed and scowled at the three of them.

"You can't talk like that," Kravetz said.

"Why not? They don't speak English."

"They don't speak Hebrew, either," Ravit said. "Only to pray. God forbid you wipe your ass in God's Hebrew."

Now a woman pushing a baby carriage approached, her young daughter slowly walking at her side.

"Like a queen, her wig glistens in the sunlight, a wig this gorgeous you wouldn't dare cover with a babababushka. . . ."

The girl lowered her head and sped up.

Shawn began to jump around singing, "Crucify-i-i-i-i me, Crucify-i-i-i-i me."

"Stop it," Kravetz said.

"Crucify-i-i-i-i me," Shawn continued.

Ravit grabbed him, pressed close, and whispered in his ear, "Be a good boy."

"You're gonna start a riot," Kravetz said, stepping away.

"Hey, that's cool," Shawn said.

"So I get stoned here instead of Thailand," Ravit said matter-of-factly.

"This isn't fucking Disneyland," Kravetz said.

"No. It's the fucking Holyland," Shawn said. "And you're playing Goofy."

At that moment, Kravetz hated Shawn, as he had hated him a thousand times before. But he knew that Shawn only wanted to have fun, and that he was trying to draw him out of his gloom. He really didn't understand, he hadn't seen the anger in the eyes of those men. And if Ravit was supposed to be a gift for him, like the Montreal cocktail waitress had been, he was not interested.

A gray-bearded man wearing a rumpled suit and black hat burst out of a building and charged toward them, calling Ravit a whore. His clenched fists looked like steel hammers, and he cursed at Shawn from beneath the sign. "She's not a whore," Shawn said. "She's the Virgin Mary." Kravetz was afraid somebody would get hurt, and pulled Ravit close to him by the shoulders. She was stronger than he thought, and pushed him away. Kravetz fell to the ground and he heard prayers from all around, as he scrambled to pick up his glasses. When Kravetz looked up again he saw that Shawn had his camera ready, aimed at the man, and that the man had covered his face with his hat to protect himself against breaching the Second Commandment forbidding graven images. And now Ravit unbuttoned the rest of her shirt, and pulled it open. She leaned close to the man, and blew a dramatic kiss at him, her bra and tattooed midriff bared for all to see.

Then the clickclickclickclickclickclick of Shawn's Nikon.

That was *A Marriage Made in Heaven,* and the beginning of FLICK Photos and Postcards.

Come Hither, Woman, Thy Breasts Are as Comely as Doves

Shawn thought it was so clever to spell the name FLICK in all capital letters, giving the illusion of the word FUCK as in the smudgy old comic books. He found a man named Sammi Shaloub who ran a camera store in East Jerusalem and who let Shawn use his darkroom for his black and white photos and would develop Shawn's color prints without asking any questions.

While Kravetz was busy studying, Shawn wandered through the city with his cameras trying to catch gold in his crosshairs. During his first week, he had been cursed in the Church of the Holy Sepulcher where he had an Australian girl, on the last leg of her three-year walkabout, slip out of her dress and lie on the Stone of Unction, smoking a cigarette where the body of Christ had been laid after he was removed from the cross. An Orthodox monk had chased him out with a burning censer into the stone courtyard, shouting "American" and "Fuck."

"It's like a dirty butcher's slab," Shawn had told Kravetz of the Stone of Unction, "and these pilgrims are tongue kissing it."

At the Dome of the Rock where the Prophet Muhammad had begun his night journey to heaven, where Muslims prostrate themselves in prayer, he snapped a Swedish girl he had just met, face to the ground, dress thrown over her head, bare behind in the air, praying to the mighty Allah. *The Ass of an Angel* even got a quiet "tsk, tsk" from Sammi Shaloub.

Shawn found two urchins throwing rotten fruit at frightened tourists outside of the Jaffa Gate and he convinced them to sell his provocative postcards for two dollars each, and before long he had a squad of six kids selling his photos throughout the city.

It was a rainy December day and Shawn had been staying with Kravetz for more than a month. The Old City was only twenty minutes from their King George Street apartment and they made the journey together about twice a week in search of sickeningly sweet Nablus-style *kanafi,* thick Turkish coffee, prickly pears, and any old trinket that caught their eyes. Shawn had bought a bullwhip on his last trip to the Old City and chased Kravetz all the way home, snapping the whip at him as he ran.

The streets were slick and luminous, seeming almost to glow in the gray light, and they passed a fruit stand and carpet and souvenir shops that sold olive-wood camels and manger scenes. They passed people in the streets, Arabs, Jews, and Christians, and Kravetz looked in every face as it passed, swearing that he saw something in each that reminded him of Jana. A boy carrying a large wooden tray of pita bread on his head bumped into Kravetz and mumbled something in Arabic that Shawn figured must be about Kravetz's mother. A shopkeeper shouted out "Special price," and waved a checkered kaffiyeh at Kravetz and Shawn as they descended deeper into the city. They reached a small mosque where, through the open door, they could see a man stretched out in prayer on the floor. Shawn had raised his camera and began to focus, but Kravetz said, "Let's go."

They arrived at a darkened shop where old black and white photographs dating from the time of the Ottomans and the British mandate hung in the window. Kravetz could see photos of a sheep market outside of Damascus Gate, slick water buffaloes trudging through the malarial Hula swamp, pilgrims dragging crosses down the Via Dolorosa, a man with an impossibly large mustache smoking from a water pipe. Shawn entered the store followed by Kravetz, and greeted the man behind the counter, who, it seemed, had been sleeping with his head in his arms.

"Welcome," the man said, jumping up.

The room smelled of old books and coffee, and a large color photo of the Dome of the Rock hung behind him. The man pulled back a curtain and disappeared for a moment, returning with a folded paper in his hand.

Shawn was looking at some color photographs of young boys throwing stones at Israeli soldiers. Kravetz could hear him chuckle, "Now that is what I call punk."

"Five hundred dollars," the man said, unfolding the piece of paper. "Only five hundred dollars. Look. Look," the man said.

Kravetz could see what looked like Hebrew letters and a bloodstain, with a hole in the middle of the page.

"You remember the prime minister," the man said. "Terrible thing."

"Robert Capa," Shawn said. "Bullshit pedestrian portraits. Look at this shit," Shawn said.

He flipped through a book of photos dating from the first days of the State of Israel. Pioneers, Kravetz thought, and smiled.

"Look," Shawn said. "Man building a fucking house, street scene Tel Aviv, ugly face no shirt, ugly face sun hat, rabbi, man with gun, eyepatch, ugly, ugly, ugly. These pictures are boring and ugly," Shawn said.

From the time he was a kid, Kravetz had always thought that Moshe Dayan in his eyepatch looked dashing. "And I suppose you are here to capture the beauty of Jerusalem's golden light," Kravetz said. "Its majestic architecture, from Herod to Süleyman the Magnificent . . ."

"No," Shawn said, shaking his head. "I'm here to be interesting. This shit is boring."

The man leaned in close to Kravetz, holding the page close to his face. He could see Hebrew lettering on the page.

"The Song of Peace," the man said.

"There will never be peace," Shawn said, picking up a book.

"Look," the man said. "The Song of Peace."

Kravetz remembered that the prime minister had been awkwardly singing the Song of Peace at the rally, only moments before he had been killed. He had folded the page and placed it in his breast pocket. "Only three hundred dollars," the man said.

"Let me see that," Kravetz said.

"No. No," the man said. "You can't touch it."

"Look at this," Shawn called. He waved an old leather-bound book. "A guide book."

"Two hundred fifty," the man said. "Look. The bullet hole. A Jewish bullet hole."

"Check this out," Shawn said, mumbling something in mangled Hebrew. "I have many gold pieces and many treasures . . ."

"That is a pilgrims' guide book to the holy city from the time of the Crusaders," the man said. He had a mustache that was just beginning to turn gray, and he wore a thick pair of glasses. He pulled Kravetz closer to him by the shoulder and said, "For you, two hundred fifty. That is his real blood. Smell it."

Kravetz turned away. He had lost sixty dollars in a shell game in Times Square when he was sixteen and had no interest in being ripped off again. He turned back to Shawn.

"What else does it say?"

Shawn laughed. "Here. This one is great. 'Come Hither, Woman, Thy Breasts Are as Comely as Doves.' Do you think that would work?"

"You've gotten away with worse," Kravetz said.

"You know, it's the Crusaders who fucked this place up in the first place," Shawn said. The man quietly folded the paper and put it back in his breast pocket. "You know, you've seen these Arabs with blond hair or blue eyes walking around. That's because they've been fucked by Crusaders, probably raped in the name of Christ."

"Come on," Kravetz said.

"You are living in the land of the perennially fucked," Shawn said. "A fantasy land of ghosts and fucking kooks."

"That's ridiculous," Kravetz said.

"The place was built directly on the ashes of the Holocaust."

"Bullshit," Kravetz said.

"It wasn't? So was that a picnic over there in Europe?

When the world stops feeling guilty about what happened over there, Israel will be wiped off the map."

"I don't believe that," Kravetz said.

"Let's go, man, this place stinks," Shawn said, walking toward the door.

"Yes, yes, you go," the man said. "But first you must buy. I have the bullets," the man added, reaching into his pocket. "Look how they have been flattened."

"So this is the golden Medina," Shawn said.

"Yeah, why not?"

"Bullshit. Even Herzl, your father of modern Zionism, said the only thing special about a Jewish state would be that the prostitutes would be Jewish, the thieves would be Jewish. . . ."

"It's not that . . ." Kravetz started to say.

"No, it's worse," Shawn said. "Living next door to terrorists, Scud missiles flying overhead, religious fanatics." He pulled the door open, looked at the man, and said, "This is a fucking garage sale. I'm outta here," Shawn said, curling his lips into a scowl.

Kravetz followed Shawn out into the street, not looking at the man as he left. Kravetz felt like arguing with Shawn, but by the time he caught up to him, Shawn was smiling. A pair of Arab women walked toward Shawn and Kravetz with their faces covered.

"Check it out, man." Shawn tried to say, "Come hither, woman, thy breasts are as comely as doves," as the two women passed.

"That's ancient Hebrew," Kravetz said. "They're not going to understand that."

The two women passed, ignoring Shawn and Kravetz. Shawn shouted down the street after them, "Your breasts are like two pillows, like two water balloons, two floppy, flapping, bouncing titties."

"Shut up," Kravetz said.

"They don't understand," Shawn said. "It's like the time we were in Montreal and we would point at our wrist, as if we're asking for the time."

"They knew you were asking them to suck your dick."

Now another woman walked toward them, carrying a string bag in her arms.

"Come on," Shawn said, "you try. We're going to get you laid."

"No way. That's obnoxious."

"Do you want me to get you laid or not?" Shawn said.

Two summers earlier, Jana had told Kravetz that she was going upstate for the summer solstice with some of her friends and that he couldn't come. "It's sort of a Baltic Bash," she had said.

"Tribalism," Shawn had said to Kravetz. "That cunt will never really accept you because you are not part of her tribe. Worse still, you're a Jew. She's probably cheating on you right now. Huh, some of that Polish kielbasa."

"You're an asshole," Kravetz said. "You're talking about my girlfriend?"

"Then why doesn't the bitch want you to go?"

Shawn was always putting doubts into Kravetz's head. At first Kravetz thought it was only jealousy, since Shawn never seemed to have a girlfriend for very long. But this time Kravetz was worried that something was going to happen. When Jana returned from the weekend away, she said the weekend was fine, but she drank too much. That worried Kravetz even more, and then he noticed the hair.

He told Shawn that she always had an inch-long black hair on her left breast, and when she came back from her trip it was gone.

"The bitch cut it off," Shawn said, "because she knew she was going to get fucked. I'll bet she shaved her bikini line, too, for the first time in a year."

That weekend Kravetz and Shawn got drunk at Haymakers and Shawn introduced Kravetz to Holly Jaundice, the singer of a local punk band.

"Have fun," Shawn called after them as they stumbled out of the bar.

And now in Jerusalem, Shawn called down the street after the woman, mangling the ancient Hebrew as he shouted.

"Shut up," Kravetz said. "Will you just shut up."

Christmas Day, Kravetz decided he should have called Jana to wish her a "Merry Christmas." Shawn had taken an Arab taxi to Bethlehem, hoping to catch some hysterical pilgrims in Manger Square. He still hadn't returned. Kravetz had picked up the phone several times and even dialed Jana's number, but always hung up before anyone answered. He thought that, somehow, thinking about her with the phone in his hand would be enough to make her pick up the phone and call him. He just wanted to hear her talk like old times, the way they used to. He wanted to apologize and to hear her say, "Me too." Sometimes his hand slipped down and he began to stroke himself, but he couldn't think of Jana. It just made him too sad, as if she were a ghost he couldn't get his arms around.

So You Should Never Forget

New Year's Eve, Kravetz and Shawn went to Elijah's Cup for drinks. The bar was packed, and loud Israeli music boomed from the speakers. They found a table near the back of the bar and sat down. Kravetz could tell that Shawn had slept with at least two or three of the girls they had passed by the way they stiffened as he walked past.

"To a new year," Shawn said. "This one's on me."

Kravetz noticed a graffito etched into the table — The sex life of the Egyptian Sphinx was lonely / reserved for Egyptian Kinx — and said, "Don't worry about it."

"At least let me buy you a beer. You won't even let me give you money for rent."

"That's so I can throw you out whenever I want," Kravetz said, laughing.

Shawn did not laugh. "I'm buying you a beer."

They drank two or three beers, and Shawn hugged the waitress, saying, "Sylvester *Tov!*" Kravetz always felt good up until three beers, and looked around the room hopefully. It was only later that he began to feel gloomy.

A large crowd had gathered across the bar at the table where the infamous Asher was sitting in his usual seat. People stood on chairs and climbed onto each other's shoulders. They sang "Auld Lang Syne," and swayed rhythmically.

"What's going on?" Shawn said, grabbing his camera before Kravetz could answer.

Shawn pressed his head between a pair of thighs, and Kravetz could see that Asher had a skinny, blond German-looking guy pinned to the table. Now the crowd was chanting,

"Go! Go! Go! Go!" as Asher dipped a needle into a bottle of India ink. His eyes looked washed out and distant, as gray as dirty ice. Kravetz had heard stories about Asher, but never believed them. He raised his tattooed arm in the air, and jabbed the needle into the German's arm shouting, "Never forget! Never forget! Never forget!" The crowd roared with laughter, and Shawn burrowed his way through the crowd, onto the table. "I need light," he called. "Move back!"

But the crowd only moved closer, as Asher continued to jab away at the poor German's arm. Kravetz could hear Shawn saying, "Perfect. Fucking perfect," and imagined the title *So You Should Never Forget* appearing at the top of the postcard. And suddenly Asher was aware of his surroundings, and he reached up to grab Shawn by the neck with his cleaver-like hand.

"You," he said, pulling Shawn close. The German was still pinned to the table with his other massive hand. "Do you remember . . ."

"What?" Shawn said, his nasal voice rising.

"Do you remember?" Asher asked, pulling Shawn closer.

Kravetz tumbled onto the table over the top of Shawn, landing on Asher's arm. "Yes, he remembers! That's what the camera is for," Kravetz said.

"All right, break it up!" a black bouncer from Chicago said, pulling bodies away. "Everybody back to your tables before I bust some heads!" He turned to Asher. "Let's go," and he led Asher out of the bar.

"You saved me," Shawn said, running his fingers through his hair. "Fuck. I hope there was enough light."

"We're even, okay," Kravetz said.

Later, they were dancing at The Shelter, which was decorated like a 1950s fallout shelter. It was a new year, and Kravetz was drunk, as bodies spun all around him. He saw Shawn jumping around to the Ramones' "I Wanna Be Sedated" and felt his own blood pumping through him. Shawn appeared a few moments later, sweating, with a girl on his arm. "Stuart!" he shouted, "this is Amy!"

"Hi!" she said, extending her hand. She wore her blonde hair in a long ponytail, red lipstick, and a short skirt. The strobe light made her face look sunken and sickly. "Wanna dance?" She pulled Kravetz into the swaying mass of bodies, where soldiers' M-16s slapped against their arching backs as they danced. Two girls wearing gas masks and bikinis bounced past them.

Shawn called out, "You owe me, buddy!"

She put her arms around him and he smelled her beery breath. He thought of Amichai's lines again: "People use each other / as healing for their pain. They put each other / on their existential wounds, / on the eye, on the cunt, on mouth and open hand. / They hold each other hard and won't let go." And he thought of taking her up his dark, noisy elevator, sliding his hand in her pants as he fumbled for the keys to his apartment. But it wasn't Jana, and she wouldn't say, "Thanks for fingering me," and she wouldn't say, "I really love you," after he fucked her. He turned to look in Amy's face but she was looking away toward a group of her friends dancing on the bar.

A few minutes later, Kravetz pulled Shawn outside into the cool damp air. His heart thumped so hard he thought he might throw up. Shawn lit a cigarette and mopped his face with the corner of his shirt. "What's going on?"

"I think I'm going to call Jana."

"What do you mean? Aren't you having fun?"

"Yeah, I guess," Kravetz said. "It's just, having my arms around that girl made me think of her. You know what I mean?"

"Bullshit," Shawn said as an army jeep drove past, its blue light flashing. He pulled his Polaroid out of his jacket pocket. He aimed the camera at Kravetz and snapped a shot.

"I'm going to call her," Kravetz said, ignoring the picture. He walked away from The Shelter.

"Do you want her to think you're weak?" Shawn called after him.

"I just want her to think of me."

"Come back here and look at this picture," Shawn called. "I don't want you to ever forget what the face of defeat looks like."

"I'm calling her," Kravetz said weakly, though he realized now that Shawn was right — he couldn't call her.

Dead Souls

It was a day before the Palestinian elections, and a cold January rain was falling from the gray sky. Jews both supporting and opposed to the Oslo peace plan took to the streets in full force. With Palestinians voting in their contested half of Jerusalem something was bound to happen, and Shawn planned to catch it on film. Shawn made Kravetz a breakfast of hard-boiled eggs, yogurt, and cucumbers. He wore no shirt when he served it to Kravetz. He had a Star of David that he had gotten five summers earlier at the port of Haifa tattooed on his right shoulder, a Misfits skull on his left. The tattoos looked strange to Kravetz now, though he had said they were cool when he first saw them, and had once wanted a local band's name tattooed on *his* arm.

"Do you have to smell everything before you eat it?" Shawn said.

Shawn smoked a cigarette as Kravetz ate.

"Do you mind if I come with you today?" Kravetz said, ignoring the question.

"Oh, now you want to be my assistant. You look like a groupie wearing that 'Peace Now' T-shirt."

"It's just I don't have classes today," Kravetz said.

The phone rang in the hallway, and Kravetz dropped his spoon into his yogurt. "You get it," he said to Shawn.

Shawn reappeared a few minutes later.

"Who was it?" Kravetz asked.

"Nobody."

"What do you mean, nobody? It had to be somebody."

"Shut up and eat," Shawn said.

"No, I want to know who it was. I pay the phone bill. Who was it?"

"Fine," Shawn said, lighting a cigarette and taking a slow drag. "It was Jana."

"What?" Kravetz shouted. "Why didn't you give me the phone?"

"She called for me," Shawn said.

"Bullshit," Kravetz croaked.

"It's true."

"She hates you," Kravetz said, his voice breaking. "She thinks you're arrogant and manipulative. She hates you." Kravetz covered his mouth with his hand, and then buried his head in the other hand. "You think you're fucking Sid Vicious."

"Ouch," Shawn said. "Are you coming, man?"

Kravetz didn't say anything.

"Fine. I'll see you later."

After Shawn left, Kravetz dialed Jana's number and it rang and rang, but nobody answered. It was the middle of the night in New York. He lay on his bed and stared at the ceiling, as the morning sun shined into his eyes, and he convinced himself that Jana must have called Shawn to speak about her and Stuart. They'd been together almost four years. You don't just love somebody and then never speak to them again.

Shawn stayed out all day taking pictures. Kravetz wandered into Shawn's dark room. He kept the iron shutters closed so the room smelled like an ashtray. Both carpets were rolled up in the corner, exposing the cracked, tiled floor. Half-finished incense sticks and *yahrtzeit* candles in small tin cups with the prime minister's face pasted on the front were strewn about the room. Shit, he even fucks to the light of memorial candles, Kravetz thought. He saw photos taped to the walls, and piled on his desk; a naked girl on a camel, another with some sheep, one with huge breasts and her arms outstretched as if she were waiting to be crucified. It's all crap, Kravetz thought.

Kravetz phoned Jana every night for three weeks, but nobody ever answered. When he heard her low voice on the machine he was reminded of conversations they had had. The first time she had said, "You have a beautiful prick," or the time she had innocently asked, "Do love and loathe mean the same thing?" He remembered the time she had cried to him about how she missed her grandfather in Riga, and how her voice had cracked, and how he had heard her accent seep in.

Some nights he heard girlish laughter from the next room and Shawn imitating their accents in his high nasal voice. One night Shawn knocked on Stuart's door and announced, as he swayed under the weight of alcohol, "You can now call me Doctor Professor Moses Kink. Here are my ten commandments of kink. . . ."

He had slathered gel in his hair so it stood up in devil-locks at the front like two horns.

"Shut the fucking door," Kravetz said. "What is it? A German or a Swede this time?"

"All by my lonesome tonight," Shawn said.

"Tell me," Kravetz said, sitting up in bed. "How many?"

"What?" Shawn said, smiling. "How many what?"

"Good night," Kravetz said, turning away from Shawn.

"All right, my son," Shawn said. He was never able to resist talking about himself. "The Doctor Professor Kink has had say, seventy-five, give or take. . . ."

"Give or take what?"

"Do you want to see the Polaroids?" Shawn said, twisting the horns on his head. He disappeared into his room for a moment. "I've got them all." He returned with a small shoe box cradled in his arms. He began flinging the photos at Kravetz. "Here. This one cried because she was too tight. This one bit. This one, this was the fat one." He kept firing the Polaroids at Kravetz. "This one was married, this one . . ."

"Shit," Kravetz said. He had only slept with one woman before Jana and one while he was with her.

Shawn's back stiffened and he became serious. "What? Since I was thirteen, that's less than ten a year. About point seven one two six five four women per month. Do the math. It's not that much. Seriously."

"That's crazy," Kravetz said.

"They meant nothing. They're dead. They're photos in a box."

"When are you going to leave?" Kravetz asked, surprising himself.

"What? 'Cause you're not getting fucked? That's weak. Take them all, then," Shawn said, throwing the entire box at Kravetz. He slammed his door and then opened it again. "When I've got enough for a show. That's when I'll leave."

Kravetz was shaking and couldn't sleep, so he went for a walk. He didn't even bother to pick up the Polaroids before he tiptoed out the door. He wore only a light T-shirt and shivered as he moved down the street in his checked slippers. A taxi passed and someone shouted out the window at him. He passed a lotto booth and for a moment wanted to smash the annoying face on the lotto ad. He knew that walking kept him from crying, so he walked as far as Rehavia Park and the Monastery of the Cross. Kravetz reached a clearing and lay on the damp ground beneath the stars. It seemed that the sky was lower than he'd ever seen it before, tilting dangerously close to the tops of trees and buildings, or maybe Jerusalem itself was rising into the heavens. Looking up into the blinking sky, he thought of Jana and how she had said that each star represents someone's soul and how she had once reached out toward the sky, grabbed at the darkness, and swallowed his soul in one gulp. And now he thought of Gogol and his trip to Jerusalem, and how after Gogol's return to Russia he had destroyed the second part of his masterpiece, *Dead Souls*, and then killed himself. Lying there in the grass, with the stars seemingly just out of reach, Kravetz never wanted to go home again.

King of the Pigs

It was a little after ten o'clock the next night when Kravetz entered Elijah's Cup. He and Shawn had made a silent peace, with the understanding that after Shawn had enough photos and a title shot that would burn into people's memories, he would return to New York. It was a Monday and Kravetz had studied all morning at the library on Mount Scopus then had gone straight to work at the cafe. He was damp with sweat and his shirt clung to his skin though it was only February. Shawn sat at a table in the corner with Shmuelik and a slim bearded man who wore a knitted *kippah* on his head. Elijah's Cup was silent, profoundly silent; Kravetz could hear the bearded man's New York accent and his laughter before the twanging thump and hand claps of Hebrew *mizrachi* music filled the room. The New Yorker was speaking loudly.

". . . you have them voting in East Jerusalem, next thing you know —"

The bearded man was cut off by Shmuelik. "Amalek as your next-door neighbor."

"Stuart, you know Shmuelik," Shawn said, offering Kravetz a seat at the table. "This is Mr. Berger."

Mr. Berger shook Kravetz's hand and popped an olive in his mouth. His beard was close cropped and he wore an expensive gold watch on his wrist. "I've still got to drive to Efrat tonight. I'd better be going." He stood up and Kravetz could see a pistol in his belt.

"Nice to meet you," Kravetz said.

Shmuelik, too, stood up and walked Mr. Berger to the door.

"So, what do you think?" Shawn said, sipping his beer.

"What do I think of what?" Kravetz said.

"Do you know where I can get a pig?" Shawn asked.

"What are you talking about?" Kravetz could see Shmuelik and the bearded man embracing as they parted ways.

"A pig," Shawn said. "You can't get a fucking pig in Israel. Isn't it illegal or something to breed them?"

"It's illegal to breed them *on* the land," Kravetz said. "But I know some kibbutzim in the north who have them on platforms, you know, *above* the land."

"Fuckin' A. Russians I bet."

"What do you need a pig for?"

"Business," Shawn said, hoisting his drink.

"Hey, Shawn? I was thinking . . ."

"Don't talk about her. Tonight we're celebrating."

The next morning Shawn was gone by the time Kravetz woke up. He didn't return for a few days, and when he finally burst through the apartment door whooping, "My masterpiece!" Kravetz was not surprised. He knew Shawn was up to something.

"That was the easiest ten grand I ever made. Come on, you want to help me put them up?"

Kravetz didn't raise his eyes from his book.

"Put that book down," Shawn said. "Look!"

He held a glossy full-color poster in his hand with a pig wearing an Arab headdress, propped up on his hind legs. There was Arabic writing across the top of the poster, and the words "Muhammad, King of the Pigs" written in English along the bottom.

"Holy shit!" Kravetz said. "What the hell is that?"

"Ten thousand dollars," Shawn said, smiling. "Two days work. And bacon, too."

From the look in the pig's eyes, Kravetz wondered if Shawn had drugged it.

"Mr. Berger?" Kravetz asked.

"Yeah," Shawn said. "The Security Council of Judea and Samaria. They've got deep pockets. If you help me poster, there will be something for you, too."

"Poster?"

"Yeah, man. I've got five hundred to put up around the city by tomorrow morning."

"Give me that," Kravetz said, lunging at the poster.

"Why, you want to help?" Shawn said, extending the poster. Kravetz reached for it. "Psych!" Shawn said, and ran down the hall. "Are you going to help or aren't you?"

Suddenly, Kravetz felt old, like he was Shawn's father. Maybe he was making too big a deal about things. He had become so serious since Jana had left him, and spent too much time with his nose buried in books. He carried Amichai's poetry with him everywhere he went, as if it were a bible of heartbreak. "Good luck," Kravetz said, flopping back onto his bed.

"Shukran, habib," Shawn called in Arabic. "Thanks, pal."

Neither Shawn nor Kravetz heard the bomb when it went off three days later; bus number eighteen, a route that went through the heart of the city, blown up during the morning rush hour by a suicide bomber. The lucky number eighteen, or *chai* for life. Twenty-four people dead. Kravetz thought it was ironic that of all the numbers, of all the bus routes to choose, the bomber chose the one symbolizing life.

When Kravetz woke Shawn and told him the news, Shawn could only fumble for his camera and say, "Shit. Missed it."

Kravetz remembered a line from Amichai's poetry about the three languages of the holy city: Hebrew, Arabic, Death.

The Bombshell

In the days following the bombing, Shawn followed Kravetz to the rally at Zion Square, not to pay condolences to the dead and maimed, but to catch someone with their pants down.

When a man led a sheep on a leash into the square, chanting, "Like sheep to the slaughter. We're not sheep!" Shawn ran to him, but was stopped by a border policeman who said, "No photos. Only press."

Though people were told not to gather in large groups, the crowds chanted and called for peace. Heavily armed soldiers snaked through the crowds; two soldiers stood at each bus stop, checking bags for bombs.

"It's just like Europe before the war," Shawn said. "Can't you see the writing on the wall. This is *Kristallnacht* all over again."

"So leave, if you're so afraid," Kravetz said. "Go home."

"Why don't you?" Shawn said, blowing smoke in Kravetz's face. "Huh?"

"This is home," Kravetz said.

"Fuckin' idealist."

"Yeah, so?" Kravetz said, clenching his fists. He felt like he was in fourth grade all over again. "Go home, if you're afraid."

"I never said I was afraid, asshole. It's just, violence breeds hysteria," Shawn said. "And hysteria makes good photos. I'm going for a drink."

Kravetz went home and lay on his bed, throwing a tennis ball against the ceiling. He could hear a man coughing from the floor below, deep retching coughs that went on for minutes before he was silent. Kravetz wondered if the man had died. He picked up the shoe box from under his bed and began flipping through Shawn's Polaroids. The photos looked so cheap, bad lighting and red eyes, most of the women mugged for the camera and looked drunk out of their skulls. He thinks he's fucking Gene Simmons, Kravetz thought. The group seemed to be made of equal parts blonde and brunette with a redhead or two thrown in. Kravetz recognized some of the girls but could not recall their names. One of the pictures was stuck to the back of another and he pulled it off.

It was Jana.

Kravetz went numb. He hadn't seen her since May and her face, puckered and drunk, looked cheap and foreign. Could it really be her? She hated Shawn, thought he was a phony and an asshole. And suddenly, without any warning, he just burst out, one loud wrenching cry, his eyes burned, his throat swollen, his saliva as thick as cotton.

He didn't even hear Shawn come in. He was breathing heavily, as if he had taken the stairs.

Shawn walked forward and took a deep breath that made him look like a bulldog. "You're not going to cry again over the Slovakian slut. She's a Jew killer," Shawn said.

Kravetz could tell that Shawn was drunk. "You found her," Shawn said.

Through blurry eyes Kravetz could not tell if Shawn was smirking or biting his lips from nerves.

"Why?" Kravetz said.

"These Slavic bitches," Shawn said. "All of them, Russians, Latvians, Czechs, every last fucking one of them — Jew killers."

"What are you talking about?" Kravetz said.

"You know what I'm talking about. You know how they killed our grandparents and our great-grandparents, and their parents. Made us live in ghettos." Shawn slurred most of these words out. "Any Jew who consorts with these types must hate himself, must have a death wish."

"But I loved her, and she loved me," Kravetz said.

"Bullshit. Take a look at yourself, Poochie. What kind of Jew would fuck a pogromist pig?"

"She was going to live with me. I don't know."

"You scared the shit out of her. You're too fucking serious and intense," Shawn said. "You pressured her. Practically forced her under the weight of guilt."

Kravetz didn't say a word. He had never been so wounded in his life before.

And now Shawn's voice became as hard as it had ever been. "I did it for you, man. I don't give a shit about her. Yeah, she called a few times trying to find you, but I never told her shit. I told her to fuck off, but she kept calling. Don't you understand we're on the same side here. I only did it to get back at her for you."

"Get out!" Kravetz shouted. "Get out of here! I want you out of here now!"

"Don't you get it?"

Kravetz threw the tennis ball at Shawn, then threw the half-empty box of Polaroids at him.

"Don't freak out. I did it for you, man. The cunt hurt

you, so I got her back. Come on." Shawn stuck out his fist and said, "Kids are united . . ."

"Get the fuck out of here," Kravetz said, batting his hand away. "Asshole! Fucking grow up."

"Bro, listen . . ." Shawn began to say.

"Go to sleep," Kravetz said. "I don't want to see your face in the morning."

Lucky 18

The next morning Kravetz was woken by a ground-shaking boom that rattled even the walls of his apartment. He lay in bed, unable to move, with the horrible silence filling his ears, thinking, "There're no sirens, so it can't be," and when he heard the sirens he thought, "That's not enough sirens for a bombing." And he prayed, or muttered what he thought was a prayer. He could hear Shawn in the next room, shouting, "Get dressed, let's go!" as the sirens wailed outside. Shawn burst into Stuart's room, buttoning his pants. His shirt was open and his camera hung around his neck. He threw open Stuart's steel shutters, and they could hear sirens racing down Azza Street, and others from the Hadassah Hospital on Mount Scopus moving toward the rising smoke on Jaffa Street, just at the other side of Independence Park.

"Get up, bitch," Shawn said. "We're going to miss the whole thing."

"It's bus eighteen again," Kravetz said. He felt hollowed out inside, and could barely breathe. He thought of Jana, and Shawn thrusting against her, and Jana with her eyes wide open, saying, "Uh-huh. Uh-huh, uh-huh, uh-huh, uh-huh," as he pushed into her. Kravetz imagined Shawn's tongue all over Jana like some absurd pink fish flopping about her body. Then he thought of the bombing, and imagined bodies scattered about the streets like torn-up rag dolls. He didn't want to move. He just wanted to close his eyes and open them again to the misty rain falling out of the gray sky.

Shawn pulled Kravetz out of bed onto the floor. "Let's go," he said, his voice rising nasally. Kravetz wanted to run at Shawn, throw him to the floor, and strangle him, squeeze every breath of life out of him. But then he thought of the twisted metal of bus eighteen, and cried out, "It's your fault! It's your fault, you fucker!"

Shawn was rushing around the room, grabbing Stuart's clothes. "We've still got a five-minute walk, let's go!"

"They were throwing stones in East Jerusalem, calling for a holy war," Kravetz shouted as he pulled on a pair of pants. "A fucking jihad because of your picture."

"Have you ever seen a dead person before?" Shawn asked calmly, lighting a cigarette.

"Well," Kravetz said. He had thought that Jana was as good as dead to him, but he knew she still walked and talked and kissed and fucked. Out the window he could see smoke rising into the sky to meet the gray clouds. And he wondered what lay beyond the clouds.

"Boo!" Shawn said, waving his arms in Stuart's face. "Let's go."

A moment later Kravetz was dressed and he was smoking one of Shawn's cigarettes. He felt delirious, almost drunk with some sort of sickened excitement. No, he never had seen a dead person before and he wondered at what moment the soul left the body, and whether if you watched carefully enough you could see it escaping its earthly bonds.

They ran through the park and the sirens kept coming from all around. Shawn tripped over a stone at the entrance to an old Muslim tomb where men traded blow jobs after dark. He lay in the grass. "I'm dying, Stuey! I'm dying!"

"Come on," Kravetz said.

"Go on without me."

"Your lens cap is off, dick," Kravetz said, running ahead.

"Wait for me, you freak."

The rain was falling harder when they arrived at Jaffa Street. Hundreds of people crowded around the steaming carcass of the bus, which was flattened and twisted like some giant insect. A police line pushed the crowds back. Religious men dressed in black shook their fists, chanting that peace with the Arabs is suicide. Men dressed in white jumpsuits were picking through the debris for body parts. Kravetz had read about these men in the newspaper the past week, how it was their job to gather every hair, tooth, and drop of blood for a proper Jewish burial. Atop the Generali Building *Hesed shel Emet* volunteers scraped body parts from the face of a winged stone lion. Shawn stood on a garbage can and pulled Kravetz up with him. Kravetz held Shawn around the waist and could feel his warm behind against him. All the windows were shattered along Jaffa Street. A woman hung her head out the window and wailed.

"There's one," Shawn said. "Look."

Kravetz could see a black charred body lying on the road behind the bus and then another, a woman tangled inside the bus, beneath a seat back. He could see her colorful wool dress hiked up high on her bleeding thigh, and he swore he saw her move, just for a second. He saw a green apple on the ground nearby that seemed to be miraculously untouched.

"I'm going down there," Shawn said, jumping from the garbage can.

"What? How?" Kravetz said.

Shawn smiled and flashed him his fake foreign press id card and said, "Don't leave home without it." And he ran off through the crowd.

Kravetz was too stunned to move and just stood where he was until a man climbed up on the can next to him and whispered in his ear, "Oslo is dead."

Stuart's throat clenched, as if he would cry, but he could only cough. Shawn had weaseled his way through the barrier and had moved in close to the bus, snapping shots next to CNN, UPI, the AP. This was it, Lucky Eighteen, the shot they'd both been waiting for. And Shawn was down in front at the second bus eighteen bombing, kneeling next to the lady with the wool dress. Kravetz could see him pull away the seat back and before Shawn turned to flash the thumbs-up sign, Kravetz could see there was no upper part of her body. He leaned over and threw up, a thin viscous fluid that tasted like tobacco, like Jana's kisses, like five thousand years, like the dying peace process. When he looked up again, Shawn had it in the can, his centerpiece shot, the woman with her skirt hiked up, his prize winner, a lament, or celebration of . . . something they didn't fully understand.

Glossary

Allah: Muslim name for God.

Am Yisrael Chai: Hebrew for "The people of Israel live."

Amalek: A nomadic tribe of the Hebrew Bible, hostile to Israel. Amalek has come to be known as the archetypal enemy of the Jews throughout history, including the Nazis and the Palestinians in the twentieth century.

Babi Yar: A ravine in the Ukrainian capital Kiev in which nearly 34,000 Jews were massacred on September 29–30, 1941.

Baksheesh: Charity to beggars in the Middle East; also used in reference to political corruption and bribery.

Baruch Hashem: Hebrew for "Praised be God."

Beshert: Yiddish word meaning "destiny," often used among Orthodox Jews to describe a preordained soul mate.

Chmelnicki: Bogdan Chmelnicki, a Cossack leader (1595–1657) led a Cossack rebellion in what is now Ukraine. It has been estimated that anywhere between 100,000 and 500,000 Jews were massacred in hundreds of communities in Poland.

Elohim: Hebrew for "God."

Fellahin: Plural for farmer or agricultural worker in Arabic.

Fuul: Egyptian dish of mashed fava beans, olive oil, parsley, onion, garlic, and lemon juice.

Hamsa: A hand-shaped amulet popular in North Africa and the Middle East. It is believed to ward off the evil eye.

Hamsiin: A hot desert wind blowing from Egypt up through Israel from about March to May.

Haram: Arabic for sanctuary or holy site in Islam.

Hijab: The head covering traditionally worn by Muslim women.

Huppa: A canopy under which a Jewish couple stands during a wedding ceremony symbolizing the privacy of the home. It is considered a basic requirement for a Jewish wedding.

Inshallah: Arabic for "God willing."

Kaffiyeh: A traditional cloth headdress worn by Arab men.

Kanafi: A Middle Eastern desert made with white cheese and honey.

Kashrut: The set of Jewish dietary laws.

Kippah: A skullcap, also known as a yarmulke, worn by religiously observant Jewish men to fulfill the requirement to cover their heads.

The Kotel: The Western Wall; the remaining Western Wall of the Temple built by King Herod on the site of Solomon's Temple.

Kristallnacht: Night of Broken Glass. A pogrom against Jews in Germany and Austria on November 9–10, 1938, in which stores owned by Jews and synagogues were vandalized and the windows were broken.

Ma'ariv service: Jewish evening prayer service.

Mazel: Hebrew for "luck." Literally means "star."

Mea Shearim: One hundred gates; one of the oldest neighborhoods in the new city of Jerusalem, populated by ultra-Orthodox Jews.

Mezuzah: A piece of parchment contained within a decorative case affixed to the doorposts of Jewish homes. Two verses from the book of Deuteronomy are inscribed upon the parchment.

Mikvah: A bath used for ritual immersion in Judaism.

Minyan: Traditionally a group of ten Jewish males required to conduct a communal service. In Reform and most Conservative communities, women are now counted.

Mitzvah: Commandment. Any of the 613 commandments Jews are obligated to observe.

Mizrachi: Refers to Jews from the Middle East and North Africa.

Moloch: The name of an ancient Semitic deity associated with sacrifice of children by their parents.

Moshiach: A term that means "anointed" and that was traditionally applied to many different kinds of leaders in ancient Israel including prophets, priests, and kings. More commonly it came to mean a political leader descended from the House of David who would bring peace. The word "Messiah" is the English (King James) attempt at transliteration.

Motek: Hebrew for "sweetheart" or "sweetie."

Muezzin: In Islam, the person chosen to lead the call to prayer from one of the mosque's minarets.

Mukhtar: Title given to the head of a village or neighborhood in the Arab world.

Nigun: A wordless religious Jewish melody, often improvised, with repetitive sounds instead of lyrics.

Nudnik: Yiddish for "a pest" or "a nuisance."

Palmach: Strike force. The elite fighting force for the Haganah in pre-state Israel before the establishment of the Israeli Defense Forces.

Pogrom: An organized massacre of Jews in Eastern Europe.

Portzim: Stormers; a unit of the Palmach.

Rashi: An acronym for the medieval French Rabbi, Rabbi Shlomo Itzhaki.

Rebbe: Leader of a Hasidic group.

Sefer Torah: The Torah, or the Five Books of Moses; the holiest book in Judaism.

Sephardi: Originally referred to a Jew expelled from the Iberian Peninsula in the fifteenth century. Now, it refers to Jews from Spanish-speaking countries. Seen historically in Israel as a second-class citizen by the more educated, European Ashkenazi Jews.

Shaddai: The Almighty. An ancient name of God commonly used in Hebrew scripture.

Sheheheyanu: A common Jewish prayer from the Talmud said on joyous occasions.

The Shema: An affirmation of Judaism and of faith in one God and a central prayer in Jewish prayer services, taken from the book of Deuteronomy. Many observant Jews consider this to be the most important prayer in Judaism.

Shesh besh: Backgammon.

Shiduch: A system of matchmaking in which Jewish Orthodox singles are introduced to each other for the purpose of marriage.

Shmatte: Yiddish for a rag or shabby garment.

Shuk: Outdoor fruit and vegetable marketplace; refers to Shuk Mahane Yehuda in Jerusalem.

Shukran: Arabic for "thank you."

Simcha: Hebrew for "joy" or "gladness." Also means "a festive occasion."

Streimel: A fur hat worn by married ultra-Orthodox Jewish men on Jewish holidays and other festive occasions.

Tchotchkes: Yiddish for "useless knickknacks."

Tefillin: A set of leather straps and small leather boxes containing verses from the Torah worn by observant Jews once a day during morning prayers, except on certain holidays and the Sabbath.

Tehillim: The Hebrew name for the book of Psalms.

Tishri: A month on the Jewish calendar that falls during September and October. Many holidays occur during this month including the High Holidays of Rosh Hashanah and Yom Kippur.

Treif: Non-kosher food.

Tschuva: Hebrew for "repentance, return."

Tzitzis: Fringes or tassels found on a prayer shawl worn by observant Jews.

Wadi: A valley or dry riverbed that fills during the rainy season.

Yala: Arabic for "Let's go," or "hurry up." Commonly used in Hebrew conversation.

Yam Ha Melach: Hebrew for the Dead Sea. Literally "Salt Sea."

Yeled: Hebrew for "child."

Yeshiva bocher: A young man studying at a Jewish religious seminary.

The Ascent of Eli Israel
Jonathan Papernick

READING GROUP GUIDE
DISCUSSION QUESTIONS

1. Why do you think Papernick decided to start the collection with a story set in 1948 when the remaining six stories were set during the 1990s? Does "Malchyk" effectively set up themes presented throughout the rest of the book?

2. Is "An Unwelcome Guest" pro-Jewish or pro-Palestinian, anti-Israeli or anti-Arab, or even-handed in its approach? Please cite examples from the story to support your belief.

3. *The New York Times Book Review* wrote that "An Unwelcome Guest" is "an encapsulation of the dread that haunts nearly every Jew—whether hawk or dove—in Israel and the diaspora." Do you agree or disagree with this statement? Why?

4. Do you think readers' perspectives on the collection of stories differ depending on their religion and whether the reader identifies personally with the Jewish religion and culture?

5. The best short stories have endings that are both surprising and inevitable. Many of these stories, such as "An Unwelcome Guest," "The Art of Correcting," and "The King of the King of Falafel," have surprise endings. Did these endings feel inevitable? Were you able to foresee the ending? If so, did this diminish or enhance your reading of the story?

6. The Jerusalem Syndrome is a psychological disorder in which victims suffer delusions and psychotic episodes triggered by a visit to the city of Jerusalem. Is the story "The Ascent of Eli Israel" primarily about a man of faith who has been called by God, or about a sick man suffering from mental illness? At what point in the story do these two themes intersect most sharply?

7. Eli Haller is a murderous monster who draws readers into his world and allows them to walk in his shoes for a while. Did you find him sympathetic throughout the story despite his horrifying actions? Why or why not?

8. If the story "The Ascent of Eli Israel," continued for another five or ten pages, what do you think might happen next?

9. What does the story "For as Long as the Lamp Is Burning" say about the nature of memory and its burden? Is there ever a time when it might be best to forget?

10. Is *The Ascent of Eli Israel* a violent book? At a time when graphic and gratuitous descriptions of violence are standard in much popular fiction for purposes of mere shock and titillation, does Papernick succeed in portraying violence in a considered, human manner? Does he accomplish this? If so, how?

11. The dreamlike city of Jerusalem is very much a character in these stories. In which of these stories does the city's magical qualities most affect the characters and their actions? Please cite specific examples from the stories.

Q&A with Jonathan Papernick

What are the biggest challenges of keeping a short story short?

A: Trying to tell a complete story that reflects all of the world, not just a fragment of it. I try to manage this by rigorously forcing myself to compress and expand my story simultaneously.

If you could take a writing class with any short fiction writer, dead or alive, who would it be and why? And further, what would you hope the first lecture would be called?

A: I know this is kind of childish, but I would love to take a writing class with Philip Roth, not just because of what I hope he could teach me but also so he knows that I actually exist. Maybe his first lecture would be called "Becoming Zuckerman: A How-to Guide."

Is there a short story you would consider to be perfectly crafted?

A: I think the short story "Bullet in the Brain" by Tobias Wolff is pretty damn near perfect, though there are a few lines that I would cut, given the chance. Even after one hundred readings I still get a physical reaction reading the final line of the story. "Going to Meet the Man" by James Baldwin, I think, is absolutely perfect. I'm still amazed that he is able to conjure such sympathy in such a horrifying, monstrous character as the racist sheriff.

William Faulkner prioritized writing forms thusly: "Maybe every novelist wants to write poetry first, finds he can't, and then tries the short story, which is the most demand-

ing form after poetry. And failing at that, only then does he take up novel writing." Do you agree or disagree, and why?

A: I hope I don't come off as arrogant paraphrasing Flannery O'Connor, who, when asked why she writes short stories, quipped "because I'm good at it." I actually find novel writing to be significantly harder than short story writing since rather than juggling one or two balls at a time you need to juggle seven or eight or more. With short story writing it is possible to contain the entire story in your mind, whereas writing a novel is a sloppy, frustrating act, full of despair and fear. My first novel took me four years to write, and I still can't believe that I was able to stick with it to completion. Writing that novel was definitely the hardest thing I ever did. Short stories, on the other hand, though never easy, at least fit into my realm of understanding and basic competence.

I read a very moving, thoughtful, and funny piece in *The Good Man Project* about your quest to become a perfect Jew after the birth of your son. So, I have to ask, did you become more perfect?

Perhaps I've succeeded, but perhaps not. My oldest son is four years old now, and I struggle every day to be a good father both to him and to his younger brother, but, with exhaustion and stress and pressure to write a good book on top of everything, I really don't know if I'm doing as good a job as I possibly can. As far as being a better Jew, the only truly tangible test that I have had to face recently is related to the death of my mother. I'm an only child, and I did what an only child with a single mother has to do, and I took care of business and gave her a proper and honorable Jewish burial, and for that I feel that I'm finally and irrevocably a man. But I don't know if I am mourning in the proper manner. Our relationship was complicated, as all parent/child relationships are, but I am not saying Kaddish every day. In fact, I've only said Kaddish for her once but think about it every day, and I hope that the community at large does not judge me for that. On the other hand, I think I honor her life by being a good father and helping her grandchildren become better people.

Can you talk about the difference for you in writing short stories versus writing the novel? Which is more satisfying to you? What's your writing process like?

I love writing short stories, and I find it immensely satisfying, like solving a complex puzzle. When I write a short story I usually have a question that I need to answer. My characters show me the way. I usually end up in a surprising and deeply satisfying place. Often times, my short stories actually come from the title alone. What I like about short stories is that I can contain all of my ideas in my head at once whereas writing a novel I need to plan and research and persist. If writing short stories is like a sprint, writing a novel is like running one hundred marathons. I find writing a novel to be immensely difficult, and though my first novel turned out much better than I ever could've imagined, I feel like the blood and sweat that I put into it never really paid off the way that I hoped it would. But I would hate to pigeonhole myself as just a short story writer or a novelist. I love to write and that feeling of hitting your stride and immersing yourself deeply in a work is the best feeling in the world.

There's a great quote from you: "You've got to play being a writer before you are a writer. You've got to convince yourself that you are one before you have the chutzpah to do it." So, what convinced you?

In some strange way, I think I always thought I was a writer going all the way back to second grade. I did identify myself as a writer all the way back then, even though I had very little talent, even for my age. I was never a prodigy in my class, or even singled out as a good writer by any of my teachers all the way up through high school. My eleventh grade creative writing teacher actually told me that I was "not a very strong writer." So, I guess some sort of inner confidence kept pushing me onward. I certainly don't believe in destiny, because there's just too much hard work involved. I really don't know what else I could do in this world. I certainly don't have the talent to play shortstop for the Toronto Blue Jays. I wrote a couple of bad novels before I was ever published, and I was young and arrogant enough to believe I was really writing something quite important. In some ways that youthful naïveté allowed me to get a couple apprentice manuscripts under my belt before I realized that I had no idea what the hell I was doing. By that time I knew I could never write anything as bad as I had already written, so I had clearly established a floor for myself with those works.

There are few things more terrifying than staring down at a blank page or a blank screen. Writing is a supreme act of creation, and one really has to convince oneself that one is capable of creating an entire world in order to do it. You really need to psych yourself up and make yourself believe that you can accomplish anything. I think in many ways I need to convince myself that I'm up to the task every time I sit down to write. I guess looking at my books on my shelves and getting positive feedback from my readers helped convince me for a short time that I am indeed a writer. But I need a booster shot of confidence quite often, so I'm certainly open to any compliments anyone might have about my writing.

IN PRAISE OF SLOWNESS

CARL HONORÉ

IN PRAISE OF
SLOWNESS

Challenging the Cult of Speed

HarperOne
An Imprint of HarperCollins*Publishers*

HarperOne

IN PRAISE OF SLOWNESS: *Challenging the Cult of Speed.* Copyright © 2004 Carl Honoré. All rights reserved. Printed in the United States of America. No part of this book may be used or reproduced in any manner whatsoever without written permission except in the case of brief quotations embodied in critical articles and reviews. For information address HarperCollins Publishers,
10 East 53rd Street, New York, NY 10022.

HarperCollins books may be purchased for educational, business, or sales promotional use. For information please write: Special Markets Department, HarperCollins Publishers, 10 East 53rd Street, New York, NY 10022.

HarperCollins Web site: http//www.harpercollins.com

HarperCollins®, 🏭®, and HarperOne™ are trademarks of HarperCollins Publishers.

First HarperCollins paperback edition published in 2005

Library of Congress Cataloging-in-Publication Data is available.

ISBN: 978–0–06–075051–0

09 10 11 RRD(H) 10

To Miranda, Benjamin and Susannah

CONTENTS

There is more to life than increasing its speed.

GANDHI

THE AGE OF RAGE

*People are born and married, and live and die, in the
midst of an uproar so frantic that you would think
they would go mad of it.*
—WILLIAM DEAN HOWELLS, 1907

ON A SUN-BLEACHED AFTERNOON in the summer of
1985, my teenage tour of Europe grinds to a halt in a square
on the outskirts of Rome. The bus back into town is twenty
minutes late and shows no sign of appearing. Yet the delay
does not bother me. Instead of pacing up and down the sidewalk, or calling the bus company to lodge a complaint, I slip
on my Walkman, lie down on a bench and listen to Simon
and Garfunkel sing about the joys of slowing down and making the moment last. Every detail of the scene is engraved on
my memory: two small boys kick a soccer ball around a
medieval fountain; branches scrape against the top of a stone
wall; an old widow carries her vegetables home in a net bag.

Fast-forward fifteen years, and everything has
changed. The scene shifts to Rome's busy Fiumicino

Airport, and I am a foreign correspondent rushing to catch a flight home to London. Instead of kickin' down the cobblestones and feelin' groovy, I dash through the departure lounge, silently cursing anyone who crosses my path at a slower pace. Rather than listen to folk music on a cheap Walkman, I talk on a mobile phone to an editor thousands of miles away.

At the gate, I join the back end of a long lineup, where there is nothing to do except, well, nothing. Only I am no longer capable of doing nothing. To make the wait more productive, to make it seem less like waiting, I start skimming a newspaper. And that is when my eyes come upon the article that will inspire me eventually to write a book about slowing down.

The words that stop me in my tracks are: "The One-Minute Bedtime Story." To help parents deal with time-consuming tots, various authors have condensed classic fairy tales into sixty-second sound bites. Think Hans Christian Andersen meets the executive summary. My first reflex is to shout Eureka! At the time, I am locked in a nightly tug-of-war with my two-year-old son, who favours long stories read at a gentle, meandering pace. Every evening, though, I steer him towards the shortest books and read them quickly. We often quarrel. "You're going too fast," he cries. Or, as I make for the door, "I want another story!" Part of me feels horribly selfish when I accelerate the bedtime ritual, but another part simply cannot resist the itch to hurry on to the next thing on my agenda—supper, emails, reading, bills, more work, the news bulletin on television. Taking a long, languid stroll through the world of Dr. Seuss is not an option. It is too slow.

So, at first glance, the One-Minute Bedtime series sounds almost too good to be true. Rattle off six or seven "stories," and still finish inside ten minutes—what could be better? Then, as I begin to wonder how quickly Amazon can ship me the full set, redemption comes in the shape of a counter-question: Have I gone completely insane? As the departure lineup snakes towards the final ticket check, I put away the newspaper and begin to think. My whole life has turned into an exercise in hurry, in packing more and more into every hour. I am Scrooge with a stopwatch, obsessed with saving every last scrap of time, a minute here, a few seconds there. And I am not alone. Everyone around me— colleagues, friends, family—is caught in the same vortex.

In 1982 Larry Dossey, an American physician, coined the term "time-sickness" to describe the obsessive belief that "time is getting away, that there isn't enough of it, and that you must pedal faster and faster to keep up." These days, the whole world is time-sick. We all belong to the same cult of speed. Standing in that lineup for my flight home to London, I begin to grapple with the questions that lie at heart of this book: Why are we always in such a rush? What is the cure for time-sickness? Is it possible, or even desirable, to slow down?

In these early years of the twenty-first century, everything and everyone is under pressure to go faster. Not long ago, Klaus Schwab, founder and president of the World Economic Forum, spelled out the need for speed in stark terms: "We are moving from a world in which the big eat the small to one in which the fast eat the slow." That warning resonates far beyond the Darwinian world of commerce. In these busy, bustling times, everything is a race against the clock. Guy Claxton, a British psychologist, thinks acceleration is now second nature to us: "We have developed an inner psychology of speed, of saving time and maximizing efficiency, which is getting stronger by the day."

But now the time has come to challenge our obsession with doing everything more quickly. Speed is not always the best policy. Evolution works on the principle of survival of the fittest, not the fastest. Remember who won the race between the tortoise and the hare. As we hurry through life, cramming more into every hour, we are stretching ourselves to the breaking point.

Before we go any further, though, let's make one thing clear: this book is not a declaration of war against speed. Speed has helped to remake our world in ways that are wonderful and liberating. Who wants to live without the Internet or jet travel? The problem is that our love of speed, our obsession with doing more and more in less and less time, has gone too far; it has turned into an addiction, a kind of idolatry. Even when speed starts to backfire, we invoke the go-faster gospel. Falling behind at work? Get a quicker Internet connection. No time for that novel you got at Christmas? Learn to speed-read. Diet not working? Try liposuction. Too busy to cook? Buy a microwave. And yet some things cannot, should not, be sped up. They take time; they need slowness. When you accelerate things that should not be accelerated, when you forget how to slow down, there is a price to pay.

The case against speed starts with the economy. Modern capitalism generates extraordinary wealth, but at the cost of devouring natural resources faster than Mother Nature can replace them. Thousands of square miles of Amazonian rainforest are cleared every year, while over-trawling has put sturgeon, Chilean sea bass and many other fish on the endangered species list. Capitalism is getting too fast even for its own good, as the pressure to finish first leaves too little time for quality control. Consider the computer industry. In recent years, software manufacturers have made a habit of rushing out their products before they have been fully tested. The result is an epidemic of crashes, bugs and glitches that costs companies billions of dollars every year.

Then there is the human cost of turbo-capitalism. These days, we exist to serve the economy, rather than the other way round. Long hours on the job are making us unproductive, error-prone, unhappy and ill. Doctor's offices are swamped with people suffering from conditions brought on by stress: insomnia, migraines, hypertension, asthma and gastrointestinal trouble, to name but a few. The current work culture is also undermining our mental health. "Burnout used to be something you mainly found in people over forty," says one London-based life coach. "Now I'm seeing men and women in their thirties, and even their twenties, who are completely burned out."

The work ethic, which can be healthy in moderation, is getting out of hand. Consider the spread of "vacationitis," the aversion to taking a proper holiday. In a Reed survey of five thousand UK workers, 60% said they would not be using their full vacation entitlement in 2003. On average, Americans fail to use a fifth of their paid time off. Even illness can no longer keep the modern employee away from the office: one in five Americans turns up for work when he should be tucked up in bed at home or visiting a doctor.

For a chilling vision of where this behaviour leads, look no further than Japan, where the locals have a word—*karoshi*—that means "death by overwork." One of the most famous victims of *karoshi* was Kamei Shuji, a high-flying broker who routinely put in ninety-hour weeks during the Japanese stock market boom of the late 1980s. His company trumpeted his superhuman stamina in newsletters and training booklets, turning him into the gold standard to which all employees should aspire. In a rare break from Japanese protocol, Shuji was asked to coach senior colleagues in the art of salesmanship, which piled extra stress onto his pinstriped shoulders. When Japan's stock bubble burst in 1989, Shuji worked even longer hours to pick up the slack. In 1990, he died suddenly of a heart attack. He was twenty-six.

Though some hold up Shuji as a cautionary tale, the work-till-you-drop culture still runs deep in Japan. In 2001, the government reported a record 143 victims of *karoshi*. Critics put Japan's annual death toll from overwork in the thousands.

Long before *karoshi* kicks in, though, a burned-out workforce is bad for the bottom line. The National Safety

Council estimates that job stress causes a million Americans to miss work every day, costing the economy over $150 billion annually. In 2003, stress replaced backache as the leading cause of absenteeism in Britain.

Overwork is a health hazard in other ways, too. It leaves less time and energy for exercise, and makes us more likely to drink too much alcohol or reach for convenience foods. It is no coincidence that the fastest nations are also often the fattest. Up to a third of Americans and a fifth of Britons are now clinically obese. Even Japan is piling on the pounds. In 2002, a national nutrition survey found that a third of Japanese men over thirty were overweight.

To keep pace with the modern world, to get up to speed, many people are looking beyond coffee to more potent stimulants. Cocaine remains the booster of choice among white-collar professionals, but amphetamines, otherwise known as "speed," are catching up fast. Use of the drug in the American workplace has jumped by 70% since 1998. Many employees favour crystal methamphetamine, which delivers a surge of euphoria and alertness that lasts for most of the workday. It also spares the user the embarrassing garrulousness that is often a side effect of snorting coke. The catch is that the more potent forms of speed are more addictive than heroin, and coming down from a hit can trigger depression, agitation and violent behaviour.

One reason we need stimulants is that many of us are not sleeping enough. With so much to do, and so little time to do it, the average American now gets ninety minutes less shut-eye per night than she did a century ago. In southern

7

Europe, spiritual home of *la dolce vita,* the afternoon siesta has gone the way of the traditional nine-to-five job: only 7% of Spaniards still have time for a post-prandial snooze. Not sleeping enough can damage the cardiovascular and immune systems, bring on diabetes and heart disease, and trigger indigestion, irritability and depression. Getting less than six hours of kip a night can impair motor coordination, speech, reflexes and judgment. Fatigue has played a part in some of the worst disasters of the modern era: Chernobyl, the Exxon *Valdez,* Three Mile Island, Union Carbide and the space shuttle *Challenger.*

Drowsiness causes more car crashes than alcohol. In a recent Gallup poll, 11% of British drivers admitted to falling asleep at the wheel. A study by the US National Commission on Sleep Disorders blamed half of all traffic accidents on tiredness. Put that together with our penchant for speeding, and the result is carnage on the roads. Annual traffic fatalities now stand at 1.3 million worldwide, more than double the figure for 1990. Though better safety norms have cut the death toll in developed countries, the UN predicts that traffic will be the third leading cause of death in the world by 2020. Even now, more than forty thousand people die and 1.6 million are injured on European roads every year.

Our impatience makes even leisure more dangerous. Every year, millions of people around the world suffer sports- and gym-related injuries. Many are caused by pushing the body too hard, too fast, too soon. Even yoga is not immune. A friend of mine recently strained her neck by attempting a yogic headstand before her body was ready for it. Others suffer worse mishaps. In Boston, Massachusetts, an impatient teacher broke a pupil's pelvic bone by forcing her into the splits position. A man in his thirties now has a permanent numb patch in his right thigh after tearing a sensory nerve during a yoga session at a fashionable studio in Manhattan.

Inevitably, a life of hurry can become superficial. When we rush, we skim the surface, and fail to make real connections with the world or other people. As Milan Kundera wrote in his 1996 novella *Slowness,* "When things happen too fast, nobody can be certain about anything, about anything at all, not even about himself." All the things that bind us together and make life worth living—community, family, friendship—thrive on the one thing we never have enough of: time. In a recent ICM poll, half of British adults said their hectic schedules had caused them to lose touch with friends.

Consider the damage that living in the fast lane can inflict on family life. With everyone coming and going, Post-it stickers on the fridge door are now the main form of communication in many homes. According to figures released by the British government, the average working parent spends twice as long dealing with email as playing with her children. In Japan, parents now book their kids into twenty-four-hour child-minding centres. All over the industrial world, children come home from school to empty houses where there is no one to listen to their stories, problems, triumphs or fears. In a *Newsweek* poll of

American adolescents carried out in 2000, 73% said parents spend too little time with their teenagers.

Perhaps kids suffer most from the orgy of acceleration. They are growing up faster than ever before. Many children are now as busy as their parents, juggling diaries packed with everything from after-school tutoring to piano lessons and football practice. A recent cartoon said it all: two little girls are standing at the school bus stop, each clutching a personal planner. One says to the other, "Okay, I'll move ballet back an hour, reschedule gymnastics, and cancel piano . . . you shift your violin lesson to Thursday and skip soccer practice . . . that gives us from 3:15 to 3:45 on Wednesday the 16th to play."

Living like high-powered grown-ups leaves little time for the stuff that childhood is all about: messing around with friends, playing without adult supervision, day-dreaming. It also takes a toll on health, since kids are even less able to cope with the sleep deprivation and stress that are the price of living hurried, hectic lives. Psychologists who specialize in treating adolescents for anxiety now find their waiting rooms packed with children as young as five suffering from upset stomachs, headaches, insomnia, depression and eating disorders. In many industrial countries, teenage suicides are on the rise. And no wonder, given the burden many face at school. In 2002, Louise Kitching, a seventeen-year-old in Lincolnshire, England, fled an examination hall in tears. The star pupil was just about to write her fifth exam of the day, having had only a ten-minute break between papers.

If we carry on at this rate, the cult of speed can only get worse. When everyone takes the fast option, the advantage of going fast vanishes, forcing us to go faster still. Eventually, what we are left with is an arms race based on speed, and we all know where arms races end up: in the grim stalemate of Mutually Assured Destruction.

Much has already been destroyed. We have forgotten how to look forward to things, and how to enjoy the moment when they arrive. Restaurants report that hurried diners increasingly pay the bill and order a taxi while eating dessert. Many fans leave sporting events early, no matter how close the score is, simply to steal a march on the traffic. Then there is the curse of multi-tasking. Doing two things at once seems so clever, so efficient, so modern. And yet what it often means is doing two things not very well. Like many people, I read the paper while watching TV—and find that I get less out of both.

In this media-drenched, data-rich, channel-surfing, computer-gaming age, we have lost the art of doing nothing, of shutting out the background noise and distractions, of slowing down and simply being alone with our thoughts. Boredom—the word itself hardly existed 150 years ago—is a modern invention. Remove all stimulation, and we fidget, panic and look for something, anything, to do to make use of the time. When did you last see someone just gazing out the window on a train? Everyone is too busy reading the paper, playing video games, listening to iPods, working on the laptop, yammering into mobile phones.

Instead of thinking deeply, or letting an idea simmer in the back of the mind, our instinct now is to reach for the nearest sound bite. In modern warfare, correspondents in the field and pundits in the studio spew out instant analyses of events as they occur. Often their insights turn out to be wrong. But that hardly matters nowadays: in the land of speed, the man with the instant response is king. With satellite feeds and twenty-four-hour news channels, the electronic media is dominated by what one French sociologist dubbed "le fast thinker"—a person who can, without skipping a beat, summon up a glib answer to any question.

In a way, we are all fast thinkers now. Our impatience is so implacable that, as actress-author Carrie Fisher quipped, even "instant gratification takes too long." This partly explains the chronic frustration that bubbles just below the surface of modern life. Anyone or anything that steps in our way, that slows us down, that stops us from getting exactly what we want when we want it, becomes the enemy. So the smallest setback, the slightest delay, the merest whiff of slowness, can now provoke vein-popping fury in otherwise ordinary people.

The anecdotal evidence is everywhere. In Los Angeles, a man starts a fight at a supermarket checkout because the customer ahead of him is taking too long to pack his groceries. A woman scratches the paintwork of a car that beats her to a parking spot in London. A company executive tears into a flight attendant when his plane is forced to spend an extra twenty minutes circling Heathrow airport before landing. "I want to land now!" he shouts, like a spoiled child. "Now, now, now!"

A delivery van stops outside my neighbour's house, forcing the traffic behind to wait while the driver unloads a small table. Within a minute, the forty-something businesswoman in the first car begins thrashing around in her seat, flailing her arms and snapping her head back and forth. A low, guttural wail escapes from her open window. It is like a scene from *The Exorcist*. I decide she must be having an epileptic fit, and run downstairs to help. But when I reach the sidewalk, it turns out she is simply annoyed at being held up. She leans out the window and screams at no one in particular, "If you don't move that fucking van, I'll fucking kill you." The delivery man shrugs as if he has seen it all before, slides behind the wheel and drives off. I open my mouth to tell Screaming Woman to lighten up a little, but my words are drowned out by the sound of her tires skidding on the asphalt.

This is where our obsession with going fast and saving time leads. To road rage, air rage, shopping rage, relationship rage, office rage, vacation rage, gym rage. Thanks to speed, we live in the age of rage.

After my bedtime-story epiphany at the airport in Rome, I return to London with a mission: to investigate the price of speed and the prospects for slowing down in a world obsessed with going faster and faster. We all moan about frenzied schedules, but is anybody actually doing anything about it? Yes, it turns out. While the rest of the world roars on, a large and growing minority is choosing not to do everything at full-throttle. In every human endeavour you can think of, from sex, work and exercise to food, medicine and urban design, these rebels are doing the unthinkable— they are making room for slowness. And the good news is that decelerating works. Despite Cassandra-like mutterings from the speed merchants, slower, it turns out, often means better—better health, better work, better business, better family life, better exercise, better cuisine and better sex.

We have been here before. In the nineteenth century, people resisted the pressure to accelerate in ways familiar to us today. Unions pushed for more leisure time. Stressed-out urbanites sought refuge and restoration in the countryside. Painters and poets, writers and craftsmen looked for ways to preserve the aesthetics of slowness in the machine age. Today, though, the backlash against speed is moving into the mainstream with more urgency than ever before. Down at the grass roots, in kitchens, offices, concert halls, factories, gyms, bedrooms, neighbourhoods, art galleries, hospitals, leisure centres and schools near you, more and more people are refusing to accept the diktat that faster is always better. And in their many and diverse acts of deceleration lie the seeds of a global Slow movement.

Now is the moment to define our terms. In this book, Fast and Slow do more than just describe a rate of change. They are shorthand for ways of being, or philosophies of life. Fast is busy, controlling, aggressive, hurried, analytical, stressed, superficial, impatient, active, quantity-over-quality. Slow is the opposite: calm, careful, receptive, still, intuitive, unhurried, patient, reflective, quality-over-quantity. It is about making real and meaningful connections—with people, culture, work, food, everything. The paradox is that Slow does not always mean slow. As we shall see, performing a task in a Slow manner often yields faster results. It is also possible to do things quickly while maintaining a Slow frame of mind. A century after Rudyard Kipling wrote of keeping your head while all about you are losing theirs, people are learning how to keep their cool, how to remain Slow inside, even as they rush to meet a deadline at work or to get the children to school on time. One aim of this book is to show how they do it.

Despite what some critics say, the Slow movement is not about doing everything at a snail's pace. Nor is it a Luddite attempt to drag the whole planet back to some pre-industrial utopia. On the contrary, the movement is made up of people like you and me, people who want to live better in a fast-paced, modern world. That is why the Slow philosophy can be summed up in a single word: balance. Be fast when it makes sense to be fast, and be slow when slowness is called for. Seek to live at what musicians call the *tempo giusto*—the right speed.

One leading proponent of deceleration is Carlo Petrini, the Italian founder of Slow Food, the international movement dedicated to the very civilized notion that what we eat should be cultivated, cooked and consumed at a relaxed pace. Though the dinner table is its chief battlefront, Slow Food is much more than an excuse for long lunches. The group's manifesto is a call to arms against the cult of speed in all its forms: "Our century, which began and has developed under the insignia of industrial civilization, first invented the machine and then took it as its life model. We are enslaved by speed and have all succumbed to the same insidious virus: Fast Life, which disrupts our habits, pervades the privacy of our homes and forces us to eat Fast Food."

On a baking summer afternoon in Bra, the small Piedmontese city that is home to the headquarters of Slow Food, I meet Petrini for a chat. His recipe for life has a reassuringly modern twang. "If you are always slow, then you are stupid—and that is not at all what we are aiming for," he tells me. "Being Slow means that you control the rhythms of your own life. You decide how fast you have to go in any given context. If today I want to go fast, I go fast; if tomorrow I want to go slow, I go slow. What we are fighting for is the right to determine our own tempos."

That very simple philosophy is gaining ground in many arenas. In the workplace, millions are pushing for—and winning—a better balance between work and life. In the bedroom, people are discovering the joy of slow sex, through Tantra and other forms of erotic deceleration. The notion that slower is better underlies the boom in exercise regimes—from yoga to Tai Chi—and alternative medicines—from herbalism to homeopathy—that take a gentle, holistic approach to the body. Cities everywhere are revamping the urban landscape to encourage people to drive less and walk more. Many children are moving out of the fast lane, too, as parents lighten their schedules.

Inevitably, the Slow movement overlaps with the anti-globalization crusade. Proponents of both believe that turbo-capitalism offers a one-way ticket to burnout, for the planet and the people living on it. They claim we can live better if we consume, manufacture and work at a more reasonable pace. In common with moderate anti-globalizers, however, Slow activists are not out to destroy the capitalist system. Rather, they seek to give it a human face. Petrini himself talks of "virtuous globalization." But the Slow movement goes much deeper and wider than mere economic reform. By taking aim at the false god of speed, it strikes at the heart of what it is to be human in the era of the silicon chip. The Slow creed can pay dividends when applied in a piecemeal fashion. But to get full benefit from the Slow movement, we need to go further and rethink our approach to everything. A genuinely Slow world implies nothing less than a lifestyle revolution.

The Slow movement is still taking shape. It has no central headquarters or website, no single leader, no political party to carry its message. Many people decide to slow down without ever feeling part of a cultural trend, let alone a global crusade. What matters, though, is that a growing minority is choosing slowness over speed. Every act of deceleration gives another push to the Slow movement.

Like the anti-globalization crowd, Slow activists are forging links, building momentum and honing their philosophy through international conferences, the Internet and the media. Pro-Slow groups are springing up all over the place. Some, such as Slow Food, focus mainly on one sphere of life. Others make a broader case for the Slow philosophy. Among these are Japan's Sloth Club, the US-based Long Now Foundation and Europe's Society for the Deceleration of Time. Much of the Slow movement's growth will come from cross-pollination. Slow Food has already given rise to spinoff groups. Under the Slow Cities banner, more than sixty towns in Italy and beyond are striving to turn themselves into oases of calm. Bra is also the home of Slow Sex, a group dedicated to banishing haste from the bedroom. In the United States, the Petrini doctrine has inspired a leading educator to launch a movement for "Slow Schooling."

My aim in this book is to introduce the Slow movement to a wider audience, to explain what it stands for, how it is evolving, what obstacles it faces and why it has something to offer us all. My motives, however, are not entirely selfless. I am a speedaholic, and so this book is also a personal journey. By the end of it, I want to recapture some of the serenity I felt waiting for that bus in Rome. I want to be able to read to my son without watching the clock.

Like most people, I want to find a way to live better by striking a balance between fast and slow.

CHAPTER ONE

DO EVERYTHING FASTER

*We affirm that the world's magnificence has been
enriched by a new beauty: the beauty of speed.*
—FUTURIST MANIFESTO, 1909

WHAT IS THE VERY FIRST THING you do when you wake
up in the morning? Draw the curtains? Roll over to snug-
gle up with your partner or pillow? Spring out of bed and
do ten push-ups to get the blood pumping? No, the first
thing you do, the first thing everyone does, is check the
time. From its perch on the bedside table, the clock gives us
our bearings, telling us not only where we stand vis-à-vis
the rest of the day, but also how to respond. If it's early, I
close my eyes and try to go back to sleep. If it's late, I spring
out of bed and make a beeline for the bathroom. Right
from that first waking moment, the clock calls the shots.
And so it goes, on through the day, as we scurry from one
appointment, one deadline, to the next. Every moment is
woven into a schedule, and wherever we look—the bedside
table, the office canteen, the corner of the computer screen,

our own wrists—the clock is ticking, tracking our progress, urging us not to fall behind.

In our fast-moving modern world, it always seems that the time-train is pulling out of the station just as we reach the platform. No matter how fast we go, no matter how cleverly we schedule, there are never enough hours in the day. To some extent, it has always been so. But today we feel more time pressure than ever before. Why? What makes us different from our ancestors? If we are ever going to slow down, we must understand why we accelerated in the first place, why the world got so revved up, so tightly scheduled. And to do that, we need to start at the very beginning, by looking at our relationship with time itself.

Mankind has always been in thrall to time, sensing its presence and power, yet never sure how to define it. In the fourth century, St. Augustine mused, "What is time then? If nobody asks me, I know; but if I were desirous to explain it to one that should ask me, plainly I do not know." Sixteen hundred years later, after wrestling with a few pages of Stephen Hawking, we understand exactly how he felt. Yet even if time remains elusive, every society has evolved ways of measuring its passage. Archaeologists believe that over twenty thousand years ago European ice age hunters counted the days between lunar phases by carving lines and holes in sticks and bones. Every great culture in the ancient world—the Sumerians and the Babylonians, the Egyptians and the Chinese, the Mayans and the Aztecs—created its own calendar. One of the first documents to roll off the Gutenberg printing press was the "Calendar of 1448."

Once our ancestors learned to measure years, months and days, the next step was to chop time into smaller units. An Egyptian sundial dating from 1500 BC is one of the oldest surviving instruments for dividing the day into equal parts. Early "clocks" were based on the time it took for water or sand to pass through a hole, or for a candle or a dish of oil to burn. Timekeeping took a great leap forward with the invention of the mechanical clock in thirteenth-century Europe. By the late 1600s, people could accurately measure not only hours, but also minutes and seconds.

Survival was one incentive for measuring time. Ancient civilizations used calendars to work out when to plant and harvest crops. Right from the start, though, timekeeping proved to be a double-edged sword. On the upside, scheduling can make anyone, from peasant farmer to software engineer, more efficient. Yet as soon as we start to parcel up time, the tables turn, and time takes over. We become slaves to the schedule. Schedules give us deadlines, and deadlines, by their very nature, give us a reason to rush. As an Italian proverb puts it: Man measures time, and time measures man.

By making daily schedules possible, clocks held out the promise of greater efficiency—and also tighter control. Yet early timepieces were too unreliable to rule mankind the way the clock does today. Sundials did not work at night or in cloudy weather, and the length of a sundial hour varied from day to day thanks to the tilt of the earth. Ideal for timing a specific act, hourglasses and water clocks were hopeless at telling the time of day. Why were so many duels, battles and other events in history held at dawn? Not because our ancestors were partial to early rises, but because dawn was the one time that everyone could identify and agree on. In the absence of accurate clocks, life was dictated by what sociologists call Natural Time. People did things when it felt right, not when a wristwatch told them to. They ate when hungry, and slept when drowsy. Nevertheless, from early on, telling time went hand in hand with telling people what to do.

As long ago as the sixth century, Benedictine monks lived by a routine that would make a modern time manager proud. Using primitive clocks, they rang bells at set intervals throughout the day and night to hurry each other from one task to the next, from prayer to study to farming to rest, and back to prayer again. When mechanical clocks began springing up in town squares across Europe, the line between keeping time and keeping control blurred further. Cologne offers a revealing case study. Historical records suggest that a public clock was erected in the German city around 1370. In 1374, Cologne passed a statute that fixed the start and end of the workday for labourers, and limited their lunch break to "one hour and no longer." In 1391, the city imposed a curfew of 9 P.M. (8 P.M. in winter) on foreign visitors, followed by a general curfew of 11 P.M. in 1398. In the space of one generation, the people of Cologne went from never knowing for sure what time it was to allowing a clock to dictate when they worked, how long they took for lunch and when they went home every night. Clock Time was gaining the upper hand over Natural Time.

Following the trail blazed by the Benedictines, modern-minded Europeans began using daily schedules to live and work more efficiently. As a philosopher, architect, musician, painter and sculptor during the Italian Renaissance, Leon Battista Alberti was a busy man. To make the most of his time, he began each day by drawing up a schedule: "When I get up in the morning, before anything else I ask myself what I must do that day. These many things, I list them, I think about them, and assign to them the proper time: this one, this morning, that one, this afternoon, the other, tonight." You just know Alberti would have loved a Personal Digital Assistant.

Scheduling became a way of life during the Industrial Revolution, as the world lurched into overdrive. Before the machine age, no one could move faster than a galloping horse or a ship at full sail. Engine power changed everything. Suddenly, with the flick of a switch, people, information and materials could travel across great distances faster than ever before. A factory could churn out more goods in a day than an artisan could make in a lifetime. The new speed promised unimaginable excitement and prosperity, and people lapped it up. When the world's first passenger steam train made its maiden voyage in Yorkshire, England, in 1825, it was greeted by a crowd of forty thousand and a twenty-one gun salute.

Industrial capitalism fed on speed, and rewarded it as never before. The business that manufactured and shipped its products the fastest could undercut rivals. The quicker you turned capital into profit, the quicker you could re-invest it for even greater gain. Not by accident did the expression "to make a fast buck" enter the language in the nineteenth century.

In 1748, at the dawn of the industrial era, Benjamin Franklin blessed the marriage between profit and haste with an aphorism that still trips off the tongue today: Time is money. Nothing reflected, or reinforced, the new mindset more than the shift towards paying workers by the hour, instead of for what they produced. Once every minute cost money, business found itself locked in a never-ending race to accelerate output. More widgets per hour equalled more profit. Staying ahead of the pack meant installing the latest time-saving technology before your rivals did. Modern capitalism came with a built-in imperative to upgrade, to accelerate, to become ever more efficient.

Urbanization, another feature of the industrial era, helped quicken the pace. Cities have always attracted energetic and dynamic people, but urban life itself acts as a giant particle accelerator. When people move to the city, they start to do everything faster. In 1871, an anonymous diarist wrote of the British capital: "The wear and tear of nerve-power and the discharge of brain-power in London are enormous. The London man lives fast. In London, man rubs out, elsewhere he rusts out. . . . The mind is ever on the stretch with rapid succession of new images, new people, and new sensations. All business is done with an increased pace. The buying and the selling, the counting and the weighing, and even the talk over the counter, is all done with a degree of rapidity and sharp practice. . . . The slow and prosy soon find they have not a chance; but after a while, like a dull horse in a fast coach, they develop a pace unknown before."

As industrialization and urbanization spread, the nineteenth century brought an endless parade of inventions designed to help people travel, work and communicate more swiftly. Most of the fifteen thousand machines registered at the US Patent Office in 1850 were, as one Swedish visitor noted, "for the acceleration of speed, and for the saving of time and labour." London opened the first underground subway line in 1863; Berlin switched on the first electric tram in 1879; Otis unveiled the first escalator in 1900. By 1913, Model T Fords were rolling off the world's first assembly line. Communications also sped up as the telegraph debuted in 1837, followed by the first transatlantic cable in 1866 and, a decade later, by the telephone and the wireless radio.

None of the new technology could be fully harnessed, however, without accurate timekeeping. The clock is the operating system of modern capitalism, the thing that makes everything else possible—meetings, deadlines, contracts, manufacturing processes, schedules, transport, working shifts. Lewis Mumford, the eminent social critic, identified the clock as "the key machine" of the Industrial Revolution. But it was not until the late nineteenth century that the creation of standard time unlocked its full potential. Before then, each town kept time by the solar noon, that eerie moment when shadows vanish and the sun appears to be directly overhead. The result was an anarchic mishmash of local time zones. In the early 1880s, for

instance, New Orleans was twenty-three minutes behind
Baton Rouge, eighty miles to the west. When no one could
travel faster than a horse, such absurdities hardly mattered,
but now trains crossed the landscape quickly enough to
notice. To make efficient rail schedules possible, nations
began harmonizing their clocks. By 1855, most of Britain
accepted the time transmitted by telegraph from the Royal
Observatory in Greenwich. In 1884, twenty-seven nations
agreed to recognize Greenwich as the prime meridian,
which eventually led to the creation of global standard
time. By 1911, most of the world was on the same clock.

Persuading the early industrial workers to live by the
clock was not easy. Many laboured at their own speed, took
breaks on a whim or failed to show up for work at all—a
disaster for factory bosses paying hourly wages. To teach
workers the new time discipline demanded by modern capitalism, the ruling classes set about promoting punctuality as
a civic duty and a moral virtue, while denigrating slowness
and tardiness as cardinal sins. In its 1891 catalogue, the
Electric Signal Clock Company warned against the evils of
failing to keep pace: "If there is one virtue that should be
cultivated more than any other by him who would succeed
in life, it is punctuality: if there is one error to be avoided,
it is being behind time." One of the firm's clocks, the aptly
named Autocrat, promised to "revolutionize stragglers and
behind-time people."

Punctuality got a big boost when the first windup alarm
clocks hit the market in 1876. A few years later, factories
began installing clocks for workers to punch at the beginning

and the end of each shift, embedding the "time is money" principle in a daily ritual. As the pressure mounted to make every second count, the portable timepiece became a status symbol. In the US, the poor joined clubs that raffled off one watch each week. Schools also backed the punctuality drive. A lesson in the 1881 edition of McGuffey's Readers warned children of the horrors that tardiness could unleash: train crashes, failed businesses, military defeat, mistaken executions, thwarted romances: "It is continually so in life, the best laid plans, the most important affairs, the fortunes of individuals, honour, happiness, life itself are daily sacrificed because somebody is behind time."

As the clock tightened its grip and technology made it possible to do everything more quickly, hurry and haste seeped into every corner of life. People were expected to think faster, work faster, talk faster, read faster, write faster, eat faster, move faster. One nineteenth-century observer quipped that the average New Yorker "always walks as if he had a good dinner before him, and a bailiff behind him." In 1880, Nietzsche detected a growing culture " . . . of hurry, of indecent and perspiring haste, which wants to 'get everything done' at once."

Intellectuals began to notice that technology was shaping us as much as we shaped it. In 1910, Herbert Casson, a historian, wrote that " . . . with the use of the telephone has come a new habit of mind. The slow and sluggish mood has been sloughed off . . . life has become more tense, alert, vivid." Casson would not be surprised to learn that spending long hours working on computers can make people impatient with anyone who fails to move at the speed of software.

The culture of hurry cranked up a notch at the end of the nineteenth century thanks to a proto-management consultant by the name of Frederick Taylor. At the Bethlehem Steel Works in Pennsylvania, Taylor used a stopwatch and a slide rule to work out how long every single task should take to the nearest fraction of a second, and then arranged them for maximum efficiency. "In the past, the man has been first," he declared, ominously. "In the future, the System must be first." But though his writings were read with interest all over the world, Taylor himself enjoyed mixed success putting his brand of "Scientific Management" into practice. At the Bethlehem Steel Works, he taught one worker to move four times more pig iron in a day than the average. Many other employees quit, though, complaining of stress and fatigue. Taylor was a hard man to get along with, and was eventually fired in 1901. But though he lived out his final years in relative obscurity, a hate figure for the unions, his creed—schedule first, man second—left an indelible mark on the Western psyche. And not just in the workplace. Michael Schwarz, who produced a 1999 TV documentary on Taylorism, said: "Taylor may have died in ignominy, but he probably had the last laugh, because his ideas about efficiency have come to define the way we live today, not just at work but in our personal lives as well."

Around the same time as Taylor was calculating how many hundredths of a second it took to change a light bulb,

Henry Olerich published a novel called *A Cityless and Countryless World,* which depicted a civilization on Mars where time is so precious that it has become the currency. A century later, his prophecy has virtually come true: time is now more like money than ever before. We even talk about being "time-rich" or, more often, "time-poor."

Why, amid so much material wealth, is time-poverty so endemic? Much of the blame rests with our own mortality. Modern medicine may have added an extra decade or so to the three score years and ten originally laid down in the Bible, but we still live under the shadow of the biggest deadline of all: death. No wonder we feel that time is short and strive to make every moment count. But if the instinct to do so is universal, then why are some cultures more prone than others to race against the clock?

Part of the answer may lie in the way we think about time itself. In some philosophical traditions—Chinese, Hindu and Buddhist, to name three—time is cyclical. On Canada's Baffin Island, the Inuit use the same word—*uvatiarru*—to mean both "in the distant past" and "in the distant future." Time, in such cultures, is always coming as well as going. It is constantly around us, renewing itself, like the air we breathe. In the Western tradition, time is linear, an arrow flying remorselessly from A to B. It is a finite, and therefore precious, resource. Christianity piles on pressure to put every moment to good use. The Benedictine monks kept a tight schedule because they believed the devil would find work for idle hands to do. In the nineteenth century, Charles Darwin summed up the Western obsession with making the most of every minute with a stern call to action: "A man who wastes one hour of time has not discovered the meaning of life."

In Japan's native Shinto religion, which exists in harmony with the local form of Buddhism, time is cyclical. Yet after 1868, with almost superhuman zeal, Japan set about catching up with the West. To create a modern capitalist economy, the Meiji government imported the Western clock and calendar, and began promoting the virtues of punctuality and making the most of time. The cult of efficiency deepened after the Second World War left Japan in ruins. Today, when you stand at Shinjuku station in Tokyo and watch commuters run to catch a train when another will be along in two minutes, you know the Japanese have swallowed the idea of time as a finite resource.

Consumerism, which Japan has also mastered, is another powerful incentive to go fast. As long ago as the 1830s, the French writer Alexis de Tocqueville blamed the shopping instinct for jacking up the pace of life: "He who has set his heart exclusively upon the pursuit of worldly welfare is always in a hurry, for he has but a limited time at his disposal to reach, to grasp, and to enjoy it." That analysis rings even more true today, when all the world is a store, and all the men and women merely shoppers. Tempted and titillated at every turn, we seek to cram in as much consumption and as many experiences as possible. As well as glittering careers, we want to take art courses, work out at the gym, read the newspaper and every book on the bestseller list, eat out with friends, go clubbing, play sports, watch hours of television, listen to music, spend time with the family, buy all the newest fashions and gadgets, go to the cinema, enjoy intimacy and great sex with our partners, holiday in far-flung locations and maybe even do some meaningful volunteer work. The result is a gnawing disconnect between what we want from life and what we can realistically have, which feeds the sense that there is never enough time.

My own life fits the pattern. Children are a lot of work, and the only way to survive parenthood is to downsize your diary. But I find this hard. I want to have it all. So instead of cutting back on my hobbies, I contrive to squeeze them into a schedule that is already bursting at the seams. After slipping off for an extra tennis game, I then spend the rest of the day rushing to catch up. I drive faster, walk faster and skip through the bedtime stories.

Like everyone else, I look to technology to help me buy more time, and with it the chance to feel less hurried. But technology is a false friend. Even when it does save time, it often spoils the effect by generating a whole new set of duties and desires. When the washing machine arrived in the early twentieth century, it freed housewives from hours of knuckle-shredding toil. Then, over the years, as standards of hygiene rose, we started washing our clothes more often. Result: the overflowing laundry basket is as much a feature of the modern household as the pile of bills on the front doormat. Email is another example. On the plus side, it brings people together like never before. But ease of use has led to rampant overuse, with everyone clicking "send" at the drop of a hat. Each day, the information superhighway carries over five billion emails, many of them superfluous memos, rude jokes and spam. For most of us, the result is a daily hike up Email Mountain.

With so much pressure on our time, even the most dedicated apostle of slowness finds it hard not to hurry. Take Satish Kumar, a former Jain monk who walked all the way to Britain from his native India in the 1960s and has since travelled much of the world on foot. Today, he lives in Devon, in southwestern England, where he publishes *Resurgence,* a bimonthly magazine that espouses many of the ideas dear to the Slow movement. I meet Kumar on a perfect summer evening in London's Hyde Park. A small, lean figure in a linen suit, he walks serenely through the straining hordes of in-line skaters, joggers and speed-walkers. We sit in the shade beneath a tree. Kumar removes his socks and shoes and sinks his well-travelled feet into the long grass. I ask him about time-sickness.

"It is a Western disease to make time finite, and then to impose speed on all aspects of life," he says. "My mother used to tell me: 'When God made time he made plenty of it'—and she was right."

But your mother lived her whole life in rural India, I point out. Surely the pressure to speed up, to beat the clock, is irresistible in the modern world.

"Yes, that is true to an extent. Living here, I too succumb to hurry, to speed. Sometimes there is no other way to meet the deadlines for the magazine. Living in the West, one constantly struggles not to be dominated by the clock."

An airplane rumbles plaintively overhead. Kumar glances at his watch. His next appointment, a book launch, is starting in fifteen minutes. "It's time to go," he says, with a weak smile. "I don't want to be late."

Time-sickness can also be a symptom of a deeper, existential malaise. In the final stages before burnout, people often speed up to avoid confronting their unhappiness. Kundera thinks that speed helps us block out the horror and barrenness of the modern world: "Our period is obsessed with the desire to forget, and it is to fulfill that desire that it gives over to the demon of speed; it picks up the pace to show us that it no longer wishes to be remembered, that it is tired of itself, sick of itself; that it wants to blow out the tiny trembling flame of memory."

Others think speed is an escape not from life but from death. Mark Kingwell, a professor of philosophy at the University of Toronto, has written perceptively on the modern cult of speed. When we meet over coffee, he steers the conversation away from rocket engines and broadband Internet. "Despite what people think, the discussion about speed is never really about the current state of technology. It goes much deeper than that, it goes back to the human desire for transcendence," he says. "It's hard to think about the fact that we're going to die; it's unpleasant, so we constantly seek ways to distract ourselves from the awareness of our own mortality. Speed, with the sensory rush it gives, is one strategy for distraction."

Like it or not, the human brain is hardwired for speed. We get a kick from the danger, the buzz, the thrilling, throbbing, heady surge of sensory input that comes from going fast. Speed triggers the release of two chemicals—epinephrine and norepinephrine—that also course through the body during sex. Kundera is right on the money when he talks about "the ecstasy of speed."

And not only do we enjoy going fast, we get used to it, we become "velocitized." When we first drive onto a motorway, 70 miles per hour seems fast. Then, after a few minutes, it feels routine. Pull onto a slip road, brake to 30 mph and the lower speed seems teeth-gnashingly slow. Velocitization fuels a constant need for more speed. As we get used to 70 mph, we are tempted to lean a little harder on the accelerator, to push the speedometer up to 80 mph or 90 mph or higher. In 1899, a Belgian engineer built the first car designed purely to break speed records. Shaped like a torpedo, and propelled by two electric motors, the vehicle bore a name that summed up our yearning to go faster and faster: La Jamais Contente—Never Happy.

The curse of velocitization reaches beyond the open road. Take Web surfing. We are never happy with the speed of our Internet connection. When I first began surfing the Net with a broadband modem, it seemed lightning fast. Now it feels run-of-the-mill, even a little sluggish. When a page fails to load instantly, I lose patience. Even a delay of two or three seconds is enough to make me click the mouse to hurry things along. The only answer seems to be a faster connection.

As we go on accelerating, our relationship with time grows ever more fraught and dysfunctional. Any medical textbook will tell you that a microscopic obsession with detail is a classic symptom of neurosis. The relentless drive to shave time into ever smaller pieces—it takes five hundred million nanoseconds to snap your fingers, by the way—makes us more aware of its passage, more eager to make the most of it, more neurotic.

The very nature of time seems to have changed, too. In the old days, the Bible taught that "To every thing there is a season, and a time to every purpose under the heaven"—a time to be born, to die, to heal, to weep, to laugh, to love and so on. In *Don Quixote,* Cervantes noted that *"Que no son todos los tiempos unos"*—not all times are the same. In a 24/7 world, however, all time is the same: we pay bills on Saturday, shop on Sunday, take the laptop to bed, work through the night, tuck into all-day breakfasts. We mock the seasons by eating imported strawberries in the middle of winter and hot cross buns, once an Easter treat, all year round. With cellphones, Blackberrys, pagers and the Internet, everyone and everything is now permanently available.

Some argue that a round-the-clock culture can make people feel less hurried by giving them the freedom to work and run errands whenever they want to. That is wishful thinking. Once the boundaries are swept away, competition, greed and fear encourage us to apply the time-is-money principle to every single moment of the day and night. That is why even sleep is no longer a haven from haste. Millions study for exams, learn foreign languages and brush up on management techniques by listening to tapes while they doze. On the Sleep Learning website, the assault on what used to be the one time when we could slow down without feeling guilty is dressed up as an exciting opportunity for self-improvement: "Your non-waking hours—one third of your life—are now non-productive. Tap this huge potential for advancing your career, health and happiness!"

So great is our neurosis about time that we have invented a new kind of therapist to help us deal with it. Enter the time management gurus. Some of their advice, proffered in countless books and seminars, makes sense. Many recommend doing fewer things in order to do them better, a core tenet of the Slow philosophy. Yet most fail to attack the root cause of our malaise: the obsession with saving time. Instead, they indulge it. In 2000, David Cottrell and Mark Layton published *175 Ways to Get More Done in Less Time*. Written in breathless, get-on-with-it prose, the book is a manual for maximizing efficiency, for acceleration. Tip number 141 is simply: "Do Everything Faster!"

And in those three words, the authors neatly sum up what is wrong with the modern world. Think about it for a minute: Do Everything Faster. Does it really make sense to speed-read Proust, make love in half the time or cook every meal in the microwave? Surely not, but the fact that someone could write the words "Do Everything Faster" underlines just how far we have gone off the rails, and how urgently we need to rethink our whole way of life.

It is not too late to put things right. Even in the era of the one-minute bedtime story, there is an alternative to doing everything faster. And though it sounds like a paradox, the Slow movement is growing quickly.

CHAPTER TWO

SLOW IS BEAUTIFUL

For fast-acting relief from stress, try slowing down.
—LILY TOMLIN, AMERICAN ACTRESS AND COMEDIENNE

WAGRAIN, A RESORT TOWN nestled deep in the Austrian Alps, moves at a slow pace. People come here to escape the hurly-burly of Salzburg and Vienna. In the summer, they hike the wooded trails and picnic beside mountain streams. When the snow falls, they ski through the forests, or down the steep, powdery slopes. Whatever the season, the Alpine air fills the lungs with the promise of a good night's sleep back in the chalet.

Once a year, though, this small town does more than just live at a slow pace. It becomes a launch pad for the Slow philosophy. Every October, Wagrain hosts the annual conference of the Society for the Deceleration of Time.

Based in the Austrian city of Klagenfurt, and boasting a membership that stretches across central Europe, the Society is a leader in the Slow movement. Its more than one thousand members are foot soldiers in the war against the cult of doing everything faster. In daily life, that means slowing down when it makes sense to do so. If a Society member is a doctor, he might insist on taking more time to chat to his patients. A management consultant could refuse to answer work calls on the weekend. A designer might cycle to meetings instead of driving. The Decelerators use a German word—*eigenzeit*—to sum up their creed. *Eigen* means "own" and *zeit* means "time." In other words, every living being, event, process or object has its own inherent time or pace, its own *tempo giusto.*

As well as publishing earnest papers on man's relationship with time, the Society stirs up debate with tongue-in-cheek publicity stunts. Members patrol city centres wearing sandwich boards emblazoned with the slogan "Please hurry up!" Not long ago, the Society called on the International Olympic Committee to award gold medals to the athletes with the slowest times.

"Belonging to the Slow movement does not mean that you must always be slow—we take planes, too!—or that you must always be very serious and very philosophical, or that you want to spoil everybody else's fun," says Michaela Schmoczer, the Society's very efficient secretary. "Seriousness is okay, but you don't need to lose the humour."

With that in mind, the Decelerators regularly run "speed traps" in town centres. Using a stopwatch, they time pedestrians going about their daily business. People caught covering 50 metres in less than thirty-seven seconds are pulled over and asked to explain their haste. Their punishment is to walk the same 50 metres while steering a complicated tortoise marionette along the pavement. "It is always a huge success," says Jurgen Adam, a schoolteacher who ran a speed trap in the German city of Ulm. "Most people have not even thought about why they are going so fast. But once we get them talking about speed and time, they are very interested. They like the idea of slowing down. Some even return later in the day asking to walk the turtle a second time. They find it so soothing."

At the Society's annual conference in 2002, seventy members from Germany, Austria and Switzerland descended on Wagrain to spend three days putting the world to rights over wine and Wiener schnitzel. Dress is casual, as is the timekeeping. A slogan pinned up in the main meeting room speaks volumes: The beginning is when the time is right. Translation: many of the workshops start late. Thanks to a printing slip-up, a whole thirty-minute slot is missing from the Saturday program. When I point out the anomaly to a delegate, he looks perplexed. Then he shrugs, smiles and says: "Oh well. Easy come, easy go."

Don't get the wrong idea. The Decelerators are not flaky relics from the hippie era. Far from it. They are the kind of concerned citizens you find at neighbourhood watch meetings around the world—lawyers, consultants, doctors, architects, teachers. Nevertheless, the conference does occasionally tip into farce. At one workshop, held in a hotel lobby, two shaggy philosophy students lead a discussion about the art of doing absolutely nothing. A dozen members convene about ten minutes after the official start time.

They sit without speaking, shifting uncomfortably in their fold-up chairs. Only the distant whir of a vacuum cleaner, echoing up a nearby stairwell, disturbs the silence.

Elsewhere in the hotel, though, others explore more pragmatic ways of slowing down. One entrepreneur gives a workshop on his blueprint for the world's first Slow hotel. "Most vacations are so stressful nowadays," explains Bernhard Wallmann, a large, middle-aged man with puppy-dog eyes. "It starts with the journey by plane or car, then you rush around seeing as many sights as possible. You check your email in an Internet café, you watch CNN or MTV on the hotel television. You use your mobile to check in with friends or colleagues back home. And then at the end you return more tired than when you left." Tucked away in an Austrian national park, his three-hundred-bed Slow Hotel will be different. Guests will travel to a nearby village by steam train, and then on to the hotel by foot or in a horse-drawn carriage. All hurry-inducing technology—televisions, cellphones, laptops, Palm Pilots, cars—will be banned. Instead, guests will enjoy simple, Slow pleasures such as gardening, hiking, reading, yoga and spa treatments. Guest speakers will come to talk about time, speed and slowness. As Wallmann lays out his vision, some of the Decelerators balk. It's too big, too elitist, too commercial, they cry. But Wallmann, who wears the polished black shoes of a man who means business, is undeterred. "There is a great hunger for slowness in the world now," he tells me later, between mouthfuls of apple strudel. "I think the time is right for a hotel that really lets people slow down in every way."

Opting out of the culture of speed involves a leap of faith—and it is always easier to leap when you know others are leaping, too. Erwin Heller, a property lawyer from Munich, tells me that meeting other members of the Society for the Deceleration of Time helped him take the plunge. "I felt that the constant acceleration of everything was bad, but when you are alone, you always suspect that you might be wrong, and that everybody else is right," he says. "Knowing there are many other people thinking the same way, and even acting on it, has given me the confidence to slow down."

The Society members are not alone. Around the world, people are banding together into pro-Slow groups. More than seven hundred Japanese people now belong to the Sloth Club, which advocates less hurried, more environmentally friendly living. The group runs a café in Tokyo that serves organic food, stages candlelight concerts and sells T-shirts and coffee mugs bearing the slogan "Slow is beautiful." Tables are deliberately spaced farther apart than is normal in Japan, to encourage people to relax and linger. Thanks in part to the Sloth Club, deceleration is now hip in Japan. The nation's advertisers use the English word "slow" to sell everything from cigarettes and holidays to apartment blocks. Admiration for the easygoing lifestyle of Mediterranean Europe is so widespread that one commentator talks of the "Latinization of the Japanese people."

In 2001, one of the Sloth Club's founders, an anthropologist and environmental activist named Keibo Oiwa, published a survey of the various campaigns for slowness around the world. The book was called *Slow Is Beautiful,* and is already into its twelfth print run. When I visit Oiwa at his office at the Meiji Gakuin University outside Tokyo, he is just back from a well-attended three-day workshop on slowness held by the Hyogo prefecture. "More and more people in Japan, especially young people, are realizing that it is okay to be slow," he says. "For us that represents a total sea change in attitudes."

On the other side of the Pacific, from its headquarters in San Francisco, the Long Now Foundation is adding to the groundswell. Its members warn that we are so busy sprinting to keep up with the daily grind that we seldom lift our gaze beyond the next deadline, the next set of quarterly figures. "Civilization is revving itself into a pathologically short attention span," they say. To make us slow down, to open our eyes to the long view and the big picture, the Foundation is building huge, intricate clocks that tick once a year and measure time over ten millennia. The first, a beautiful beast of bronze and steel, is already on display at the Science Museum in London, England. A second, much larger clock will eventually be carved into a limestone cliff near Great Basin National Park in eastern Nevada.

Many Long Now supporters work in the technology sector. Danny Hillis, who helped invent supercomputers, is on the board. Among the corporate donors are high-tech giants such as PeopleSoft, Autodesk and Sun Microsystems, Inc. Why are players from the fastest industry on earth backing an organization that promotes slowness? Because they, too, have realized that the cult of speed is out of hand.

Today's pro-Slow organizations belong to a tradition of resistance that started long before the industrial era. Even in the ancient world, our ancestors chafed against the tyranny of timekeeping. In 200 BC, the Roman playwright Plautus penned the following lament:

> The Gods confound the man who first found out
> How to distinguish the hours—confound him, too
> Who in this place set up a sundial
> To cut and hack my days so wretchedly
> Into small pieces!
>
> . . . I can't (even sit down to eat) unless the sun gives leave.
> The town's so full of these confounded dials . . .

As mechanical clocks spread across Europe, protest was never far behind. In 1304, Daffyd ap Gwvilyn, a Welsh bard, fumed: "Confusion to the black-faced clock by the side of the bank that awoke me! May its head, its tongue, its pair of ropes, and its wheels moulder; likewise its weights and dullard balls, its orifices, its hammer, its ducks quacking as if anticipating day and its ever restless works."

As timekeeping wormed its way into every corner of life, satirists poked fun at the European devotion to the clock. In *Gulliver's Travels* (1726), the Lilliputians decide that Gulliver consults his watch so often that it must be his god.

As industrialization gathered pace, so, too, did the back-lash against clock-worship and the cult of speed. Many denounced the imposition of universal time as a form of slavery. In 1884, Charles Dudley Warner, an American editor and essayist, gave vent to the popular unease, echoing Plautus in the process: "The chopping up of time into rigid periods is an invasion of individual freedom and makes no allowances for differences in temperament and feeling." Others complained that machines were making life too fast, too hectic, less humane. The Romantic movement of artists, writers and musicians that swept across Europe after 1770 was partly a reaction against the modern culture of hustle and bustle, a harking back to a lost idyllic era.

Right through the Industrial Revolution, people sought ways to challenge, restrain or escape the accelerating pace of life. In 1776, the bookbinders of Paris called a strike to limit their working day to fourteen hours. Later, in the new factories, unions campaigned for more time off. The standard refrain was: "Eight hours for work, eight hours for sleep, eight hours for what we will." In a gesture that underscored the link between time and power, radical unionists smashed the clocks above the factory gates.

In the United States, meanwhile, a group of intellectuals known as the Transcendentalists exalted the gentle simplicity of a life rooted in nature. One of their number, Henry David Thoreau, retired to a one-room cabin beside Walden Pond near Boston in 1845, from which he decried modern life as a treadmill of "infinite bustle . . . nothing but work, work, work."

In 1870, the British-based Arts and Crafts movement turned away from mass production to embrace the slow, meticulous handwork of the artisan. In cities across the industrial world, weary urbanites found solace in the cult of the rural idyll. Richard Jeffries made a career of writing novels and memoirs about England's green and pleasant land, while Romantic painters such as Caspar David Friedrich in Germany, Jean-Francois Millet in France and John Constable in England filled their canvases with soothing country scenes. The urban desire to spend a little time resting and recharging the batteries in Arcadia helped bring about the emergence of modern tourism. By 1845, there were more tourists than sheep in Britain's Lake District.

In the late nineteenth century, physicians and psychiatrists began calling attention to the deleterious effects of speed. George Beard got the ball rolling in 1881 with *American Nervousness,* which blamed fast living for everything from neuralgia to tooth decay and hair loss. Beard argued that the modern obsession with punctuality, with making every second count, made everyone feel that "a delay of a few minutes might destroy the hopes of a lifetime."

Three years later, Sir James Crichton-Browne blamed the high tempo of modern life for the sharp rise in the number of deaths in England from kidney failure, heart disease and cancer. In 1901, John Girdner coined the term "newyorkitis" to describe an illness whose symptoms included edginess, quick movements and impulsiveness. A year later, a Frenchman named Gabriel Hanotaux prefigured modern environmentalism by warning that the reckless pursuit of speed was hastening the depletion of the world's coal reserves: "We are burning our way during our stay in order to travel through more rapidly."

Some of the fears articulated by the early critics of speed were patently absurd. Doctors claimed that passengers travelling on steam trains would be crushed by the pressure, or that the mere sight of a speeding locomotive would drive onlookers insane. When bicycles first became popular in the 1890s, some feared that riding into the wind at high speed would cause permanent disfigurement, or "bicycle face." Moralists warned that bikes would corrupt the young by enabling them to enjoy romantic trysts far from the prying eyes of their guardians. However risible these misgivings turned out to be, it was nevertheless clear by the end of the nineteenth century that speed really did take a toll. Thousands were dying every year in accidents involving the new vessels of velocity—bicycles, cars, buses, trams, trains, steamships.

As the pace of life accelerated, many spoke out against the dehumanizing effects of speed. Octave Mirbeau, a French writer, observed in 1908, "(Our) thoughts, feelings, and loves are a whirlwind. Everywhere life is rushing insanely like a cavalry charge. . . . Everything around a man jumps, dances, gallops in a movement out of phase with his own." Through the twentieth century, resistance to the cult of speed grew, and began to coalesce into broad social movements. The counterculture earthquake of the 1960s inspired millions to slow down and live more simply. A similar philosophy gave birth to the Voluntary Simplicity movement. In the late 1980s, the New York–based Trends Research Institute identified a phenomenon known as downshifting, which means swapping a high-pressure, high-earning, high-tempo lifestyle for a more relaxed, less consumerist existence. Unlike decelerators from the hippie generation, downshifters are driven less by political or environmental scruples than by the desire to lead more rewarding lives. They are willing to forgo money in return for time and slowness. Datamonitor, a London-based market research firm, expects the number of downshifters in Europe to rise from twelve million in 2002 to over sixteen million by 2007.

These days, many people are seeking refuge from speed in the safe harbour of spirituality. While mainstream Christian churches face dwindling congregations, their evangelical rivals are thriving. Buddhism is booming across the West, as are bookstores, chat rooms and healing centres dedicated to the eclectic, metaphysical doctrines of New Ageism. All of this makes sense at a time when people crave slowness. The spirit, by its very nature, is Slow. No matter how hard you try, you cannot accelerate enlightenment. Every religion teaches the need to slow down in order to connect with the self, with others and with a higher force. In Psalm 46, the Bible says: "Be still then, and know that I am God."

In the early twentieth century, Christian and Jewish clerics lent moral weight to the campaign for a shorter workweek, arguing that workers needed more time off in order to nourish their souls. Today, the same plea for slowness is once again emanating from pulpits around the world. A Google search turns up scores of sermons railing against the demon speed. In February 2002, at the First Unitarian Church in Rochester, New York, Reverend Gary James made an eloquent case for the Slow philosophy. In a sermon entitled "Slow Down!" he told his congregation that life "requires moments of intense exertion and quickened pace. . . . But it also requires a pause now and then—a Sabbath moment to assess where we are going, how quickly we wish to get there—and, more important, why. Slow can be beautiful." When Thich Nhat Hanh, a well-known Buddhist leader, visited Denver, Colorado, in 2002, more than five thousand people came to hear him speak. He urged them to slow down, "to take the time to live more deeply." New Age gurus preach a similar message.

So does that mean we have to be spiritual, or "New Age-y," to be Slow? In our cynical, secular world, it is a question that matters. Many people, including me, are wary of any movement that promises to open the door to spiritual nirvana. Religion has never been a big part of my life, and many New Age practices strike me as mumbo-jumbo. I want to slow down without being bullied into finding God or embracing crystals and astrology. Ultimately, the success of the Slow movement will depend on how smoothly it can reconcile people like me with decelerators of a more spiritual bent.

It will also depend on the economic case for saying no to speed. How much, if any, material wealth will we have to sacrifice, individually and collectively, in order to live Slow? Are we able, or willing, to pay the price? And to what extent is slowing down a luxury for the affluent? These are big questions that the Slow movement must answer.

If they are to make any headway at all, pro-Slow campaigners must root out the deep prejudice against the very idea of slowing down. In many quarters, "slow" remains a dirty word. Just look at how the *Oxford English Dictionary* defines it: "not understanding readily, dull, uninteresting, not learning easily, tedious, slack, sluggish." Hardly the sort of stuff you would put on your CV. In our hyped-up, faster-is-better culture, a turbocharged life is still the ultimate trophy on the mantelpiece. When people moan, "Oh, I'm so busy, I'm run off my feet, my life is a blur, I haven't got time for anything," what they often mean is, "Look at me: I am hugely important, exciting and energetic." Though men seem to like speed more than women, both sexes indulge in faster-than-thou one-upmanship. With a mixture of pride and pity, New Yorkers marvel at the slower pace of life elsewhere in the United States. "It's like they're on vacation all the time," sniffs one female Manhattanite. "If they tried to live like that in New York, they'd be toast."

Perhaps the greatest challenge of the Slow movement will be to fix our neurotic relationship with time itself. To teach us, in the words of Golda Meir, the former Israeli leader, how to " . . . govern the clock, not be governed by it." This may already be happening, below the radar. As the Curator of Time at the Science Museum in London, David

Rooney oversees a splendid collection of five hundred time-keeping devices, ranging from ancient sundials and hour-glasses to modern quartz watches and atomic clocks. Not surprisingly, the bespectacled twenty-eight-year-old has a claustrophobic relationship with time. On his wrist he wears a terrifyingly accurate radio-controlled watch. An antenna hidden in the wristband receives a daily update from Frankfurt. If the watch misses a signal, the number 1 appears in the lower left corner of the screen. If it misses the next day's signal, the number changes to 2, and so on. All of this accuracy makes Rooney very anxious indeed.

"I feel a real sense of loss when I miss my signal," he tells me as we wander round the museum's Measuring Time exhibit, raising our voices to be heard over the persistent tick-tock-tick-tock. "When the counter on the watch reaches 2, I get worried. Once it went to 3, and I had to leave it in a drawer at home. I get stressed knowing it's just a millisecond out."

Rooney knows this is not healthy behaviour, but he sees hope for the rest of us. The historical trend towards embracing ever more accurate timepieces has finally come to an end with the radio-controlled watch, which failed to catch on as a consumer product. People would rather put style ahead of accuracy by wearing a Swatch or a Rolex. Rooney thinks this reflects a subtle shift in our feelings about time.

"In the Industrial Revolution, when life became ruled by work, we lost control over our use of time," he says. "What we're seeing now is maybe the beginnings of a reaction against that. People seem to have reached the point where they don't want to have their time diced up into smaller and smaller pieces, with greater and greater accuracy. They don't want to be obsessed with time, or a slave to the clock. There may be an element of 'the boss keeps time, so I don't want to.'"

A few months after our meeting, Rooney decided to tackle his own obsessive timekeeping. Instead of fretting over mislaid milliseconds, he now wears a 1960s windup watch that is usually around five minutes off. "It's my own reaction against too much accuracy," he tells me. Rooney deliberately chose a windup watch to symbolize regaining the upper hand over time. "If you don't wind it every day, it stops, so you're in control," he says. "I feel like time is working for me now, rather than the other way round, which makes me feel less pressured. I don't hurry so much."

Some people are going even further. On a recent trip to Germany, my interpreter raved about the benefits of not wearing a watch at all. He remains scrupulously punctual, thanks to the clock on his mobile phone, but his former obsession with minutes and seconds is waning. "Not having a watch on my wrist definitely makes me more relaxed about time," he told me. "It is easier for me to slow down, because time is not always there in my line of vision saying, 'No, you must not slow down, you must not waste me, you must hurry.'"

Time is certainly a hot topic these days. How should we use it? Who controls it? How can we be less neurotic about it? Jeremy Rifkin, the American economist, thinks it could be the defining issue of the twenty-first century. "A battle is brewing over the politics of time," he wrote in his 1987 book *Time Wars*. "Its outcome could determine the future course of politics around the world in the coming century." It will certainly help to determine the future of the Slow movement.

CHAPTER THREE

FOOD: TURNING THE TABLES ON SPEED

We are what we eat.
—Ludwig Feuerbach, nineteenth-century
German philosopher

Have you ever seen *The Jetsons*, the old American cartoon about life in the distant, high-tech future? It gave many children their first glimpse of what the twenty-first century might look like. The Jetsons were a traditional family of four who inhabited a world where everything was super-fast, ultra-convenient and totally manmade. Spaceships blazed across the sky, couples vacationed on Venus, robots dashed through the domestic chores. When it came to cooking, the Jetsons left McDonald's in the dust. At the push of a button, their "home food dispenser" spat out synthetic servings of lasagna, roast chicken and chocolate brownies. The family lapped it up. Sometimes, the Jetsons just ate pills for dinner.

Even growing up in a foodie household, I remember liking the idea of an all-in-one meal pill. I imagined gulping it down and heading straight back outside to play with my friends. Of course, the idea of instant food was not invented by *The Jetsons*—it is an inevitable fantasy in a culture desperate to do everything faster. In 1958, four years before the first episode of *The Jetsons* was made, *Cosmopolitan* magazine predicted, without a hint of sadness, that one day every meal would be prepared in the microwave, which first hit the consumer market in the early 1950s. To remind us of a time when cooking was less rushed and more real, we would spray artificial aromas—think fresh bread, sizzling sausages, roasted garlic—around the kitchen. In the end, the *Cosmo* prophecy turned out to be only half true: these days we are in too much of a hurry to bother with the fake smells. Food, like everything else, has been hijacked by haste. Even if the instant meal pill remains the stuff of sci-fi fantasy, we have all taken a leaf out of the Jetsons' cookbook.

Hurry took its place at the dinner table during the Industrial Revolution. In the nineteenth century, long before the invention of the drive-thru burger bar, one observer summed up the American way of eating as "gobble, gulp and go." Margaret Visser notes, in *The Rituals of Dinner,* that industrializing societies came to prize speed as a "sign of control and efficiency" in formal dining. By the late 1920s, Emily Post, the doyenne of American etiquette, decreed that a dinner party should last no longer than two and a half hours, from the first ring of the doorbell to the departure of the last guest. Today, most meals are little more than refuelling pit stops. Instead of sitting down with family or friends, we often eat solo, on the move or while doing something else—working, driving, reading the newspaper, surfing the Net. Nearly half of Britons now eat their evening meal in front of the TV, and the average British family spends more time together in the car than they do around the table. When families do eat together, it is often at fast-food joints like McDonald's, where the average meal lasts eleven minutes. Visser reckons that communal dining is too slow for the modern world: "In comparison with acting out a sudden whim to consume a microwaved mug of soup within the next five minutes, eating together with friends can come to seem a formal, implacably structured and time-consuming event . . . whereas being in one's own personal hurry must be free and preferable."

The acceleration at the table is mirrored on the farm. Chemical fertilizers and pesticides, intensive feeding, antibiotic digestive enhancers, growth hormones, rigorous breeding, genetic modification—every scientific trick known to man has been deployed to cut costs, boost yields and make livestock and crops grow more quickly. Two centuries ago, the average pig took five years to reach 130 pounds; today, it hits 220 pounds after just six months and is slaughtered before it loses its baby teeth. North American salmon are genetically modified to grow four to six times faster than the average. The small landowner gives way to the factory farm, which churns out food that is fast, cheap, abundant and standardized.

As our forebears moved into the cities and lost touch with the land, they fell in love with the idea of fast food for a fast age. The more processed, the more convenient, the better. Restaurants in the 1950s gave tinned soups pride of place on the menu. At Tad's 30 Varieties of Meals, an American chain, diners cooked frozen meals at tableside microwave ovens. Around the same time, the big fast-food chains began applying the ruthless logic of mass production that would eventually bring us the 99-cent hamburger.

As life got faster, people rushed to replicate the convenience of fast food at home. In 1954, Swanson unveiled the first TV dinner—a highly processed, all-in-one platter containing turkey with cornbread dressing and gravy, sweet potatoes and buttered peas. Husbands angry that their wives no longer cooked from scratch deluged the company with hate mail, but the cult of convenience rolled on like a juggernaut. Five years later, another classic culinary time-saver, the instant noodle, made its debut in Japan. Everywhere food came to be marketed less for its flavour and nutritional value than for how little time it took to make. Uncle Ben's famously wooed harried housewives with the slogan: "Long grain rice that's ready in . . . five minutes!"

Once microwave ovens colonized kitchens in the 1970s, cooking was measured in seconds. Suddenly, Swanson's original TV dinner, which took twenty-five minutes to cook in a conventional oven, looked sundial slow. The cake-mix market collapsed like a bungled soufflé because not enough people were willing to sacrifice thirty minutes to work up the recipe. Today, even the simplest fare, from scrambled eggs to mashed potatoes, comes in an instant format. Supermarkets stock ready-made versions of almost every meal under the sun—curries, hamburgers, roast meats, sushi, salads, stews, casseroles, soups. To keep pace with its impatient customers, Uncle Ben's developed microwaveable rice that's ready in two minutes.

Of course, attitudes to food are not the same everywhere. Americans devote less time than anyone else—about an hour a day—to eating, and are more likely to buy processed food and to dine alone. Britons and Canadians are not much better. In southern Europe, where good food is still seen as a cultural birthright, people are nevertheless learning to eat with Anglo-Saxon haste during the week. In Paris, which fancies itself the world capital of fine dining, cafés specializing in *réstauration rapide* are stealing trade from the laidback bistros of yesteryear. At Goûts et Saveurs, in the ninth arrondissement, lunch is a twenty-minute affair where the wine is poured as soon as you sit down and the food comes straight from the microwave. At the Hôtel Montalembert on the Left Bank, the chef serves a three-course lunch on a single airline-style tray.

Nearly two hundred years ago, Anthelme Brillat-Savarin, the legendary French gastronome, remarked that "The destiny of nations depends upon the manner in which they feed themselves." That caveat is more apt today than ever before. In our haste, we feed ourselves badly, and suffer the consequences. Obesity rates are rocketing, in part because we wolf down processed food packed with sugar and fat. We all know the results of picking produce before it reaches full ripeness, shipping it across the planet in refrigerated containers and then ripening it artificially: avocadoes that go from rock hard to rotten overnight; tomatoes that taste like cotton wool. In the pursuit of low costs and high turnover, industrial farms do damage to livestock, the environment and even the consumer. Intensive agriculture is now a leading cause of water pollution in most Western countries. In his bestselling exposé, *Fast Food Nation,* Eric Schlosser revealed that mass-produced American ground beef is often tainted with fecal matter and other pathogens. Thousands of Americans catch E-coli poisoning from hamburgers every year. Scratch the surface and the "cheap food" brought to us by factory farms turns out to be a false economy. In 2003, researchers at Essex University calculated that British taxpayers spend up to £2.3 billion every year repairing the damage that industrial farming does to the environment and human health.

Many of us have swallowed the idea that when it comes to food, faster is better. We are in a hurry, and we want meals to match. But many people are waking up to the drawbacks of the gobble-gulp-and-go ethos. On the farm, in the kitchen and at the table, they are slowing down. Leading the charge is an international movement with a name that says it all: Slow Food.

Rome is the capital city of a nation in love with food. On shady terraces overlooking the vine-clad hills of Tuscany, lunch stretches deep into the afternoon. As the clock strikes midnight in *osterie* up and down Italy, couples are still flirting over plates of prosciutto and handmade ravioli. Yet these days Italians often take a faster approach to food. Young Romans are more likely to grab a Big Mac on the run than to spend the afternoon making fresh pasta. Fast-food joints have sprung up all over the country. All is not lost, though. The culture of *mangiare bene* still informs the Italian psyche, and that is why Italy is at the forefront of the movement for culinary slowness.

It all started in 1986, when McDonald's opened a branch beside the famous Spanish Steps in Rome. To many locals, this was one restaurant too far: the barbarians were inside the gates and something had to be done. To roll back the fast-food tsunami sweeping across the planet, Carlo Petrini, a charismatic culinary writer, launched Slow Food. As the name suggests, the movement stands for everything that McDonald's does not: fresh, local, seasonal produce; recipes handed down through the generations; sustainable farming; artisanal production; leisurely dining with family and friends. Slow Food also preaches "eco-gastronomy"—the notion that eating well can, and should, go hand in hand with protecting the environment. At its heart, though, the movement is about pleasure.

Petrini thinks this is a good starting point for tackling our obsession with speed in all walks of life. The group's manifesto states: "A firm defence of quiet material pleasure is the only way to oppose the universal folly of Fast Life. . . . Our defence should begin at the table with Slow Food."

With its very modern message—eat well and still save the planet—Slow Food has attracted seventy-eight thousand members in more than fifty countries. In 2001, the

New York Times Magazine named it one of the "80 ideas that shook the world (or at least jostled it a little)." Aptly enough, Slow Food takes the snail as its symbol, but that does not mean the members are lazy or sluggish. Even in the sticky heat of July, the head office in Bra, a small city south of Turin, buzzes with young, cosmopolitan staff fielding emails, editing press releases and putting the finishing touches on the newsletter that is sent to every member in the world. Slow Food also publishes a quarterly magazine in five languages and a host of respected food and wine guides. Other projects include setting up an online catalogue of every artisanal food on the planet.

All over the world, Slow Food activists organize dinners, workshops, school visits and other events to promote the benefits of taking our time over what we eat. Education is key. In 2004, Slow Food will open its own University of Gastronomic Sciences at Pollenzo, near Bra, where students will study not only the science of food, but also its history and sensual character. The movement has already persuaded the Italian state to build "food studies" into the school curriculum. In 2003, Petrini himself helped the German government lay the groundwork for a nationwide "taste education" program.

On the economic side, Slow Food seeks out artisanal foods that are on the way to extinction and helps them gain a foothold in the global market. It puts small producers in touch with one another, shows them how to slice through red tape and promotes their wares to chefs, shops and gourmets around the world. In Italy, over 130 dying delicacies have been saved, including lentils from Abruzzi, Ligurian potatoes, the black celery of Trevi, the Vesuvian apricot and purple asparagus from Albenga. Not long ago, Slow Food rescued a breed of Sienese wild boar once prized in the courts of medieval Tuscany. The pigs are now being reared—and turned into succulent sausages, salamis and hams—on a thriving Tuscan farm. Similar rescue operations are underway in other countries. Slow Food is working to save the Firiki apple and traditional olive oil–soaked ladotiri cheese in Greece. In France it has thrown its weight behind the Pardigone plum and a delicate goat's cheese called Brousse du Ruve.

As you might expect, Slow Food is strongest in Europe, which has a rich tradition of indigenous cuisine, and where fast-food culture is less entrenched. But the movement is also making strides across the Atlantic. Its American membership is eight thousand and rising. In the United States, Slow Food helped persuade *Time* magazine to run a feature on the Sun Crest peach of northern California, a fruit that tastes sublime but travels badly. After the article appeared, the small producer was inundated with buyers wanting to sample his crop. Slow Food is also leading a successful campaign to resurrect the tasty rare-breed turkeys—Naragansett, Jersey Buff, Standard Bronze, Bourbon Red—that were the centrepiece of every American family's Thanksgiving supper until bland factory-farmed birds took over.

Slow Food has not been afraid to take on the powers that be. In 1999, it raised over half a million signatures in a campaign that eventually persuaded the Italian government to amend a law that would have forced even the smallest food-maker to conform to the rigid hygiene standards used by corporate giants such as Kraft Foods. As a result, thousands of traditional producers were saved from a flood of unnecessary paperwork. With backing from Slow Food, artisanal cheese-makers formed a Europe-wide alliance in 2003 to fight for the right to work with raw milk. The campaign against pasteurization will soon cross to North America.

As part of its ecological credo, Slow Food opposes the genetic modification of foodstuffs and promotes organic farming. Nobody has conclusively proven that organic food is more nutritious or better tasting than non-organic, but it is clear that the methods used by many conventional farmers take a toll on the environment, polluting the water table, killing off other plants and exhausting the soil. According to the Smithsonian Migratory Bird Center, pesticides, directly or indirectly, kill at least sixty-seven million American birds every year. By contrast, a well-run organic farm can use crop rotation to enrich the soil and manage pests—and still be very productive.

Slow Food also fights for biodiversity. In the food industry, haste leads to homogenization: manufacturers can process inputs—be they turkeys, tomatoes or turnips—more quickly if they are all the same. So the pressure is on farmers to concentrate on single strains or breeds. Over the last century, for instance, the number of artichoke varieties grown in Italy has tumbled from two hundred to about a dozen. Besides narrowing our choice of flavours, the loss of fauna upsets delicate ecosystems. By putting our eggs in fewer baskets, we court disaster. When all you have is one breed of turkey, a single virus can wipe out the whole species.

With its love of the small, the unhurried and the local, Slow Food seems like a natural-born enemy of global capitalism. But nothing could be further from the truth. Slow Food campaigners are not against globalization per se. Many artisanal products, from Parmesan cheese to traditional soya sauce, travel well—and need overseas markets to thrive. When Petrini talks of "virtuous globalization," he is thinking of trade agreements that allow European chefs to import quinoa from a family farm in Chile, or the information technology that permits a smoked salmon specialist in the Scottish Highlands to find customers in Japan.

The virtues of globalization are on full display at the Salone del Gusto, Slow Food's biannual jamboree. Held in a former Fiat factory in Turin, Salone 2002 was the mother of all smorgasbords, attracting five hundred artisanal food producers from thirty countries. Over five waist-expanding days, 138,000 people strolled among the stalls, soaking up the wonderful aromas and sampling the exquisite cheeses, hams, fruits, sausages, wines, pastas, breads, mustards, preserves and chocolates. All over the Salone, people networked as they nibbled. A Japanese sake-maker discussed Internet marketing with a Bolivian llama herder. Bakers from France and Italy compared notes on stone-ground flours.

Everywhere you looked, someone was turning the principles of Slow Food into profit. Susana Martinez had travelled from Jujuy, a province in the remote, rugged north of Argentina, to promote yacon, an ancient Andean root that was slipping into oblivion. Sweet and crunchy, like jicama or water chestnut, yacon is easy on the waistline because its sugars pass through the human body unmetabolized. With help from Slow Food, Martinez and forty other families are now growing it on small, organic plots for export. Orders are flooding in from overseas, with posh restaurants in Spain eager to put the root on the menu and Japanese retailers clamouring for crates of yacon jam. At Salone 2002, Martinez was upbeat. "When you look around the Salone, at all the different producers, you realize that you don't have to be big and fast to survive," she said. "You can be small and slow and still be successful. More and more people in the world want to eat things that are produced in a natural, non-industrial way."

With so much emphasis on eating, you might expect everyone at the Salone to be of Pavarotti proportions. Far from it. There is a lot more surplus flesh wobbling round your average Dunkin' Donuts. But the sensual pleasures of the table are definitely more important to the Slow Food crowd than being able to swap dresses with Calista Flockhart. That is why Elena Miro, an Italian fashion designer who specializes in clothes for larger women, had a stall at Salone 2002. A curvy young model named Viviane Zunino was handing out brochures when I visited. She scoffed at the catwalk queens who live on mineral water and salad leaves. "Diets just make people unhappy," she said. "One of the most beautiful things in life is taking the time to sit round the table with friends and family to enjoy really good food and wine." A middle-aged man with an

enormous belly waddled past, breathing heavily and dab-
bing his forehead with a silk handkerchief. We watched him
make a beeline for the biscuits lathered with jalapeño jelly at
the US stall. Zunino smiled: "There are limits, though."

The Slow Food movement is part of a much broader
backlash against the high-speed, high-turnover culture of
the global food industry. After half a century of relentless
growth, McDonald's recorded its first losses in 2002 and
immediately began closing overseas branches. All over the
world, consumers are steering clear of the golden arches
because they find the food inside uninspiring and
unhealthy. For many, boycotting the Big Mac is a way of
saying no to the global standardization of taste. As Philip
Hensher, a British commentator, noted, people are finally
waking up to the fact that "their own culture does not, and
will not, depend on a burnt hamburger in a calcium-
peroxide-flavoured bun." On home turf, McDonald's faces
an avalanche of lawsuits from Americans claiming its food
made them obese.

Across the world, food-makers of all stripes are proving
that small and slow are not only beautiful, but profitable,
too. Fifteen years ago, for instance, two large companies,
Miller and Busch, dominated the US beer market. Today,
fifteen hundred craft breweries make beer following Slow
Food principles. Artisanal bakers are also making a comeback and showing that time is an essential ingredient of
good bread. Most use stone-ground flour, rather than the
cheaper, industrial equivalent, which passes through high-
speed rollers that destroy many of the natural nutrients.

Real bakers also favour longer proving times—anywhere from sixteen hours to three days—to let the dough ferment and develop flavour. The result is bread that tastes better and is more nutritious. A local bakery can also help people reconnect with their community. Round the corner from my house in London, two former publishers opened the Lighthouse Bakery in 2001. Apart from making heavenly bread, one of their aims was to create a social hub. The line-up on Saturday morning is now the perfect place to bump into neighbours and catch up on local gossip.

Chickens are also enjoying more slowness nowadays. Living a measly four weeks, most of it in cramped coops, the factory-farmed chicken produces meat with as much taste and texture as tofu. More and more farmers, though, are now raising poultry in the Slow style. At the Leckford Estate in Hampshire, England, the chickens spend up to three months roaming freely round the farm. At night, they sleep in spacious sheds. The birds produce meat that is firm, juicy and flavourful. To win back consumers fed up with industrial broilers, Japanese farmers are also returning to slower growing, better tasting breeds of chickens, such as the Akita hinaidori and the Nagoya cochin.

Nothing, however, illustrates the spread of the Slow Food gospel better than the renaissance of the traditional farmers' market. In towns and cities across the industrial world, and often a few blocks from large supermarkets, farmers are once again selling their fruits, vegetables, cheeses and meats directly to the public. Not only do consumers like putting a face to the food, but the produce usually tastes better. The fruit and vegetables are seasonal, left to ripen naturally, and travel only short distances. Nor is the farmers' market a plaything for the gourmet minority. Prices are often lower than in supermarkets, which spend a fortune on transport, advertising, staff and storage. The three thousand farmers' markets in the United States now turn over more than $1 billion in annual revenue, allowing nearly twenty thousand farmers to opt out of the industrial food chain altogether.

Many people are going one step further and cultivating their own produce. All over Britain, young urbanites are queuing up to rent small plots of land from their local authorities. At the "allotments" near my house, you can see yuppies stepping out of BMW Roadsters to check on their rocket, carrots, new potatoes and chillies.

As consumers become more discerning, everyone is forced to raise their game. Ambitious restaurants make a point of cooking with ingredients sourced directly from local farms. Manufacturers sell higher grade convenience and takeout food. Supermarkets clear shelf space for cheeses, sausages and other goods made by artisanal producers.

A common denominator in all of these trends is flavour. Industrial methods knock much of the natural taste out of food. Consider the case of cheddar cheese. The factory-made stuff on sale in supermarkets tends to be boring and predictable. Artisanal cheddar, made by hand with natural ingredients, offers a kaleidoscope of subtle flavours that vary from one batch to the next.

Neal's Yard Dairy, in London's Covent Garden, stocks around eighty cheeses from small producers in Britain and Ireland. The shop is a feast for the senses. Behind the counter and along the painted wooden shelves, crumbly Wensleydales jostle with creamy Stiltons, giving off a delightful aroma. Flavour is king here. Neal's Yard sells a range of artisanal cheddars, each with its own distinct character. The one made by Keen's is soft, a little waxy, with sharp, grassy notes. Montgomery cheddar is drier, firmer, with a nutty, savoury taste. Lincolnshire Poacher is smooth and mellow, with a hint of Alpine sweetness. A Scottish cheddar from the Isle of Mull, where grass is scarce and the cows mainly survive on draff from a local brewery, is much paler than the rest, with a wild, almost gamey taste.

When it comes to pleasure, factory cheese simply cannot compete. Most leave little impression on the taste buds. The flavours in an artisanal cheese, by contrast, develop slowly in the mouth, and then linger, tickling the palate like a fine wine. "Often a customer will taste a cheese, not be very impressed, and then move on down the counter," says Randolph Hodgson, the founder and manager of Neal's Yard Dairy. "After a few seconds, though, the flavour hits them. Their head suddenly turns and they say: 'Wow, that actually tastes really nice.'"

Producing food in a Slow manner is just the beginning. Even in these convenience-mad times, many of us are setting aside more time for cooking and eating. People are flocking to cookery holidays in Thailand, Tuscany and other exotic locations. Young Italians are signing up for courses to learn the kitchen tricks that *mamma* failed to teach them. North American companies arrange for their staff to cook a sumptuous meal together as a team-building exercise. Celebrity chefs such as Nigella Lawson, Jamie Oliver and Emeril Lagasse rule the airwaves and sell millions of recipe books. True, many of their fans are voyeurs, munching on Pot Noodle or Domino's Pizza while watching the stars work their magic in the kitchen. But their message—slow down and enjoy making and eating your food—is sinking in, even in some of the most hurried places on earth.

In Japan, where fast food is endemic, Slow Food is on the rise. There is a trend among the young to cook for fun. After years of gulping down dinner in front of the television, some Japanese people are rediscovering the joys of communal dining. Retailers report growing sales of the *chabudai,* a small, round portable table that diners kneel at together.

The Slow Food gospel is also gaining ground in hurry-up New York. When I visit, the city is its usual seething self. People move through the streets with energy and purpose, despite the heavy summer heat. At midday, everyone seems to grab a stuffed bagel or a salad on the hop. The first magazine I pick up has an article claiming that the average business lunch has been downsized to thirty-six minutes. And yet some New Yorkers are making more time for food. Take Matthew Kovacevich and Catherine Creighton, a thirty-something married couple who work together in a Manhattan marketing firm. Like many denizens of the Big Apple, they used to have only a nodding acquaintance with their kitchen. Warming up prepared soups or stirring canned sauces into pasta was the nearest they got to cooking, and supper was often takeout eaten in front of the TV. Then a holiday in southern Europe changed everything.

When I visit their apartment in Brooklyn, we sit at the dining room table, sipping California chardonnay and eating organic goat's cheese topped with homemade red pepper jelly. Matthew, a burly thirty-one-year-old, explains his conversion to gastronomic slowness with the fervour of the true believer: "In the States, we think we do things better because we do them faster. And it's very easy to get sucked into that lifestyle. But when you see how the French or the Italians eat, how much time and respect they give to food, you realize how wrong the American way can be."

Fresh off the plane from Europe, Matthew and Catherine set about living by the Slow Food manual. Instead of grazing in the kitchen, or snacking alone in front of the TV, they now try, whenever possible, to sit down together for a home-cooked supper. Even when the workday stretches to twelve hours, the couple still makes room for Slow Food touches. That might mean pairing a supermarket roast chicken with a homemade salad. Or even just setting the table to dine on takeout pizza.

Everything they eat tastes better now, and food is a feature of most weekends. They spend Saturday mornings browsing in the farmers' market in Grand Army Plaza. Catherine bakes pies with whatever fruit is in season—strawberry and rhubarb, blueberry, peach, apple—and

Matthew makes his own pesto. Producing his delicious barbecue sauce takes all of Sunday morning, a long, slow dance of chopping, grating, stirring, simmering, tasting, seasoning and just plain waiting. "A lot of the pleasure is in the fact that you don't hurry it," he says.

Cooking can be so much more than just a chore. It connects us with what we eat—where it came from, how the flavours work, what it will do for our health. Making food that gives pleasure to other people can be a real joy. When you have enough time for it, when hurry is not part of the recipe, cooking is also a wonderful way to unwind. It has an almost meditative quality. Slowing down with food makes the rest of Matthew's life seem less frantic. "It's easy in a city like New York to get so wound up that you end up rushing everything," he says. "Cooking gives you a little oasis of slowness. It re-grounds you and that helps you avoid the superficiality of urban life."

Matthew and Catherine feel a Slow approach to food has strengthened their relationship, too, which is not surprising. There is something in the nature of cooking and eating together that forms a bond between people. It is no accident that the word "companion" is derived from Latin words meaning "with bread." A relaxed, convivial meal has a calming, even civilizing, effect, smoothing away the smash-and-grab haste of modern life. The Kwakiutl people of British Columbia warn that fast eating can "bring about the destruction of the world more quickly by increasing the aggressiveness" in it. Oscar Wilde expressed a similar sentiment with a typically barbed aphorism:

"After a good dinner one can forgive anybody, even one's own relations."

Sharing a meal can do more than just help us get along better. Studies in several countries suggest that children from families that regularly eat together are more likely to succeed at school and less liable to suffer from stress or to smoke and drink at an early age. Taking the time to eat a proper meal can also pay dividends in the workplace, where desktop dining rules. Jessie Yoffe, who works for an accountancy firm in Washington, DC, used to lunch in front of her computer. She felt her workaholic boss would disapprove if she took time to eat outside the office, even on quiet days. Then, one afternoon, she was munching on a salad while perusing a contract when she realized she had just read the same paragraph six times without taking any of it in. She decided then and there to start leaving the office for a lunch break, no matter what her boss said. On most days, she now spends half an hour eating in a nearby park or café, often with a friend. She has lost 5 pounds, and uncovered new reserves of energy. "It's funny, because you think that if you spend less time at your desk you'll get less work done, but that isn't what happens," says Yoffe. "I find that taking time to eat relaxes me, and I get a lot more done in the afternoons than I did before." Without mentioning the new lunching regime, her boss recently complimented Yoffe on the improvement in her work.

Eating at a gentle pace is also good for the waistline, because it gives the stomach time to tell the brain that it is full. Dr. Patrick Serog, a nutritionist at Bichat Hospital in

Paris, says, "It takes fifteen minutes for the brain to register the signal that you have eaten too much, and if you eat too quickly, that signal comes too late. You can easily eat more than you need without knowing it and that's why it is better to eat slowly."

As any seasoned dieter will tell you, changing what we eat and the way we eat it is not easy. But it is possible to wean people off the Fast approach to food, especially if you catch them young. Some British schools now take children to farms to learn where their meals come from. Others encourage them to cook and design menus for the school cafeteria. When given the choice, many kids choose real food that takes time to prepare over processed snacks.

In Canada, Jeff Crump spends a lot of time re-educating young palates. Despite growing up in a family where home cooking meant hot dogs, Crump is now head chef at a restaurant based in a farmers' market outside Toronto. At thirty-one, he is also the leader of Slow Food Ontario. "I'm living proof that with a little curiosity anyone can learn to love good food," he says. On a warm September evening, I join Crump on the culinary campaign trail. The scene is a cooking school in downtown Toronto. Fifteen children, aged from nine to sixteen, sit on stools round a wooden table in the main classroom. Most are from middle-class families where busy parents serve up processed food with a side order of guilt. The children are here to compare Kraft Dinner with a Slow Food version of the same dish.

Dressed in pristine chef whites, Crump begins by assembling the ingredients for a real macaroni and cheese—milk, butter, eggs, cheese, pasta, salt and pepper. Alongside them, he empties out the contents of a box of Kraft Dinner—dried macaroni with a sachet of bright orange flavouring powder. As he talks about the chemicals in processed food, his assistant whips up a batch of Kraft Dinner on the stainless steel stove, boiling the pasta and then stirring in the powder with some milk and butter. When it is ready, Crump removes his own homemade macaroni and cheese, prepared earlier, from the oven. The taste test begins. Silence descends as the children sample the rival pastas, then all hell breaks loose as the amateur critics noisily compare notes. Twelve of the fifteen prefer the Slow Food version. Sarah, a thirteen-year-old, says: "When you have Kraft Dinner by itself you don't really think about what it tastes like, you just eat it. But when you have it side by side on the plate with real macaroni and cheese you realize how much it tastes like chemicals. It's gross. Jeff's is way better. It tastes like cheese is supposed to taste." Afterwards, Crump hands out copies of his recipe. Several children hope it will replace Kraft Dinner at home. Sarah vows to cook it herself. "I'll definitely make this," she says, tucking the recipe into her knapsack.

Some critics dismiss Slow Food as a club for affluent epicureans—and when you watch members spending hundreds of dollars on truffle shavings at the Salone del Gusto, it is easy see why. But charges of elitism are actually wide of the mark. Fine dining is just one aspect of the movement. Slow Food has plenty to offer those on a tight budget, too.

After all, eating Slow does not always mean eating expensively. Fruit and vegetables often cost less at farmers' markets. As demand grows, and efficiency improves, the price of organic food is coming down. In Britain, co-operatives are springing up in deprived areas, offering produce from local farms—as well as tips on how to cook it—at affordable prices. Cooking at home is also a surefire way to save money. Meals made from scratch tend to be cheaper—as well as tastier—than the ready-made alternative. Pre-scrambled eggs cost twenty times more than uncooked ones from a carton.

On the other hand, many Slow foods, by their very nature, are pricier than their mass-produced rivals. A burger made with organic beef from grass-fed cattle will never be as cheap as a Whopper, and a free-range chicken will always cost more than the factory-farmed equivalent. That is the price we pay for eating better. The trouble is that the world has grown accustomed to cheap food. Half a century ago, the average European family spent up to half its income on feeding itself. Today that figure is nearer 15%, and is even lower in Britain and North America. Italians spend 10% of their income on their cellphones, versus 12% on what they eat. Yet change is stirring. In the post–mad cow disease era, polls show a strong willingness to spend more money and time on food.

Inspired by the growing appetite for culinary deceleration, and eager to put the Petrini principles to the test, I set off in pursuit of the perfect Slow Food meal. My quest takes me to Borgio-Varezzi, a bustling resort town just along the coast from Genoa. It is high summer, and the streets leading to the beach are thronged with Italian holi-daymakers, padding in and out of the bars and *gelaterie* in flip-flops. I pick my way through the crowds and walk up the hill to the narrow, cobbled streets of the old quarter. My destination is Da Casetta, a family-run restaurant singled out for special praise by the Slow Food guide.

I arrive at opening time, 8 P.M., to confirm my booking for later in the evening. Already, the first customers of the night, a young couple, are at the door. Cinzia Morelli, a member of the family, gently turns them away. "I'm sorry, but we're still preparing the antipasti," she says. "You could have a drink, or maybe go for a walk outside until we're ready." The couple take the delay in stride and stroll off into the old quarter with indulgent smiles that seem to say: we know the meal will be worth the wait.

An hour and a half later, I return for my own dinner, full of great expectations and an even greater appetite. The antipasti are ready now, arrayed like a flotilla of ships on a side table in the dining room. Cinzia steers me towards the wooden deck outside, where the tables look onto a scene straight from an Italian holiday brochure. Da Casetta nestles at the bottom of a sloping, tree-lined piazza. To one side, an eighteenth-century church rises above the red-tiled rooftops, its bells tolling lazily every half hour. Down in the cobbled square, nuns dressed in white huddle in small groups, whispering like schoolgirls. Couples canoodle in the shadows. Children's laughter spills from the balconies overhead.

My dining companion drifts into Da Casetta twenty-five minutes late. Vittorio Magnoni is a twenty-seven-year-old textile merchant and a member of the Slow Food movement. It's nearly 10 P.M., and he is in no hurry to order.

Instead, he settles into the chair opposite mine, lights a cigarette and launches into a report of his recent holiday in Sicily. He tells how the local fishermen catch tuna by stringing a single net between ships. Then he describes the various ways the fish is served up at the dinner table on shore—sliced into thin carpaccio, grilled with lemon, bobbing in hearty soups.

His descriptions are so mouth-watering that we are both relieved to see the waiter arrive. His name is Pierpaolo Morelli, and he looks like John McEnroe without the receding hairline. Pierpaolo explains how Da Casetta embodies the Slow Food ethos. Most flowers, vegetables and fruits on the menu come from the family garden. The dishes are all traditional Ligurian, assembled by hand, slowly and with *passione*. No one pops in for a quick bite on the fly. "This is the opposite of fast food," declares Pierpaolo. Even as he speaks, I notice the couple who arrived too early for the antipasti sitting a few tables away. The man is popping what looks like a shrimp into the woman's mouth. She eats it slowly, teasingly, and then places her hand on his cheek.

After ordering the food, we mull over the wine list. Pierpaolo returns to help us out. Muttering the names of our chosen dishes under his breath, he strokes his chin and looks up at the night sky for inspiration. After what seems an eternity, he finally delivers his verdict. "I have the perfect wine for your meal—a local Ligurian white," he says.

"It is *pigato*, with a little *vermentino* mixed in. I know the man who makes it."

The wine comes swiftly, and is exquisite, fresh and light. Then a plate of mixed antipasti arrives. It is a delightful medley: a tiny pizza; a sliver of asparagus torte; zucchini stuffed with egg, mortadella, parmesan, potato and parsley. Arranged in a small pile in the centre of the plate are the jewels in the crown: baby onions, or *cipolline*, roasted with vinegar. They are ambrosia, firm and yielding, sweet and tangy. "My father picked them in the garden this morning," says Pierpaolo, en route to another table.

Despite our hunger, we eat slowly, savouring every mouthful. All around us, wine flows, aromas waft, laughter dances on the cool evening air. A dozen conversations blur into a low, sweet, symphonic hum.

Vittorio shares the Italian passion for food and loves to cook. His speciality is pappardelle with prawns. While we eat, he talks me through its preparation, step by step. Detail is everything. "For the tomatoes, you must use the small ones from Sicily," he says. "And you cut them in half, no more." His other signature dish is spaghetti with clams. "You should always, always, strain the juice that comes from cooking the clams, to remove all the little hard bits," he says, wielding an imaginary sieve. As we wipe the antipasti plates clean with crusty homemade bread, we compare risotto recipes.

Now it's time for the *primo piatto*. Mine is *testaroli* with porcini mushrooms. Testaroli is a flat pasta cooked once, chilled, sliced, and then cooked again. Somehow it manages to be al dente and pleasingly squishy at the same time. The mushrooms, gathered locally, are earthy but light. The combination is sublime. Vittorio has chosen a different Ligurian speciality: *lumache alla verezzina*—snails in a nutty sauce. Another triumph.

Our conversation drifts away from food. Vittorio explains how northern Italians are more modern-minded than their southern cousins. "When I go to Naples, they can tell just by looking at me that I am from the north," he says. We talk about that other great Italian passion, *calcio,* or soccer. Vittorio reckons his favourite team, Juventus, still has what it takes to win European glory, despite having sold Zinedine Zidane, the midfield maestro that many regard as the world's best player. Then things get personal. Vittorio reveals that, like many Italian men, he still lives with *mamma.* "Life is very comfortable in an Italian family— you get your meals cooked, your clothes washed," he says, smiling. "But I have a fiancée now, so eventually I will move in with her."

Delighted with his snails, Vittorio starts singing the praises of Slow Food. He especially enjoys getting together with fellow members for meals that go on for hours. Vittorio sums up the Slow Food take on the modern world: "McDonald's is not genuine food; it fills you up without sustaining you. I think people are tired of eating things that have no taste, no history, no link with the land. They want something better."

As if on cue, Pierpaolo appears at my elbow with the main course: *cappon magro,* a Slow Food delicacy if ever there was one. The dish consists of layers of mixed seafood, *salsa verde,* potato and smoked tuna. With all the boning and de-shelling, cleaning and chopping, it takes four people three hours to make a dozen servings of real *cappon magro.* It is worth every minute, though: the dish is an *opera d'arte,* a work of art, the perfect marriage of sea and land.

We're halfway through this masterpiece when Vittorio drops a bombshell. "I have to tell you something," he says, a little sheepishly. "I sometimes eat at McDonald's." A stunned silence descends. A man at a nearby table, until now in thrall to his roast rabbit, looks up as though Vittorio has just broken wind.

"You what?" I say. "But isn't that heresy? Like a rabbi eating a ham sandwich?"

Loosened up by the wine, and emboldened by his own candour, Vittorio tries to explain his apostasy. "In Italy, there are very few options for those times when you want to eat fast: you either sit down in a restaurant for a meal or you eat a slice of pizza or you have a sandwich in a dirty bar," he says. "You can say a lot of things against McDonald's, but at least it is clean."

He pauses for a sip of wine. The man with the roast rabbit is listening intently now, his eyebrows crinkled like those of a cartoon character.

"I always feel a bit guilty after eating somewhere like McDonald's," says Vittorio. "But I think other Slow Food members eat there, too. They just keep quiet about it."

With that dirty little secret hanging in the air, we polish off the *cappon magro.* It is now time for dessert. Pierpaolo?

Pierpaolo? Ah, there he is, cleaning up a broken glass underneath a neighbouring table. He glides over to talk us through the *dolci*. A few minutes later, the desserts arrive— a chocolate torte with a dollop of mascarpone and zabaione cream; apple sorbet; strawberry bavaroise. All are exquisite, especially when paired with a local Malvasia wine, which is sweet, smooth and the colour of maple syrup. "Delicious," purrs Vittorio.

Wilde was right about the power of a good dinner to make one forgive anything. As we slide into post-prandial nirvana, that glorious state when the appetite is calmed and all is right in the world, Vittorio's McDonald's confession already seems like a distant memory. We drink strong espressos in companionable silence. Pierpaolo brings a bottle of grappa and two small glasses. After some more sipping and chatting, we are the only customers left in Da Casetta. The rest of the Morelli clan come out of the kitchen onto the deck for some fresh air. The mood is mellow and magnanimous.

I look at my watch. It is 1:25 A.M.! I have spent four hours at the table without ever once feeling bored or restless. Time has floated by imperceptibly, like water in a Venetian canal. Perhaps because of that, the meal has turned out to be one of the most memorable of my life. As I write these words, more than a year later, I can still recall the bittersweet smell of the *cipolline,* the delicate sea notes of the *cappon magro,* the sound of leaves ruffling in the darkened piazza.

In the afterglow of dinner at Da Casetta, it is easy to imagine that the future belongs to Slow Food. Yet the movement faces some serious obstacles. To start with, the global food industry is structured to favour high-turnover, low-cost production—and food manufacturers, long-distance transport companies, fast-food giants, advertising firms, supermarkets and industrial farms all have an interest in keeping it that way. In most countries, subsidy systems, regulations and supply chains are stacked against the Slow producer.

Fans of the status quo argue that industrial farming is the only way to feed the world's population, which is forecast to peak at ten billion in 2050. This seems logical: we need to accelerate output to make sure no one goes hungry. Yet the way we farm now is clearly unsustainable. Industrial agriculture ravages the environment. Some experts now believe the best way to the feed the world is to return to smaller-scale mixed farming, which strikes an eco-friendly balance between crops and livestock. Already, similar thinking is starting to sink in at the European Union level. In 2003, the EU finally agreed to reform its Common Agricultural Policy to reward farmers more for the quality, rather than the quantity, of their output and for safeguarding the environment.

When it comes to modifying our own behaviour, Slow Food is realistic. It recognizes that every meal cannot be a four-hour banquet of handmade delicacies. The modern world simply does not allow it. We live in fast times, and taking a Fast approach to food is often the only option. Sometimes all we want or need is a sandwich on the run. Yet it is possible to work some of the Slow Food ideas that inform the menu at Da Casetta into our own kitchens. The place to start is with the raw materials. Local, seasonal produce. Meat, cheese and bread from conscientious producers. Maybe even a few herbs, like mint, parsley and thyme, grown in the garden or on the balcony.

The next step is to cook more. After a long, bruising day at work, our reflex is to throw a ready-made meal in the microwave or call out for Thai food. But sometimes that reflex is just that: a reflex. It can be overcome; we can find the time and energy to do a little chopping, frying and boiling. In my experience, taking a deep breath and just heading into the kitchen can be enough to get over the I-can't-be-bothered-to-cook hump. And once there, the payoff is more than just gastronomic. As the crushed garlic slides into the pan of hot oil and starts to sizzle, I can feel the stresses of the day melting away.

Cooking a meal need not be a long and laborious affair. Anyone can rustle up a homemade supper in less time than it takes to have a pizza delivered. We're not talking about a *cappon magro*. A Slow dish can be quick and simple. A book stall at the Salone del Gusto stocked a magazine with recipes, from tomato pasta to mushroom soup, that took as little as fifteen minutes to prepare. Another way round the time crunch is to cook more than you need when you can and freeze the surplus. So instead of heating up a ready-made meal or phoning for a curry, you can defrost a homemade dish. In our house, we order a lot less takeout—and therefore save a fortune—now that the freezer is stocked with our own chili con carne and lentil dahl.

Certainly, we can all benefit from taking a Slow approach to the way we eat. Food is harder to enjoy when scoffed down on the run or in front of the television or computer. It becomes fuel. Savouring food is easier when you slow down and pay attention to it. I appreciate my supper a lot more at table than I do balancing it on my lap in front of the evening news or *Friends*.

Few of us have the time, money, energy or discipline to be a model Slow Foodie. Such is life in the fast-paced twenty-first century. Yet more and more of us are learning to slow down. Slow Food has captured the public imagination and spread across the planet because it touches on a basic human desire. We all like to eat well, and are healthier and happier when we do. Anthelme Brillat-Savarin put it best in his 1825 masterpiece *The Physiology of Taste:* "The pleasures of the table are for every man, of every land, of every place in history or society; they can be a part of all our other pleasures and they last the longest, to console us when we have outlived the rest."

CHAPTER FOUR

CITIES: BLENDING OLD AND NEW

The tide of life, swift always in its course,
May run in cities with a brisker force,
But nowhere with a current so serene,
Or half so clear, as in the rural scene.
—WILLIAM COWPER, 1782

AFTER MY MEETING WITH CARLO PETRINI, I set off on a walking tour of Bra. Even on a normal workday, the headquarter city of Slow Food seems like the perfect place to get away from it all. Locals linger over coffee at sidewalk tables, gossiping with friends or watching the world drift by. In the shady, tree-lined squares, where the air smells of lilac and lavender, old men sit like statues on the stone benches. Everyone has time to say a warm *"buon giorno."*

And no wonder. By local decree, *la dolce vita* is now the law of the land here. Inspired by Slow Food, Bra and three other Italian towns signed a pledge in 1999 to transform themselves into havens from the high-speed frenzy of the modern world. Every aspect of urban life is now recast in line with the Petrini principles—pleasure before profit, human beings before head office, Slowness before speed. The movement was christened Citta Slow, or Slow Cities, and now has more than thirty member towns in Italy and beyond.

For a denizen of chaotic, breathless London, putting the words "slow" and "city" side by side is instantly appealing. To see if the movement is more than just a pipe dream or a marketing ruse, I arrange to interview Bruna Sibille, deputy mayor of Bra and a driving force within Citta Slow. We meet in a conference room on the first floor of the town hall, a handsome fourteenth-century palazzo. Sibille stands at the window, admiring the view—a sea of red terracotta rooftops, skewered by the occasional church tower, stretching into the distance. As a young man cycles languidly through the piazza below, her mouth curls into a satisfied smile.

"The Slow movement was first seen as an idea for a few people who liked to eat and drink well, but now it has become a much broader cultural discussion about the benefits of doing things in a more human, less frenetic manner," she tells me. "It is not easy to swim against the tide, but we think the best way to administer a city is with the Slow philosophy."

The Citta Slow manifesto contains fifty-five pledges, such as cutting noise and traffic; increasing green spaces and pedestrian zones; backing local farmers and the shops, markets and restaurants that sell their produce; promoting technology that protects the environment; preserving local aesthetic and culinary traditions; and fostering a spirit of hospitality and neighbourliness. The hope is that the reforms will add up to more than the sum of their parts, that they will revolutionize the way people think about urban living. Sibille talks with zeal of "creating a new climate, an entirely new way of looking at life."

In other words, a Slow City is more than just a fast city slowed down. The movement is about creating an environment where people can resist the pressure to live by the clock and do everything faster. Sergio Contegiacomo, a young financial consultant in Bra, waxes lyrical about life in a Slow City. "The main thing is that you do not become obsessed with time. Instead you enjoy each moment as it comes," he says. "In a Slow City you have the licence to relax, to think, to reflect on the big existential questions. Rather than get caught up in the storm and speed of the modern world, where all you do is get in the car, go to work, then hurry home, you take time to walk and meet people in the street. It's a little bit like living in a fairy tale."

Despite their pining for kinder, gentler times, the Citta Slow campaigners are not Luddites. Being Slow does not mean being torpid, backward or technophobic. Yes, the movement aims to preserve traditional architecture, crafts and cuisine. But it also celebrates the best of the modern world. A Slow City asks the question: Does this improve our quality of life? If the answer is yes, then the city embraces it. And that includes the very latest technology. In Orvieto, a Slow City perched on a hilltop in Umbria, electric buses glide silently through the medieval streets. Citta Slow uses a snazzy website to promote its philosophy of *buon vivere,* or living well. "Let's make one thing very clear: being a Slow City does not mean stopping everything and turning back the clock," explains Sibille. "We do not want to live in museums or demonize all fast food; we want to strike a balance between the modern and the traditional that promotes good living."

Slowly but surely, Bra is working its way through the fifty-five pledges. In its *centro storico,* the city has closed some streets to traffic, and banned supermarket chains and lurid neon signs. Small family-run businesses—among them shops selling handwoven fabrics and speciality meats—are granted the best commercial real estate. City Hall subsidizes building renovations that use the honey-coloured stucco and red-tile roofing typical of the region. Hospital and school canteens now serve traditional dishes made from local organic fruit and vegetables instead of processed meals and produce from distant suppliers. To guard against overwork, and in keeping with Italian tradition, every small food shop in Bra closes on Thursdays and Sundays.

Locals seem pleased with the changes. They like the new trees and benches, the pedestrian precincts, the thriving food markets. Even the young are responding. The pool hall in Bra has turned down the pop music in deference to the Slow ethos. Fabrizio Benolli, the affable owner, tells me that some of his young customers are starting to look beyond the high-octane, one-size-fits-all lifestyle promoted by MTV. "They are beginning to understand that you can also have fun in a tranquil, Slow way," he says. "Instead of gulping down a Coke in a loud bar, they are learning how nice it can be to sip local wine in a place where the music is low."

Joining Citta Slow is helping member towns cut unemployment and breathe life into flagging economies. In Bra, new shops selling artisanal sausages and handmade chocolates, along with food festivals featuring local delicacies such as white truffles and Dolcetto red wine, draw thousands of tourists. Every September, the town is clogged with stalls run by speciality cheese-makers from across Europe. To meet the surging demand for high-quality food from both foreigners and locals, fifty-eight-year-old Bruno Boggetti has expanded his delicatessen. He now sells a wider array of local goodies—roasted peppers, truffles, fresh pasta, peppery olive oil. In 2001, he turned his basement into a cellar stocked with regional wines. "The Slow movement has helped me transform my business," he tells me. "Instead of always grabbing the cheapest and fastest thing, which is what globalization encourages, more people are deciding it is better to slow down, to reflect, to enjoy things made by hand rather than machine."

Citta Slow even hints at turning the demographic tables. In Italy, as in other countries, the young have long fled rural areas and small towns for the bright lights of the big city. Now that the charm of high-speed, high-stress urban living is wearing off, many are returning home in search of a calmer pace of life. A few urbanites are also joining the influx. At the counter of a *gelateria* in Bra, I bump into Paolo Gusardi, a young IT consultant from Turin, a seething industrial city 30 miles north of here. He is looking for an apartment in the *centro storico.* "Everything is rush, rush, rush in Turin, and I'm tired of it," he says, between mouthfuls of mint chocolate ice cream. "The Slow vision seems to offer a real alternative." Gusardi plans to work most of the week in Bra, designing websites and business software, and only commute into Turin when he has to see someone face to face. His main clients have already given him the green light.

Nevertheless, these are early days for Citta Slow, and in every member city deceleration remains very much a work in progress. Some of the obstacles that the movement will face are already apparent. In Bra, even as life gets sweeter, many locals still find work too hectic. Luciana Alessandria owns a leather goods store in the *centro storico.* She feels as stressed as she did before the town signed up to Citta Slow. "It's all very well for politicians to talk about slow this and slow that, but in the real world it is not so easy," she scoffs. "If I want to afford a decent standard of living, I have to work hard, very hard." To some extent, Citta Slow is a victim of its own success: the promise of Slow living draws tourists and outsiders, which brings speed, noise and bustle.

Citta Slow campaigners have also found that some reforms are easier to sell than others. Efforts to curb noise pollution are thwarted by the Italian penchant for shouting into mobile phones. In Bra, the hiring of more traffic cops has failed to extinguish that other national passion: driving too fast. As they do in other Slow Cities, cars and Vespas speed through the streets that are still open to them. "I am afraid people continue to drive badly here, just like in the rest of Italy," sighs Sibille. "Traffic is one part of life where it will be hard to make Italians slow down."

At the very least, though, Citta Slow has opened up another front in the worldwide battle against the culture of speed. By 2003, twenty-eight Italian towns were officially designated Slow Cities, with another twenty-six working towards certification. Inquiries are also flowing in from the rest of Europe and as far away as Australia and Japan. Two towns in Norway (Sokndal and Levanger) and one in England (Ludlow) have already joined the movement, with two German towns (Hersbruck and Geimende Schwarzenbruck) soon to follow. At the end of our interview, Sibille is in high spirits. "It is a long-term process, but bit by bit we are making Bra into a better place to live," says the deputy mayor. "When we are finished, everyone will want to live in a Slow City."

That may be going a little too far. Citta Slow, after all, is not for everyone. A strong emphasis on preserving local cuisine will always make more sense in Bra than it does in Basingstoke or Buffalo. What's more, the movement is limited to towns with fewer than fifty thousand inhabitants. For many in Citta Slow, the urban ideal is the late-medieval city, a rabbit warren of cobbled streets where people come together to shop, socialize and eat in charming piazzas. In other words, the sort of place most of us will only ever see on holiday. Nevertheless, the movement's core idea—that we need to take some of the speed and stress out of urban living—is feeding into a global trend.

In chapter 1, I described the city as a giant particle accelerator. That metaphor has never been more apt than it is today. Everything about urban life—the cacophony, the cars, the crowds, the consumerism—invites us to rush rather than relax, reflect or reach out to people. The city keeps us in motion, switched on, constantly in search of the next stimulus. Even as they thrill us, though, we find cities alienating. Not long ago, a poll found that 25% of Britons do not even know their neighbours' names. Disillusionment with urban life goes back a long way. In 1819, Percy Bysshe Shelley observed, "Hell is a city much like London." A few decades later, Charles Dickens chronicled the squalid underbelly of the fast-growing, fast-paced cities of industrialized Britain. In 1915, Booth Tarkington, a Pulitzer-winning American novelist, blamed urbanization for turning his native Indianapolis into an impatient inferno: "Not quite so long ago as a generation, there was no panting giant here, no heaving, grimy city . . . there was time to live."

Throughout the nineteenth century, people looked for ways to escape the tyranny of the town. Some, like the American Transcendentalists, moved to remote corners of the countryside. Others made do with occasional bursts of back-to-nature tourism. But cities were here to stay, and so campaigners sought to make them more liveable, with reforms that echo today. One measure was to import the slow, soothing rhythms of nature by building public parks. Central Park in New York City, which Frederick Olmstead set about creating in 1858, became a model for North American towns. From the early twentieth century, planners sought to build neighbourhoods that struck a balance between urban and rural. In Britain, Ebenezer Howard launched the Garden City movement, which called for small, self-supporting towns with a central park and a greenbelt of farmland and forests. Two garden cities were built in England—Letchworth in 1903 and Welwyn in 1920—before the idea crossed the Atlantic. In the United States, where the automobile was already king of the urban jungle, architects designed Radburn, New Jersey, a city where residents would never need to drive.

As the twentieth century rumbled on, planners experimented with a range of styles, notably the suburb, to combine the dynamism of city life with the slower feel of the countryside. Yet their reforms have largely failed, and urban life feels faster and more stressful than ever. The yearning to escape grows stronger every day, which is why *A Year in Provence*, Peter Mayle's account of moving his family from England to an idyllic village in France, sold millions of copies worldwide after its publication in 1991 and spawned legions of imitators. Today, we are assailed by books and documentaries about urbanites who go to raise chickens in Andalusia, make ceramics in Sardinia or run a hotel in the Scottish Highlands. Demand is brisk for weekend cottages in the wilderness outside North American cities. Even the Japanese, who have long derided the countryside as anti-modern, are discovering the charms of cycling past rice paddies and hiking in the mountains. Once scorned for its slow pace of life, the country's Okinawa region is now a magnet for city slickers eager to shift out of the fast lane.

The cult of rural tranquility is probably most pronounced in Britain, where urbanization started early, and
where fifteen hundred people now flee the cities to the
countryside every week. British estate agents try to make
urban areas sound more attractive by promising a "village
atmosphere"—code for small shops, green spaces and walkable streets. In London, suburbs built along Garden City
principles command a premium price. British newspapers
are packed with teasing columns written by townies who
have set up home in their own little slice of Arcadia. Some
of my thirty-something friends have made the jump, swapping the metropolis for muddy wellies. While most still
commute into the city for work, they spend the rest of their
time living, or trying to live, like characters in an H. E.
Bates novel.

Of course, we cannot all move out of London or Tokyo
or Toronto. And, when push comes to shove, most of us
probably don't really want to. We like the buzz of the big
city and regard a retreat to the countryside as something for
our twilight years. To some extent, we agree with what
Samuel Johnson said in 1777: " . . . when a man is tired of
London, he is tired of life; for there is in London all that life
can afford." Yet most of us wish urban living were a little less
frenetic. Which is why Citta Slow captures the imagination,
and why its ideas are catching on around the world.

Tokyo is a shrine to speed, a humming jungle of
concrete skyscrapers, neon signs and fast-food joints. At
lunchtime, salarymen stand in noodle bars, gulping down
large bowls of soup. The Japanese even have a proverb to

sum up their admiration for speed: "To eat fast and defe-
cate fast is an art." Nevertheless, many Japanese are now
embracing the idea that slower can be better when it comes
to urban design. Leading architects are putting up buildings that explicitly set out to help people decelerate. Due
for completion in 2006, the Shiodome district now taking
shape in downtown Tokyo is designed to be an oasis of
"Slow Life." Leisure facilities—a theatre, a museum and
restaurants—will nestle among the shining new office
blocks. To encourage shoppers to dawdle, the Shiodome
mall has wide halls lined with designer chairs that cry out
to be sat on.

The Slow principle is also gaining ground in the residential housing market. Most Japanese real estate developers churn out cookie-cutter homes of mediocre quality.
Getting a property to market quickly is top priority.
Recently, though, buyers have started to rebel against the
hurry-up, off-the-rack approach. Many are now forming
co-operatives that give them full control over planning,
design and construction. Though the hands-on approach
can add up to six months to the average building time for
a new property, more Japanese now accept that patience is
the price to pay for a decent home. Applications to join
what some call "Slow Housing" co-operatives have surged,
and even mainstream developers are starting to offer clients
more choice.

Tetsuro and Yuko Saito are a poster couple for the slower
building trend. In spring 2002, the two young editors
moved into the handsome four-storey apartment block

built by their co-operative in Bunkyo, a well-to-do neighbourhood in central Tokyo. The building, which looks onto a Shinto shrine, took sixteen months to construct instead of the standard year. Every apartment has its own bespoke layout and style, from traditional Japanese to sci-fi futurism. The Saitos went for open-plan minimalism—all white walls, steel banisters and spotlights. The couple had plenty of time to get the details just right, including where to put the cupboards, staircase and kitchen. They were also able to install stylish hardwood flooring throughout and a miniature garden on the balcony. The final product puts most Japanese apartments to shame.

"It was definitely worth waiting for," says Tetsuro, smiling over a steaming mug of green tea. "When we were building it, some of the residents became impatient with the process—there was so much talking and debate—and they wanted to speed things up. But by the end everyone understood the benefits of doing it slowly."

In a city where many would struggle to pick their neighbours out of a lineup, the Saitos are on friendly terms with their fellow residents. And their bank balance is healthier, too: cutting out the developer saved the co-operative a fortune on building costs. The only disappointment is that as soon as the Saitos leave the building they are straight back on the turbo-treadmill that is Tokyo. "We may have built our homes slowly," says Yuko. "But the city itself is still very fast, and it is hard to imagine that changing."

It is a familiar lament: big cities are fast and always will be. There is no point trying to slow them down, right? Wrong.

In large cities all over the world, people are successfully applying tenets of the Slow philosophy to urban living.

One example is the "urban time policies" that started in Italy in the 1980s and have now spread to Germany, France, the Netherlands and Finland. Such policies aim to make daily life less hectic by harmonizing operating hours in everything from schools, youth clubs and libraries to medical clinics, shops and offices. In Bra, the City Hall now opens on Saturday mornings to allow people to deal with bureaucratic procedures at a more leisurely pace. Another Italian city, Bolzano, has staggered the starting times for schools to ease the morning rush for families. To lighten the time pressure on working mothers, doctors in Hamburg now offer appointments after 7 P.M. and on Saturday morning. Another example of Slowing urban life is the war on noise. To promote peace and tranquility, a new European Union directive obliges all large cities to cut noise levels after 7 P.M. Even Madrid has launched a campaign to persuade its famously loud citizens to pipe down.

When it comes to making cities less fast, however, campaigners have identified the almighty automobile as the chief foe. More than any other invention, the car expresses and fuels our passion for speed. A century ago, we thrilled to the record-breaking exploits of La Jamais Contente and its rivals. Today, television commercials show the latest sedans, Jeeps and even minivans zooming through dramatic landscapes, spraying dust or water in their wake. In the real world, speeding is the most common form of civil disobedience. Millions buy radar detectors so they can speed with impunity. Websites give tips on how to evade detection by the police. In the UK, pro-car militants vandalize roadside speed cameras. People who would otherwise never dream of breaking the law routinely make an exception when it comes to speeding. I know, because I do it myself.

Speeding makes hypocrites of us all. We know that traffic accidents kill three thousand people every day—more than the number that died in the terrorist attacks on the World Trade Centre—and cost us billions of dollars. And we know speeding is often a factor. Yet still we drive too fast. Even at the Salone del Gusto 2002, the world's greatest gastronomic celebration of Slow, speeding was on the menu. One of the festival's sponsors, the Italian automaker Lancia, showed off a turbo sedan that could accelerate from 0–100 km/h in 8.9 seconds. Fresh from cooing over Parmesans aged gently in mountain huts and porcini gathered by hand from forest floors, Slow Food delegates, mainly men, took turns sitting at the wheel of the car, their faces lit up with dreams of making like Michael Schumacher on the *autostrada*. I smiled wryly at the scene, until I remembered the old saying about people in glass houses. Not long before the Salone, I was caught speeding on an Italian highway. My destination that day: the four-hour Slow Food dinner at Da Casetta.

There are many reasons—or excuses—for speeding. In a busy world, where every second counts, we drive fast to keep ahead, or just to keep up. Many modern cars are built for speed, gliding along smoothly in higher gears while labouring in lower ones. And then there is the excuse that no one ever gives to the traffic cop as he writes out a ticket: speeding down a road, weaving in and out of traffic, is actually rather fun; it gets the adrenaline pumping. "The truth is that we're all Italians behind the wheel," says Steven Stradling, professor of transport psychology at Edinburgh's Napier University. "We all drive with the heart as well as the head."

Even when traffic travels at a reasonable clip, or comes to a complete stop, cars still dominate the urban landscape. Outside my house in London, both sides of the street are permanently lined with parked vehicles. They form a Berlin Wall that cuts people off from each other—small children are invisible from the other side of the street. With SUVs, cars and vans storming up and down, the pedestrian feels alienated. The whole scene says cars first, people second. Once, when repaving work emptied the street for a couple of days, the atmosphere transformed. People lingered on the sidewalks and fell into conversation with strangers. I met two of my neighbours for the first time that week. And mine is not a unique experience. Studies around the world show a direct correlation between cars and community: the less traffic that flows through an area, and the more slowly it flows, the more social contact among the residents.

I do not mean to demonize cars. I drive one myself. The trouble is that driving has gained too much ascendancy over walking. For decades, urban life has been haunted by the words of Georges Pompidou, a former president of France: "We must adapt the city to the car, and not the other way round." Finally, though, the tables are turning.

By tackling the culture of speeding and reconfiguring the urban landscape to cut car use to a minimum, cities of all sizes are adapting to put people first.

Let's start with the war on speeding.

Reckless driving is almost as old as the car itself. In 1896, Bridget Driscoll, a housewife from Croydon, became the first pedestrian in the world to be knocked down and killed by a motor vehicle. She stepped off a London curb straight into the path of a car travelling at 4 mph. Before long, the death toll was soaring on roads everywhere. In 1904, four years before the Model T Ford brought motoring to the masses, the British parliament imposed a 20 mph limit on public highways. The war against speeding had begun.

Today, the push to slow traffic is stronger than ever. Governments everywhere are laying speed bumps, narrowing streets, lining roads with radar cameras, synchronizing traffic lights, cutting speed limits and launching media campaigns against fast driving. Like other fronts in the battle for Slow, the backlash against speeding is raging at the grassroots. In the British countryside, cars hurtle down narrow lanes and through picturesque hamlets, endangering the lives of cyclists, ramblers and horseback riders. Fed up with the speed demons, many villages now erect their own 30 mph speed limit signs until the authorities make it official.

In urban areas, residents are tackling the speeding culture with a campaign of civil obedience. In 2002, a plucky American grandmother named Sherry Williams posted a sign on her front lawn in Charlotte, North Carolina. It urged drivers to sign a pledge promising "to observe the speed limit on every neighbourhood street as if it were my own, as if the people I love the most—my children, my spouse, my neighbours—live there." Before long, hundreds of people signed up, and the local police threw their weight behind the campaign. Within months, Car Smart, a Web-based automobile dealership, took up the cause, giving Williams a national platform. Now, thousands of people across the United States have taken her "Pledge to Slow Down."

Another populist anti-speeding campaign sweeping the United States is the Neighbourhood Pace Program, which started in Australia. Its members pledge to drive at the speed limit, and in so doing act as "mobile speed bumps" for the traffic behind them. Similar schemes have drawn adherents across Europe.

The battle against speeding has even broken into primetime TV. In a recent British show, motorists caught driving too fast in a school zone were given a choice between paying the fine and facing the local children. Those who chose the latter sat ashen-faced at the head of a classroom, fielding poignant questions from kids as young as six: How would you feel if you ran me over? What would you say to my parents if you killed me? The drivers were visibly shaken. One woman wept. All went away vowing never to break the speed limit again.

Before we go any further, though, let's shoot down one of the great driving myths: that speeding is a reliable way to save time. True, on a long journey on a traffic-free highway you will arrive earlier at your destination. But the benefit on a short trip is minimal. For example, it takes just under two-and-a-half minutes to drive two miles at 50 mph. Crank up the speed to a reckless 80 mph, and you arrive fifty-four seconds earlier, barely enough time to check your voice mail.

On many journeys, speeding will not save any time at all. The spread of synchronized traffic signals means that drivers who flout the speed limit come up against more red lights. Weaving in and out of heavy traffic is often counter-productive, partly because lane speeds are constantly changing. Yet even knowing that speed is a false economy is unlikely to slow people down. The problem with most anti-speeding measures, from radar traps to narrowed roads, is that they rely on coercion. In other words, people slow down only because they must—to avoid damaging their car, being flashed by a roadside camera or rear-ending the vehicle in front of them. As soon as the coast is clear, they speed up again, sometimes even faster than before. The only way to win the war on speeding is to go deeper, to recast our whole relationship with speed itself. We need to *want* to drive more slowly.

This brings us back to one of the central questions facing the Slow movement: How do we curb the instinct to accelerate? In driving, as in life, one way is to do less, since a busy schedule is a prime cause of speeding. Another is to learn to feel comfortable with slowness.

To help people kick the acceleration habit, the English county of Lancashire runs a Speeders Anonymous–style program. In 2001, local police began offering a choice to anyone caught driving up to 5 mph over the limit: attend our one-day course, or pay the fine and take the points on your licence. Around a thousand people now opt to go through the Speed Awareness Program every month.

On a grey Monday morning, on a grey industrial estate outside Preston, I join the latest eighteen recruits. Speeding is clearly a classless crime. My group ranges from stay-at-home mothers and career women to blue-collar workers and pinstriped businessmen.

Once the participants have settled down with cups of tea and coffee, they start to compare experiences. Shame is tinged with defiance. "I wasn't really going *that* fast," sniffs a young mother. "I mean, it wasn't like I was a danger to anyone." A couple of people nod in sympathy. "I shouldn't even be here," grumbles the man on my left. "I got done late at night when there was nobody on the roads."

A hush falls as the teacher, a brusque northerner named Len Grimshaw, enters the room. He kicks off by asking us to list the most common reasons for speeding. We come up with the usual suspects: deadlines; running late; distractions on the road; the flow of traffic; quiet engines. "The one thing no one ever does here is blame themselves—it's always someone or something else that makes us drive too fast," says Grimshaw. "Well, that's rubbish. Speeding is our fault. We choose to speed. So we can choose not to."

Then come the ugly statistics. A car travelling at 35 mph takes 21 feet longer to stop than when it is travelling at 30 mph. A pedestrian hit by a car doing 20 mph stands a 5% chance of dying; at 30 mph that figure jumps to 45%; at 40 mph it is 85%. Grimshaw talks a lot about the modern obsession with saving time. "We're all in such a hurry nowadays that we speed in order to save a minute and a half," he says. "Is it really worth the risk of ruining your life or someone else's just to arrive ninety seconds earlier?"

We spend much of the morning deconstructing photographs of standard road scenes, teasing out the visual clues that tell us to slow down. Balloons tied to a front gate? A child might run into the street from a birthday party. Muddy tracks on the road? A heavy construction vehicle could reverse blindly into our path. A roadside café? The driver in front of us might suddenly pull over for a snack. None of this is rocket science, says Grimshaw, but the faster we drive the fewer clues we pick up.

After lunch, we head outside for some in-car training. My instructor is Joseph Comerford, a slight, bearded, rather intense man in his forties. We climb into his small Toyota Yaris. He drives first, touring the local suburbs, always within the speed limit. To a speedaholic like me, it feels like we're crawling. When we hit an open stretch of highway, I can feel my right foot itching to slam down the gas pedal. Comerford gently accelerates to the speed limit and then holds steady. As he cruises serenely along, he delivers a running commentary on what a driver should be looking out for: sports fields, bus stops, pedestrian crossings, changes in the colour of the road paving, dips in the curb, playgrounds, shop fronts. He rattles through the list like an auctioneer. My head spins. There is so much to take in.

Then it is my turn. My plan is to obey the speed limit, but I am surprised by how easily, how instinctively, I fail to do so. Each time the speedometer inches above the limit,

Comerford tells me off. He is especially hard when I drive through a school zone 8 mph too fast. I protest that the road is clear and that it is summer vacation anyway. But my excuses have a hollow ring. I know he is right. Gradually, as the afternoon wears on, I begin to adjust. I start to keep an eye on the speedometer. I scan for the clues we were taught in the classroom, delivering my own running commentary. Eventually, my speed starts to fall without my even noticing. What I do notice is that the impatience I usually feel at the wheel has eased.

At the end of our session, I am ready for a large slice of humble pie. Other participants seem equally chastened. "You won't catch me speeding again after that," says one young woman. "Too right," mumbles another. But will it last? Like prison inmates released back into the community, we will face the same old temptations and pressures. Will we remain on the road to rehabilitation? Or will we lunge back into the fast lane?

If Peter Holland is anything to go by, the Speed Awareness Program has a promising future. Holland is a forty-year-old BBC journalist. In the bad old days, breaking the speed limit was almost a badge of honour for him. "I always used to be the first on the scene, speeding all the way," he recalls. "I felt I had to hurry to beat deadlines, but there was also a sort of macho kick to getting there before anybody else." Even a collection of expensive speeding tickets failed to slow him down.

Then the BBC asked him to file a report on the Speed Awareness Program. Holland arrived at the classroom ready to poke fun. But as the day wore on, the message began to filter through. For the first time in his life, he started to question his inner roadrunner. The turning point came during his in-car training, when he raced through a residential area without noticing a school sign. "That suddenly brought everything home to me because I have two kids of my own," he says. "Even on the way back to the BBC office from the course, I knew my driving would never be the same again."

Holland filed an admiring report, and began putting what he had learned into practice. Now when he takes the wheel, safety comes first. He scans the road with the hungry eyes of a Speed Awareness instructor and has not broken the speed limit once since finishing the course. Nor has he missed a single interview or news scoop. Better still, slowing down on the road has helped him rethink the pace of the rest of his life. "Once you start asking questions about speed, that five-letter word, in the car, then you start asking the same questions about life in general: Why am I in such a hurry? What is the point of rushing just to save a minute or two?" he says. "When you're a calmer driver, you're calmer with your family, your work, with everything. I am a much calmer person in general now."

While not everyone finds the Speed Awareness Program a life-changing epiphany, the course clearly makes a difference. Follow-up studies reveal that most graduates are still actively choosing to drive within the speed limit. Councils around Britain are moving to copy the scheme. My own experience is also encouraging. Eight months after taking the course, I am less impatient at the wheel. I observe more and feel in better control of the car. Even in and around London, where the road code is survival of the fastest, driving is no longer the white-knuckle ride it used to be. My gas bills have fallen, too. Okay, I am no Peter Holland: I still drive too fast sometimes. But like many of the other graduates of the Speed Awareness Program, I am starting to mend my ways.

When it comes to making urban areas more liveable, though, learning to obey the speed limit is just the start. As Citta Slow proved, you also have to give less space to the car. To that end, cities everywhere are pedestrianizing roads, laying bicycle lanes, cutting parking, imposing road tolls and even banning traffic outright. Every year, many European cities hold car-free days. Some even empty the streets once a week. Every Friday night, traffic is cleared from swathes of central Paris to make way for an army of in-line skaters. Rome banned traffic for the whole of December 2002 from the fashionable shopping district known as Trident. In 2003, London began charging drivers £5 per day to enter the city centre during weekdays. Overall traffic is down by a fifth, turning the British capital into a much more welcoming place for cyclists and pedestrians. Other major cities are now studying the London charging scheme.

At the same time, planners are redesigning residential neighbourhoods to put people ahead of cars. In the 1970s, the Dutch invented the Woonerf, or "living street," a residential area with lower speed limits; reduced parking;

benches and play areas; more trees, bushes and flowers; and sidewalks that are on the same level as the road. The net result is a pedestrian-friendly environment that encourages slower driving, or no driving at all. The scheme is so successful that cities all over the world are copying it.

In traffic-blighted Britain, residents have banded together to turn more than eighty areas into Woonerf-style "Home Zones." One of the pilot projects is a five-street enclave in Ealing, a neighbourhood in west London. As part of the scheme, the local council has laid speed bumps and has slightly raised the entrances to the area and paved them with reddish bricks. It has also made most of the streets level with the sidewalks. Cars now park in staggered clusters on one side of the road or the other, so that drivers seldom see an acceleration-inducing straightaway and the sidewalks are rarely separated by two rows of vehicles. Many of the cars are parked at an angle to the curb, which narrows the space left for driving. The net result is that the area feels more relaxed and inviting than my own, even though the Victorian houses are virtually identical. Children skateboard and play soccer on the road. Cars that do pass through travel more slowly. As it has in neighbourhoods elsewhere, the war on traffic has brought people together. Instead of politely ignoring each other, as Londoners tend to do, the residents of this corner of Ealing now throw street parties, hold rounders and softball tournaments in the nearby park and socialize in the evenings. Charmion Boyd, a mother of three, hopes the car culture is in retreat. "People have become more aware of what driving does to the way of life in an area," she says. "A lot of us now think twice before hopping in the car."

Yet turning all of London into a Slow-friendly Home Zone is not an option—at least not in the short term. There are simply too many cars. The traffic that once flowed through the streets around Boyd's home has not disappeared—it just pours through the surrounding roads. Moreover, the hop-in-the car reflex will persist in cities like London as long as public transport remains so poor.

To wean North America off the car will be even harder. Cities in the New World are built for the automobile. Millions of North Americans live in suburbs where a long drive is the only way to get to work, school or shopping. And even when the distances are short, driving remains the default mode. In my old neighbourhood in Edmonton, Alberta, people think nothing of driving 300 yards to the convenience store. Mainstream suburban design reflects and reinforces the car-first mentality. Some streets do not even have sidewalks, and most houses have a driveway and multi-vehicle garage out front.

Suburbia is often a lonely, transient place, where people know the neighbours' cars better than they know the neighbours themselves. Suburban living is also unhealthy. All that driving eats time, forcing people to hurry everything else, and making it harder for them to get exercise. Research published in the *American Journal of Public Health* in 2003 showed that Americans who live in the most sprawling suburbs weigh on average 6 pounds more than those living in more compact areas.

As the demand for car-free, slower living grows, the appetite for traditional suburbs is waning. In the United States, recent census data suggest that the population flow to suburbia began to slow in the 1990s. North Americans are tired of long, stressful commutes, and many are choosing to live in rejuvenated city centres, where they can walk and cycle. A prime example is Portland, Oregon. Barred by law from expanding outwards in the 1970s, local leaders set about regenerating the downtown with pedestrian-friendly neighbourhoods linked by light-rail lines. The result may be the most liveable city in the US. Instead of charging off to out-of-town malls in SUVs, locals shop and socialize on foot, creating the kind of vibrant street life that Citta Slow would be proud of. With refugees from Los Angeles pouring in, and planners across the country taking note, Portland has been dubbed an "Urban Mecca" by the *Wall Street Journal*.

Portland is a sign of things to come. Across North America, urban planners are designing town centres and residential neighbourhoods that put people ahead of cars without sacrificing the creature comforts of the modern world. Many do so under the banner of New Urbanism, a movement that began in the late 1980s. The archetypal New Urbanist development evokes the streetcar suburbs of the early twentieth century, which many regard as the high-water mark of American urban design. It has walkable neighbourhoods with a generous sprinkling of public spaces—squares, parks, bandstands—and a blend of mixed-income housing, schools, leisure facilities and businesses.

Buildings are set close together and near the street to foster a feeling of intimacy and community. To calm traffic, and encourage walking, the streets are narrow and flanked by wide, tree-lined sidewalks. Garages are tucked out of view in lanes running behind the houses. Yet New Urbanism, like Citta Slow, is not about hiding inside a sepia-tinted vision of yesteryear. Rather, the aim is to use the best technology and design, old or new, to make urban and suburban life more relaxed and convivial—more Slow.

New Urbanism is nudging into the mainstream. The movement's annual conference now draws two thousand delegates from North America and beyond. At last count, more than four hundred New Urbanist projects are underway in Canada and the United States, ranging from the building of brand new neighbourhoods to the restoration of established downtown cores. The US Department of Housing and Urban Development now applies New Urbanist principles in projects across the country, and even conventional developers are snatching some of the movement's design ideas, such as hiding garages behind homes. Markham, an affluent town north of Toronto, plans every new neighbourhood along New Urbanist lines.

New Urbanism has its critics. Perhaps because the movement harks back to the days before the car ruled the roost, designers tend to favour traditional architecture. That often means a mix of mock Victorian, Georgian and Colonial, with lots of porches, picket fences and gabled roofs. Some scorn New Urbanism as a retreat from the real world into a twee land of make-believe—a charge that sometimes rings true. Seaside, a showpiece New Urbanist town on the Gulf coast of Florida, served as the faux neighbourhood in the movie *The Truman Show*. And you can't get more unreal than that.

Aesthetics is not the only target. Many New Urbanist developments have struggled to attract enough businesses to create a thriving commercial centre, forcing locals to work and shop elsewhere. And because public transport is often patchy, that trip into the outside world is usually made by car, via the sort of high-speed, high-stress arterial roads that are anathema to Slow living. Another problem is that many developers produce watered-down versions of New Urbanism—borrowing a few cosmetic touches while ignoring the core principles on street layout—and thus give the movement a bad name. Tom Low, an architect and town planner in Huntersville, North Carolina, thinks the time has come to reaffirm New Urbanist principles, and even augment them with a few ideas from Slow Food and Citta Slow. He proposes a new, improved movement called "Slow Urbanism."

New Urbanism certainly has a long way to go. Many current projects have a trial-and-error feel about them. But for anyone hoping to put "slow" and "city" in the same sentence, the movement clearly has promise. That is plain the moment I arrive in Kentlands, one of the jewels in the New Urbanist crown.

Built in the 1990s in Gaithersburg, Maryland, Kentlands is an island of calm in a sea of suburban sprawl. Every detail on the 352-acre site is calculated to slow people down, to encourage them to walk, mingle and smell the roses. There are three lakes, plenty of mature trees, parks, playgrounds and squares with gardens and pavilions. Many of the two thousand homes—a mix of Colonial, Georgian and Federal styles—have front porches with comfortable chairs and well-tended flower pots. Cars move gingerly, even apologetically, through the narrow streets, before vanishing into garages hidden in the back lanes. The fastest thing you are likely to see here is a local fitness fanatic in-line skating through the quiet roads like a bat out of hell.

But that does not mean that Kentlands is a lifeless bedroom community. Far from it. Unlike a conventional suburb, it has a Main Street with around sixty shops and businesses to meet every need: a tailor, a grocer, a dentist, law firms, opticians, a holistic healing centre, two beauty salons, an art gallery, a post office, a pet store, a dry cleaners, a handful of real estate agents, a pottery shop and an accountant. The Market Square contains two office buildings, a wine bar, a coffee house, more than twenty restaurants, a vast organic supermarket, a health club for children and a cinema.

With so much to do on their doorstep, the people of Kentlands have fallen in love with that very un-American activity: walking. Young mothers push prams to Main Street for a latte and a little light shopping. Children walk to school and then to soccer practice, swimming lessons and piano class. In the evening, Kentlands is abuzz, the streets thronged with people on foot, chatting with friends, heading off for a meal or a movie, or simply ambling around. It could almost be a scene from *Pleasantville*.

So who are the contented citizens of Kentlands? People of all ages who want to live a little more as one does in a Slow City. The more affluent live in houses, the less so in apartments. Almost everyone is a refugee from conventional suburbia. The Callaghan family fled to Kentlands from a car-choked suburb just over a mile away. Today, Missy, Chad and their teenage son, Bryan, live in a house that would not look out of place in a Norman Rockwell painting: a large porch with generous rocking chairs; the American flag hanging from a post by the front door; a white picket fence; a front yard bursting with nandinas, burberries, hollies and laurels. In their last home, the Callaghans had to drive more than 6 miles to reach the nearest restaurant, supermarket or bookstore. In Kentlands, they can walk to Main Street in five minutes. Like everyone else here, Missy loves the slower pace. "In a normal suburb, you get into the car for everything, and that means you're rushing all the time," she says. "But here we walk everywhere, which makes things a lot more laid back. It also creates a strong community. We're not the social butterflies of the neighbourhood or anything, but we know people all over Kentlands because we meet them out walking."

The neighbourhood is tightly knit in an old-fashioned kind of way. Parents look out for each other's children in the streets. Crime is so low—when everyone knows everyone else, intruders stick out—that some residents even leave their doors unlocked. There is also a fine-tuned grapevine. Reggi Norton, an acupuncturist at the healing centre on Main Street, thinks Kentlands has entered a virtuous circle:

slower living leads to stronger community, which in turn encourages people to relax and slow down even further. "When you have good communal bonds, people feel they belong," she says. "And that has a calming influence on the way they live their lives."

How far does that influence reach? Most people in Kentlands still have to commute by car to jobs in the big bad world outside the development. Yet living Slowly at home can take the edge off the manic modern workplace. As a vice-president of safety and security with the Marriott hotel chain, Chad Callaghan puts in a fifty-hour week, plus plenty of business travel. He also spends forty minutes a day commuting by car. Back in conventional suburbia, he spent most evenings indoors, usually flopped down in front of the TV. Today, he and Missy go for a walk almost every evening. Or they sit on the front porch, reading and shooting the breeze with passersby. Kentlands is the ultimate chill-out after a hard day at the office.

"When I come home, I can really feel the stress start to slough off, I can feel my blood pressure going down," says Chad. "And I suppose there is some residual effect in the other direction: I go to the office in a more relaxed frame of mind. And if I'm feeling really stressed at work, I think of Kentlands, and it makes me feel good."

Callaghan also finds that he does some of his best thinking while strolling in the neighbourhood. "When I'm walking around here, I lose myself in thought," he says. "If I'm having some issue at work, often I find that I solve the problem without even noticing I'm thinking about it."

Kentlands is not perfect. The mass exodus of commuters every day drains much of the life from the place, though a planned office park nearby may go some way towards fixing that. Several spaces for shops and businesses still lie empty. And purists gripe that some of the streets could be more pedestrian-friendly. But the drawbacks are dwarfed by the benefits. Indeed, the people of Kentlands share an almost cult-like devotion to their relaxed lifestyle. Property seldom comes on the market, and when it does a local resident usually snaps it up. Even divorcing couples tend to find separate homes within the neighbourhood. Kentlands is also very popular with non-residents. Many come from conventional suburbs to walk around Main Street and the Market Square in the evenings. Some send letters begging residents to sell up so they can move in. Over the last decade, house prices have doubled in Kentlands. "The lifestyle here may not be for everyone, but the demand for homes is growing all the time," says Chad Callaghan. "Obviously a lot of people nowadays want a place where they can live more simply, more slowly."

Near the end of my stay in Kentlands, something happens to confirm the view that New Urbanism, or at least a version of it, is a good thing for North America. To remind myself what a conventional suburb feels like, I set out on foot to explore one on the other side of Gaithersburg. It is a perfect day for a walk. Birds play tag across a cloudless autumn sky. A light breeze riffles through the trees. The neighbourhood is neat and affluent—and as lively as a graveyard. Every house has a garage out front, and many have a vehicle or two parked in the driveway. From time to time, someone emerges from a front door, jumps into a car and drives off. I feel like an interloper. After about twenty minutes, a police cruiser pulls up at the curb beside me. The officer in the passenger seat leans out the window and says, "Good morning, sir. Everything okay?"

"Everything's fine," I reply. "I'm just taking a walk."

"A what?"

"A walk. You know, like a stroll. I wanted to stretch my legs a little."

"Do you live in this neighbourhood?"

"No, I'm from out of town."

"Figures," he laughs. "Folks don't do much walking round here."

"Yeah, everyone seems to be driving," I say. "Maybe they should walk more."

"Maybe so." As the squad car pulls away, the officer adds, with gentle irony, "You enjoy that walk now, ya hear."

Across the street, a network of underground sprinklers splutters into life, spraying clouds of water over the local baseball field. I stand alone on the sidewalk, amused and appalled. I have just been stopped by the police—for walking.

Later that same day, Kentlands is also pretty quiet. Most residents are away at work. But there are people on the streets, and they are walking. Everyone says a friendly "hello." I bump into Anjie Martinis, who is taking her two little boys to the shops. She and her husband are just about to sell their local row house and move into a larger home a few streets away. We talk about the trials and tribulations of parenthood, and the fact that Kentlands is good place to raise children. "You'd love living here," she says. And you know what? I think she may be right.

CHAPTER FIVE

MIND/BODY: *MENS SANA IN CORPORE SANO*

This art of resting the mind and the power of dismissing from it all care and worry is probably one of the secrets of energy in our great men.
—CAPTAIN J. A. HADFIELD

ON A CRISP, SPRING MORNING, deep in the Wiltshire countryside, walking seems like the most natural thing in the world. Cattle graze gently in the rolling green fields. Locals trot by on horseback. Birds swoop low above the dense woodlands. The hustle and bustle of city life seems a million miles away. As I stroll along a country lane, gravel scrunching underfoot, I can feel myself shifting down a gear or two, which is as it should be. I am here to learn how to slow down my mind.

In the war against the cult of speed, the front line is inside our heads. Acceleration will remain our default setting until attitudes change. But changing *what* we think is just the beginning. If the Slow movement is really to take root, we have to go deeper. We have to change the *way* we think.

Like a bee in a flower bed, the human brain naturally flits from one thought to the next. In the high-speed workplace, where data and deadlines come thick and fast, we are all under pressure to think quickly. Reaction, rather than reflection, is the order of the day. To make the most of our time, and to avoid boredom, we fill up every spare moment with mental stimulation. When did you last sit in a chair, close your eyes and just relax?

Keeping the mind active makes poor use of our most precious natural resource. True, the brain can work wonders in high gear. But it will do so much more if given the chance to slow down from time to time. Shifting the mind into lower gear can bring better health, inner calm, enhanced concentration and the ability to think more creatively. It can bring us what Milan Kundera calls "the wisdom of slowness."

Experts think the brain has two modes of thought. In his book *Hare Brain, Tortoise Mind—Why Intelligence Increases When You Think Less,* Guy Claxton, a British psychologist, calls them Fast Thinking and Slow Thinking. Fast Thinking is rational, analytical, linear, logical. It is what we do under pressure, when the clock is ticking; it is the way computers think and the way the modern workplace operates; it delivers clear solutions to well-defined problems. Slow Thinking is intuitive, woolly and creative. It is what we do when the pressure is off, and we have the time to let ideas simmer at their own pace on the back burner. It yields rich and subtle insights. Scans show the two modes of thought produce different waves in the brain—slower alpha and theta waves during Slow Thinking, faster beta ones during Fast Thinking.

Relaxation is often a precursor to Slow Thinking. Research has shown that people think more creatively when they are calm, unhurried and free from stress, and that time pressure leads to tunnel vision. In one study, carried out in 1952, participants were asked to encrypt simple phrases into a basic code. Sometimes the researcher handed over the words with no comment, but sometimes he asked them, "Can you do it a little bit faster?" Invariably, the participants floundered when asked to speed up. In a separate study, Canadian researchers found that hospital patients awaiting surgery come up with less creative endings for similes such as "as fat as . . ." or "as cold as . . . ."

These findings match my own experience. My eureka moments seldom come in a fast-paced office or a high-stress meeting. More often they occur when I am in a relaxed state—soaking in the bath, cooking a meal or even jogging in the park. The greatest thinkers in history certainly knew the value of shifting the mind into low gear. Charles Darwin described himself as a "slow thinker." Albert Einstein was famous for spending ages staring into space in his office at Princeton University. In the stories of Arthur Conan Doyle, Sherlock Holmes weighs up the evidence from crime scenes by entering a quasi-meditative state, "with a dreamy vacant expression in his eyes."

Of course, Slow Thinking on its own is just indulgence without the rigours of Fast Thinking. We have to be able to seize, analyze and evaluate the ideas that surface from the subconscious—and often we must do so quickly. Einstein appreciated the need to marry the two modes of thought: "Computers are incredibly fast, accurate, and stupid. Human beings are incredibly slow, inaccurate, and brilliant. Together they are powerful beyond imagination." That is why the smartest, most creative people know when to let the mind wander and when to knuckle down to hard work. In other words, when to be Slow and when to be Fast.

So how can the rest of us access Slow Thinking, especially in a world that prizes speed and action? The first step is to relax—put aside impatience, stop struggling and learn to accept uncertainty and inaction. Wait for ideas to incubate below the radar, rather than striving to brainstorm them to the surface. Let the mind be quiet and still. As one Zen master put it, "Instead of saying 'Don't just sit there; do something' we should say the opposite, 'Don't just do something; sit there.'"

Meditation is one way to train the mind to relax. It lowers blood pressure and generates more of the slower alpha and theta waves in the brain. And research shows that the effects last long after the meditating ends. In a 2003 study, scientists at the University of California San Francisco Medical Centre found that the Buddhist mix of meditation and mindfulness affects the amygdala, the area of the brain linked to fear, anxiety and surprise, making adherents more serene and less likely to lose their cool.

Meditation is not new. People of all faiths have been using it for thousands of years in the quest for inner harmony or spiritual enlightenment, which may explain why it has a slightly flaky image. To many, meditation evokes monks with shaved heads chanting "om" in mountaintop temples or New Age types sitting smugly in the lotus position.

Yet such prejudice is starting to look outdated. Meditation is going mainstream. Ten million Americans now practise it regularly, and meditation rooms are popping up all over the industrial world, from airports, schools and prisons to hospitals and offices. Stressed-out, speed-ravaged professionals, among them die-hard agnostics and atheists, are flocking to spiritual retreats where meditation is on the menu. Some of the least flaky people on earth, including Bill Ford, the CEO and chairman of Ford Motors, are now committed meditators.

To see how meditation works, and how it might fit into the Slow movement, I sign up for the first three days of a ten-day retreat in rural Wiltshire. The course is run by the International Meditation Centre (IMC), a worldwide Buddhist network that started in Burma in 1952. The British branch opened in 1979, and now occupies a converted red-brick farmhouse and its outbuildings. A modern pagoda rises up from the landscaped garden, its golden spires glinting in the spring sunshine.

I arrive on a Friday afternoon with some trepidation. Will I be able to sit still for hours on end? Will I be the only person not wearing a sarong? My fellow retreaters, forty in total, hail from all over the world—Britain, Germany, France, Australia, the United States. On the tables in the cafeteria, bottles of Kikkoman soya sauce jostle with jars of crunchy peanut butter and small pots of Marmite. Many of the participants are practising Buddhists, with shaved heads and the colourful sarongs that are the national dress in Burma. But others are not. They have simply come, like me, in search of a quiet place to learn the art of meditation.

In the first group session, we gather in a long, narrow room. The lighting is soft. A framed photograph of Sayagyi U Ba Kin, the founder of the IMC network, hangs on the front wall, below a plaque declaring in Burmese and English: "Truth Must Triumph." Wrapped in blankets, and arranged in four rows, the students sit or kneel on cushioned floor mats. At the head of the class, the teacher perches cross-legged on a stool. He is Roger Bischoff, a mild-mannered Swiss man who bears a strong resemblance to Bill Gates.

Bischoff explains that we are about to embark on the Eightfold Noble Path as taught by the Buddha. The first step is to purify our actions by observing a moral code: no killing, no stealing, no sex (during our stay), no lying, no drugs or alcohol. Next comes the meditation. The aim is to develop our concentration for the first five days, and then, in the next five days, to use that concentration to gain insight and wisdom. In an ideal world, the students will achieve—or at least be on the road to—enlightenment by Day 10.

Everything at the Centre is designed to relax and still the mind. Many of the stimuli that keep us buzzing in the modern world are banned. So there is no television, no radio, no reading material, no Internet, no phones. We also observe Noble Silence, which means no chitchat. Life is pared back to the basics: eating, walking, sleeping, washing and meditating.

There are many ways to meditate. Most involve focusing the mind on a single point: an object, such as a candle or a leaf; a sound or a mantra; or even a concept, such as love, friendship or growing old. The technique at IMC seems simple enough. Close the eyes and breathe in and out through the nose, fixing all attention on a point just above the upper lip. In a gentle, mellifluous voice, Bischoff tells us to slow right down, to relax and focus our minds on the soft touch of the breath just below the nose. This is not as easy as it sounds. My mind seems to have a mind of its own. After five or six breaths, it shoots off like a pinball, ricocheting noisily from one thing to the next. Every time I draw my concentration back to the breath, another barrage of unconnected thoughts comes stampeding through my head—work, family, sports highlights, snippets from pop songs, anything and everything. I begin to worry that there is something wrong with me. Everyone else seems so still and focused. As we all sit there in silent rows, like galley slaves on a ghost ship, I feel the urge to giggle, or shout something silly, like "Fire!"

Thankfully, though, Bischoff interviews the students twice a day to clock their progress. This is the only time we are permitted to speak, and since it occurs in full view of the whole class, eavesdropping is easy. To my relief, it turns out that everyone else is struggling to achieve stillness of mind. "I feel like I just can't slow down," says one young man, despair in his voice. "I'm craving activity."

Bischoff offers a steady stream of encouraging words. Even the Buddha had trouble stilling his mind, he tells us. The main thing is not to force it. If you feel tense or agitated, then go lie down, have a snack in the kitchen or take a walk. Outside, the grounds resemble those of a convalescent hospital, with students slowly picking their way through the gardens.

The meditation clearly has an effect, though, even on the fastest, most stress-addled mind. I feel wonderfully mellow at the end of the first evening. And as the weekend progresses, I begin to slow down without even trying. By Saturday night, I notice that I am taking more time to eat and brush my teeth. I have started walking, instead of running, up the stairs. I am more mindful of everything—my body, its movements, the food I eat, the smell of the grass outside, the colour of the sky. By Sunday night, even the meditation itself is starting to seem within reach. My mind is learning to be quiet and still for longer. I feel less impatient and hurried. In fact, I am so relaxed I do not want to leave.

Without my realizing it, my brain has also been engaged in some very useful Slow Thinking. By the end of the weekend, ideas for work are bursting up from my subconscious mind like fish jumping in a lake. Before returning to London, I sit in the car scribbling them down.

Is it possible to transfer that meditative calm from a retreat to the real world? The answer turns out to be a qualified yes. Obviously, the temptation to accelerate is far greater in London than it is in deepest Wiltshire, and few who pass through the IMC program reach a state of perfect Zen. Nevertheless, meditation can take the edge off a hectic urban life.

After my stint at the Wiltshire retreat, I speak to a number of people to find out what meditating does for them. One is Neil Pavitt, a forty-one-year-old advertising copywriter from Maidenhead, outside London. He started attending retreats at IMC in the early 1990s and gradually became a practising Buddhist. He now sets aside an hour every evening to meditate.

Meditation provides a bedrock of calm that helps him to negotiate the choppy, fast-moving waters of the advertising world. "It's like a rock, something that I can always rely on. A solid thing that gives me a grounding, a centre where I can always return to for strength," he says. "If things get really busy or stressful at work, I'll just take five or ten minutes to do some breathing exercises, and that will bring back the calm to my mind."

Pavitt also finds that meditation unlocks the door to Slow Thinking. "It's good for the creative part of work because it clears and calms the mind," he says. "I often find that meditation helps to make a problem become much clearer, or it helps good ideas come up to the surface."

Other ways of meditating deliver similar results. More than five million people worldwide now practice transcendental meditation, a simple technique that takes fifteen to twenty minutes twice a day. Though invented in 1957 by an Indian yogi, TM is not anchored to any religious tradition, which is why it appeals to people like Mike Rodriguez, a

Chicago-based management consultant. "I liked the idea of calming my mind without having any spiritual or religious baggage attached to it," he says. Before TM, Rodriguez felt overwhelmed by the pace and pressure of work. Now he feels like an unflappable corporate warrior. "Everything can be spinning around me at a 100 miles an hour—the phones, the email, requests from clients—but I don't get swept up in it so much anymore," he says. "I'm like an island of calm in an ocean of craziness."

Like Pavitt, Rodriguez feels more creative: "I feel that I come up with more imaginative solutions for my clients now. When you give your mind a chance to slow down, it can really come up with some good stuff."

There is even evidence that meditating can make you happy. In 2003, scientists at the University of Wisconsin at Madison scanned the brains of people with a long experience of Buddhist practice. They found that their left prefrontal lobes, the area of the brain linked with feel-good emotions, were unusually active. In other words, they were physiologically happier. One hypothesis is that regular meditation gives the left prefrontal load a permanent boost.

The findings do not surprise Robert Holford. Every year, the fifty-six-year-old psychoanalyst makes time in his busy schedule to attend a ten-day IMC retreat in Wiltshire. In between, he tries to meditate daily. Meditation gives his mind the confidence to steer clear of dark thoughts. "A still mind is like a taste of freedom," he says. "It's like you're sitting on the bank and also in the river at the same time—

you're engaged with life but you have a wider view of it all, as well. That makes you feel lighter and happier."

Despite my earlier skepticism, meditation is now part of my routine. I take short breaks—around ten minutes at a time—to meditate in the middle of the day, and it makes a difference. I return to my desk relaxed and clear-headed. Though such things are hard to measure, I think meditation is making me more mindful, more able to enjoy the moment—more Slow.

Meditation can pay physical dividends, too. Although the Western philosophical tradition drove a wedge between mind and body after René Descartes in the seventeenth century, the two are clearly connected. Clinical studies suggest that meditating may help keep the body in good working order. Doctors increasingly recommend it to patients as a way to cope with a range of conditions: migraines, heart disease, AIDS, cancer, infertility, high blood pressure, irritable bowel syndrome, insomnia, stomach cramps, premenstrual syndrome, even depression. A five-year study in the United States found that people who practise transcendental meditation are 56% less likely to be hospitalized.

The fitness world has also discovered the link between mind and body and the role that slowness plays in keeping both in good shape. Of course, the idea of slow exercise goes against the modern grain. The twenty-first-century gym is a temple of sound and fury. Egged on by a thumping soundtrack, people huff and puff on the cardio machines and in aerobics classes. I once saw a gym instructor wearing a T-shirt that said "Go Fast. Go Hard. Or Go Home." In other words, the only way to build a better body is to pump the heart rate up to the top of the target zone.

Or is it? Many of the exercise regimes that emerged centuries ago in Asia are based on slowing down the body and stilling the mind—a combination that can offer wider benefits than simply sweating away on a StairMaster.

Take yoga, an ancient Hindu regimen of physical, spiritual and mental exercises that seeks to bring body, mind and spirit into harmony. The word "yoga" means "unite" in Sanskrit. In the West, though, we tend to focus on the physical side of the discipline—the breathing control, the slow, fluid movements, the postures, or *asanas.* Yoga can do wonders for the body, firming and toning muscles, fortifying the immune system, boosting blood circulation and increasing flexibility.

But the physical payoff is just the beginning. Many Eastern exercise regimes teach people to extend the moment by easing them into a relaxed state of readiness. Even in martial arts such as karate, judo and kendo, with their lightning-fast kicks and punches, combatants learn to maintain a core of slowness. If the mind is racing, if they feel anxious and rushed, they are vulnerable. Through his own inner stillness, the martial arts expert learns to "slow down" his opponents' moves in order to counter them more easily. He must be Slow on the inside to be fast on the outside. Western athletes call this "being in the zone." Even when performing an act of skill at high speed, they remain unflustered and unrushed. John Brodie, a former star quarterback for the San Francisco 49ers, sounds like a Zen master when he talks of staying serene in the heat of battle: "Time seems to slow way down, in an uncanny way, as if everyone were moving in slow motion. It seems as if I have all the time in the world to watch the receivers run their patterns, and yet I know the defensive line is coming at me just as fast as ever."

Yoga can help achieve that core of stillness. It seeks to sustain a person's *chi*—the life force, or energy—which can be hampered by stress, anxiety, illness and overwork. Even those who dismiss the idea of *chi* as mystical claptrap often find that yoga helps them develop a Slow frame of mind. Through the unhurried, controlled movements, they acquire more self-awareness, concentration and patience.

In a world craving inner calm, as well as the perfect body, yoga is therefore manna from heaven. People do it everywhere nowadays, from offices and hospitals to fire departments and factories. Recent surveys suggest that the number of Americans practising yoga has trebled since 1998 to around fifteen million, among them many professional athletes. Every newspaper travel supplement is packed with advertisements for yoga holidays in exotic locations. My son does yogic exercises at his nursery in London. In many gyms, yoga has knocked aerobics off its perch as the fitness class of choice. Even Jane Fonda, the original Queen of Huff and Puff, now makes yoga videos.

Mark Cohen credits yoga with making him healthy and Slow. As a thirty-four-year-old trader on Wall Street, he lives in the fast lane. His job is all about split-second

decisions and, in his spare time, he plays two of the speedi-
est sports around, basketball and hockey. Like many people, he used to scorn yoga as a hobby for wimps who
could not do "real" sports. However, when a woman he
fancied invited him to her class, he held his nose and went
along. On the first night, he was amazed by how hard it
was to bend his body into some of the *asanas,* and yet how
relaxed he felt afterwards. Even though he decided the
woman was not for him, he signed up for a yoga class
nearer his apartment. After a few months of instruction,
he was much more flexible. He felt stronger, and his posture improved so much that he threw away the fraying
lumbar cushion that had been a permanent fixture on the
back of his office chair. He also feels his balance and speed
have improved on the basketball court and in the hockey
rink. What Cohen most likes about yoga, though, is its
relaxing, meditative quality. "When I do the poses, everything inside me slows right down," he says. "After the
class, I feel mellow but also really clear-headed." That
feeling spills over into the rest of his life. "You should see
me at work now," he says. "When things get crazy, I'm
just Mr. Calm."

Yoga also eases Cohen into Slow Thinking mode. Often
he arrives at class feeling stressed about a problem at work.
After an hour of relaxing his mind and slowly bending his
body this way and that, a solution sometimes comes to
him. "My mind must be working through stuff on a subconscious level when I do yoga," he says. "Some of my
greatest ideas hit me when I'm walking home after class."

Others rave about the energy yoga gives them. Dahlia Teale works in a hairdressing salon in New Orleans, Louisiana, and used to go to the gym four days a week to take aerobics classes and work out on the cardio machines. In 2002, she joined a yoga class with a friend. Right away, she felt energized. "I used to come out of the gym a lot of the time feeling exhausted," she says. "With yoga it's the opposite—I get an energy high that lasts for a long time." Teale has cancelled her gym membership and now stays fit through a combination of yoga, walking and cycling. She has lost 6 pounds.

Chi Kung is another Eastern exercise regime whose Slow approach to the mind and body is winning converts. Sometimes described as "yoga with meditation and move-ment," Chi Kung is a generic term for a range of ancient Chinese exercises that promote health by circulating *chi* round the body. In a standing position, and using the pelvic area as a fulcrum, practitioners move slowly through a series of postures that elongate the limbs. Slow, deep breathing is also important. Chi Kung is not about pump-ing up the heart rate and sweating profusely; it is about control and awareness. It can improve balance, strength, posture and rhythm of movement. Even more than yoga, it helps to achieve a relaxed mind while in an active state. Chi Kung has many branches, ranging from martial arts such as Kung Fu to the much gentler Tai Chi.

In the West, people are using Chi Kung as a way to play sports better. Mike Hall gives golf and squash lessons in Edinburgh, Scotland, and slowness is his watchword. He claims that by using Chi Kung to still his mind he can actually see the yellow dot on the squash ball as it hurtles towards him. Through the slow, controlled movements of Chi Kung, his students learn to move fluidly on the squash court, instead of lurching hither and thither. And they develop a calmness of mind that makes them feel they have enough time to play any shot. "The paradox is that you are in motion and still at the same time," Hall tells me over the phone.

To see this paradox in action, I arrange to visit his squash club in Edinburgh. A former professional soccer player, Hall is a stocky forty-five-year-old with sandy hair and a slight lisp. He is just finishing off a lesson as I arrive. Right away he stands out from the crowd. While others flap and flail around the court, Hall moves with the liquid grace of a tango dancer. Even when he lunges to make an awkward return, he seems to flow. I am reminded of that famously counterintuitive piece of advice from Jackie Stewart, the Formula One hero: sometimes to be faster you have to be slower.

When the lesson is over, Hall takes me through a few Chi Kung exercises, urging me to think about the movements and to remain fluid. He always comes back to the importance of keeping a steady centre, both in the trunk of the body and in the mind. "For most people, the problem in squash is not being fast enough," he says. "It's being slow enough." It all sounds a little corny, which gives me an extra incentive to take Hall down a peg or two when we finally enter the court to play a game. From the first rally, though, I find myself on the back foot. Hall covers the whole court with very little effort at all. He wins 9–2.

Afterwards, his next pupil, an amazingly fit seventy-two-year-old business professor named Jim Hughes, tells me how Chi Kung is helping him to conquer his addiction to hurry. "Things don't change overnight, but working with Mike has done wonders for my squash game," he says. "I don't do so much pointless rushing about as I used to." Chi Kung has also helped take some of the haste out of his working life. On consulting jobs, Hughes used to rush into giving his clients feedback. In the classroom, he raced through the material with one eye on the clock. Now, thanks to Chi Kung, he takes a Slow approach. That means setting aside the time he needs to teach his pupils at a suitable pace and waiting for the right moment to discuss a client's weaknesses. "Instead of yielding to my first reflex, which is to act as soon as possible, I now slow down and give myself the space to consider the options," says Hughes. "I'm sure I'm a better professor and a better consultant for it."

The morning after our one-sided contest on the squash court, Hall takes me to knock some golf balls around a local park. The weather is vintage Edinburgh, grey and drizzly. Hall watches me play a few shots with a nine-iron. We then perform some Chi Kung exercises together. Hall talks again about the importance of remaining calm and still inside. He also tells me that studies have shown that swinging too fast actually causes the golf club to decelerate as it hits the ball. A slower, rhythmical swing delivers better control and more power. I pick up the nine-iron, determined to put his words into action. Right away, my swing feels smoother, stronger.

Later I compare notes with Lindsay Montgomery, the fifty-year-old chief executive of the Scottish Legal Aid Board and a lifelong golfer. When he first started taking lessons from Hall, he was skeptical about Chi Kung and its promise to harness the power of slowness. Six months later, to his amazement, he had shaved nearly three strokes off his handicap. "Chi Kung gives you a different sense of timing and tempo," he says. "I tend to do everything very quickly—that's my personality. But slowing my swing down has made it much smoother. Chi Kung has taught me not to rush, and that has made me a better golfer."

The East is not the only source of slow, mindful forms of exercise. In 1930s Britain, Joseph H. Pilates devised a strengthening regime based on three very yogic principles: precise movements, concentration and controlled breathing. In a modern Pilates class, people perform special exercises to strengthen the core muscles around the spine and thus improve flexibility, endurance and posture. Though not rooted in a spiritual or meditative tradition, Pilates can also deepen mental concentration and focus. Tiger Woods, the American golfer, practices Pilates and meditation.

Meanwhile, Western sports scientists are coming around to the idea that exercising more slowly can yield better results. The harder we work out, the more quickly our heart beats, and the more fat we burn. But beyond a certain point, the faster-is-better equation no longer applies. Dr. Juul Achten, a research fellow at the University of Birmingham, has found—and other studies have since confirmed—that we burn the most fat per minute when our heart beats at 70% to 75% of its maximum rate. The average person can reach that state by power-walking or jogging lightly. Work out harder than that, pushing the heart rate closer to its maximum, and the body starts using more carbohydrates to fuel itself. In other words, the gym rat pounding manically away on the StairMaster is probably burning less fat than the shrinking violet exercising more slowly on the neighbouring machine. The tortoise and the hare metaphor helps to explain. "The hare looks like he's achieving more because he's going faster," says Dr. Achten. "But in the race to burn fat, I would put my money on the tortoise to win."

Against that backdrop, walking, the oldest form of exercise, is making a comeback. In the pre-industrial era, people mostly travelled on foot—and that kept them fit. Then came engine power, and people got lazy. Walking became the transport of last resort, a "forgotten art" in the words of the World Health Organization.

As we saw in the last chapter, though, planners across the world are redesigning suburbs and city centres to make more room for pedestrians. My London borough, Wandsworth, has just launched its own Walking Strategy. There are many good reasons to walk. One is that it is free: you don't need to take classes or hire a personal fitness instructor to learn how to stroll in the park. Many of the journeys we make by car could just as easily—and sometimes more easily—be made on foot. Walking can boost fitness and guard against heart disease, stroke, cancer and osteoporosis. And it is less likely to cause injury than more strenuous exercise.

Travelling on foot can also be meditative, fostering a Slow frame of mind. When we walk, we are aware of the details around us—birds, trees, the sky, shops and houses, other people. We make connections.

Walking can even help ease the itch to accelerate. In a car, train or plane, where the engine always holds out the promise of more power, more speed, we feel tempted to go faster, and treat every delay as a personal affront. Because our bodies come with a built-in speed limit, walking can teach us to forget about acceleration. It is inherently Slow. In the words of Edward Abbey, the *enfant terrible* of American environmentalism: "There are some good things to say about walking. . . . Walking takes longer, for example, than any other form of locomotion except crawling. Thus, it stretches time and prolongs life. Life is already too short to waste on speed. . . . Walking makes the world much bigger and therefore more interesting. You have time to observe the details."

Alex Podborski could not agree more. The twenty-five-year-old used to ride a scooter to his job at a travel agency in central London. Then, in 2002, when his Vespa was stolen for the third time, he decided to try commuting on foot. Now, he spends twenty-five minutes walking to and from work. His route takes him across Hyde Park, where he does some of his best thinking. He smiles at people along the way, and generally feels more connected to the city.

Instead of arriving at the office all pumped up after navigating the rush hour traffic, Podborski strolls in relaxed and ready for anything. "Walking is my chill-out time," he says. "It sets me up for the day and winds me down at the end of it." It also pays dividends on the fitness front. Since taking up walking, Podborski feels healthier and leaner. "I'm never going to model underwear for Calvin Klein," he says, with a wry smile. "But at least my beer gut is getting smaller."

For a more contemporary take on Slow exercise, look no further than SuperSlow, the weightlifting movement sweeping North America and beyond. Before you skip ahead to the next chapter, though, let's lay to rest a common misconception: pumping iron does not turn everyone into the Incredible Hulk. SuperSlow makes the average person stronger and leaner without piling on the muscle. And since muscle takes up around 30% less space than fat, many people drop a dress size or two after hitting the weights. *Vanity Fair,* a bible for those who favour beauty over bulk, named SuperSlow one of the hottest workouts of 2002. *Newsweek, Men's Health, Sports Illustrated for Women* and the *New York Times* have also jumped on the bandwagon.

When I first start sifting through the media reports, the glowing testimonials sound too good to be true. Lifting weights at the conventional speed never did this much for me or anyone else I know. Could slowing down really make that big a difference?

The SuperSlow movement's headquarters is tucked away in an anonymous strip mall not far from the airport in Orlando, Florida. When I arrive, Ken Hutchins, the man who founded SuperSlow in the early 1980s, is busy on the phone, explaining to someone in Seattle how to become a certified trainer. The delay gives me a chance to inspect the Before and After photographs on the office walls. Bearded, middle-aged Ted took 6 inches off his waist in ten weeks. Thirty-something Ann shed 7 inches from her thighs in under three months. The photos are shot in the warts-and-all style favoured by medical textbooks—no air-brushing, no artsy lighting, no touching up. I find this reassuring. It suggests that SuperSlow is winning converts through results rather than slick marketing.

Hutchins himself is tall, and blessed with the ramrod posture of a four-star general (he once worked as a surgical technician in the US Air Force). He is fit, without being muscle-bound. We settle into a couple of chairs and start talking about the folly of the Do Everything Faster culture. "The modern mentality is that doing something slowly means it's not intense or productive—and that applies to exercise, too," says Hutchins. "People think that unless you're performing a frenzied activity like aerobics you're not getting any benefit. But actually the opposite is true. It is the slowness that makes exercise so productive."

How does it work? A SuperSlow adherent takes twenty seconds to lift and lower a weight, compared to the conventional six seconds. The slowness eliminates momentum, forcing the muscles to work to complete exhaustion. That, in turn, encourages them to rebuild more quickly and thoroughly. Weightlifting can also make bones stronger and denser, a godsend for young and old. A study published in the June 2001 issue of the *Journal of Sports Medicine and Physical Fitness* concluded that SuperSlow boosted strength 50% more than conventional weight training, at least over the short term. But power is only part of it. Building muscle is also a good way to slim down because it boosts the body's metabolism, forcing it to burn more calories all day long. Put on some muscle, keep your diet steady, and the fat starts falling off.

SuperSlow has the added advantage of taking very little time. The workout is so intense that it never lasts more than twenty minutes. Beginners need to rest three to five days between sessions, more experienced lifters even longer. Since little, if any, sweating occurs—fans keep the temperature in the studio low—many SuperSlow clients work out in their office clothes. Slower turns out to be faster. And safer, too: with its smooth, controlled movements, SuperSlow minimizes the risk of injury.

A SuperSlow workout can also trigger a flurry of other health benefits ranging from higher levels of HDL, the good cholesterol, to stronger, more mobile joints. Hutchins claims that SuperSlow is enough to keep the average person fit and healthy, and that any extra sport is merely a hindrance. Just mention the phrase "cardio workout" and he rolls his eyes. Not everyone agrees, though. Both the American Heart Association and the US Surgeon General's office recommend a mixture of strength training and conventional aerobic exercise.

Despite the absence of a definitive clinical study of SuperSlow, the anecdotal evidence is winning people over in droves. In the United States, professional and collegiate sports teams have reportedly woven elements of SuperSlow philosophy into their exercise regimes, as have the Special Forces, the FBI, the civilian police and paramedics. Doctors and physiotherapists rave about it. Across North America, SuperSlow gyms are drawing a cross-section of society, from pensioners and teenage couch potatoes to desk-bound yuppies and ladies who lunch. Almost every day someone calls the headquarters in Orlando to find out how to become a certified trainer. Studios have opened in Australia, Norway, India, Israel and Taiwan.

Why has SuperSlow taken twenty years to move into the mainstream? Perhaps because it can be hard to love. For a start, lifting weights is less likely to deliver the endorphin high you get from other forms of exercise. Pumping iron at a snail's pace also hurts like hell. If you follow the SuperSlow regime to the letter, it can feel more like a duty than a delight. Listen to Hutchins' description of the perfect SuperSlow studio: " . . . low-distraction furnishings with pale wall colours, no music, no plants, no mirrors, no socializing, dim lighting, continuous ventilation, low temperature, low humidity. . . . Also integral to the ideal environment (is) a strict clinical demeanour."

At the end of our interview, Hutchins guides me into his studio for a SuperSlow workout. Cool, silent and sterile, the room is as welcoming as a silicon chip factory. Clipboard and stopwatch in hand, Hutchins directs me to a leg press machine. He comes down on my first attempt at chitchat like a ton of bricks. "We're not here to socialize," he snaps. "All you need to say is yes or no to my questions." I clam up and start pushing. At first, the weight seems light enough, but as the set drags on, it begins to feel unbearably heavy. Halfway through the second rep, my thighs are trembling, the muscles burning like never before. My instinct is to speed up, to get it over with, but Hutchins is having none of that. "Slow down," he scolds. "Don't get excited. Stay calm and keep breathing. It gets easier when you stay focused." After six reps, my thigh muscles are utterly spent. The next three machines mete out the same punishment to my biceps, calves and pectorals. Then it is over. "That took fifteen minutes and thirty seconds," says Hutchins, clicking his stopwatch. "How do you feel?" Shattered. Wiped out. Take your pick. My legs are jelly, my throat parched. But it is a novel kind of post-workout fatigue—not panting or breathless. I am not even sweating. A few minutes later, I am heading back to the car with a spring in my step.

As I drive away, I ask myself: Would I want to do it again? The honest answer has to be no. The results may be amazing, but it all feels so—let's use Hutchins' own word—clinical. I have read, however, that other SuperSlow trainers take a more relaxed approach. Curious, I hop on a plane to check out a thriving SuperSlow studio in New York.

Nestled seven floors above Madison Avenue, in midtown Manhattan, the Ultimate Training Centre looks much more like a conventional gym: mirrors on the walls, music on the sound system, banter in the air. The owner, Lou Abato, has a ponytail and a ready smile. A photograph of him meeting Arnold Schwarzenegger occupies pride of place on the windowsill by the reception desk, just past the shelves piled high with muscle magazines. Abato has a superhero physique and competes in bodybuilding competitions, yet his training regime is minimalism itself: one SuperSlow workout every week—and nothing else. "People find it hard to believe, but it's all you need," he tells me.

Ultimate Training, however, is not a mecca for musclemen. Almost all Abato's clients are Manhattan professionals. First up, at 8:30 A.M., is a middle-aged construction lawyer and three-year veteran of SuperSlow named Jack Osborn. He emerges from the locker room in a white tank top and blue shorts. Apart from a slight paunch, he looks fit. Abato straps him into the same type of leg press machine I tried with Hutchins, and the session begins. Osborn grunts and grimaces his way through the reps. His breathing quickens, his eyes bulge, his limbs quiver. I feel his pain. Abato reminds him not to seek refuge in speed: "Slow now, slow it right down. Don't rush it." And so it goes on. Around twenty minutes later, Osborn is back in his charcoal suit, telling me how SuperSlow has helped him shed 10 pounds and conquer chronic back pain, and given him deep reserves of energy. "I feel like I have a completely new body," he says. On a hunch, I ask him if lifting weights very slowly also pays psychological dividends. Has it taught him to tackle the New York rat race with a Slow frame of mind? His face lights up. "It's not the reason I started SuperSlow, but it's definitely one of the benefits," he says. "I get a kind of meditative calmness here that carries over through the day. If I have a major meeting or court date, I make sure I still work out with SuperSlow, so that I go in focused, with a clear mind and in control." Osborn recently excelled in a very tricky case, and gives at least some of the credit to lifting weights slowly. "Even when things got crazy, as they tend to do during trial, I felt centred and calm. I was able to manage the client, the judge and the other attorneys on the case," he says. "As well as the physical benefits, SuperSlow has helped to make me more successful in court."

That is quite an endorsement. Could Abato's other clients possibly be as gung-ho? Yes, it turns out. After Osborn heads back to the office, Mike Marino, a fifty-one-year-old management consultant, tells me how nine months of SuperSlow helped slash his body fat by nearly 50%. Tall, trim and tanned, he seems to have stepped from the pages of a men's clothing catalogue. Like Osborn, he sees SuperSlow as a vaccine against the New Yorker's natural urge to rush everything. "It has definitely taken some of the edge off my hurried lifestyle," he says. "If I had a big problem in life, my instinct was always to try to go fast, to get it over with as soon as possible. Now I approach things in a much more meditative way, which helps in consulting work."

Client after client tells the same tale of stronger, tauter, pain-free bodies—and many credit SuperSlow with giving them the inner calm to keep their heads in the Manhattan melee. SuperSlow turns out to be Slow in every sense of the word.

After thanking Abato for his help, I take the elevator back down to the street. Outside, on the sidewalk, a chic young woman with expensively coiffured hair is raving about SuperSlow into her cellphone. I pretend to rifle through my bag in order to eavesdrop. "Trust me, you'll love it," she coos into the handset. "Slow is the new fast."

CHAPTER SIX

MEDICINE: DOCTORS AND PATIENCE

Time is a great healer.
—ENGLISH PROVERB, FOURTEENTH CENTURY

WE ARE NOW IN A WAITING ROOM at the Chelsea and Westminster hospital in London. I have come to see a specialist about a nagging pain in my lower right leg. Even after months of swelling and discomfort, my spirits are high. The hospital has good associations for me—both my children were born here—and the orthopaedic department is among the best in Britain.

The waiting room is packed. People limp on crutches from the toilet to the magazine stand and back. They move warily in their seats. Several are confined to wheelchairs. Above the door leading into the ward, an electronic notice board informs us that the clinic is running forty-five minutes behind schedule. Engrossed in an old copy of *Cosmopolitan,* I am vaguely aware of patients coming and going.

When my name is called, an orderly steers me into the examination room, where a young consultant is waiting at a desk. My heart sinks. Everything, including the coffee stain on his tie, says: Hurry up! After a mumbled greeting, he launches straight into a breathless interrogation. Where is the pain? When did it start? When does it hurt? He wants quick, concise answers. When I try to elaborate, he cuts me short, repeating his question more firmly. We are at logger-heads. I want to build a complete picture of the injury—changes in my sports routine, how the pain has evolved, the impact of painkillers and stretching, the effect on my pos-ture—but Dr. Hurry wants to tick a few boxes and finish his shift. During the brief physical examination, he glances at his watch—twice. Unable to identify the cause of the pain, he tells me to continue popping painkillers and puts me down for an MRI scan and a blood test. I have more questions, but my time is up. I leave the surgery nursing a bad case of consultation interruptus.

Many of you will know the feeling. In hospitals and clin-ics across the world, doctors are under pressure to deal with patients quickly. In Britain's overburdened National Health Service, the average GP visit lasts around six minutes. Even in well-funded private hospitals, doctors are prey to the hurry bug. Pagers keep them constantly on their toes, prac-tising what some call "beeper medicine." The result is a medical culture built on the quick fix. Rather than take the time to listen to patients, to probe all aspects of their health, state of mind and lifestyle, the conventional doctor tends to home in on the symptoms. Often, the next step is to reach for technology—scans, medication, surgery. It is all about fast results on a tight schedule, and patients collude in the hurry. In a world where every second counts, we all want—no, we expect—to be diagnosed, treated and cured as quickly as possible.

Of course, speed is often crucial in medicine. We've all watched *ER*. If you don't remove a diseased appendix, or staunch a bullet wound, or administer an insulin injection in time, the patient will die. But in medicine, as in so many other walks of life, faster is not always better. As many doctors and patients are realizing, it often pays to be Slow.

The backlash against Fast medicine is gaining momentum. Doctors everywhere are pushing for more time with their patients. Medical schools are putting a greater emphasis on talking and listening as tools of diagnosis. A mounting body of research shows that patience is often the best policy. Take infertility. Doctors usually recommend in vitro fertilization, with all its risks, if a woman fails to conceive after one year of trying. But a 2002 study in seven European cities found that one year is simply not enough. Given an extra twelve months, most healthy females will conceive. Indeed, the study found that over 90% of women in their late thirties became pregnant within two years if their partner was also under forty.

Disillusioned with conventional health care, millions of people are turning to complementary and alternative medicine (CAM), which draws on the unhurried, holistic healing traditions that still hold sway in much of the developing world. CAM is a broad movement that includes medical philosophies ranging from traditional Chinese and Indian Ayurveda to Arabic Unani. Among the better-known alternative treatments are homeopathy, herbalism, aromatherapy, acupuncture, massage and energy healing. Osteopaths and chiropractors are also classified as CAM practitioners.

To what extent alternative medicine works remains the subject of fierce debate. Scientific proof of its safety and efficacy is hard to come by. Skeptics, and they are legion, dismiss CAM as quackery dolled up with candles and crystals. If it works at all, they say, it is only as a placebo: people believe they will be cured, so they are. Nevertheless, the medical establishment is paying more attention to CAM than ever before. Conventional hospitals and research institutes across the globe are putting traditional therapies through rigorous trials. And though the jury is still out, preliminary evidence suggests that some CAM really does work. For example, many doctors accept that acupuncture can relieve pain and nausea, even though they are not sure how to explain it.

While the experts hunt for scientific proof in the lab, people are voting with their feet. The global market for CAM tops US$60 billion a year. About half the population of North America now seeks care outside the mainstream health system. Nearly 80% of pain clinics in Germany, where CAM is widespread, offer acupuncture. In Britain, complementary practitioners now outnumber GPs. Unable to find what they want at home, Westerners are flocking to China and other countries known for traditional medicine.

In Beijing, one hospital now runs a separate ward for foreigners. Others offer all-inclusive tour packages—visit the
Great Wall *and* a Chinese herbalist!

Yet even the most zealous fans of CAM do not think that
it can—or should—completely replace the Western tradition. There are certain conditions, such as infections and
trauma, that conventional medicine will always be better at
treating. Even in China you don't find herbalists rushing to
treat the victims of car accidents. Its supporters claim that
where CAM can help most is precisely where Western medicine fails: in the handling of chronic illnesses ranging from
asthma and heart disease to back pain and depression.
Right now, the trend is to pair up the most effective
Western and CAM treatments to create an entirely new tradition of "integrative medicine." CAM courses are already
multiplying in conventional medical schools across the
developed world, and centres for integrative medicine have
sprung up in blue-chip US universities such as Harvard,
Columbia and Duke. In 2002, the World Health
Organization launched a global campaign to blend the best
of CAM into mainstream medicine.

One of Europe's leading providers of integrative medicine is the Hale Clinic, which occupies four floors of a
Regency terrace in central London. When it opened in
1987, the clinic was seen as a haven for New Agers. Today,
all kinds of people, from company directors to chemistry
teachers, come here for acupuncture, aromatherapy or to
have their chakras balanced. Customers young and old
browse in the basement bookshop, or line up for herbal and

homeopathic remedies in the dispensary. "When we started, complementary medicine was seen as strange and revolutionary, something for rebels to try," says Teresa Hale, the clinic's founder. "Now it is accepted in the mainstream. We even have hospitals referring patients to us." Among its staff of a hundred, the Hale Clinic has several conventionally trained doctors, including a couple of GPs. In 2003, a London hospital invited one of the clinic's healers to work with its cancer patients.

Part of the attraction of complementary medicine is that it eschews the quick fix, and treats patients as people, rather than as a sack of symptoms. Most CAM therapies are by nature Slow. They work in harmony with the body and mind, coaxing rather than coercing the patient into healing. Relaxation, which lowers blood pressure and reduces pain, anxiety and depression, is often at the core of the treatment, as is urging people to live at a balanced pace. At the Hale Clinic, practitioners from all disciplines encourage their patients to be Slow—to work less, to eat in a more leisurely fashion, to meditate, to spend more time with family and friends, to take up contemplative hobbies, or simply to find a moment each day to walk in the park.

By and large, CAM practitioners take much more time than their mainstream rivals can afford. A homeopath will spend up to two hours with a patient, building rapport, listening attentively, sifting through the answers to tease out the root cause of the ailment. Massage and acupuncture sessions usually last an hour, during which the practitioner talks to and touches the patient. It may sound trite, but in a world where everyone is constantly dashing around, and real connections between people are few and far between, a little tender loving care goes a long way. It may even trigger healing mechanisms in the body. In the words of Ingrid Collins, a British consultant psychologist, "When you give patients time and attention, they can relax into healing."

Research seems to bear this out. In one American study, a psychotherapist worked alongside a GP, lending a sympathetic ear during consultations. He asked questions that went far beyond the usual symptoms checklist. What are your feelings about the illness? How has it affected the people around you? Patients loved the attention, and some went on to recover from long-term conditions. This brings us back to the link between mind and body. In the last chapter, we saw how slower forms of exercise lead to what the Romans called *mens sana in corpore sano*. Now, the medical world is coming round to the holistic idea that people's mental state can affect their physical well-being. And once you accept that a patient is a person with moods, hang-ups and a story to tell, it is no longer enough to run through a checklist of symptoms and reach for the prescription pad. You have to take the time to listen. You have to make a connection.

Mainstream medicine is making room for Slowness in many ways. One is in the growing willingness to use relaxation in healing. To help patients unwind, more and more hospitals steer them towards soothing activities such as gardening, painting, making music, knitting and spending time with pets. Another trend is to recognize the healing effects of Mother Nature. A recent study at Texas A&M University found that having a view of green spaces from the bedside window helped patients recover from surgery more quickly and with fewer painkillers. So hospitals are installing outdoor gardens, revamping wards to provide more sunlight, plants and green views and broadcasting footage of dolphins swimming in the sea or streams gurgling through sun-dappled forests on in-house TV channels.

Conventional doctors are embracing Slow-style therapies in growing numbers. Some use meditation, yoga and Chi Kung to treat cancer, carpal tunnel syndrome, osteoarthritis, diabetes, hypertension, asthma and epilepsy, as well as mental health problems. Others use SuperSlow weightlifting to rehabilitate patients with cardiac problems and osteoporosis. Many GPs now refer their patients to chiropractors, acupuncturists, osteopaths, herbalists and homeopaths. And although CAM treatments usually take longer to work, sometimes the Slow approach brings faster results. Consider two rival methods of treating the pain caused by a pinched nerve along the spine. A Western doctor would probably dash off a prescription for anti-inflammatory drugs, which would take time to kick in. An Ayurvedic practitioner, however, could zap the pain immediately with a Marma massage, which focuses on special sites where flesh, veins and bones meet up.

Some mainstream doctors are going one step further by retraining in CAM therapies. Take Catherine Watson. She used to work as a research technician for a major pharmaceutical company, developing drugs to treat the immune system. After years in the lab, however, she grew disenchanted with the sledgehammer approach of conventional medicine. Western drugs often blitz the symptoms of a disease, without curing the underlying problem. And many cause collateral damage—side effects that require even more drugs. "I just felt there had to be another way," says Watson. In 1999, she left her well-paid job at the pharmaceutical company to study Western herbalism. Her background gave her a head start, since many modern drugs are derived from natural herbs. Watson now runs a thriving herbalism practice at her home in Hertfordshire, just outside London. Her speciality is treating skin and digestive problems. Sometimes her herbal concoctions work alone, but for other conditions, such as asthma, they act in tandem with conventional medicine. With every patient, though, Watson takes a Slow approach. She usually devotes at least an hour to the initial consultation, and makes it clear that her remedies take time. "Sometimes you get a quick result, but usually herbalism works gradually, by chipping away at a condition," she says. "It is normally slower than conventional medicine, but in the end the results are more effective than people imagine, and without the side effects I saw all too often in the pharmaceutical industry."

Often CAM is a last resort for patients failed by Western medicine. Nik Stoker, a twenty-seven-year-old advertising manager in London, used to suffer from excruciating menstrual pains. Every month, her hormones went haywire, waking her in the night with hot flushes and condemning her to chronic fatigue in the day. Her emotions yo-yoed wildly, and she found it hard to work. Eventually, her doctor put her on the contraceptive Pill, a common remedy for menstrual pains. For years, she bounced from one brand of Pill to the next, never curing the problem, and suffering side effects. The drugs made her feel like she was carrying a cannonball in her stomach and legs. Sometimes she could hardly walk. "I felt like I was going bananas," she says. When scans and even investigative surgery failed to pinpoint the source of her woes, doctors offered little sympathy, telling her that all women suffered menstrual pains and that the only thing for it was a hot water bottle and a good rest. "They made me feel like I was just moaning, you know, just wasting their time," she says.

In desperation, Stoker went to see Tom Lawrence, an acupuncturist-cum-herbalist recommended by a friend. It was her first foray into CAM, but his relaxed, holistic approach put her at ease right away. The first consultation lasted more than an hour, during which Stoker talked and talked and talked, not only about her symptoms but also about her diet, career, mood, social life and hobbies. Lawrence wanted a complete picture. Stoker felt someone was finally listening to her. The treatment itself was a long way from Medicine 101. To realign and rebalance the energy lines coursing through her body, Lawrence inserted a forest of needles into her lower legs and wrists. He asked Stoker to stop eating dairy products, and made her some capsules containing a dozen herbs, including field mint, angelica root and liquorice. Mainstream medics may scoff at the methods, but the results are real enough. After her first appointment, Stoker felt less tense than she had in years. A dozen sessions later, the menstrual pains had more or less cleared up. Her life is transformed. "I'm a different person now," she says.

Like many patients who reach beyond conventional medicine, Stoker thinks CAM has healed both her body and her mind. She feels less irritable now, more able to cope with stress and the fast pace of life in London. "You know that sickly, worked-up feeling you get when you have a million things to do and you don't even know where to start?" she says. "Well, I don't get that so much anymore. I have a lot more calmness and clarity of mind."

As long as CAM remains on the medical fringe, however, patients will have to negotiate a minefield of misinformation. There are plenty of charlatans eager to cash in on the fashion for alternative therapies, promising "holistic" care and then delivering a pale imitation of it. It takes years to learn the techniques of Shiatsu or Ayurvedic massage, yet unqualified hairdressers offer them as a post-cut extra. Often the improper use of CAM therapies is nothing more than an expensive waste of time. But sometimes it can do real damage. Some studies suggest that St. John's wort, a herbal remedy for depression, can interfere with drugs used to treat cancer and HIV. And some CAM cures have been very misleadingly sold: in China, the herb *ma huang* (ephedra) is the traditional remedy for short-term respiratory congestion, but American companies marketed it as a dietary aid and energy booster. The result was a string of deaths, heart attacks and strokes.

Gradually, though, law and order is coming to what some regard as the Wild West of medicine. Governments are drawing up codes of practice and establishing minimum standards for some CAM practices. In 2001, the UK finally set up an official register of osteopaths. A dozen US states have passed laws to license naturopaths, healers who practice a range of alternative therapies from homeopathy to herbalism. Critics warn that the "formalization" of CAM could stifle innovation—even the most ancient healing tradition is always evolving. Even if that is true, though, winning an official seal of approval will bring benefits, not least funding from the public purse.

At the moment, most people pay for CAM out of their own pockets. And many treatments are not cheap. In London, a single session of acupuncture can cost over US$60 dollars. Persuading the state to pick up the tab will not be easy. At a time when the cost of health care is skyrocketing, governments are in no mood to extend coverage to new treatments, especially those supported by scant scientific evidence. That is why CAM is often treated more as a luxury than a necessity. Against a backdrop of economic hard times, the state medical insurance scheme in Germany has cut back the number of alternative treatments it covers.

Yet there may be an economic case for spending public money on at least some CAM therapies. To start with, alternative medicine can be cheaper than conventional rivals. A course of Shiatsu massage might fix a back problem that would otherwise lead to expensive surgery. In Germany, St. John's wort is now used to treat more than half of all cases of depression. Studies show the herb has fewer side effects than prescription antidepressants. And at 25 cents a day it is a lot cheaper than Prozac.

CAM may be able to lower health care budgets in other ways, too. The holistic mind-body approach favoured by many practitioners puts the stress on prevention, which is cheaper than cure. CAM also seems to excel at treating chronic illnesses, which gobble up around 75% of all health spending in the industrialized world. In the United States that adds up to nearly a trillion dollars a year.

The number crunchers are taking note. In Britain, where the state medical system is notoriously cash-strapped, hospitals are starting to fund treatments such as aromatherapy, homeopathy and acupuncture. Around 15% of American hospitals offer some form of CAM. In 2003, for the first time, two naturopathic physicians were appointed to the committee that decides which treatments the US Medicare program will fund.

Many private companies now build CAM into their benefit packages. Microsoft will pay for its employees to see a naturopath. On both sides of the Atlantic, meanwhile, leading insurance companies are footing the bill for a growing number of CAM treatments. Chiropractic care and osteopathy top the list, but many private health care plans now cover homeopathy, reflexology, acupuncture, biofeedback, massage therapy and herbal remedies. A half-dozen US states now oblige insurers to cover at least some alternative therapies. In Europe, insurance companies already offer lower life insurance premiums to people who meditate regularly.

Nevertheless, acceptance from the insurance industry is not the only guarantee that an alternative therapy actually works. At the Hale Clinic, Danira Caleta practises what must be one of the slowest and most gentle forms of medicine, reiki, which involves channelling energy by holding the hands above the body. The aim is to work in harmony with the patient, activating his or her "internal doctor." Though insurance companies shy away from reiki, more than a hundred hospitals in the United States now offer it, and Caleta is deluged with people willing to pay from their own pockets.

Marlene Forrest turned to her for help in 2003. The fifty-five-year-old had been diagnosed with breast cancer, and was facing a double mastectomy. Memories of her father's death after an operation ten years earlier had sent her into a panic, and her mind was racing from one dark scenario to the next. To calm herself down, and to prepare her body for surgery, Forrest booked an appointment with Caleta.

Caleta combines reiki with other techniques to heal and relax. She starts off by steering the patient through a deep-breathing exercise, and then uses guided meditation to help them visualize a peaceful scene in nature. "People who live in cities respond especially well to making that connection with nature," she says. "It really calms them down."

After five sessions with Caleta, Forrest's anxiety melted away, and she went into hospital feeling serene. As she lay in the ward, waiting to go under the knife, she worked through the breathing exercises, the meditation and the visualization. When the porters came to wheel her into the theatre, she was actually smiling. "I just felt so relaxed," she says. "Like I was ready for anything."

Following the operation, Forrest, who runs a retirement home in London, made such a miraculous recovery that hospital staff dubbed her "superwoman." Apart from a tiny initial dose, she needed no painkillers at all. "The nurses and the doctors were amazed," she says. "They kept looking in on me to see if I needed any morphine, but I didn't. They said I must be brave or have a high pain threshold, but that wasn't it at all; I simply wasn't in any pain." The breast-care nurse was so impressed she urged Caleta to treat more cancer patients.

Caleta's brand of healing is not only for the clinically unwell. It can also help people develop a Slow frame of mind. Just ask David Lamb. In 2002, the busy, thirty-seven-year-old textile agent came down with labyrinthitis, an inflammation of the inner ear that causes dizziness. Unhappy with the care on offer from his GP, he booked a few sessions with Caleta, who shaved four weeks off his recovery time. What really impressed Lamb, though, was the slowing, soothing effect that the treatment had on his mind. Long after the labyrinthitis cleared up, he continues to visit Caleta every three weeks. "Everyone has to find a way of dealing with the stress and the fast pace of life in London," he says. "For some people it's yoga, for others it's the gym or gardening. For me it's reiki." An hour under Caleta's hands usually helps Lamb de-stress and slow down. Her healing touch has also led him to rethink his priorities. "Reiki slows you down by making you think about the things that are really important in your life—your kids, your partner, your friends," he says. "It makes you realize that rushing about trying to land the next big deal, earn more money or buy a bigger house is actually pretty meaningless." Which does not mean that Lamb plans to give up his job and join a commune. Not a chance. Instead, he uses the slowness of reiki to cope better in the fast-moving business world. Before big meetings, when his head is spinning, he stills his mind with the visualization and breathing exercises. Not long ago, he visited Caleta to calm his nerves two days before negotiating a large contract with an overseas supplier. On the big day, he strode confidently into the meeting, made his case lucidly, and closed the deal. "I am a businessman, and I like to make money, but there is a right way to do it," he says. "Even if you're in an aggressive environment, you can approach it calmly. Reiki gives you an edge by bringing out that calmness. A calm mind gives you more confidence, more power."

Not surprisingly, Caleta is branching out from hospitals and clinics to the workplace. She recently treated Esther Porta, a thirty-year-old consultant at a leading PR agency in London. For the second time in five years, Porta had come down with optic neuritis, a nasty inflammation of the optic nerve that triggers a temporary loss of vision. Thanks to Caleta, her recovery was so quick and so thorough that even her doctor was astounded. When colleagues noted how well she looked, Porta owned up to using a healer. Rather than smirking, the company brass wanted to know more. One member of the board has suggested bringing Caleta into the office to help the whole staff slow down and boost their health.

Intrigued by the rave reviews, and fed up with the failure of physiotherapy, sports massage and medication to fix my leg, I decide to give reiki a try. Caleta arranges to put me through the paces on a Monday afternoon at the Hale Clinic. She is a reassuring presence, a forty-three-year-old Australian with laughing eyes and an easy smile. The treatment room is small and white, with a tall window looking out onto the back of the building behind. There are no crystals, no star charts, no incense sticks, none of the New Age trappings I was expecting. Instead, it looks very much like my GP's office.

Caleta begins by asking me about all kinds of things that never came up in my hurried consultation with the orthopaedic specialist: my diet, work routine, emotional state, family life, sleeping pattern. She also listens closely to a blow-by-blow account of how the pain in the leg has shifted and changed. When there is nothing more to say, I lie down on the treatment table, and close my eyes.

The first step is to slow down my breathing. Caleta tells me to inhale deeply through the nose, allowing the abdomen to expand, and then exhale through the mouth. "It's a Chi Kung technique, to get the energy circulating again," she says. Then we move on to the guided meditation. Caleta talks me into a beautiful beach scene: a tropical sun; blue sky; a gentle breeze; warm sand underfoot; a lagoon of still, translucent, turquoise water; an emerald jungle dotted with red hibiscus and yellow and white frangipani. "It's absolutely spectacular," she whispers. "And you feel a sense of freedom, openness, stillness, tranquility, peace." This is true. I can almost feel myself floating on my back in the warm water, gazing up at the sky. Caleta then asks me to imagine a white ball of healing light moving up through my body.

By the time she is ready to start the reiki, I have forgotten the meaning of the word "stress." She rubs her hands together and holds them above various parts of my body to get the blocked energy flowing again. Though I cannot see her, I know where she is standing from the strange heat. It seems to come from within me, as though something has been activated deep inside my body. In my lower back, the heat is faint, no more than a whisper of warmth. When Caleta holds her hands above my right leg, it feels positively hot.

The session lasts an hour and leaves me feeling pleasantly mellow, yet also alert and energized, ready for anything. My leg, though, is unchanged. "It takes time," says Caleta, reading the disappointment in my face. "The body heals itself at its own pace, so you have to be patient. You can't rush it." This neat summary of the Slow philosophy somehow fails to give me hope for the leg, and I leave the clinic with mixed feelings.

A few days later, though, a breakthrough occurs. The pain in my leg has eased off, and the swelling is down, too. It is the first clear sign of progress in months. I cannot explain it with science, and neither can my orthopaedic surgeon when I meet him again a week later. Maybe

Caleta's willingness to take the time to listen helped kick-start the healing. Or maybe it is possible to use universal energy to help the body repair itself. Whatever the explanation, reiki seems to work for me. My next appointment is already booked.

CHAPTER SEVEN

SEX: A LOVER WITH A SLOW HAND

*Most men pursue pleasure with such breathless haste
that they hurry past it.*
—Søren Kierkegaard (1813–1855)

There are some things a person never lives down. In an interview a few years ago, Sting confessed to a fondness for Tantric sex, and raved about making love to his wife for hours on end. In an instant, the English rocker was the butt of a million jokes. Commentators wondered how he found time to write songs, or how his wife could still walk. By the time Sting tried to play down his dabblings in Tantra, it was already too late. He was forever fixed in the public imagination as the priapic pop star. Even today, DJs introduce his songs with snide references to never-ending nooky.

Sting should have known better. There is something inherently ludicrous about taking courses to improve your sexual performance. And Tantra, a mystical blend of yoga, meditation and sex, is a particularly easy target for scorn. It conjures images of hirsute hippies romping in the nude. In an episode of *Sex in the City*, Carrie and the girls attend a Tantric workshop. After a long, slow buildup, the male instructor accidentally shoots his seed into Miranda's hair. She spends the rest of the episode manically wiping her bangs with tissues.

But Tantra has more to offer than just cheap laughs. All over the world, people are warming to the very Tantric idea that slower sex is better sex. Most of us could certainly devote more time to making love. That may seem, at first glance, like an odd assertion. After all, the modern world is already saturated with sex. From movies and the media to advertising and art, everything is laced with erotic themes and imagery. You get the feeling everyone is at it all the time. Only they're not. Even if we spend a big chunk of the day watching, talking, fantasizing, joking and reading about sex, we spend very little time actually doing it. A large study carried out in 1994 found that the average American adult devoted a meagre half an hour per week to making love. And when we finally do get down to it, it is often over before it really gets started. Though statistics on sexual behaviour must always be taken with a pinch of salt, academic surveys and anecdotal evidence suggest that an awful lot of couplings have a whiff of the wham-bam-thank-you-ma'am about them. Published in the early 1950s, the historic *Kinsey Report* famously estimated that 75% of American husbands reach climax within two minutes of penetration.

Fast sex is not a modern invention—it goes way back, and probably has its roots in the survival instinct. In prehistoric days, copulating quickly made our ancestors less vulnerable to attack, either by a wild beast or a rival. Later, culture added extra incentives to hurry the sex act. Some religions taught that intercourse was for procreation rather than recreation: a husband should climb on, do his duty and climb off again.

Things are supposed to be different now. The modern world likes to take the Woody Allen view that sex is the most fun you can have without laughing. So why do we still rush it? One reason is that the biological urge to fornicate fast remains hardwired into the human, or at least the male, brain. Our rapid pace of life must take some of the blame, too. Busy schedules militate against long, languid sessions of erotic play. At the end of a hard day, most people are too worn out for sex. Working fewer hours is one way to free up energy and time for sex, which is why couples make love more on vacation. But fatigue and time pressure are not the only reasons for fast sex. Our hurry-up culture teaches that reaching the destination is more important than the journey itself—and sex is affected by the same finishing line mentality. Even women's magazines seem more obsessed with orgasm—how intense, how often—than with the foreplay that triggers it. In their book, *Tantra: The Secret Power of Sex,* Arvind and Shanta Kale wrote, "One of the first victims of Western man's unseemly haste is his sex life. Efficiency is measured by the speed with which a person completes an act effectively, and an effective act of sex is an act which results in orgasm. . . . In other words, the quick-er   the   orgasm the more effective the intercourse." Pornography takes the Western obsession with closing the deal to its ultimate con-clusion, reducing sex to a blur of frenzied pumping crowned by the all-important "money shot."

The modern world has little patience for anyone who fails to keep up with the sexual pace. Many women—40%, according to some surveys—suffer from lack of sexual desire or pleasure. True to our quick-fix culture, the phar-maceutical industry insists that a Viagra-style pill can put things right. But genital blood flow may be a red herring. Maybe the real problem is speed. A woman needs more time to warm up, taking on average twenty minutes to reach full sexual arousal, compared with ten minutes or under for a man. Most women, like the Pointer Sisters, pre-fer a lover with a slow hand.

Let's not get carried away, though. Speed has its place between the sheets. Sometimes a swift roll in the hay is all you want or need. Long live the quickie. But sex can be so much more than a sprint to orgasm. Making love slowly can be a profound experience. It can also deliver fantastic orgasms.

That is why the Slow philosophy is now making inroads into bedrooms across the world. Even lads' magazines have started urging readers to seduce their partners with long, laidback erotic encounters, complete with candles, music, wine and massage. Over twelve straight weeks in 2002, *Weekly Gendai,* Japan's leading men's title, filled its pages with articles on lovemaking in the twenty-first century. The tone was serious, even a little didactic, because the aim was to teach readers the art of intimacy, sensuality and slowness. "A lot of Japanese men have the idea that the best sex you can have is fast, macho, American-style sex," says Kazuo Takahashi, a senior editor at the magazine. "We wanted to show that there is another way to have a physical relationship." One article in the series hailed the tradition of "slow sex" in Polynesia. The author explained how Polynesian lovers spend ages stroking and exploring each other's bodies. When it comes to orgasm, quality takes precedence over quantity.

The sex series was a big hit in Japan. *Weekly Gendai*'s circulation shot up by 20%, and letters from grateful readers flooded in. One thanked the magazine for giving him the courage to talk openly to his wife about sex. He was shocked to learn that vigorous, energetic lovemaking did not always ring her bell, and that she would prefer to take things at a more Polynesian pace. He gave it a try, and now their marriage and sex life are better than ever.

Around the same time as commuters on the Tokyo subway were reading about the joys of erotic deceleration, an official Slow Sex movement sprang to life in Italy. Its founder is Alberto Vitale, a Web marketing consultant based in Bra, the home of Slow Food. In a textbook example of the cross-fertilization within the Slow movement, Vitale decided that the Petrini principle—taking time leads to greater sensual pleasure—could be transplanted from the dinner table to the bedroom. In 2002, he founded Slow Sex to rescue lovemaking from "the breakneck speed of our crazy and vulgar world." Membership quickly hit three figures, with an even gender split, and is still rising.

After a long day of interviewing Slow Food activists, I meet Vitale at a sidewalk café in Bra. He is a slim, owlish thirty-one-year-old. As soon as the drinks are ordered, he begins telling me why his days as a Latin Lothario are over. "In our consumer culture, the aim is to sleep with someone quickly and then move on to the next conquest," he says. "Listen to men talking—it's all about the number of women, the number of times, the number of positions. It's all about numbers. You go to bed with a checklist of things you have to get through. You're too impatient, too self-centred, to really enjoy the sex."

Vitale crusades against the culture of the quick shag. He gives talks on the joys of Slow sex to social clubs around Piedmont. He has plans to convert his website (www.slow-sex.it) into a forum for discussing all aspects of erotic deceleration. Slowing down has done wonders for his own sex life. Instead of racing through his favourite positions, Vitale now takes time to indulge in extended foreplay, to whisper to his partner, to look into her eyes. "If you look around the world, there is a growing desire to slow down," he says. "In my opinion, the best place to start is in bed."

Nothing highlights the yearning for slower sex more than the worldwide Tantra boom. During the sexual revolution of the 1960s and 1970s, a few pioneers dabbled in Tantric techniques. Now others are catching up. Every day, twelve thousand people navigate through the blizzard of Internet porn to visit Tantra.com. Undeterred by the ridicule heaped on Sting, couples of all ages are flocking to Tantric sex workshops.

So what exactly is Tantra? The word itself comes from Sanskrit, and means "to extend, expand or weave." Invented five thousand years ago in India, and later embraced by Buddhists in Tibet and China, Tantra is a spiritual discipline that treats the body as an instrument of prayer. Just as the Christian mystics reached out to God through self-flagellation, the Tantrikas used slow, mindful sexual union as the path to enlightenment. In other words, Tantric sex, in its purest form, is not just normal sex slowed down. It is about using sexual energy to forge a perfect spiritual union with your partner, and with the universe.

Tantric philosophy teaches that the human body circulates energy through the seven chakras that run up and down the spine, from the genitals to the crown of the head. With a mixture of meditation, yogic exercises, controlled breathing and unhurried foreplay, couples learn to contain and channel their sexual energy. During intercourse, the man prolongs his erection through slow, measured thrusting. Men also learn to have an orgasm without ejaculating. With its stress on sharing, intimacy and slowness, Tantra is very female-friendly. Indeed, the man is meant to treat the woman as a goddess, gently stoking her arousal without seeking to take it over or impose his own pace. In the end, however, the spoils are shared evenly. When Tantra works, both partners achieve, in the words of Tantra.com, a "higher state of consciousness" and a "realization of the blissful nature of the Self." If that all sounds a little too corny for comfort, the carnal payoff is pretty amazing, too: Tantra teaches both men and women to surf the waves of multiple orgasm for as long as they like. If a couple remains together—and who wouldn't after that?—their sexual fire will burn brighter, instead of fizzling out, as the years pass.

The modern urge to slow down in the bedroom, as elsewhere, has its roots in the nineteenth century. As industrialization cranked up the pace, people began to look East for a slower alternative. A growing interest in Oriental philosophies brought Westerners into contact with Tantra. An early fan of what came to be known as "sacred sex" was Alice Bunker Stockham, one of the first female doctors in the United States. After studying Tantra in India, she returned home to promote the control of orgasm as a route to physical ecstasy, emotional bonding, better health and spiritual fulfilment. She coined the term *karezza,* which derives from an Italian word meaning "caress," to describe her secularized version of Tantra. Her sex tips first appeared in 1883 in a book called *Toktology,* which Tolstoy later translated into Russian. Others followed in Stockham's footsteps, defying Victorian taboos to publish books and manuals on the art of slow, mindful lovemaking. In *Hell on Earth Made Heaven: The Marriage Secrets of a Chicago Contractor,* George Washington Savory gave Tantric sex a Christian spin.

More than a century later, my own journey into Tantra gets off to a halting start. As I begin the research, my first instinct is to smirk, or run away. The New Age jargon, the chakras, the self-help videos hosted by men with ponytails—it all seems so cheesy. I'm not sure I'm ready to harmonize my inner man or awaken my divinity, or even if I know what either of those things means. And do we really have to call the penis a lingam, or "wand of light"?

When you think about it, though, Tantra is not as goofy as it sounds. Even the most down-to-earth among us knows that sex is more than just a very pleasant muscle spasm. It can forge deep emotional bonds; it can pull us out of our-selves, letting the mind float free in a timeless present. Occasionally, it offers a glimpse of the profound, the tran-scendent. When people talk about their most intense moments of sexual ecstasy, they often use spiritual metaphors: "I felt like I was flying like an eagle." "I crawled into my partner's body." "I saw the face of God." Tantra seeks to develop that link between the sexual and the spiritual.

In the ancient world, people spent years purifying and mastering their body and mind before a Tantric guru would even give them the time of day. Only once their "inner psychic energies" were awakened could they begin to study the sexual techniques. Nowadays, anyone can start learning Tantric lovemaking tomorrow. And this being a consumer society, there are workshops to suit every taste. Some are more spiritual than others. Many Western instructors blend in techniques from the Kama Sutra and other sacred-sex texts. Not surprisingly, the purists accuse the reformers of peddling "Tantra Lite." But even if that is so, who cares? What is wrong with modified Tantra if it works? Even if people fail to reach a higher plane of consciousness, or to realign their chakras, they can still benefit from the basic sexual philosophy. After all, once you strip Tantra of its mystical baggage, you are left with the rudiments of good sex: tenderness, communication, respect, variety and slowness.

Even hardened skeptics succumb to the charms of Tantra. In 2001, Val Sampson, a forty-something journalist, went to write a feature on Tantric sex for the London *Times*. She dragged her husband along to the workshop, expecting that both of them would giggle all the way through. Instead, they found that the simple breathing exercises actually worked, and that the message about honouring your partner with slow, sharing sex struck a chord. "It was a revelation," Sampson tells me when we meet at her gym in Twickenham, on the outskirts of London. "I really had no idea that there was another approach to sex that was about giving time to each other, about bringing your head and your heart completely into the sexual relationship."

Sampson and her husband promptly signed up for a Tantra weekend. Now they are converts. In 2002, Sampson published a book called *Tantra: The Art of Mind-Blowing Sex*, a how-to guide written for people who normally run a mile from anything New Age. Her view is that we can all decide how deeply we want to explore the mystical side of sexuality. "I think it's equally valid to follow Tantra as a spiritual path or simply to improve your sex life," she says. "In the end, you'll probably get to the same place, anyway."

At the end of our chat, Sampson gives me the phone

number of her Tantric teacher, the improbably named Leora Lightwoman. I call her that evening. Lightwoman is taken with the idea of a book on slowing down, and invites me to join her next workshop.

Two months later, on a blustery Friday evening, my wife and I arrive at an old warehouse in north London. We ring the bell, and the door clicks open. Voices float up the stairwell from the basement on a wave of incense. One of the workshop assistants—they are called "angels"—greets us on the landing. He is in his thirties and has a crooked smile and a ponytail. He wears a white vest and cream-coloured yoga trousers and smells strongly of armpit. He reminds me of the host of a particularly toe-curling Tantra video I have seen. My heart sinks.

We remove our shoes and enter the basement, a large whitewashed room decked out with ethnic throws. My worst fear—that everyone in the workshop would be a macrobiotic vegan or an aromatherapist or both—turns out to be way off the mark. There are a few archetypal New Agers, in sarongs and beads, but most of the thirty-two participants are ordinary folk in comfortable street clothes. There are doctors, stockbrokers, teachers. One man has come straight from his trading desk in the City. Many have never been to a self-improvement workshop before.

Lightwoman is at pains to put everyone at ease. A graceful, elfin figure with cropped hair and large eyes, she speaks slowly, as though rolling each sentence around inside her head before releasing it. She starts the workshop by explaining a little about Tantra, and then asks us to introduce ourselves and say why we are here. The singletons claim to be on a journey of self-discovery. The couples have come to deepen their relationships.

Once the ice is broken, we start with a little Kundalini shaking. This involves closing the eyes and vibrating the body from the knees up. The aim is to relax and get your inner energy flowing. I don't know about the energy, but I certainly feel less tense after about ten minutes of wobbling around. We then move on to the showpiece event of the evening, the Awakening of the Senses. "In the modern world, when everyone is in a hurry, we often do not take enough time to use our senses," says Lightwoman. "This is about rediscovering your senses and bringing them back to life."

Everyone puts on a blindfold and holds hands with a partner. After a few minutes, my wife and I are guided across the room and made to sit on some cushions on the floor. The only sound is the gentle rustling of angels escorting people back and forth. Instead of fidgeting, I can feel myself surrendering to the moment, going with the flow. In a soft voice, Lightwoman asks us to listen closely. The silence is then broken by the ring of a Tibetan bell. Deprived of other sensory input, my mind is free to concentrate on the ringing. The sound—clear, rich, noble— feels as if it is washing over me. I want it to go on forever. Other sounds—hands beating on drums, maracas, a didgeridoo—have a similar effect. For a moment it occurs to me that I could stand being blind if my ears could always bring me this much pleasure. The ceremony continues, moving on to the sense of smell. The angels wave richly scented objects beneath our noses—cinnamon, rose water, oranges. The aromas are intense and exciting. To awaken our taste buds, the angels then pop morsels of food—chocolate, strawberries, mango—into our mouths. Again the result is a sensory explosion.

Touch is the final leg of the journey. The angels run feathers up and down our arms, and nuzzle our necks with furry toys, which is a lot nicer than it sounds. We are then given an object to explore with our hands. Mine is a bronze statuette of a woman. My fingers probe every nook and cranny, trying to draw a mental picture. We are then asked to investigate our partner's hands with the same spirit of wonder. This sounds lame, but actually turns out to be rather moving. As I slowly explore my wife's hands, I remember doing the same a long time ago, in the early days of our relationship, in the doorway of a bistro in Edinburgh.

Later, we remove our blindfolds to find the room darkened and everyone sitting on cushions in a large circle. In the middle, the objects used in the ceremony are artfully arranged on a red blanket draped over some boxes and dotted with candles. It looks like a luxury cruise liner sailing into port on a summer evening. A warm glow envelops the room. One man, a lawyer who came to the workshop simply to please his wife, is blown away. "That was really beautiful," he mutters. "Really beautiful." I know how he feels. My senses are tingling. The evening has passed in the blink of an eye. I can hardly wait to come back for more.

The next morning, though, my plans go disastrously awry. Our daughter is rushed to hospital with a chest infection, and my wife has to drop out of the course to be with her. It is a big blow for us both. Nevertheless, I decide to carry on alone, turning up on Saturday morning as a singleton.

The awkwardness of opening night has given way to an easy camaraderie. It helps that the workshop is as far from a swingers' party as you can imagine. There is no overt sexual touching or nudity. Respect is a top priority for Lightwoman. Indeed, she expels a single man from our workshop for showing a little too much interest in the female participants.

After another round of Kundalini shaking, we pair off for a series of exercises designed to teach the art of slow, loving sensuality. One is called Yes-No-Maybe-Please. Partners take turns touching each other, with the touchee delivering a running commentary to the toucher: Yes means "I like that"; No means "Try something else"; Maybe means "I'm not sure"; Please means "Mmm, more of the same." In Tantra, each time couples make love they should explore each other's bodies as if for the first time. For this exercise, my partner is a slightly shy young woman. Because the standard erogenous zones are off limits, we are free to investigate areas often neglected in the heat of the moment— knees, calves, ankles, feet, shoulders, the base of the neck, elbows, the spine. We start off tentatively, but gradually find a groove. It is all very sweet and sensual.

Other exercises foster the same Slow ethic. We dance sensually, breathe in unison and stare into each other's eyes. Striving to create intimacy with a total stranger feels a bit weird to me, but the principle—slow down and make a connection with your partner—is clearly working for many participants. Couples who arrived with ho-hum body language are now holding hands and canoodling. It makes me miss my wife.

The toughest exercise of the weekend is designed to strengthen the pubococcygeus, the cluster of muscles that run from the pubic bone to the tailbone. These are what you flex to push out the final few drops of urine. Lightwoman calls them the "love muscle." Strengthening them can deliver more intense orgasms for both sexes, and can help men separate ejaculation from the spasms that accompany it, paving the way for the multiple orgasm.

Lightwoman asks us to combine a love muscle workout with controlled breathing. While clenching and releasing the pubococcygeus, we imagine moving our breath up through the seven chakras, starting at the perineum and finishing at the crown of the head. Even if, like me, you are skeptical about the whole chakras thing, the exercise is very relaxing, and strangely affecting.

For many, though, the highlight of the weekend is a manoeuvre called streaming. In the normal course of things, sex culminates with a genital orgasm that lasts a few seconds. Tantra seeks to extend and intensify the ecstasy by releasing the sexual energy from the groin and spreading it around. This is known as the full-body orgasm. In both sexes, streaming is a technique for clearing out the channels through which energy flows. It works like this. After some Kundalini shaking, you lie on your back with your knees in the air and feet flat on the ground. As you slowly open and close your legs, the shake is supposed to start again at your knees and then work its way up your body. Your partner can help the energy flow by waving a hand above the shake and slowly coaxing it in the right direction. It sounds kooky, but let me tell you that streaming does exactly what it says on the packet. In a word: Wow! Almost as soon as I lie down the shaking takes over, as if something has invaded my body. It moves up through my pelvis into my solar plexus. At first the movements are violent, and a little scary, reminding me of the *Alien* movies, where characters convulse and contort before the monster bursts out of their chests. But the fear is short-lived. Before long, the shaking induces a feeling of elation and ecstasy. And I am not alone. All around, people are crying out in joyful release. It is a genuinely remarkable moment. Afterwards, the couples lie entwined, stroking each other languidly.

Tantra is not something you master in a weekend. It takes time. The basic exercises require practice—at the very least, my love muscle still needs work—and there are many more techniques to learn. But my first brush with Tantra suggests that, whatever you think about the New Age, it can open the door to better sex, deeper intimacy and self-awareness.

To find out more about the sexual pot of gold at the end of the rainbow, I speak to a number of graduates from Tantra workshops. Most give it rave reviews. The Kimbers are an affable middle-aged couple from Rickmansworth, just outside London. Cathy, fifty-two, does marketing for trade fairs; Roger, forty-eight, owns and runs an electrical engineering business that manufactures ventilation systems for large buildings. They have been married thirty years. As in many long-term relationships, sex slipped down the priority list as children came along—they have two sons—and work took off. The Kimbers were often too busy or too tired or too stressed for bedroom fireworks. When they did make love, it seldom lasted very long.

In 1999, however, Cathy decided to make a change. She felt her whole life was racing along like a runaway locomotive, and she wanted to slow down. Tantra seemed like a good place to start, so she signed up for Lightwoman's introductory workshop. As the weekend drew near, the Kimbers began to get cold feet. Roger, a down-to-earth type with a natural aversion to the airy-fairy, dreaded being lectured on chi and chakras. The prospect of taking part in the Awakening of the Senses filled Cathy with panic. How could she, a textbook Type-A personality, possibly sit still, doing nothing, for all that time? The Kimbers took a leap of faith, though, and the weekend turned out to be a revelation for them both. Roger was blown away by the streaming. And Cathy loved the Awakening of the Senses. "I felt so much sensual pleasure," she says. "I came out of there floating on air, with an incredible feeling of peace." The couple has since done four Tantric workshops.

Along the way, their sex life has undergone a renaissance with a capital R. Now, at least one evening a week, they retreat upstairs to a small room set aside for Tantric trysts. One of the teachings of Tantra is to create a "sacred space" for sex, which can mean as little as using scents or coloured lights in the bedroom. The Kimbers' room is a secular shrine decorated with mystical objects and personal mementoes—stone sculptures of guardian angels, favourite books, Tibetan bells, lots of candles, family photographs and a ceramic figurine made years ago by their younger son. A dreamcatcher hangs from the ceiling. In soft candlelight, and with essential oils burning, the Kimbers spend hours massaging and caressing each other, and breathing in unison. When they finally do make love, the earth is guaranteed to move. Both now experience deeper and more intense orgasms. Thanks to the relaxation, pelvic exercises and breathing techniques he learned through Tantra, Roger can extend his for two or three minutes. "It's amazing," he says, smiling. "You just don't want it to stop."

Sex is not always a multi-hour affair in the Kimber household. Like other fans of Tantra, the couple still enjoys a quick fumble under the sheets. But even fast sex packs a bigger bang than it used to.

Earth-shattering orgasms are just part of the payoff. A whole new world of tenderness and intimacy has opened up for the Kimbers. Snuggling together on the sofa in their front room, they look like a couple of newlyweds. "Tantra has added a lot of depth to our relationship," says Roger. "Sex is more spiritual and from the heart now." Cathy nods. "People can be married for twenty years and not really know each other because they are just skimming along the surface," she says. "Through Tantra, Roger and I have really come to know each other in a profound way."

Before you rush off to sign up for a weekend workshop,

though, remember that Tantra is a double-edged sword. On one hand, it can inject fresh fizz into a relationship gone flat. But by forcing people to slow down and look deeply at themselves and their partners, it can also expose irreconcilable differences. Halfway through my workshop, one man dropped out. His wife told me he was storming around the house in tears, shouting that their relationship was ruined.

Tim Dyer, a thirty-seven-year-old restaurant manager in Bristol, England, knows the feeling. In 2002, he and his fiancée, a high-flying product developer, attended a Tantra workshop. They had been together three years and wanted to kick-start their dwindling sex life before embarking on marriage. Instead of setting them on the path to the perfect orgasm, however, the workshop made it clear that their relationship was built on sand. Dyer felt uneasy looking deeply into his fiancée's eyes. By the end of the weekend, the couple were quarrelling in hushed tones during exercises. A few weeks later, they broke up.

Earlier, we heard Milan Kundera's warning that people in the fast lane cannot be sure of anything, not even their own hearts. Dyer could not agree more. "I look back now, and I can see that we were both living such busy lives that we never had time to really notice that our relationship had gone pear-shaped," he says. "What Tantra does is slow you down and make you aware of things. And I guess that when we slowed down we realized that we weren't really the love of each other's lives after all." Relieved to have dodged a marriage that was destined for the divorce courts, Dyer is now single again. And he has learned from his mistakes.

Armed with a little Tantric wisdom, he plans to make more time for the sensual and intimate side of any future relationship. "I've learned that the best sex is about making connections, and you can't make real connections if you're in a hurry," he says. "The next time I fall for someone, I want that slowness, that awareness from the beginning."

If he sticks with it, Dyer may find that decelerating in the bedroom helps to bring slowness to other parts of his life. Tantra has certainly done that for the Kimbers. Cathy has mellowed and become more patient with the delays of daily life. Roger, meanwhile, has chosen to work fewer hours. With so much love and so many great orgasms to be had at home, he feels, not surprisingly, less inclined to spend long hours chained to his desk. "Work just doesn't seem to matter so much anymore," he says. He has even started running his business along Slow lines. Having long prided itself on speed of delivery, his company is now less obsessed with filling orders as quickly as possible. Easing the strain on the workforce was one reason for the shift. Has the company fallen prey to quicker rivals? On the contrary, product standards have risen, and orders are still coming in. "Slowing down doesn't have the disastrous results people think it does," says Roger. "It can actually do some good. That does not mean we can't turn on the gas when we have to, but we don't have to all the time."

It should come as no surprise to hear a businessman drawing a link between work and love. Being married to the job takes a toll on our intimate relationships, but the harm also flows in the other direction. According to US research, employees with marital problems lose on average fifteen workdays a year, costing American companies nearly seven billion dollars a year in lost productivity. The solution put forward by the Slow movement is as simple as it is appealing: Spend less time working and more time indulging in slow sex.

WORK: THE BENEFITS OF WORKING LESS HARD

Cannot the labourers understand that by over-working themselves they exhaust their own strength and that of their progeny, that they are used up and long before their time come to be incapable of any work at all, that absorbed and brutalized by this single vice they are no longer men but pieces of men, that they kill within themselves all beautiful faculties, to leave nothing alive and flourishing except the furious madness for work.
—PAUL LAFARGUE, *THE RIGHT TO BE LAZY* (1883)

THERE WAS A TIME, NOT SO LONG AGO, when mankind looked forward to a new Age of Leisure. Machines promised to liberate everyone from the drudgery of work. Sure, we might have to put in the odd shift at the office or factory, monitoring screens, twiddling dials, signing invoices, but the rest of the day would be spent hanging out and having fun. With so much free time on our hands, words like "hurry" and "haste" would eventually fall out of the language.

Benjamin Franklin was among the first to envision a world devoted to rest and relaxation. Inspired by the technological breakthroughs of the latter 1700s, he predicted that man would soon work no more than four hours a week. The nineteenth century made that prophecy look foolishly naive. In the dark satanic mills of the Industrial Revolution, men, women and even children toiled for fifteen hours a day. Yet at the end of the nineteenth century, the Age of Leisure popped up once again on the cultural radar. George Bernard Shaw predicted that we would work two hours a day by 2000.

The dream of limitless leisure persisted through the twentieth century. Dazzled by the magical promise of technology, the man in the street dreamed of a life spent lounging by the pool, waited on by robots that not only mixed a mean martini but also kept the economy ticking over nicely. In 1956, Richard Nixon told Americans to prepare for a four-day workweek in the "not too distant future." A decade later, a US Senate subcommittee heard that by 2000 Americans would be working as little as fourteen hours per week. Even in the 1980s, some predicted that robotics and computers would give us all more free time than we would know what to do with.

Could they have been more wrong? If we can be sure about anything in the twenty-first century, it is that reports of the death of work have been greatly exaggerated. Today, the Age of Leisure looks as feasible as the paperless office. Most of us are more likely to put in a fourteen-hour day than a fourteen-hour week. Work devours the bulk of our waking hours. Everything else in life—family and friends, sex and sleep, hobbies and holidays—is forced to bend around the almighty work schedule.

In the industrialized world, the average number of hours worked began a steady decline in the middle of the 1800s, when six-day weeks were the norm. But over the last twenty years two rival trends have taken hold.

While Americans work as much as they did in 1980, Europeans work less. By some estimates, the average American now puts in 350 hours more on the job per year than his European counterpart. In 1997, the United States supplanted Japan as the industrialized country with the longest working hours. By comparison, Europe looks like a slacker's paradise. Yet even there the picture is mixed. To keep up with the fast-paced, round-the-clock global economy, many Europeans have learned to work more like Americans.

Behind the statistical averages, the grim truth is that millions of people are actually working longer and harder than they want to, especially in Anglo-Saxon countries. One in four Canadians now racks up more than fifty hours a week on the job, compared to one in ten in 1991. By 2002, one in five thirty-something Britons was working at least sixty hours a week. And that is before one adds in the long hours we spend commuting.

Whatever happened to the Age of Leisure? Why are so many of us still working so hard? One reason is money. Everyone needs to earn a living, but the endless hunger for consumer goods means that we need more and more cash.

So instead of taking productivity gains in the form of extra time off, we take them in higher incomes.

Technology, meanwhile, has allowed work to seep into every corner of life. In the age of the information superhighway, there is nowhere to hide from email, faxes and phone calls. Once you can tap into the company database from home, access the Internet from an airplane, or take a call from the boss at the beach, everyone is potentially on duty all the time. I know from experience that working from home can easily slide into working all the time. In a recent interview, Marilyn Machlowitz, the author of *Workaholics* (1980), claimed that in the twenty-first century the pressure to be "always-on" is universal: "Workaholics used to be the people who would work anytime, anywhere. What has changed is that it has become the norm to be on call 24/7."

There is also a lot more to do in most jobs. After years of re-engineering and downsizing, companies expect employees to shoulder the workload left behind by their laid-off colleagues. With the fear of unemployment hanging over offices and factories, many people regard putting in long hours as the best way to prove their worth. Millions go to work even when too tired or ill to be effective. Millions more never take their full vacation entitlement.

This is madness. While some people like to work long hours, and should be allowed to do so, it is wrong to expect everyone else to keep pace. Working too hard is bad for us and for the economy. A 2002 study carried out at Kyushu University in Fukuoka, Japan, found that men who work sixty hours a week are twice as likely to have a heart attack as men who put in forty hours. That risk is trebled for those who sleep less than five hours a night at least twice a week.

Workplace stress is not all bad. In limited doses, it can concentrate the mind and boost productivity. But too much of it can be a one-way ticket to physical and mental breakdown. In a recent poll, more than 15% of Canadians claimed that job stress had driven them to the brink of suicide.

Companies also pay a heavy price for imposing a long-hours culture. Productivity is notoriously hard to measure, but academics agree that overwork eventually hits the bottom line. It is common sense: we are less productive when we are tired, stressed, unhappy or unhealthy. According to the International Labour Organization, workers in Belgium, France and Norway are all more productive per hour than are Americans. The British clock up more time on the job than do most Europeans, and have one of the continent's poorest rates of hourly productivity to show for it. Working less often means working better.

Beyond the great productivity debate lies what may be the most important question of all: What is life for? Most people would agree that work is good for us. It can be fun, even ennobling. Many of us enjoy our jobs—the intellectual challenge, the physical exertion, the socializing, the status. But to let work take over our lives is folly. There are too many important things that need time, such as friends, family, hobbies and rest.

For the Slow movement, the workplace is a key battlefront. When the job gobbles up so many hours, the time left over for everything else gets squeezed. Even the simple things—taking the kids to school, eating supper, chatting to friends—become a race against the clock. A surefire way to slow down is to work less. And that is exactly what millions of people around the world are seeking to do.

Everywhere, and especially in the long-hours economies, polls show a yearning to spend less time on the job. In a recent international survey by economists at Warwick University and Dartmouth College, 70% of people in twenty-seven countries said they wanted a better work-life balance. In the United States, the backlash against workaholism is gathering steam. More and more blue-chip firms, from Starbucks to Wal-Mart, face lawsuits from staff allegedly forced to put in unpaid overtime. Americans are snapping up books that show how a more leisurely approach to work, and to life in general, can bring happiness and success. Recent titles include *The Lazy Way to Success, The Lazy Person's Guide to Success* and *The Importance of Being Lazy.* In 2003, US campaigners for shorter working hours held the first national Take Back Your Time Day on October 24, the date when, according to some estimates, Americans have worked as much as Europeans do in a year.

All over the industrial world, recruitment managers report that younger applicants have started asking questions that would have been unthinkable ten or fifteen years ago: Can I leave the office at a reasonable hour in the evening? Is it possible to trade income for more vacation time? Will I have control over my working hours? In interview after interview, the message is coming through loud and clear: we want to work, but we want to have a life, too.

Women are especially eager for work-life balance. Recent generations have been reared to believe it is their right and duty to have it all: family, career, house, rewarding social life. But "having it all" has turned out to be a poisoned chalice. Millions of women have recognized their own frazzled selves in the American collection of essays *The Bitch in the House* and in *I Don't Know How She Does It*, Allison Pearson's best-selling novel about a working mother struggling to run a hedge fund and a home. Fed up with trying to be "super-woman," women are leading the charge to renegotiate the rules of the workplace. Attitudes are changing. At smart dinner parties, alpha females are now just as likely to boast about the length of their maternity leave as the size of their bonus. Even high flyers with no kids can be heard advocating a four-day workweek.

Janice Turner, a *Guardian* columnist, recently noted that taking the Slow road can be bittersweet for the modern woman: "How cruel for a generation of women educated to succeed and fill every hour with purposeful activity to discover that happiness isn't, after all, about being the fastest and busiest. What awful irony that contentment, more often than not, is about slowing down: taking pleasure in a bedtime story, not skipping pages to phone New York."

Everywhere, vote-hungry politicians are leaping on the work-life bandwagon. In 2003, the Parti Québécois in Canada proposed a four-day workweek for parents of young children. Whether such promises ever reach the statute books remains to be seen. Many politicians, as well as companies, simply pay lip service to work-life balance. Yet the fact that they bother to do so at all hints at a cultural sea change.

The shift is particularly striking in Japan, which once terrorized the world with its fearsome work ethic. A decade of economic stagnation has brought job insecurity, and with it a new way of thinking about work and time. More and more young Japanese people are eschewing long hours on the job for longer spells of leisure. "For years, parents in Japan screamed at their children to go faster, work harder, do more, but now people are saying enough is enough," says Keibo Oiwa, the author of *Slow Is Beautiful*. "The new generation is realizing that you do not have to work incredibly long hours, that it is not so bad to be slow." Instead of becoming a cog in the corporate wheel—a "salaryman"— many young Japanese people now prefer to drift from one temporary job to the next. Pundits talk of Generation Fureeta, a coinage based on the English word *free* and the German word *arbeiter* (worker).

Consider Nobuhito Abe, a twenty-four-year-old university graduate in Tokyo. While his father toils more than seventy hours a week for a bank, he works part-time at a convenience store, spending the rest of the day playing baseball and video games, or hanging out downtown. Abe, smiling under a mop of hennaed hair, says that a life ruled by work is not for him or his friends. "My generation is finally realizing what people in Europe realized long ago— that it is crazy to let a job take over your life," he says. "We

want to be in control of our own time. We want the freedom to be slow." The Fureeta are hardly a role model for
the future—most fund their relaxed lifestyle by sponging
off hard-working parents. But their refusal to embrace the
furious madness for work points to a cultural shift. Even
Japanese officialdom is changing tack. In 2002, the government called for shorter working hours. New legislation has
already made it easier to job-share. Japan still has a long
way to go, but the trend towards working less has begun.

Continental Europe has moved furthest down the road
to cutting work hours. The average German, for instance,
now spends 15% less time on the job than in 1980. Many
economists reject the claim that working less creates more
jobs by spreading the work around. But everyone agrees
that trimming work hours generates more time for leisure,
traditionally a higher priority among continental Europeans.
In 1993, the EU laid down a maximum workweek of forty-
eight hours with workers given the right to work longer if
they wish. At the end of the decade, France took the boldest
step so far to put work in its place by cutting the workweek
to thirty-five hours.

In practice, France stipulated that no one should work
more than 1,600 hours per year. Since the implementation
of *les 35 heures* was negotiated at the company level, the
impact on workers varies. Many French people now work
shorter days throughout the year, while others work the
same or even longer weekly hours but get extra days off. A
mid-ranking French executive can aspire to nine weeks
or more of annual vacation. Though some professions—

among them senior business executives, doctors, journalists and soldiers—are exempted from the thirty-five-hour rule, the net effect is a leisure revolution.

For many French people, the weekend now starts on Thursday, or ends on Tuesday. Legions of office staff desert their desks at 3 P.M. While some use the extra leisure time to veg out—sleeping or watching TV—many more have broadened their horizons. Enrolment in art, music and language classes has risen sharply. Tour operators report a boom in short trips to London, Barcelona and other European hot spots. Bars and bistros, cinemas and sports clubs are packed with people. The surge in leisure spending gave the economy a much-needed shot in the arm. But beyond the economic numbers, the shorter workweek has revolutionized people's lives. Parents spend longer playing with their children, friends see each other more often, couples have more time for romance. Even that favourite French pastime, adultery, has benefited. Paul, a married accountant in southern France, tells me that the thirty-five-hour workweek allows him to indulge in an extra tryst each month with his mistress. "If cutting the workload gives more time for love, then it has to be a good thing, *n'est-ce pas?*" he says, with a wolfish grin.

Fans of the new regime are certainly easy to find. Take Emilie Guimard. The Paris-based economist now enjoys a couple of three-day weekends a month, on top of her six weeks of annual paid vacation. She has taken up tennis, and started reading the Sunday edition of *Le Monde* from cover to cover. Many of her long weekends are spent touring museums across Europe. "I now have time for things that make my life richer, and that is good for me and for my employers," she says. "When you are relaxed and happy in your personal life, you work better. Most of us in the office feel we are more efficient on the job than we used to be."

Many bigger companies have grown to love the thirty-five-hour week. On top of the tax breaks they received for hiring more workers, the new regime allowed them to negotiate more flexible ways of working. Staff at large manufacturers, such as Renault and Peugeot, have agreed to work longer hours when production peaks and shorter hours when it slumps.

So the Cassandras who warned that the thirty-five-hour week would send the French economy into instant meltdown have been proved wrong. The gross domestic product has grown, and unemployment, though still above the EU average, has fallen. Productivity also remains high. Indeed, some evidence suggests that many French workers are more productive now. With less time on the job, and more leisure to look forward to, they make greater efforts to finish their work before clocking off.

There are, however, some pretty large flies in the ointment. Small businesses find the thirty-five-hour week a real burden, and many have put off implementing it until the deadline in 2005. Funding the tax breaks that underpin the system has blown a hole in state finances. Meanwhile, business leaders moan that the leisure revolution has made France uncompetitive. There is some truth in this. The flow of foreign investment into France has slowed in recent years, as companies opt to put their money into nations with cheaper labour. The thirty-five-hour week must take some of the blame. Indeed, the French experience points up the dangers of taking a unilateral stand against the culture of long working hours in a globalized economy.

Nor has the thirty-five-hour regime been a blessing for all workers. Many have found their wages held down to off-set the higher costs of doing business. In both the private and public sectors, employers have often failed to hire enough new staff, leaving existing employees to cram the same tasks as before into less time. Blue-collar workers get an especially raw deal. Restrictions on overtime have cut their income, and many have lost control over when they can take their vacations. To workers who actually want to put in longer hours, the system is anathema.

With so much invested in the idea of *les 35 heures,* the French attitude to time itself has taken on a more obsessive edge. The state enforces the thirty-five-hour week with nit-picking inspectors, who count cars in company parking lots and look for lights on in offices after 6 P.M. Employers are more likely to frown on coffee and toilet breaks. Some French shops now have to shut early so that staff can leave bang on the official closing time.

The system is flawed, and everybody knows it. In 2002, the new right-wing government took the first step towards rolling back the thirty-five-hour regime by easing restrictions on overtime. In a landmark poll in September 2003, a slight majority of French citizens said the country should return to a thirty-nine-hour week. Thirty-six percent wanted the

switch to be permanent, 18% thought it should be temporary. But though critics claim a counter-reformation is
underway, a full-scale repeal will not come easily. Having
spent years and large sums of money implementing the
thirty-five-hour week, companies in France are loath to
reopen the complex and divisive negotiations that brought it
about. What's more, support for the philosophy that underlies the system—less work, more leisure—remains strong.

The lesson for other countries, especially those with a
less *dirigiste* culture, is that a one-size-fits-all approach to
cutting the workweek has serious drawbacks, which is why
the battle to work less takes a different form elsewhere.

Other European countries have used collective bargain-
ing to push down working hours in individual sectors of
the economy. The Netherlands is often held up as a
paragon of this piecemeal approach. Today, the Dutch
work fewer hours than almost any industrial nation. Their
standard workweek has fallen to thirty-eight hours, with
half the labour force working thirty-six hours in 2002.
A third of Dutch workers are now part-time. Crucial to
the change was legislation passed in the 1990s that gave
the Dutch the right to force their employers to let them
work fewer hours in return for less pay. Such meddling in
the labour market makes orthodox economists shudder.
But it has worked. The Netherlands combines prosperity
with an enviable quality of life. Compared to Americans,
the Dutch spend less time commuting, shopping and
watching television and more time socializing, studying,
looking after their children, and pursuing sports and

hobbies. Other countries, notably Japan, have started studying the "Dutch model."

Even where lawmakers are loath to intervene in the labour market, people are taking a personal stand against the round-the-clock work ethic. In 2002, Suma Chakrabarti, one of the most gifted senior civil servants in Britain, accepted his latest post as permanent secretary at the Department of International Development on the understanding that he would work forty hours a week and not a second more. Why? So he could have breakfast with his six-year-old daughter every morning and read her a bedtime story in the evening. Across the Atlantic, President George W. Bush makes no apologies for his short workday and laid-back weekends. And for every headline-grabbing high flyer that has started cutting back on work, millions of ordinary people are doing the same. Though working less often means earning less money, more and more of us think that is a price worth paying. A recent survey in Britain found that twice as many people would prefer to work fewer hours than win the lottery. A similar study in the United States revealed that, given the choice between two weeks' vacation and two weeks' extra pay, twice as many Americans would choose the time off. Across Europe, part-time work has shed its "McJob" stigma to become an increasingly popular lifestyle choice. A 1999 survey found that 77% of temp workers in the EU had chosen to work fewer hours in order to have more time for family, hobbies and rest.

At the top of the corporate food chain, more and more high achievers are choosing to work freelance or as independent contractors. This allows them to work hard when they choose and still have time to recharge their batteries, enjoy hobbies and hang out with the family. Many are refugees from the dotcom boom. Dan Kemp spent three years putting in ninety-hour weeks as a project manager for a software company in Silicon Valley. The long hours put such a strain on his marriage that his wife threatened to leave him and take their twin daughters with her. When the company went belly up in 2001, and Kemp found himself back on the job market, he decided to scale back. Now, he works four days a week, helping companies manage their IT systems. He still earns a comfortable wage and now has enough time for his family and his golf. So far he has not detected any disapproval or contempt from full-time colleagues. "If anything they envy my lifestyle," he says.

As it turns out, people who cut their work hours often take a smaller hit financially than they expect. That is because spending less time on the job means spending less money on the things that allow us to work: transport, parking, eating out, coffee, convenience food, childcare, laundry, retail therapy. A smaller income also translates into a smaller tax bill. In one Canadian study, some workers who took a pay cut in return for shorter hours actually ended up with more money in the bank at the end of the month.

Sensing which way the wind is blowing, companies across the industrial world have started offering their staff the chance to get off the long-hours treadmill. Even in fast-moving, cut-throat industries, employers have twigged that one way to boost productivity and profits is to offer staff a better work-life balance. At SAS, a leading software company based in Cary, North Carolina, staff put in a thirty-five-hour week when the workload permits and enjoy generous vacation benefits. The firm also offers a package of on-site amenities, including childcare, a health clinic, a cafeteria with a pianist, and a gym—and encourages employees to use them. SAS is regularly voted one of the best firms to work for in the United States.

Farther north, the Royal Bank of Canada (RBC) has also won plaudits for recognizing that its employees have lives outside the office. On any given day, up to 40% of RBC staff will be using a work-life program—job-sharing, flextime, reduced hours. At the bank's headquarters, a gleaming skyscraper in downtown Toronto, I meet Karen Domaratzki and Susan Lieberman, a couple of smart, energetic forty-somethings, who have moved steadily up the ranks since starting to share a job in 1997. By 2002, the pair were second in command of the division that sells banking services overseas. We meet on a Wednesday, the only day of the week when they overlap at work. Their shared office is homey. Two shelves are given over to family photos. Artwork by their children hangs on the walls.

Both women followed a similar career path. After earning MBAs, they began climbing the corporate ladder, putting in sixty-hour weeks without blinking. But once children entered the picture—they have three apiece—life became an endless, unsatisfying rush. So they decided to share a job, doing three days a week each.

The 40% pay cut turned out to be less of a blow than it sounds. It helps, of course, that Lieberman and Domaratzki both have high-earning husbands. But the extra leisure has proved to be priceless. Both women are able to spend more time with their children, making family life more relaxed and rewarding. Lieberman's six-year-old son recently urged his father to start job-sharing. The two bankers also feel closer to their communities. They now have time to chat with neighbours and local shopkeepers, help out at their children's schools and do volunteer work. Home cooking is back on the agenda, too. "Before the job-share, we used to have some pretty lousy meals," says Domaratzki, wincing at the memory.

Both women feel their whole relationship with time has taken on a healthier complexion. The itch to accelerate has gone, or at least faded. "When you have more time off to slow down and recharge, you don't take anything quite so intensely," explains Lieberman. "The whole emotional level changes, and you're just calmer in general."

For RBC, that calmness pays off in higher productivity—and more Slow Thinking. "When I come in on Wednesday, I'm fresh. I've got all my home stuff under control—the house is clean, the food is bought, the laundry is done, the children are happy," Domaratzki explains. "And during my days off I don't just rest and rejuvenate, I mull. The work plays in the back of your mind, and often because of that you make better, more thoughtful decisions when you come into the office. You're not just always reacting to things on the spot." In 2000, RBC started offering flexible working arrangements to the eleven thousand new staff it acquired through expansion into the United States.

Formally cutting work hours is not the only route to working and living better. Sometimes it is enough to purge the corporate culture of the notion that working longer always means getting more done. That is what Marriott did. In 2000, the hotel chain concluded that its managers were often staying late at the office simply because they felt it was expected of them. The result was sagging morale and burnout.

To combat the culture of "presenteeism," Marriott launched a pilot project in three hotels in the northeastern United States. Staff were told that it was okay to leave the office when the work was done, no matter what the clock said. Leading by example, senior managers began openly going home at 5 P.M., or earlier. After three months, it was clear that a cultural revolution was underway. Staff who left early, or who took time off in the middle of the day for personal reasons, no longer had to run the gauntlet of disapproving gestures and jokes. Instead, people began taking an interest in what their colleagues were doing with their spare time. On average, Marriott managers now work five hours less per week—and they are more productive. Not having to clock up long hours for the sake of it gives them extra motivation to be efficient and prompt. Bill Munck, the Marriott manager who oversaw the regime change, draws a conclusion that should be pinned up in boardrooms and factories everywhere: "One of the most important things we learned . . . was that people could be just as productive—

and sometimes even more so—when they worked fewer hours."

Nevertheless, any move against the long-hours culture faces some hefty obstacles. A CEO can create the world's most enlightened work-life scheme but if managers farther down the chain of command are unsympathetic, it fails. One American company recently introduced a raft of work-life measures with full backing from the board. After a year, though, enrollment was much lower than expected. An investigation revealed that several division leaders were putting staff off with warnings that signing up would damage their chances of promotion. "A lot of people are still very suspicious of work-life solutions," says a manager in the company's human resources department. "Changing the rules is just the beginning—you have to change people's mentality, too."

Often the barrier to work-life balance is self-inflicted. Many men still regard it skeptically. In most companies, women with children are the main users of work-life balance schemes. John Atkins, a sales manager for a large retailer in London, recently became a father. He would love to work reduced hours, but cannot bring himself to sign up for the program. "Every time I think of it, a little voice in the back of my head says, 'If you can't stand the heat get out of the kitchen,'" he says.

Another obstacle to establishing work-life balance is that everyone is different. A single twenty-five-year-old man will find it easier to work long hours than a thirty-six-year-old mother of four. He may even *want* to spend longer on the job. Companies need to find a formula for rewarding those who work more without penalizing those who work less. They also have to manage the ill will that can flare up between colleagues. Childless workers often resent work-time concessions granted to those with children. In many companies, different departments simply cannot offer the same work-life deals—and that can cause friction. At RBC, the Capital Markets division offers less flexible working arrangements simply because staff have to be on hand for the hours that the market is open.

For many companies, the long-term benefits of work-life policies, such as higher productivity and staff retention, can be overshadowed by the pressure to keep costs down in the short term. Benefit schemes often make it cheaper to over-work the few than to hire more staff. Competition also per-suades many bosses to put work before life. One British manager puts it bluntly: "We're in a cut-throat business, and if our rivals are getting seventy hours per week out of their staff, then we have to get at least that to stay in the game." Legislation may be the only way to stop the arms race in work hours.

Yet working less is just part of the Slow blueprint. People also want to decide *when* they work. They want control over their own time—and businesses who grant it to them are reaping the benefits. In our time-is-money culture, giv-ing workers dominion over the clock goes against the grain. Ever since the Industrial Revolution, the norm has been to pay people for the hours they spend on the job rather than for what they produce. But rigid timetables are out of step with the information economy, where the boundary between work and play is much more blurred than it was in the nineteenth century. Many modern jobs depend on the kind of creative thinking that seldom occurs at a desk and cannot be squeezed into fixed schedules. Letting people choose their own hours, or judging them on what they achieve rather than on how long they spend achieving it, can deliver the flexibility that many of us crave.

Studies show that people who feel in control of their time are more relaxed, creative and productive. In 2000, a British energy company hired management consultants to streamline the shift system at its call centre. Almost overnight, productivity nose-dived, customer complaints shot up and staff began leaving. By denying employees a say in when they worked, the new regime had ruined morale. Realizing its mistake, the company promptly gave staff more control over their shifts, and soon the call centre was more productive than ever. Many of the workers said that having "time autonomy" at work helped them feel less hurried and stressed both on and away from the job. Domaratzki bears witness to that at RBC: "When you have control over your own time, you feel more calm in everything you do."

I know this to be true from my own experience. In 1998, after years of freelancing, I joined the staff of a Canadian newspaper as the London correspondent. In an instant, I lost control of my time. Because I had no set working hours, I was, in theory, available 24/7. Even when my editors did not call, there was always the chance that they might. The difference in time zones meant that assignments often landed on my desk in the afternoon, leaving me just a few hours before it was time to help put my son to bed. This meant a mad dash to finish, or reading Dr. Seuss with work hanging over me. It was miserable. At the time, I found other reasons to explain why a job I had loved so much had become such a millstone. My editor was small-minded. The paper covered stories in the wrong way. The hours were too long. When I began investigating the Slow movement, however, it became clear to me that the underlying problem was that I had lost the power to decide *when* to work. So why did I stick with it for nearly three years? My reasons were the same as those that prevent many of us from leaving jobs that make us unhappy: the fear of losing a good salary, of damaging my career, of disappointing others. Eventually, the decision to leave was made for me. When the paper announced mass layoffs, I was on the list—and over the moon.

Things are so much better now. I still work the same number of hours, sometimes even more, but my relationship with time is healthier. Now that I control my own schedule, I move through the working day feeling less hurried and resentful. And away from my desk, whether reading bedtime stories or preparing the evening meal, I am less liable to seek a shortcut. Sure, my earnings are down, but that is a small price to pay for enjoying my work—and my life—again. My only regret is that I did not go back to freelancing sooner.

Of course, giving people control over their own time in the workplace will require a seismic shift in thinking. But where practical, it can, and should, be done. If deployed in the right spirit, information technology can help us do it. Instead of using Blackberrys, laptops and cellphones to extend the workday, we can use them to rearrange it. Many companies are already ceding more time autonomy to their staff. In the UK, for example, British Telecom, Bayer and Lloyds TSB now allow employees to customize their own schedules: to work from home, say, or to come in and leave the office at more convenient hours. Though it naturally lends itself more to white-collar work, time autonomy is also making inroads in the blue-collar world. Some Swiss watch factories have rearranged production to allow workers on a single shift to vary their start and finish times by up to three hours. In Gloucestershire, a nylon factory lets staff set their own hours as long as at least two workers are on duty at all times.

The benefits of working less, and working when it's convenient, are clear enough, but now let's consider why it sometimes makes sense to work more slowly. In the just-in-time, modern workplace, speed seems to be all-important. Email and cellphones demand an instant response, and a deadline lurks round every corner. A 2001 survey conducted by the European Foundation for the Improvement of Living and Working Conditions found that EU workers were under much greater time pressure than a decade ago. A third now spend all or almost all of their time rushing to meet deadlines. Of course, speed has a role in the workplace. A deadline can focus the mind and spur us on to perform remarkable feats. The trouble is that many of us are permanently stuck in deadline mode, leaving little time to ease off and recharge. The things that need slowness—strategic planning, creative thought, building relationships—get lost in the mad dash to keep up, or even just to look busy.

Erwin Heller, a member of the Society for the Deceleration of Time, enjoys the benefits of working more slowly at his law firm in Munich. Like many attorneys, he used to rush through get-to-know meetings with clients—ten minutes to suss out the brief and then straight down to tackling the case. After a while, though, he noticed that he was always placing follow-up calls to clients, and would sometimes set off in the wrong direction and have to backtrack. "Most people come to lawyers with goals that they tell you about, like money, and goals that they don't, like being acknowledged or getting justice or revenge," he says. "It takes time to get through to the hidden wishes that motivate clients, but you have to know these to do the best job for them." These days, his initial meetings last up to two hours, during which he develops a thorough grasp of the client's personality, circumstances, values, aims and fears. As a result, Heller, a lively fifty-six-year-old with a goatee and a mischievous grin, works more efficiently, and his business is booming. "Clients are always telling me that with other lawyers you get five minutes to explain what you need, you hand over the papers and you're out the door," he says. "Though it may seem very slow and old-fashioned, listening is the best policy. The worst thing is to rush into action."

Many companies are now trying to strike a balance between fast and slow at work. Often this means recognizing the limits of technology. Email, for all its speed, cannot capture irony, nuance or body language, and this leads to misunderstandings and mistakes. Slower methods of communication—walking across the office and actually talking to someone face to face, for instance—can save time and money, and build esprit de corps, in the long run. That is one reason that companies have started urging staff to think hard before they hit the send button. In 2001, Nestlé Rowntree became the first of many UK firms to introduce email-free Fridays. A year later, British Airways ran a series of TV commercials with a "slower is better" theme. In one, a group of businessmen think they have won an order from a US firm by faxing across a proposal. Their rivals end up stealing the deal by taking the time to fly over and make the pitch face to face.

Companies are also moving to make work less of a 24/7 treadmill. Ernst & Young, the accountancy firm, recently told its US employees that it was okay not to check email and voice mail over the weekend. In a similar vein, stressed-out executives are taking the heretical step of turning off their cellphones outside the office. Jill Hancock, a go-getting investment banker in London, used to take her chic, chrome-plated Nokia everywhere, and even answered calls on vacation or in the middle of a romantic dinner. She paid the price, though, in depression and chronic fatigue. When a psychologist diagnosed "mobile phone addiction" and urged her to switch off from time to time, Hancock was appalled. But eventually she gave it a try, first silencing the Nokia during her lunch break, and later on evenings and weekends when an urgent call was unlikely. Within two months, she was off the anti-depressants, her skin had cleared up and she was getting more work done in less time. At the bank, her colleagues accept that Hancock is no longer reachable around the clock. A few have even followed her example. "I didn't realize it at the time, but the fact that I was always available, always on, was grinding me down," she says. "We all need time to ourselves." Decelerating at work also prompted Hancock to make more room for Slow pursuits in the rest of her life. She has taken up yoga and now cooks a real supper, instead of a microwaved meal, at least two evenings a week.

To avoid burnout, and to promote creative thinking, business gurus, therapists and psychologists increasingly prescribe doses of slowness for the workplace. In his best-selling 2002 book, *How to Succeed in Business Without Working So Damn Hard,* Robert Kriegel suggested taking regular fifteen- to twenty-minute timeouts during the day. Dr. Donald Hensrud, director of the Mayo Clinic Executive Health program, advises, "Try shutting your office door and closing your eyes for fifteen minutes. Lean back and breathe deeply."

Even in high-speed, high-pressure industries, companies are taking steps to help their staff slow down. Some grant sabbaticals in the hope that an extended period away from the office will refresh employees and stir their creative juices. Others offer on-the-job yoga, aromatherapy and massage, or encourage workers to eat lunch away from their desks. Some firms have installed chill-out rooms. At the

Tokyo office of Oracle, the software giant, staff have access to a sound-proofed meditation room with a wooden floor bordered by smooth pebbles and Oriental objets d'art. The room's lighting is soft, and a hint of incense hangs in the air. At the flick of a switch, the soothing sounds of a babbling brook tinkle from the stereo system.

Takeshi Sato is a big fan of the eighth-floor sanctuary. As manager of the CEO's office, he works a twelve-hour day, juggling emails, meetings, phone calls and budget reports. When the pace becomes too frenetic, he leaves his desk to spend ten minutes in the meditation room. "At times in the day, I suddenly feel like I need to be slow, to relax, to let my mind become still and quiet," he tells me. "Some people might think of that as ten minutes of lost time, but I see it as ten minutes well invested. It is very important for performance to be able to switch on and off, between fast and slow. After I have been in the meditation room, my mind is sharper and calmer, which helps me make good decisions."

Other people are taking deceleration to its ultimate conclusion and actually catching forty winks during the working day. Though sleeping on the job is the ultimate taboo, research has shown that a short "power nap"—around twenty minutes is ideal—can boost energy and productivity. A recent study by NASA concluded that twenty-four minutes of shut-eye did wonders for a pilot's alertness and performance. Many of the most vigorous and successful figures in history were inveterate nappers: John F. Kennedy, Thomas Edison, Napoleon Bonaparte, John D. Rockefeller, Johannes Brahms. Winston Churchill delivered the most eloquent defence of the afternoon snooze: "Don't think you will be doing less work because you sleep during the day. That's a foolish notion helped by people who have no imagination. You will be able to accomplish more. You get two days in one—well, at least one and a half."

Napping can be especially helpful nowadays, when so many of us are not sleeping enough at night. Backed by pro-sleep groups, from the World Napping Organization to the Portuguese Association of Friends of the Siesta, snoozing in the middle of the workday is enjoying a renaissance. At its six factories in the United States, Yarde Metals encourages staff to doze during breaks. The company has built special "nap rooms" and once a year holds a collective napping session complete with buffet lunch and silly costumes. Vechta, a small city in northern Germany, urges its civil servants to take a post-prandial snooze in their office chairs or at home. From the American factory floor to the German town hall, the results are the same: happier staff, better morale, higher productivity. More on-the-job napping may be in the pipeline. In 2001, Sedus, a leading European manufacturer of office furniture, unveiled a new chair that opens up to a horizontal position to allow people to catch a few zee's at their desks.

In Spain, meanwhile, the siesta is coming back with a modern twist. Since most Spaniards no longer have time to go home at lunch for a big meal and a nap, Masajes a 1000 (Massages for 1000), a nationwide network of "siesta salons," now offers everyone from bankers to bartenders the chance to grab twenty minutes of sleep for four euros.

At the branch in Barcelona's Mallorca Street, every detail is designed to relax. The walls are painted a soothing shade of peach, and the rooms are warm and softly lit. New Age music whispers from hidden speakers. Fully clothed and kneeling facedown in ergonomically designed chairs, the customers enjoy head, neck and back massages. Once they drift off to sleep, the masseur drapes a thick woollen blanket over them and moves on. As I settle into my chair, at least three people in the room are snoring gently. A couple of minutes later, I join them.

Afterwards, on the sidewalk outside, I fall into conversation with a young salesman called Luis, who is straightening his tie after a fifteen-minute snooze. He looks as refreshed as I feel. "This is so much better than going to the gym," he says, snapping his briefcase shut. "I feel totally energized. I feel ready for anything."

CHAPTER NINE

LEISURE: THE IMPORTANCE OF BEING AT REST

*To be able to fill leisure intelligently is the
last product of civilization.*
—BERTRAND RUSSELL

IN A WORLD OBSESSED WITH WORK, leisure is a serious matter. The United Nations declared it a basic human right in 1948. Half a century later, we are inundated with books, websites, magazines, TV shows and newspaper supplements dedicated to hobbies and having fun. Leisure Studies is even an academic discipline.

How to make the best use of free time is not a new concern. Two thousand years ago, Aristotle declared that one of the central challenges facing man was how to fill his leisure. Historically, the elites, sometimes known as the "leisured classes," had more time than anyone else to ponder that question. Instead of toiling to make ends meet, they indulged in games, socializing and sport. In the modern era, however, leisure is more democratic.

During the early part of the Industrial Revolution, the masses worked too hard, or were too poor, to make the most of what free time they had. But as incomes rose, and working hours fell, a leisure culture began to emerge. Like work, leisure became formalized. Many of the things with which we fill our spare time today came into being in the nineteenth century. Football, rugby, hockey and baseball turned into spectator sports. Cities built parks for the public to stroll and picnic in. The middle classes joined tennis and golf clubs and flocked to the new museums, theatres and music halls. Better printing presses, coupled with rising literacy, fuelled an explosion in reading.

Even as leisure spread, people debated its purpose. Many Victorians saw it chiefly as an escape from work, or a means to working better. But others went further, suggesting that what we do with our free time gives texture, shape and meaning to our lives. "It is in his pleasure that a man really lives," said Agnes Repplier, an American essayist. "It is from his leisure that he constructs the true fabric of self." Plato believed that the highest form of leisure was to be still and receptive to the world, a view echoed by modern intellectuals. Franz Kafka put it this way: "You don't need to leave your room. Remain sitting at your table and listen. Don't even listen, simply wait. Don't even wait, be quite still and solitary. The world will freely offer itself to you to be unmasked. It has no choice. It will roll in ecstasy at your feet."

With so many predicting the "end of work" in the twentieth century, pundits wondered how people would cope with so much free time. Some feared we would become lazy, corrupt and immoral. John Maynard Keynes, the economist, warned that the masses would fritter their lives away listening to the radio. Others were more sanguine. In 1926, William Green, president of the American Federation of Labor, promised that shorter working hours would free men and women to pursue a "higher development of (their) spiritual and intellectual powers." Bertrand Russell, the British philosopher, predicted that many would use the extra free time for self-improvement; they would read and study, or take up gentle, reflective hobbies such as fishing, gardening and painting. In his 1935 essay, *In Praise of Idleness*, Russell wrote that a four-hour workday would make us "more kindly and less persecuting and less inclined to view others with suspicion." With so much leisure, life would be sweet, slow and civilized.

Seven decades later, though, the leisure revolution remains the stuff of fantasy. Work still rules our lives, and when we do have free time, we seldom use it to moon around in a Platonic reverie of stillness and receptivity. Instead, like earnest disciples of Frederick Taylor, we rush to fill up every spare moment with activity. An empty slot in the diary is more often a source of panic than pleasure.

Nevertheless, part of Russell's prophecy has come true: people are devoting more free time to slow, contemplative hobbies. Gardening, reading, painting, making crafts—all of these satisfy the growing nostalgia for a time when the cult of speed was less potent, when doing one thing well, and taking real pleasure from it, was more important than doing everything faster.

Crafts are a perfect expression of the Slow philosophy. As the pace of life accelerated in the nineteenth century, many people fell out of love with the mass-produced goods pouring from the new factories. William Morris and other proponents of the Arts and Crafts movement, which started in Britain, blamed industrialization for giving machines the upper hand and stifling the creative spirit. Their solution was to return to making things slowly and carefully by hand. Artisans produced furniture, textiles, pottery and other goods using traditional, pre-industrial methods. Crafts were hailed as a link to a kinder, gentler era. More than a century later, when once again technology seems to be calling the shots, our passion for the handmade is stronger than ever. You can see it in the cult of homemaking started by Martha Stewart, in the growth of the Slow Food movement and in the knitting boom sweeping across North America.

Like other household crafts, such as cooking and sewing, knitting fell out of favour in the second half of the twentieth century. Feminism denounced homemaking as a curse on womankind, a barrier to gender equality. For women struggling to get ahead in the workplace, knitting was something to keep Granny busy in her rocking chair. But now that the sexes are on a more even footing, the domestic arts of yesteryear are making a comeback.

Promoted by fashionable feminists such as Debbie Stoller, and hailed by trend spotters as "the new yoga," knitting is now officially cool. Some of the most bankable celebrities in Hollywood—Julia Roberts, Gwyneth Paltrow, Cameron Diaz—do it in their spare time. More than four million Americans under the age of thirty-five, most of them women, have taken up the hobby since 1998. In New York, you see them in their Ralph Lauren jackets and Prada shoes, knitting up a storm on the subway or in the big, comfy chairs at Starbucks. On scores of websites, knitters swap tips on everything from choosing the best wool for mittens to dealing with finger cramp. Hip new knitting shops sell glamorous yarns—think faux fur or cashmere— that were once available only to fashion designers.

Bernadette Murphy, a forty-year-old writer based in Los Angeles, caught the mood with her 2002 book, *Zen and the Art of Knitting*. She sees the return to needles and yarn as part of a wider backlash against the superficiality of modern life. "There is a great hunger in our culture right now for meaning, for things that connect us with the world and with other people, things that really nurture the soul," she says. "Knitting is one way of taking time to appreciate life, to find that meaning and make those connections."

In living rooms, college dorms and company cafeterias across North America, women join knitting circles, where they build friendships as they stitch. The sweaters, hats and scarves they produce offer an alternative to the fleeting pleasures of modern consumerism. While manufactured goods can be functional, durable, beautiful, even inspiring, the very fact that they are mass-produced makes them disposable. In its uniqueness, its quirks and imperfections, a handmade item such as a knitted shawl carries the imprint of its creator. We sense the time and care that went into the making—and feel a deeper attachment to it as a result.

"In the modern world, where it is so easy, so cheap, so quick to buy things, the things that we buy have lost their worth. What value does an object have when you can buy ten more exactly the same in an instant?" says Murphy. "When something is handmade, it means that someone has invested time in it, and that imbues it with real value."

Murphy came to knitting almost by accident. On a trip to Ireland in 1984, she tore her Achilles tendon and was unable to walk for two months. She started to knit to keep herself busy, and found it immensely calming.

Knitting is by nature Slow. You cannot push a button, turn a dial or flick a switch to knit more quickly. The real joy of knitting lies in the doing, rather than in reaching the finish line. Studies show that the rhythmic, repetitive dance of the needles can lower heart rate and blood pressure, lulling the knitter into a peaceful, almost meditative state. "The best thing about knitting is its slowness," says Murphy. "It is so slow that we see the beauty inherent in every tiny act that makes up a sweater. So slow that we know the project is not going to get finished today—it may not get finished for many months or longer—and that allows us to make our peace with the unresolved nature of life. We slow down as we knit."

Many knitters use their hobby as an antidote to the stress and hurry of modern life. They knit before and after big meetings, during conference calls or at the end of a tough day. Some claim the calming effect continues after they put down the needles, helping them keep their cool in the fast-moving workplace. Murphy finds that knitting _lps her slip into Slow Thinking mode. "I can actually feel the active part of my brain shutting down, and that helps to straighten out the tangled knot of my thoughts," she says. "It's a wonderful cure for writer's block."

Will the twenty-first century knitting boom eventually turn to bust? It is hard to say. Fashion is notoriously fickle. Knitwear may be trendy now, but what happens when chunky sweaters and funky scarves stop appearing on the cover of *Vogue?* Some knitters will probably hang up their needles and move on to the next fad. But many will carry on. In a fast-paced, high-tech world, a low-tech hobby that helps people decelerate is bound to keep its appeal.

The same goes for gardening. In almost every culture, the garden is a sanctuary, a place to rest and ruminate. *Niwa,* the Japanese word for garden, means "an enclosure purified for the worship of the gods." The act of gardening itself—planting, pruning, weeding, watering, waiting for things to grow—can help us slow down. Gardening does not lend itself to acceleration any more than knitting does. Even with a greenhouse, you cannot make plants bloom on demand or bend the seasons to suit your schedule. Nature has its own timetable. In a hurry-up world, where everything is scheduled for maximum efficiency, surrendering to the rhythms of nature can be therapeutic.

Gardening took off as a popular leisure pursuit during the Industrial Revolution. It gave urbanites a taste of the rural idyll, providing a buffer against the frenetic pace of life in the new cities. Britain, which industrialized early, led the way. In the nineteenth century, air pollution made it difficult to grow much in the centre of London and other towns, but on the urban outskirts the middle classes began assembling ornamental gardens with flowerbeds, shrubs and water features.

Fast-forward to the twenty-first century, and gardening is once again in the ascendancy. In a world where so many jobs revolve around data flickering across a computer screen, people are warming to the simple, Slow pleasure of sinking their hands into the earth. Gardening has, like knitting, shaken off its image as a pastime for pensioners to become a fashionable way for people of all ages and backgrounds to relax. *Time* magazine recently hailed the rise of "horticulture chic." Across the industrial world, garden centres and nurseries are thronged with young people on a quest for the perfect plant, shrub or ceramic pot. A 2002 survey by National Family Opinion found that a record 78.3 million Americans now spend time gardening, making it the country's leading outdoor leisure activity. The same goes for Britain, where horticultural programs command prime-time slots on television, turning green-fingered presenters such as Charlie Dimmock and Alan Titchmarsh into household names. *Gardener's Question Time,* a radio show that the BBC first aired after the Second World War, has doubled its audience since the mid-1990s.

Hip, young and urban, Matt James is the new face of gardening. His British TV show, *The City Gardener,* teaches busy urbanites how to make room for Mother Nature on their doorsteps. James believes that gardening can reconnect us to the seasons. It can also bring people together.

Gardening is not just about getting back to nature," he says. "A well-designed garden is a great place to have friends round, open a few beers, light up the barbecue. The social aspect is very important."

James inherited his passion for gardening from his mother, and has made a hobby and career of it since leaving school. What he cherishes most about working with the soil and plants is the way it slows him down. "Gardening can be incredibly frustrating when you start out—plants die on you, it seems like loads of work—but once you get past that first hump it is very peaceful and relaxing. You can turn off, be alone, let your mind wander," he says. "Nowadays, when everyone is in such a rush all the time, we need slower pastimes like gardening more than ever."

Dominic Pearson could not agree more. As a trader for a bank in London, the twenty-nine-year-old works in the fast lane. Numbers flash across his screen all day long, forcing him to make split-second decisions that could make—or cost—his employer millions. Pearson used to thrive on the high-octane buzz of the trading floor, and earned big bonuses. But when the great bull market collapsed, he started suffering from anxiety. His girlfriend suggested that gardening might help. As a lager-loving, rugby-playing man's man, Pearson had his doubts, but he decided to give it a shot.

He ripped up the crumbling patio behind his flat in Hackney, replacing the old paving stones with a small lawn. Along the borders, he planted roses, crocuses, lavender, daffodils, winter jasmine and wisteria. He also put in creeping ivy and tomatoes. Later, he filled his apartment with potted plants. Three years on, his home is a feast for the senses. On a summer afternoon, the smell in the sun-drenched garden is intoxicating.

Pearson thinks gardening makes him a better trader. While weeding or pruning, his mind goes quiet, and out of that silence come some of his best ideas for work. He is less tense on the trading floor and sleeps better at night. In almost everything he does, Pearson feels calmer, more engaged, less hurried. "Gardening is like therapy without having to pay a therapist," he says.

After a long day at work, though, most people are still more likely to reach for the television remote control than a gardening trowel or the knitting needles. Watching TV is easily the world's number one leisure activity, gobbling up much of our free time. The average American views around four hours of television a day, the average European around three. TV can entertain, inform, distract and even relax us, but it is not Slow in the purest sense of the word. It does not allow us time to pause or reflect. TV dictates the pace, and the pace is often fast—rapid-fire imagery, speedy dialogue and quick camera edits. Moreover, when we watch television, we do not make connections. On the contrary, we sit there on the sofa, soaking up images and words, without giving anything back. Most research shows that heavy viewers spend less time on the things that really make life pleasurable—cooking, chatting with family, exercising, making love, socializing, doing volunteer work.

In search of a more fulfilling lifestyle, many people are kicking the TV habit. The anti-television movement is most militant in the United States. Every year since 1995, a lobby group called the TV-Turnoff Network has encouraged people to switch off their sets for a whole week in April. In 2003, a record 7.04 million people in the US and abroad took part. Most couch potatoes who cut back their viewing find that they spend more time on genuinely Slow pursuits.

One of those is reading. Like knitting and gardening, the act of sitting down and surrendering to a piece of writing defies the cult of speed. In the words of Paul Virilio, a French philosopher, "Reading implies time for reflection, a slowing-down that destroys the mass's dynamic efficiency." Even when overall book sales are stagnant or falling, many people, particularly educated urbanites, are saying to hell with dynamic efficiency and curling up with a good book. It is even possible to talk of a reading renaissance.

Just look at the Harry Potter phenomenon. Not so long ago, conventional wisdom pronounced reading dead among the young. Books were too boring, too slow for a generation raised on Playstation. But J. K. Rowling has changed all that. These days, millions of kids all over the world devour her Harry Potter novels, the latest of which weighs in at a hefty 766 pages. And having discovered the joys of the written word, the young are now reaching for books by other authors. Reading is even a little bit cool. At the back of the school bus, kids leaf through the latest works by Philip Pullman and Lemony Snicket. Along the way, children's fiction has gone from publishing backwater to star performer, complete with huge advances and movie tie-ins. In 2003, Puffin paid Louisa Young a million pounds for *Lionboy*, a story about a kid who finds he can talk to cats after being scratched by a leopard. In Britain, sales of children's books have jumped 40% since 1998.

Another sign that reading is making a comeback is the rise of the book group. Reading circles started in the mid-1700s, partly as a way to share books, which were expensive, and partly as a social and intellectual forum. Two and a half centuries later, book groups are sprouting all over the place, including in the media. In 1998, the BBC set up a monthly *Book Club* slot on highbrow Radio 4, and then added a similar show to the World Service in 2002. Oprah Winfrey launched her famously influential Book Club in 1996. Novels featured on her show, even those by unknown authors, routinely glide to the top of the bestseller list. In 2003, after a ten-month hiatus, Oprah resurrected her Book Club with a new focus on literary classics. In the twenty-four hours after she recommended John Steinbeck's *East of Eden*, which was first published in 1952, the novel soared from number 2,356 in the Amazon sales list to number 2.

Book clubs attract busy professionals looking for an enriching way to unwind and socialize. Paula Dembowski joined a group in Philadelphia in 2002. An English literature graduate, she began reading less and less as her career in executive recruitment took off. Then, one day, the thirty-two-year-old suddenly realized that she had not picked up a novel for six months. "That was a wake-up call to me that my life was out of balance," she says. "I wanted to get back to reading, but I also saw reading as a way to generally rebalance the pace of my life." To make room for books, she started watching less TV and gradually cutting back on after-hours work engagements. "I'd forgotten how totally relaxing it is to just sit down for a whole evening with a good novel," she says. "You enter another world, and all those little worries, and the big ones, too, just melt away. Reading adds another, slower register to things."

For many people, the act of reading is Slow enough. But others are going a step further by making an effort to read less quickly. Cecilia Howard, a Polish-American writer who describes herself as "a fast-lane, type-A person," draws a parallel between reading and exercise: "My motto is that anything truly worth reading is worth reading slowly. Think of it as the mental equivalent of SuperSlow exercise. If you really want to build muscles, make your movements as slow as possible. If you want to exercise really hard, do it so slowly it's practically a standstill. And that's the way you need to read Emily Dickinson."

Amos Oz, an Israeli writer, agrees. In a recent interview, he urged us all to be less fast with books. "I recommend the art of slow reading," he said. "Every single pleasure I can imagine or have experienced is more delightful, more of a pleasure, if you take it in small sips, if you take your time. Reading is not an exception."

Reading slowly does not have to mean consuming fewer words per minute. Just ask Jenny Hartley, an English lecturer and expert on book groups. In 2000, her London-based group decided to read Charles Dickens' *Little Dorrit* in the same way it would have been read in its day—in monthly instalments spread over a year and a half. That meant resisting the modern urge to race ahead to the end, but the wait was worth it. Everyone in the group loved taking it *lento*. Having already read the novel six times for her teaching work, Hartley was pleased to find that a slower reading opened up a whole new world of detail and nuance. "When you rattle through it, you don't appreciate some of the jokes and waiting games, and the play that Dickens makes with secret stories and hidden plots," she says. "Reading it slowly is much more satisfying." In her course at the University of Surrey, Roehampton, Hartley now experiments with her students, having them devote a full semester to reading *Middlemarch*.

Thousands of miles away, on the Canadian Prairies, Dale Burnett, a professor of education at the University of Lethbridge, has come up with a high-tech version of Slow Reading. Whenever he reads a book of any substance—airport novels need not apply—he keeps a Web-based diary. After each reading session, he uploads memorable quotes and insights, basic details about the plot and characters and any reflections inspired by the text. Burnett still reads the same number of words per minute, but takes two to four times longer to finish a book. When I catch up with him, he is slowly working his way through *Anna Karenina,* reading for an hour or two, and then spending the same time again pouring his thoughts and impressions into a cyber-diary. He is bursting with enthusiasm for Tolstoy's grasp of the human condition. "I find I have a much deeper appreciation of the books I read now," he says. "Slow Reading is a bit of an antidote to the fast-paced state we're in at the moment."

The same can be said of art. Painting, sculpture, any act of artistic creation, has a special relationship with slowness. As the American writer Saul Bellow once noted, "Art is something to do with the achievement of stillness in the midst of chaos. A stillness which characterizes . . . the eye of the storm . . . an arrest of attention in the midst of distraction."

In galleries all over the world, artists are putting our relationship with speed under the microscope. Often the works seek to shift the viewer into a more still, contemplative mode. In a recent video piece, Marit Folstad, a Norwegian artist, is shown struggling to blow up a large red balloon until it explodes. Her aim is to make the viewer decelerate long enough to think. "By using a series of visual metaphors centred on the body, breathing and the extended limits of physical strain, I attempt to slow the art spectator down," she says.

In the everyday world, beyond the galleries and garrets, people are taking up art as a way to decelerate. One of the first English-language signs I see in Tokyo is for an Art Relaxation Course. Kazuhito Suzuki uses painting to slow down. As a Web designer in the Japanese capital, he lives from one deadline to the next. To ward off what he thought was an impending burnout, the twenty-six-year-old signed up for an art course in 2002. Now, every Wednesday evening, he joins a dozen other students for two or three hours of painting still lifes and models. No deadlines, no competition, no rush—just him and his art. At home, in his tiny apartment, Suzuki paints watercolours of everything from bowls of fruit to Microsoft manuals. His latest effort is of Mount Fuji on a spring morning. In his study, the easel stands just a couple of feet from his computer, yin and yang, work and play, in perfect harmony. "Painting helps me find a balance between fast and slow, so that I feel more calm, more in control," he says.

Music can have a similar effect. Singing and playing instruments, or listening to others do so, is one of the oldest forms of leisure. Music can be exhilarating, challenging, stirring. Or it can soothe and relax, which is precisely what more of us are seeking nowadays. Using music deliberately to unwind is not a new idea. In 1742, Count Kaiserling, then the Russian ambassador to the Saxon court, commissioned Bach to write some music to help him overcome his insomnia. The composer came up with the Goldberg Variations. Two and a half centuries later, even the man in the street uses classical music as a tool for relaxation. Radio stations devote entire programs to gentle, calming works. Classical compilations with words like "relaxing," "mellow," "chill-out" and "soothing" in the title are flying off the shelves.

Listeners are not the only ones hankering after a slower tempo. A growing number of musicians—around two hundred at last count—believe that we play a lot of classical music too fast. Many of these rebels belong to a movement called Tempo Giusto, whose mission is to persuade conductors, orchestras and soloists everywhere to do a very unmodern thing: slow down.

To find out more, I fly to Germany to attend a Tempo Giusto concert. On a windless summer evening, a small crowd files into a community centre on the outskirts of Hamburg. Posters on the door promise a familiar program of sonatas by Beethoven and Mozart. In the modern, sun-lit auditorium, a grand piano stands alone beneath a bank of windows. After settling into their seats, the spectators make their final preparations for the show, switching off their mobile phones and clearing their throats in the osten-tatious manner favoured by concert-goers the world over. The buildup reminds me of every recital I have ever been to—until the pianist walks in.

Uwe Kliemt is a compact, middle-aged German with a spring in his step and a twinkle in his eye. Instead of sitting down at the keyboard to start the concert, he stands in front of his gleaming Steinway and says to the audience: "I want to talk to you about slowness." Then, as he does at concerts across Europe, he delivers a mini-lecture on the evils of speed worship, adding emphasis by waving his spec-tacles like a conductor brandishing a baton. A murmur of approval ripples through the audience as Kliemt, who also happens to be a member of the Society for the Deceleration of Time, utters a neat summation of the Slow philosophy. "It is pointless to speed up everything just because we can, or because we feel we must," he declares. "The secret of life is always to look for the *tempo giusto*. And nowhere is that more true than in music."

Kliemt and his allies believe that musicians began playing faster at the dawn of the industrial era. As the world sped up, they sped up with it. In the early nineteenth century, the public fell in love with a new generation of virtuoso pianists, among them the supremely gifted Franz Liszt, who played with dazzling dexterity. For the virtuoso, cranking up the tempo was one way to flaunt his technical brilliance—and give the audience a thrill.

Advances in instrument technology may have also encouraged faster playing. In the nineteenth century, the piano came to the fore. It was more powerful and better suited to running notes together than were its predecessors, the harpsichord and the clavichord. In 1878, Brahms wrote that "on the piano . . . everything happens faster, much livelier, and lighter in tempo."

Mirroring the modern obsession with efficiency, musical teaching took on an industrial ethic. Students began practising by playing notes, rather than compositions. A long-hours culture took hold. Modern piano students can spend six to eight hours a day tickling the ivories. Chopin recommended no more than three.

In Kliemt's view, all of these trends helped to fuel the acceleration of classical music. "Think of the greatest composers in the pre-twentieth-century canon—Bach, Haydn, Mozart, Beethoven, Schubert, Chopin, Mendelssohn, Brahms," he says. "We play them all too fast."

This is not a mainstream view. Most people in the music world have never heard of Tempo Giusto, and those who have tend to scoff at the movement. Yet some experts are open to the idea that classical music suffers from too much speed. There is certainly evidence that we play some music faster than before. In a letter dated October 26, 1876, Liszt wrote that he took *"presque une heure"* to play the Beethoven Hammerklavier Sonata op. 106. Fifty years later, Arthur Schnabel needed just forty minutes. Today some pianists rattle through the same notes in thirty-five minutes.

Early composers scolded musicians for succumbing to the virus of hurry. Mozart himself threw the odd tempo tantrum. In 1778, he fired off a blistering letter to his father after hearing Abbe Vogler, a leading musician of the day, massacre his Sonata in C Major, KV 330, at a dinner soiree. "You can easily imagine the situation went beyond endurance, since I could not suppress to communicate to him, 'much too swift,'" wrote the composer. Beethoven knew exactly how Mozart felt. "There lies a curse on the virtuosos," he once moaned. "Their practised fingers are always off in a hurry together with their emotion, sometimes even with their mind." A distrust of accelerated tempo carried into the twentieth century. Mahler is said to have told budding conductors to slow down, rather than speed up, if they felt the audience was growing bored.

Like the broader Slow movement, the musicians in Tempo Giusto are not against speed itself. What they object to is the very modern assumption that faster is always better. "Speed can give you a great feeling of excitement, and there is a place for that in life and in music," says Kliemt. "But you have to draw the line, and not always use speed. It is stupid to drink a glass of wine quickly. And it is stupid to play Mozart too fast."

Yet finding the "correct" playing speed is not as easy as it sounds. Musical tempo is a slippery concept at the best of times, more an art than a science. The speed at which a piece of music is played can vary with the circumstances—the mood of the musician, the type of instrument, the nature of the occasion, the character of the audience, the venue, the acoustics, the time of day, even the room temperature. A pianist is unlikely to play a Schubert sonata in exactly the same way in a packed concert hall as she does for a few close friends at home. Even composers are known to vary the tempo of their own works from one performance to the next. Many musical compositions work well in more than one speed. Robert Donington, a British musicologist, puts it this way: " . . . the right tempo for a given piece of music is the tempo which fits, as the hand fits the glove, the interpretation of that piece *then being given by the performer.*"

But surely the great composers laid down what they considered the "right" tempo for their music? Well, not exactly. Many left behind no tempo markings at all. Almost all the instructions we have for the works of Bach were added by pupils and scholars after his death. By the nineteenth century, most composers denoted tempo with Italian words such as *presto, adagio* and *lento*—all of which are open to interpretation. Does *andante* mean the same thing to a modern pianist as it did to Mendelssohn? The arrival in 1816 of Maelzel's metronome failed to settle the matter either. Many nineteenth-century composers struggled to convert the gadget's mechanical tick-tock-tick-tock into meaningful tempo instructions. Brahms, who died in 1897, summed up the confusion in a letter to Henschel: "As far as my experience goes every composer who has given metronome marks has sooner or later withdrawn them." To make matters worse, editors down the ages made a habit of adding and altering tempo instructions on the music they published.

Tempo Giusto takes a controversial route to working out the true intentions of earlier composers. In 1980, W. R. Talsma, a Dutch musicologist, laid the movement's philosophical foundations in a book called *The Rebirth of the Classics: Instruction for the Demechanization of Music.* His thesis, derived from an exhaustive study of historical records and musical structure, is that we systematically misinterpret metronome markings. Each note should be represented by two ticks of the pendulum (from right to left and back again) rather than, as is the common practice, a single tick. To honour the wishes of pre-twentieth-century composers, therefore, we should cut playing speeds in half. Talsma, however, believes that slower pieces—think Beethoven's "Moonlight Sonata"—should not be slowed down quite so much, if at all, because since the early industrial era musicians have played them more slowly, or at the original tempo, in order to heighten their sentimentality and to accentuate the contrast with the faster passages. Not all Tempo Giusto members agree, though. Grete Wehmeyer, a German composer and author of the 1989 book *Prestississimo: The Rediscovery of Slowness in Music,* thinks that all pre-twentieth-century classical music, fast and slow, should be played at half the speed commonly used today.

Tempo Giusto musicians side with either Talsma or Wehmeyer, or they fall somewhere in between. Some pay less attention to metronome markings, focusing more on other historical evidence and what feels right. Everyone in the movement, however, agrees that a slower tempo can bring to light the inner details of a piece of music, the notes and nuances that give it its true character.

Even skeptics can be swayed. Today, the leading exponent of Tempo Giusto in orchestral music is probably Maximianno Cobra, the Brazilian-born conductor of the Europa Philharmonia Budapest Orchestra. Though Cobra's 2001 recording of Beethoven's legendary Ninth Symphony takes twice as long as mainstream renditions, it garnered some favourable reviews. One critic, Richard Elen, conceded that "there is a great deal of inner detail that this performance reveals, which usually whizzes past so fast that you can hardly hear it." Even though he disliked the slow approach, Elen grudgingly accepted that it might be closer to what Beethoven intended, and rated Cobra's performance "extremely good."

This begs a question: If indeed we do play some classical music faster than our ancestors did, is that really such a bad thing? The world changes, and sensibilities change with it. There is no escaping the fact that we have learned to love a faster musical tempo. The twentieth century was all about boosting the beat, with ragtime giving way to rock 'n' roll, disco, speed metal and eventually techno. When Mike Jahn published *How to Make a Hit Record* in 1977, his advice to would-be pop stars was that 120 beats per minute was the optimum tempo for a dance track. Anything more than 135 beats per minute, he said, would appeal only to speed freaks. By the early 1990s, drum 'n' bass music and jungle music were belting along at 170 beats per minute. In 1993, Moby, a titan of techno, released what the *Guinness Book of World Records* anointed the fastest single of all time. "Thousand" clocked in at a dizzying 1,000 beats per minute, and reduced some listeners to tears.

Classical music has also evolved. Extreme variations in tempo came into fashion in the twentieth century. Orchestras are also much louder today than they were in the past. The way we consume the classical repertoire has changed, too. In a busy, fast-paced world, who has time to sit down and listen to a symphony or an opera from start to finish? More often we reach for the edited highlights on a compilation CD. Terrified of boring their listeners, classical music radio stations jazz up their broadcasts with fast-talking DJs, Top Ten countdowns and trivia contests. Some favour shorter pieces and faster renditions; others trim the pauses that composers write into their scores.

All this affects the way we experience music from the distant past. If 100 beats per minute set pulses racing in the 1700s, it is more likely to induce a yawn in the era of Moby. In order to sell CDs and fill concert halls in the twenty-first century, maybe musicians do have to play some of the classics at a higher tempo. And maybe that is not the end of the world. Even Kliemt does not wish to outlaw faster playing. "I don't want to be dogmatic and tell everyone exactly how they should play, because there is room for variation," he says. "I just think that if people are given a chance to listen to their favourite music played more slowly, and they listen with an open mind, then they will know in their hearts that it sounds better."

My head is humming with the great tempo debate as Kliemt finally sits down at the piano in Hamburg. What follows is a cross between a concert and a seminar. Before each piece, Kliemt plays a few bars in the faster tempo favoured by mainstream pianists, and then replays the same segment at his own slower pace. Then he talks about the differences.

The first piece on the program is a well-known Mozart sonata, C Major, KV 279. I often listen to a recording of it made by Daniel Barenboim. Kliemt kicks off by playing a bit of the sonata in a tempo familiar to the modern ear. It sounds good. Then he slows down to what he regards as the *tempo giusto*. His head bobs dreamily as his fingers caress the keys. "When you play too fast, the music loses its charm, its finer points, its character," Kliemt tells us. "Because each note needs time to develop, you need the slowness to bring out the melody and the playfulness." Slowed down from the norm, Sonata KV 279 sounds odd at first. But then it starts to make sense. To my untrained ear, at least, the *tempo giusto* version sounds richer, more textured, more melodious. It works well. According to the stopwatch I have smuggled in to the concert, Kliemt gets through the three movements of the sonata in twenty-two minutes and six seconds. On my CD, Barenboim cranks out the same notes in fourteen minutes.

Like Talsma, Kliemt believes in slowing down the faster classical pieces and leaving the slower ones more or less as they are. Yet he maintains that playing in *tempo giusto* means more than just reinterpreting metronome markings. You have to get inside the music, feel out every contour, discover the natural beat of the piece, its *eigenzeit*. Kliemt sets great store by matching musical tempo to the rhythms of the human body. In 1784, Mozart published a famous sonata called "Rondo alla Turca," the Turkish March. Most modern pianists play the piece at a rollicking speed best suited to running, or at least jogging. Kliemt gives it a slower tempo that evokes soldiers marching. Dance is another touchstone. Many early works of classical music were written for dancing, which meant the powdered aristocrats of yesteryear had to be able to hear the notes in order to know when to make the next step. "In Mozart's time, music was still like a language," says Kliemt. "If you play it too quickly, nobody will understand anything."

The concert continues. Kliemt gives the same treatment to the final three pieces, a Mozart Fantasie and two Beethoven sonatas, and all three sound marvellous, not slow or ponderous or dull. After all, a musician can lower the tempo and still give the impression of speed and vivacity by playing in a highly rhythmic manner. Does slow Mozart sound better than fast Mozart? Inevitably, that is a matter of taste. Just as it is when pop stars play "unplugged" versions of their high-tempo songs on MTV. Maybe, in this fast-paced world, there is room for both. Personally, I like the Tempo Giusto style. But I also still enjoy listening to Barenboim play Mozart and Beethoven.

To find out what Josef Public thinks, I conduct a straw poll after the Hamburg recital. One man, an elderly academic with wild hair, is unimpressed. "Too slow, too slow, too slow," he mutters. Others, however, seem delighted by what they have heard. Gudula Bischoff, a middle-aged tax inspector in a cream suit and floral blouse, is a long-time admirer of Kliemt. She credits him with opening her eyes to the genius of Bach. "When you hear Uwe play, it is beautiful, a completely new way to hear music," she says, with a dreaminess not normally associated with tax inspectors. "Because you can hear the notes when he plays, the melody comes out much better, and the music seems more alive."

Kliemt has made at least one convert this evening. Among the spectators queuing up to meet him after the recital is Natascha Speidel, an earnest twenty-nine-year-old in a white turtleneck. As a violin student, she is used to rattling through pieces in the tempo favoured by mainstream players. "In music schools, technique is a big priority, so there is lots of fast playing," she tells me. "We hear things played fast, we practise fast and we play fast. A quick tempo feels comfortable to me."

"What did you think of Kliemt?" I ask.

"Wonderful," she says. "I thought a slow tempo would make it boring, but it was the opposite. The music was much more interesting because you can hear many more details than you can at a higher tempo. At the end, I looked at my watch and thought 'Wow, two hours already.' The time went a lot faster than I expected."

Speidel will not, however, be rushing out to join the Tempo Giusto movement. She still likes playing fast, and she knows that slowing down would hurt her grades at music college. It could also scupper her dream of landing a job in an orchestra. "I can't choose at the moment to play slowly in public, because people expect a faster tempo," she says. "But maybe I will play more slowly on my own sometimes. I will have to think about it."

For Kliemt, that in itself is a triumph. A seed of slowness has been planted. After the crowd melts away into the balmy evening, we linger in the parking lot, savouring the blood-orange sunset. Kliemt is in high spirits. Sure, he knows Tempo Giusto faces an uphill battle. With back catalogues to sell and reputations to protect, the heavyweights of classical music have little time for a movement that claims they have spent their whole lives playing and conducting in the wrong tempo. Even Kliemt himself is still refining his search for the *tempo giusto*. Finding the right speed can involve a lot of trial and error: some of his current recordings are faster than the ones he made ten years ago. "Maybe when I was just starting out with the idea of slowness I took it a bit far," he says. "There is still much to debate."

Nevertheless, Kliemt buzzes with a messianic zeal. Like other Tempo Giusto members, he believes the movement could be the biggest revolution to hit classical music in more than a century. And he takes heart from the progress made by other Slow campaigns. "Forty years ago, people laughed at organic farming, but now it looks like it will become the national standard in Germany," says Kliemt.

"Perhaps forty years from now, everyone will be playing Mozart more slowly."

While the Tempo Giusto movement seeks to rewrite the history of classical music, others are using musical slowness to mount a symbolic challenge to the cult of speed.

An old lighthouse on the banks of the Thames River in east London is now the venue for what may be the longest concert ever staged. The project is called Longplayer and will last a thousand years. The music is based on a twenty-minute recording of notes played on Tibetan singing bowls. Every two minutes, an Apple iMac plays six segments of the recording at different pitches, yielding a soundtrack that will never repeat itself through a full millennium of performance. Jem Finer, the creator of Longplayer, wants to take a stand against the narrow horizons of our speed-crazed world. "With everything getting faster and faster, and attention spans getting shorter, we have forgotten how to slow down," he tells me. "I wanted to make something that evokes time as a long, slow process, rather than as something to rush through." Sitting at the top of a lighthouse with views across the Thames, listening to the deep, meditative hum of the singing bowls, is very much a slowing experience. Longplayer reaches a wider audience than those who make the pilgrimage to East London. During 2000, a second iMac piped the soothing tones into the Rest Zone at the Millennium Dome across the river. Dutch national radio gave it four hours of uninterrupted airtime in 2001. Even now, Longplayer is broadcast on the Internet.

Another marathonic musical event is underway in Halberstadt, a small German town famous for its ancient organs. The local St. Burchardi Church, a twelfth-century pile that was sacked by Napoleon, is the venue for a concert that will end in the year 2640, sponsors permitting. The featured work was written in 1992 by John Cage, the avant-garde American composer. Its title, appropriately enough, is *ASLSP,* or *As Slow As Possible.* How long the piece should last has long been a bone of contention among the cognoscenti. Some thought twenty minutes enough; hardliners insisted on nothing short of infinity. After consulting a panel of musicologists, composers, organists, theologians and philosophers, Halberstadt settled on 639 years—the exact time that had passed since the creation of the town's renowned Blockwerk organ.

To do justice to Cage's piece, the organizers built an organ that will last for centuries. Weights attached to the keyboard hold down notes long after the organist has left. The *ASLSP* recital began in September 2001 with a pause that lasted seventeen months. During that time, the only sound was that of the organ bellows inflating. In February 2003, an organist played the first three notes, which will reverberate through the church until the summer of 2004, when the next two notes will be played.

The notion of a concert so slow that no one who attends opening night will live to hear the final note clearly strikes a chord with the public. Hundreds of spectators descend on Halberstadt each time an organist comes to play the next set of notes. During the long months in between, visitors flock to soak up the residual sounds echoing round the church.

I attended the *ASLSP* concert in the summer of 2002, when the bellows were still filling with air, and before the organ had been installed. Norbert Kleist, a commercial lawyer and member of the John Cage Project, was my guide. We met outside the St. Burchardi Church. Across the yard, old farm buildings had been converted into social housing and a furniture workshop. Near the church stood a modern sculpture, made up of five disjointed iron pillars. "It represents broken time," explained Kleist, as he dug a set of keys from his pocket.

We stepped through a heavy wooden door into the church, which was spectacularly empty. No pews, no altar, no icons—just a gravel floor and a high ceiling crisscrossed with wooden beams. The air was cool and smelled of old masonry. Pigeons flapped about on the windowsills overhead. Housed in a large oak box, the organ bellows squatted like a miniature power station in one of the transepts, huffing and puffing in the half-light. The whooshing sound they emitted was gentle, almost musical, like a steam engine pulling into the station at the end of a long journey.

Kleist described the 639-year rendition of *As Slow As Possible* as a challenge to the breathless, haste-ridden culture of the modern world. As we walked away from the church, leaving the organ to fill its vast lungs, he said, "Maybe this is the start of a revolution in slowness."

CHAPTER TEN

CHILDREN: RAISING AN UNHURRIED CHILD

The most effective kind of education is that a child should play amongst lovely things.
—PLATO (427–347 BC)

HARRY LEWIS IS DEAN of the undergraduate school at Harvard. In early 2001, he attended a meeting at which students were invited to air their grievances about staff at the Ivy League university. One undergraduate kicked up a memorable fuss. He wanted to double major in Biology and English, and cram all the work into three, instead of the usual four, years. He was exasperated with his academic advisor, who was unable, or unwilling, to devise a schedule to accommodate all the courses. As he listened to the student moan about being held back, Lewis felt a light bulb flash above his head.

"I remember thinking, 'Wait a minute, you need help, but not in the way you think you do,'" says the dean. "You need to take time to think about what is really important, rather than trying to figure out how to pack as much as you can into the shortest possible schedule."

After the meeting, Lewis began to reflect on how the twenty-first-century student has become a disciple of hurry. From there it was a short step to speaking out against the scourge of overstuffed schedules and accelerated degree programs. In the summer of 2001, the dean wrote an open letter to every first-year undergraduate at Harvard. It was an impassioned plea for a new approach to life on campus and beyond. It was also a neat précis of the ideas that lie at the heart of the Slow philosophy. The letter, which now goes out to Harvard freshmen every year, is entitled: *Slow Down*.

Over seven pages, Lewis makes the case for getting more out of university—and life—by doing less. He urges students to think twice before racing through their degrees. It takes time to master a subject, he says, pointing out that top medical, law and business schools increasingly favour mature candidates with more to offer than an "abbreviated and intense undergraduate education." Lewis warns against piling on too many extracurricular activities. What is the point, he asks, of playing lacrosse, chairing debates, organizing conferences, acting in plays and editing a section of the campus newspaper if you end up spending your whole Harvard career in overdrive, striving not to fall behind schedule? Much better to do fewer things and have time to make the most of them.

When it comes to academic life, Lewis favours the same less-is-more approach. Get plenty of rest and relaxation, he says, and be sure to cultivate the art of doing nothing.

"Empty time is not a vacuum to be filled," writes the dean. "It is the thing that enables the other things on your mind to be creatively rearranged, like the empty square in the 4 x 4 puzzle that makes it possible to move the other fifteen pieces around." In other words, doing nothing, being Slow, is an essential part of good thinking.

Slow Down is not a charter for slackers and born-again beatniks. Lewis is as keen on hard work and academic success as the next Harvard heavyweight. His point is simply that a little selective slowness can help students to live and work better. "In advising you to think about slowing down and limiting your structured activities, I do not mean to discourage you from high achievement, indeed from the pursuit of extraordinary excellence," he concludes. "But you are more likely to sustain the intense effort needed to accomplish first-rate work in one area if you allow yourself some leisure time, some recreation, some time for solitude."

His *cri de coeur* comes not a moment too soon. In our turbocharged world, the hurry virus has spread from adulthood into the younger years. These days, children of all ages are growing up faster. Six-year-olds organize their social lives with cellphones, and teenagers launch businesses from their bedrooms. Anxiety about body shape, sex, consumer brands and careers starts earlier and earlier. Childhood itself seems to be getting shorter, with more girls now hitting puberty before their teens. Young people today are certainly busier, more scheduled, more rushed than my generation ever was. Recently, a teacher I know approached the parents of a child in her care. She felt the boy was spending too long at school and was enrolled in too many extracurricular activities. Give him a break, she suggested. The father was furious. "He has to learn to do a ten-hour day, just like me," he snapped. The child was four.

In 1989, David Elkind, an American psychologist, published a book called *The Hurried Child: Growing Up Too Fast Too Soon*. As the title suggests, Elkind warned against the vogue for rushing kids into adulthood. How many people took notice? Apparently very few. A decade later, the average kid is more hurried than ever.

Children are not born obsessed with speed and productivity—we make them that way. Single-parent homes put extra pressure on kids to shoulder adult responsibilities. Advertisers encourage them to become consumers earlier. Schools teach them to live by the clock and use time as efficiently as possible. Parents reinforce that lesson by packing their schedules with extracurricular activities. Everything gives children the message that less is *not* more, and that faster is always better. One of the first phrases my son learned to say was: "Come on! Hurry up!"

Competition spurs many parents to rush their children. We all want our offspring to succeed in life. In a busy world, that means putting them on the fast track in everything—school, sports, art, music. It is no longer enough to keep up with the Joneses' children; now, our own little darlings have to outpace them in every discipline.

The fear that one's kids may fall behind is not new. Back in the eighteenth century, Samuel Johnson warned parents not to dither: "Whilst you stand deliberating which book your son shall read first, another boy has read both." In the 24/7 global economy, however, the pressure to stay ahead of the pack is more ferocious than ever, leading to what experts call "hyper-parenting," the compulsive drive to perfect one's children. To give their offspring a head start, ambitious parents play Mozart to them in the womb, teach them sign language before they are six months old and use Baby Webster flash cards to teach them vocabulary from their first birthday. Computer camps and motivational seminars now accept kids as young as four. Golf lessons start at two. With everyone else fast-tracking their offspring, the pressure to join the race is immense. The other day I came across an ad for a BBC foreign language course for children. "Speak French at 3! Spanish at 7!" screamed the headline. "If you wait, it will be too late!" My first instinct was to rush to the phone to place an order. My second instinct was to feel guilty for not having acted on the first.

In a cut-throat world, school is a battleground where the only thing that matters is coming top of the class. Nowhere is that more true than in East Asia, where education systems are built on the principle of "exam hell." Just to keep pace, millions of kids across the region spend evenings and weekends at institutions called "cram schools." Devoting eighty hours a week to academic work is not uncommon.

In the headlong dash for higher international test scores, schools in the English-speaking world have been especially keen to emulate the East Asian model. Over the last two decades, governments have embraced the doctrine of "intensification," which means piling on the pressure with more homework, more exams and a rigid curriculum. Often the toil starts before formal school. At his nursery school in London, my son started learning—not very successfully—how to hold a pen and write at the age of three. Private tutoring is also booming in the West, at younger and younger ages. American parents hoping to win a place in the right kindergarten send their four-year-olds to be coached on interview techniques. London tutors take children as young as three.

Intensification is not confined to schooling, either. In between lessons, many children dash from one extracurricular activity to the next, leaving them no time to relax, play on their own or let their imaginations wander. No time to be Slow.

Children increasingly pay a price for leading rushed lives. Kids as young as five now suffer from upset stomachs, headaches, insomnia, depression and eating disorders brought on by stress. Like everyone else in our "always-on" society, many children get too little sleep nowadays. This can make them cranky, jumpy and impatient. Sleep-deprived kids have more trouble making friends. And they stand a greater chance of being underweight, since deep sleep triggers the release of human growth hormone.

When it comes to learning, putting children on the fast track often does more harm than good. The American Academy of Pediatrics warns that specializing in a sport at too young an age can cause physical and psychological damage. The same goes for education. A growing body of evidence suggests that children learn better when they learn at a slower pace. Kathy Hirsh-Pasek, professor of child psychology at Temple University in Philadelphia, Pennsylvania, recently tested 120 American preschool kids. Half went to nursery schools that stressed social interaction and a playful approach to learning; the rest attended nursery schools that rushed them towards academic achievement, using what experts call the "drill and kill" style of teaching. Hirsh-Pasek found that children from the more relaxed, Slower environment turned out less anxious, more eager to learn and better able to think independently.

In 2003, Hirsh-Pasek co-authored *Einstein Never Used Flash Cards: How Our Children REALLY Learn—and Why They Need to Play More and Memorize Less.* The book is packed with research debunking the myth that "early learning" and "academic acceleration" can build better brains. "When it comes to raising and teaching children, the modern belief that 'faster is better' and that we must 'make every moment count' is simply wrong," says Hirsh-Pasek. "When you look at the scientific evidence, it is clear that children learn better and develop more rounded personalities when they learn in a more relaxed, less regimented, less hurried way."

In East Asia, the punishing work ethic that once made the region's schools the envy of the world is clearly backfiring. Pupils are losing their edge in international test scores, and failing to develop the creative skills needed in the information economy. Increasingly, East Asian students are rebelling against the study-till-you-drop ethos. Crime and suicide rates are rising, and truancy, once regarded as a Western problem, has reached epidemic proportions. Over a hundred thousand Japanese primary and junior high students play hooky for more than a month each year. Many others refuse to go to school at all.

Right across the industrial world, though, there is a growing backlash against the hurry-up approach to childhood. Lewis's *Slow Down* letter is a hit with everyone from newspaper columnists to students and staff. Parents with kids at Harvard show it to their younger children. "Apparently, it's like a bible in some families," says Lewis. Many of the ideas in *Slow Down* are gaining ground in the media. Parenting magazines run regular features on the perils of pushing youngsters too hard. Every year brings a fresh crop of books by psychologists and educators making the scientific case against the "roadrunner" approach to raising children.

Not long ago, the *New Yorker* published a cartoon that summed up the growing fear that modern youngsters are being denied a real childhood. Two primary-school boys are walking down a street, books under their arms, baseball caps on their heads. With a world-weariness beyond his years, one mutters to the other: "So many toys—so little unstructured time."

We have been here before. Like much of the Slow movement, the battle to give children back their childhood has roots in the Industrial Revolution. Indeed, the modern notion of childhood as a time of innocence and imagination grew out of the Romantic movement, which first swept across Europe in the late eighteenth century. Until then, children were seen as mini-adults who needed to be made employable as soon as possible. In education, Jean-Jacques Rousseau, the French philosopher, rang in the changes by attacking the tradition of teaching the young as though they were grown-ups. In *Emile*, his landmark treatise on schooling children in accordance with nature, he wrote: "Childhood has its own way of seeing, thinking, and feeling, and nothing is more foolish than to try to substitute ours for theirs." In the nineteenth century, reformers turned their sights on the evils of child labour in the factories and mines that powered the new industrial economy. In 1819, Coleridge coined the term "white slaves" to describe the children toiling in English cotton factories. By the late 1800s, Britain was starting to move children out of the workplace and into the classroom, to give them a proper childhood.

Today, educators and parents around the world are once again taking steps to allow young people the freedom to slow down, to be children. In my search for interviewees, I post messages on a few parenting websites. Within days, my inbox is crammed with emails from three continents. Some are from teenagers lamenting their haste-ridden lives. An Australian girl named Jess describes herself as a "rushed teen" and tells me "I have no time for anything!" But most of the emails come from parents enthusing about the various ways their kids are decelerating.

Let's start in the classroom, where pressure is mounting for a Slower approach to learning. At the end of 2002,

Maurice Holt, professor emeritus of education at the University of Colorado, Denver, published a manifesto calling for a worldwide movement for "Slow Schooling." Like others, he draws his inspiration from Slow Food. In Holt's view, stuffing information into children as fast as possible is as nourishing as wolfing down a Big Mac. Much better to study at a gentle pace, taking time to explore subjects deeply, to make connections, to learn how to think rather than how to pass exams. If eating Slow excites the palate, learning Slow can broaden and invigorate the mind.

"At a stroke, the notion of the slow school destroys the idea that schooling is about cramming, testing, and standardizing experience," Holt writes. "The slow approach to food allows for discovery, for the development of connoisseurship. Slow food festivals feature new dishes and new ingredients. In the same way, slow schools give scope for invention and response to cultural change, while fast schools just turn out the same old burgers."

Holt and his supporters are not extremists. They do not want children to learn less, or to spend the school day goofing around. Hard work has a place in a Slow classroom. Instead of obsessing over tests, targets and timetables, though, kids would be given the freedom to fall in love with learning. Rather than spend a history lesson listening to a teacher spewing dates and facts about the Cuban missile crisis, a class might hold its own UN-style debate. Each pupil would research the position of a major country on the 1962 standoff, and then make the case to the rest of the class. The children still work hard, but without the drudgery of rote learning. Like every other wing of the Slow movement, "Slow Schooling" is about balance.

Countries that take a Slower approach to education are already reaping the benefits. In Finland, children enter pre-school education at the age of six, and formal schooling at seven. They then face fewer of the high-pressure standard exams that are the bane of student life from Japan to Britain. The result? Finland routinely tops the Organization for Economic Co-operation and Development's prestigious world rankings for educational performance and literacy. And delegates from across the industrial world are flocking to study the "Finnish model."

Elsewhere, parents who want their children to learn in a Slow environment are turning to the private sector. In interwar Germany, Rudolf Steiner pioneered a brand of education that is the polar opposite of accelerated learning. Steiner believed that children should never be rushed into studying things before they are ready, and he was against teaching them to read before their seventh birthday. Instead, he believed, they should spend their early years playing, drawing, telling stories and learning about nature. Steiner also eschewed rigid timetables that forced pupils to hop from subject to subject at the whim of the clock, preferring to let them study a topic until they felt ready to move on. Today, the number of Steiner-inspired schools around the world is over eight hundred, and rising.

The Institute of Child Study Laboratory School in Toronto also takes a Slow approach. Its two hundred pupils, aged from four to twelve, are taught how to learn, how to understand, how to pursue knowledge for its own sake, free from the mainstream obsession with tests, marks and schedules. When they do sit standard exams, though, their scores are usually very high. Many have won scholarships to top universities around the world, lending credence to Holt's view that "the supreme irony of the slow school is that precisely because it provides the intellectual nourishment students need . . . good test results follow. Success, like happiness, is best pursued obliquely." Although the Laboratory School has been running since 1926, its ethos is more popular now than ever. Despite annual fees of $7,000 Canadian, more than a thousand children are on the waiting list to get in.

In Japan, experimental academies are springing up to meet the demand for a more relaxed approach to learning. One example is Apple Tree, which a group of desperate parents founded in Tokyo's Saitama prefecture in 1988. The school's philosophy is a million miles from the martial discipline, breathless competition and hothouse atmosphere of the average Japanese classroom. Pupils come and go as they please, study what they want when they want to and take no exams. Though it sounds like a recipe for anarchy, the laid-back regime actually works rather well.

On a recent afternoon, twenty pupils aged from six to nineteen climb the rickety wooden steps to the small, first-floor academy. They do not look particularly rebellious—some have dyed hair, but there are no tattoos or facial piercings to be seen. In the Japanese way, they stack their shoes neatly by the entrance before kneeling down to work at the low tables spread around the L-shaped room. Occasionally, a pupil rises to make green tea in the kitchen, or to take a cellphone call. Otherwise, everyone is hard at work, writing in notebooks or discussing ideas with the teachers or their classmates.

Hiromi Koike, a cherubic seventeen-year-old in jeans and a denim cap, wanders over to tell me why schools like Apple Tree are a godsend. Unable to keep up with the constant pressure and fast pace of traditional state education, she fell behind and became a target for the playground bullies. When she refused point-blank to attend school, her parents enrolled her in Apple Tree, where she is now working towards a high school diploma, taking four years instead of the usual three. "In normal school, you are always under so much pressure to be fast, to do everything within a set time," she says. "I much prefer being at Apple Tree, because I get to control my own schedule and learn at my own speed. It is not a crime to be slow here."

Critics warn that Slow Schooling is best suited to children who are academically able, or from families that put a high premium on education. And there is some truth in that. But elements of the Slow doctrine can also work in an average classroom, which is why some of the fastest nations are starting to change their approach to teaching. Across East Asia, governments are moving to lighten the load on students. Japan has embraced what it calls a "sunshine" approach to education. That means more freedom in the classroom, more time for creative thinking and shorter hours. In 2002, the government finally abolished Saturday—yes,

Saturday—classes. It has also started throwing its weight behind the growing number of private schools that take a more Slow approach to learning. Apple Tree finally won full government approval in 2001.

School systems in Britain are also looking at ways to ease the pressure on stressed-out pupils. In 2001, Wales scrapped the standard assessment tests for seven-year-olds. In 2003, Scotland began exploring ways to put less emphasis on formal testing. Under a new plan, English primary schools will aim to make learning more enjoyable.

Parents are also starting to question the academic hothousing that prevails in so many English private schools. Some are lobbying headmasters for less homework and more Slow time for art, music or just thinking. Others are simply yanking their kids out and moving them into schools that take a less Fast approach.

That is what Julian Griffin, an office broker in London, did. Like so many successful parents, he wanted to give his son what he thought was the best education possible. The family even moved, to be within walking distance of a top private primary school in south London. Before long, though, James, an artistic, dreamy child, began to flounder. Though good at drawing and making things with his hands, he struggled to keep up with the academic pace—the long hours in the classroom, the take-home assignments, the exams. Most parents at the school found it difficult to make their children plow through the mountain of homework, but the battles were particularly virulent in the Griffin household. James began to suffer panic attacks, and wept when his parents dropped him off at school. After two years of misery, and a fortune spent on psychologists, the Griffins decided to look for another school. All the private schools turned them down. One headmistress even suggested James might be brain-damaged. Eventually, it was the family doctor who came up with the solution. "There is nothing wrong with James," she said. "All he needs is to chill out. Send him to a state school."

British state schools do not hothouse. So in September 2002, the Griffins enrolled James in a public primary school that is popular with ambitious middle-class parents in south London. The school has been the making of James. Though he still has a tendency to daydream, he has discovered a taste for learning and now ranks in the middle of his class. He looks forward to going to school, and does his homework—about one hour a week—without a fuss. He also attends a weekly pottery class. Above all, he is happy, and his confidence is returning. "I feel like I have my son back," says Julian. Disillusioned with the hothouse culture in the private sector, the Griffins plan to send their younger child, Robert, to the same school as his brother. "He's a different character to James, and I'm sure he could take the pace in the private sector, but why should he have to?" says Julian. "What's the point of driving kids so hard that they burn out?"

Even when their children are coping fine, other parents are pulling their kids out of private schools to give them more space to flex their creative muscles. When he was four, Sam Lamiri passed the entrance exams for a top

London private school. His mother, Jo, was proud and delighted. But though Sam did well enough in his coursework, she felt the school was pushing the children too hard. A particular disappointment was the low priority given to art. The children did one hour a week on Friday afternoon—and only then if the teacher felt like it. Lamiri thought Sam was missing out. "His head was so full of facts and learning, and he was under so much pressure to get ahead academically, that he didn't have any space left to use his imagination," she says. "It wasn't at all what I wanted for my children—I wanted them to be well-rounded, interested and imaginative."

When a shift in financial circumstances meant the family had less money for school fees, Lamiri suddenly had an excuse to change things. In the middle of the 2002 school year, she moved Sam to a popular public school, and is pleased with the gentler pace and the emphasis on exploring the world through art. Sam is now happier and has more energy. He has developed a keen interest in nature, particularly in snakes and cheetahs. Lamiri also feels his creative faculties are sharper. The other day he wondered aloud what would happen if we could build a really huge staircase up into space. "Sam would never have asked something like that before," says his mother. "He talks in a much more imaginative way now."

Bucking the hothouse trend can be nerve-wracking, though. Parents who allow their children to slow down invariably suffer from the nagging fear that they may be shortchanging them. Even so, more and more are taking the plunge. "When so many other people around you are hothousing, you sometimes wonder if you've done the right thing," says Lamiri. "In the end, you just have to follow your instincts."

Other parents find that instinct tells them to pull their children out of school altogether. Home education is on the rise, with the United States leading the charge. Statistics everywhere are fuzzy, but the National Home Education Research Institute estimates that more than a million American youngsters are now being schooled at home. Other estimates include a hundred thousand children in Canada, ninety thousand in Britain, thirty thousand in Australia and eight thousand in New Zealand.

Parents choose to educate their offspring at home for a range of reasons—to shield them from bullying, drugs and other antisocial behaviour; to raise them in a particular religious or moral tradition; to give them a better education. But many see home-schooling as a way to free children from the tyranny of the timetable, to let them learn and live at their own pace. To let them be Slow. Even families that start off home-educating with a rigidly structured day usually end up taking a more fluid, freewheeling tack. On the spur of the moment, if the sun is shining, they might head off on a nature walk or to visit a museum. Earlier, we saw how having control over their own time makes people feel less rushed in the workplace. The same applies in education. Both parents and children report that the power to fix their own schedule, or choose their own tempo, helps to curb the hurry reflex. "Once you control your own hours, the pressure to rush is much less," says a home educator in Vancouver. "You just automatically slow down."

Home education is often bound up with the whole family embracing a more Slow approach to life. Many parents find that their priorities shift, as they spend less time working and more time overseeing their child's learning. "Once people start asking questions about education, you find that they start asking questions about everything—politics, the environment, work," says Roland Meighan, a British expert on home-schooling. "The genie is out of the bottle."

True to the Slow philosophy, home education does not mean dropping out or lagging behind. On the contrary, learning at home actually turns out to be highly efficient. As everyone knows, schools waste a lot of time: pupils have to travel there and back; take breaks when someone else tells them to; sit through instruction in material they have already mastered; wade through irrelevant homework. When you study alone at home, time can be put to more productive use. Research shows that home-educated children learn faster and better than their rivals in conventional classrooms. Universities love them because they combine curiosity, creativity and imagination with the maturity and gumption to tackle a subject on their own.

The fear that children will suffer socially when they abandon the classroom is also unfounded. Parents who educate at home usually set up local networks to share teaching and field trips, and to arrange social gatherings. And because home-educated children get through their coursework more quickly, they have more free time for recreation, which can include joining clubs or sports teams full of their peers from formal school.

Beth Wood, who switched to home education at the beginning of 2003, when she was thirteen, would never dream of returning to the classroom. In her early years, she attended a Steiner school near the family home in Whitstable, a small fishing port fifty miles east of London. A precociously bright child, Beth thrived in the less rigid environment. But when the size of her class expanded, and several disruptive pupils enrolled, she grew so frustrated that her mother, Claire, decided to move her. Since the local state primaries were below par, they began touring private schools in the area. Several offered Beth a scholarship, promising to throw her straight into the "accelerated learning" stream. Unwilling to put her daughter on the fast track, Claire decided to make the leap into home education. Manoeuvring Beth onto the slower road mirrored a shift in her own life: in 2000, she had quit her stressful, long-hours job as a marine insurance adjuster to set up a soap-making workshop at home.

Home education has done wonders for Beth. She is more relaxed and confident, and relishes the freedom to learn at her own pace. If she doesn't feel like studying geography on Monday, she'll tackle it later in the week. And when a subject takes her fancy, she reads up on it voraciously. Her fluid schedule, and the fact that she gets through her work twice as fast as she did at school, also leaves plenty of time for extracurricular activities: she has lots of friends, plays violin in a youth orchestra, attends a weekly art class and is the only girl on the water polo team at her local swimming pool. Perhaps the most important thing for Beth, who is tall and already looks older than her age, is that she never feels rushed or beholden to the clock. Having control over her own time gives her an immunity to time-sickness. "My friends in school are always hurried or stressed or fed up, but I never feel like that," she says. "I really enjoy studying."

Under light supervision from her mother, Beth is following the national curriculum, and even exceeding it in some subjects. History is her passion, and she has set her sights on studying archaeology at Oxford or Cambridge. Soon she will start preparing for her GCSEs, the exams that all British pupils sit at the age of sixteen. Claire thinks her daughter could whiz through them in a year, instead of the usual two, but plans to rein her in. "She could run like hell with them, but I can't see the point in rushing," she says. "If she takes it at a slower pace, and keeps a healthy balance between work and play, she'll learn a lot more."

Whenever people talk of the need for children to slow down, play is always high on the agenda. Many studies show that unstructured time for play helps younger children develop their social and language skills, their creative powers and their ability to learn. Unstructured play is the opposite of "quality time," which implies industry, planning, scheduling and purpose. It is not a ballet lesson or a soccer practice. Unstructured play is digging for worms in the garden, messing about with toys in the bedroom, building castles with Lego, horsing around with other kids in the playground or just gazing out the window. It is about exploring the world, and your own reaction to it, at your own speed. To an adult used to making every second count, unstructured play looks like wasted time. And our reflex is to fill up those "empty" slots in the diary with entertaining and enriching activities.

Angelika Drabert, an occupational therapist, visits kindergartens in Munich to talk to parents about the importance of unstructured play time. She teaches them not to hurry or over-schedule their kids. Drabert has a bag full of letters from grateful mothers. "Once you show parents that they do not need to provide entertainment and activities for every moment of the day, everyone can relax, which is good," she says. "Sometimes life has to be slow or boring for children."

Many parents are arriving at that conclusion without help from a therapist. In the United States, thousands are joining groups, such as Putting Family First, that campaign against the epidemic of over-scheduling. In 2002, Ridgewood, a town of twenty-five thousand in New Jersey, began holding an annual Ready, Set, Relax! event. On a chosen day in March, local teachers agree not to assign any homework and all sports practices, tutoring sessions and club meetings are cancelled. Parents arrange to come home from work early enough to have dinner with their children and spend time with them in the evening. The event is now a fixture on the Ridgewood calendar, and some families have started applying the Slow creed the rest of the year.

The cue to slow down often comes from children themselves. Take the Barnes family, who live in west London. Nicola, the mother, works part-time for a market research firm. Her husband, Alex, is the financial director for a publishing company. They are busy people with bulging diaries. Until recently, their eight-year-old son, Jack, was the same. He played organized soccer and cricket, took swimming and tennis lessons, and acted in a drama group. On weekends, the family trawled through art galleries and museums, attended musical events for children and visited nature study centres around London. "We ran our lives, including Jack's, like a military campaign," says Nicola. "Every second was accounted for."

Then, one afternoon in late spring, everything changed. Jack wanted to stay at home and play in his room instead of going to his tennis lesson. His mother insisted he go. As they sped across west London, screeching round corners and surging through yellow lights to avoid being late, Jack fell quiet in the back seat. "I looked in the mirror, and he was fast asleep—and that's when it hit me," Nicola recalls. "I suddenly thought: 'This is mad—I'm dragging him to something he doesn't really want to go to. I'm going to burn out my own child.'"

That evening, the Barnes family gathered round the kitchen table to downsize Jack's diary. They decided he should do no more than three extracurricular activities at a time. Jack chose soccer, swimming and drama. They also agreed to cut back on their scheduled weekend outings. As a result, Jack now has more time to potter around in the garden, meet friends in the nearby park and play in his room. On Saturdays, instead of collapsing exhausted into bed after supper, he now hosts sleepovers. On Sunday morning, he and a friend make pancakes and popcorn. Shifting down a gear did take some getting used to, at least for the parents. Nicola worried that Jack would be bored and restless, especially on weekends. Alex feared he would miss cricket and tennis. Jack, however, has blossomed on the lighter schedule. He is livelier, more talkative and has stopped biting his nails. His soccer coach thinks his passing is sharper. The head of his drama group feels Jack has more get-up-and-go. "I think he's just enjoying everything about his life more," says his mother. "I just wish we'd lightened his load sooner."

Nicola feels closer to her son now that they spend more time just hanging out together. She also finds her own life is less rushed. All that shuttling from one activity to the next was stressful and time-consuming.

The Barneses are now planning to cut back on the mother of all extracurricular activities: television. Earlier, I described cities as giant particle accelerators. It is a metaphor that can just as easily apply to TV, especially for the young. Television accelerates children's move into adulthood by exposing them to grown-up issues and turning them into consumers at a young age. Because kids watch it so much—up to four hours a day in the United States, on average—they have to rush to squeeze everything else into their schedules. In 2002, ten leading public health organizations, including the American Medical Association and the American Academy of Pediatrics, signed a letter warning that watching too much television makes youngsters more aggressive. A number of studies suggest that children exposed to violent TV or computer games are more likely to be restless and unable to sit still and concentrate.

In classrooms around the world, where more and more kids are being diagnosed with attention deficit disorder, teachers increasingly point the finger at the boob tube. Extreme visual speed on the small screen certainly has an effect on young brains. When Japanese TV broadcast a Pokémon video in 1997, the bright flashing lights triggered epileptic fits in nearly seven hundred children watching at home. To guard against lawsuits, software companies now attach health warnings to their games.

This explains why many families are saying enough is enough. In busy, wired homes around the world, parents are restricting their children's access to the small screen— and finding that life is less frantic without it. To experience a TV-free zone firsthand, I arrange to visit Susan and Jeffrey Clarke, a busy forty-something couple who live with their two young children in Toronto. Until recently, the television was the centre of their household. Rooted like zombies in front of the screen, ten-year-old Michael and eight-year-old Jessica routinely lost track of time, and ended up rushing to avoid being late. Both children gobbled down meals to get back to the box.

After reading about the anti-TV movement, the Clarkes decided to give it a try. They went cold turkey, stowing their 27-inch Panasonic in a cupboard under the stairs.

Once the initial protests died down, the results were amazing. Within a week, the children had covered the basement floor with mattresses and started putting together gymnastic routines with cartwheels and handstands. Like other TV-free families, the Clarkes suddenly found they had time on their hands, which helped take the rush out of daily life. Many of the hours once spent watching TV are now devoted to Slower pursuits—reading, playing board games, horsing around in the backyard, studying music or just chatting. Both children seem healthier and are doing better at school. Jessica finds it easier to get to sleep at night. Michael, who used to have trouble concentrating and reading, now devours books on his own.

On a recent Thursday evening, the Clarke household was enviably serene. Susan was cooking pasta in the kitchen. Michael was reading *Harry Potter and the Goblet of Fire* on a sofa in the living room. Beside him, Jeffrey flipped through the *Globe and Mail*. On the floor, Jessica was writing a letter to her grandmother.

The Clarkes are not as cloyingly virtuous as they sound. The TV set is now back in the living room, and the kids are allowed to watch the odd program. Jeffrey assures me that the house is often more chaotic than it looked on my visit. But cutting back on TV has changed the underlying tempo of family life from a frenetic *prestissimo* to a more dignified *moderato.* "There is definitely a calmness that wasn't there before," says Susan. "We still lead active, interesting lives. The difference is that we no longer rush around like headless chickens all the time."

In a world obsessed with doing everything faster, though, some will find it easier than others to bring up their children in a Slow fashion. Some forms of deceleration come at a price not everyone can afford. You need money to send a child to a private school that takes a Slow approach to learning. To make the time for home education, at least one parent has to work less, which is not an option for every family. Nevertheless, many ways to put a child on the Slow track are free. Cutting back on TV or extracurricular activities, for instance, costs nothing.

Rather than cash, though, the main barrier to Slow child-rearing—indeed to Slow anything—is the modern mindset. The urge to fast-track kids still runs deep. Instead of welcoming official efforts to ease the workload in classrooms, many Japanese parents make their children spend even longer at local cram schools. Across the industrial world, parents and politicians remain in thrall to exam results.

Rescuing the next generation from the cult of speed means reinventing our whole philosophy of childhood, much as the Romantics did two centuries ago. More freedom and fluidity in education, more emphasis on learning as a pleasure, more room for unstructured play, less obsession with making every second count, less pressure to mimic adult mores. Grown-ups can certainly do their bit by curbing the urge to hyper-parent and by setting a Slow example in their own lives. None of these steps are easy to take. But the evidence is that taking them is well worth it.

Nicola Barnes is glad her son, Jack, no longer rushes around trying to do as much as he can with every single moment of the day. "It's such an important lesson to learn, for children and adults," she says. "Life is just better when you know how to slow down."

FINDING THE *TEMPO GIUSTO*

*The whole struggle of life is to some extent a struggle
about how slowly or how quickly to do each thing.*
—STEN NADOLNY, AUTHOR OF
THE DISCOVERY OF SLOWNESS (1996)

IN 1898, MORGAN ROBERTSON published *Futility,* an
eerily prescient novel about the folly of pursuing the
transatlantic speed record at any cost. The story begins
when a company unveils the largest cruise liner ever built,
a "practically unsinkable" craft capable of travelling the
high seas at full throttle in any weather. On its maiden voyage, though, the ship slices through another vessel. A witness to the accident decries the "wanton destruction of life
and property for the sake of speed." The name of the fic-
tional ship was *Titan.* Fourteen years later, in 1912, the
Titanic slammed into an iceberg, killing more than fifteen
hundred people.

The sinking of the unsinkable *Titanic* had all the mak-
ings of a wake-up call to a world in thrall to speed. Many
hoped the tragedy would force mankind to pause for

breath, to take a long hard look at the cult of acceleration and see that the time had come to slow down a little.

It was not to be. A century later, the world is still straining to do everything faster—and paying a heavy price for it. The toll taken by the hurry-up culture is well documented. We are driving the planet and ourselves towards burnout. We are so time-poor and time-sick that we neglect our friends, families and partners. We barely know how to enjoy things any more because we are always looking ahead to the next thing. Much of the food we eat is bland and unhealthy. With our children caught up in the same hailstorm of hurry, the future looks bleak.

Yet all is not lost. There is still time to change course. Though speed, busyness and an obsession with saving time remain the hallmarks of modern life, a powerful backlash is brewing. The Slow movement is on the march. Instead of doing everything faster, many people are decelerating, and finding that Slowness helps them to live, work, think and play better.

But is the Slow movement really a movement? It certainly has all the ingredients that academics look for—popular sympathy, a blueprint for a new way of life, grassroots action. True, the Slow movement has no formal structure, and still suffers from low brand recognition. Many people slow down—working fewer hours, say, or finding time to cook—without feeling part of a global crusade. Yet every act of deceleration is grist to the mill.

Italy may be the closest thing the Slow movement has to a spiritual home. With its emphasis on pleasure and leisure, the traditional Mediterranean way of life is a natural anti-dote to speed. Slow Food, Slow Cities and Slow Sex all have Italian roots. Yet the Slow movement is not about turning the whole planet into a Mediterranean holiday resort. Most of us do not wish to replace the cult of speed with the cult of slowness. Speed can be fun, productive and powerful, and we would be poorer without it. What the world needs, and what the Slow movement offers, is a middle path, a recipe for marrying *la dolce vita* with the dynamism of the information age. The secret is balance: instead of doing everything faster, do everything at the right speed. Sometimes fast. Sometimes slow. Sometimes somewhere in between. Being Slow means never rushing, never striving to save time just for the sake of it. It means remaining calm and unflustered even when circumstances force us to speed up. One way to cultivate inner Slowness is to make time for activities that defy acceleration—medi-tation, knitting, gardening, yoga, painting, reading, walk-ing, Chi Kung.

There is no one-size-fits-all formula for slowing down, no universal guide to the right speed. Each person, act, moment has its own *eigenzeit*. Some people are content to live at a speed that would send the rest of us to an early grave. We all must have the right to choose the pace that makes us happy. As Uwe Kliemt, the Tempo Giusto pianist, says, "The world is a richer place when we make room for different speeds."

Of course, the Slow movement still faces some pretty daunting obstacles—not least our own prejudices. Even when we long to slow down, we feel constrained by a mixture of greed, inertia and fear to keep up the pace. In a world hardwired for speed, the tortoise still has a lot of persuading to do.

Critics dismiss the Slow movement as a passing fad, or as a fringe philosophy that will never go mainstream. Certainly, the call for less speed has not stopped the world's acceleration since the Industrial Revolution. And many who embraced slowness in the 1960s and 1970s spent the 1980s and 1990s racing to catch up. When the global economy starts to roar again, or when the next dotcom-style boom comes along, will all the talk of slowing down go out the window as everyone rushes to make a quick buck? Don't bet on it. More than any generation before us, we understand the danger and futility of constant acceleration and are more determined than ever to roll back the cult of speed. Demographics are also on the side of deceleration. Across the developed world, populations are aging, and as we get older most of us have one thing in common: slowing down.

The Slow movement has its own momentum. Saying no to speed takes courage, and people are more likely to take the plunge knowing they are not alone, that others share the same vision and are taking the same risks. The Slow movement provides strength in numbers. Every time a group like Slow Food or the Society for the Deceleration of Time makes headlines, it becomes a little easier for the rest of us to question speed. What's more, once people reap the rewards of slowing down in one sphere of life they often go on to apply the same lesson in others. Alice Waters, founder of the celebrated Chez Panisse restaurant in Berkeley, California, is a star of the Slow Food movement. In 2003, she began lecturing on the merits of Slow Schooling. People are connecting the dots at the grass roots level, too. After discovering the unhurried pleasures of Tantric sex, Roger Kimber cut back on his work schedule. For Claire Wood, giving up her high-powered job in insurance to make soap went hand in hand with home-educating her daughter, Beth. Using Chi Kung to slow down on the squash court taught business professor Jim Hughes to take his time on consulting jobs and in the classroom. Switching off her mobile in the evening inspired banker Jill Hancock to take up cooking. "Once you start challenging the go-go-never-stop mindset at work, you start challenging it everywhere," she says. "You just want to go deeper into things, instead of just skimming along on the surface."

That sense that something is missing from our lives underpins the global yearning for Slowness. Whether that "something" goes deeper than a better quality of life, however, remains an open question. Many find that slowing down has a spiritual dimension. But many others do not. The Slow movement is broad enough to accommodate both. In any case, the gap between the two may not be as wide as it seems. The great benefit of slowing down is reclaiming the time and tranquility to make meaningful connections—with people, with culture, with work, with nature, with our own bodies and minds. Some call that living better. Others would describe it as spiritual.

The Slow movement certainly implies a questioning of the untrammelled materialism that drives the global economy. This is why critics think we cannot afford it, or that slowing down will remain a lifestyle perk for the rich. It is true that some manifestations of the Slow philosophy—alternative medicine, pedestrianized neighbourhoods, free-range beef—do not fit every budget. But most do. Spending more time with friends and family costs nothing. Nor does walking, cooking, meditating, making love, reading or eating dinner at the table instead of in front of the television. Simply resisting the urge to hurry is free.

Nor is the Slow movement inimical to capitalism. On the contrary, it offers it a lifeline. In its current form, global capitalism forces us to manufacture faster, work faster, consume faster, live faster, no matter what the cost. By treating people and the environment as valuable assets, rather than as disposable inputs, a Slow alternative could make the economy work for us, rather than vice versa. Slow capitalism might mean lower growth, a tough sell in a world obsessed with the Dow Jones index, but the notion that there is more to life than maximizing GDP, or winning the rat race, is gaining currency, especially in richer nations, where more and more people are considering the high cost of their frenetic lives.

In our hedonistic age, the Slow movement has a marketing ace up its sleeve: it peddles pleasure. The central tenet of the Slow philosophy is taking the time to do things properly, and thereby enjoy them more. Whatever its effect on the economic balance sheet, the Slow philosophy delivers the things that really make us happy: good health, a thriving environment, strong communities and relationships, freedom from perpetual hurry.

Persuading people of the merits of slowing down is only the beginning, however. Decelerating will be a struggle until we rewrite the rules that govern almost every sphere of life—the economy, the workplace, urban design, education, medicine. This will take a canny mix of gentle persuasion, visionary leadership, tough legislation and international consensus. It will be a challenge, but it is crucial. Already there are grounds for optimism. Collectively, we know our lives are too frantic, and we want to slow down. Individually, more of us are applying the brakes and finding that our quality of life improves. The big question now is when the individual will become the collective. When will the many personal acts of deceleration occurring across the world reach critical mass? When will the Slow movement turn into a Slow revolution?

To help the world reach that tipping point, each of us should try to make room for Slowness. A good place to start is by reassessing our relationship with time. Larry Dossey, the American doctor who coined the term "time-sickness," helps patients beat the condition by teaching them to step out of time, using biofeedback, meditation or prayer to engineer "time exits." By confronting the way the clock has ruled their lives, they are able to slow down. We can all learn from this. Try to think about time not as a finite resource that is always draining away, or as a bully to be feared or conquered, but as the benign element we live in.

Stop living every second as if Frederick Taylor were hovering nearby, checking his stopwatch and tut-tutting over his clipboard.

If we become less neurotic about time, we can start putting the twenty-four-hour society to more sensible use. At the beginning of this book, I argued that a world open round the clock is a world that invites hurry. Give us the chance to do anything, any time, and we will pack our schedules to bursting. But the twenty-four-hour society is not intrinsically evil. If we approach it in a Slow spirit— doing fewer things, with less hurry—it can give us the flexibility we need to decelerate.

When it comes to slowing down, it is best to start small. Cook a meal from scratch. Take a walk with a friend rather than dashing off to buy things you don't really need at the mall. Read the newspaper without switching on the TV. Add massage to your lovemaking. Or simply take a few minutes to sit still in a quiet place.

If a small act of Slowness feels good, move on to the bigger stuff. Rethink your working hours or campaign to make your neighbourhood more pedestrian-friendly. As life gets better, you will ask yourself the same question that I often do: Why didn't I slow down sooner?

Bit by bit, my own speedaholism is on the wane. Time no longer feels like a cruel and irresistible taskmaster. Working freelance helps, as does meditating and leaving my watch in the drawer. I cook, read and switch off my cellphone more often. Taking a less-is-more approach to my hobbies—no more tennis until my children are older—has eased the pressure to rush. Reminding myself that speed is not always the best policy, that haste is often pointless and even counterproductive, is enough to curb the acceleration reflex. Whenever I catch myself hurrying for the sake of it, I stop, take a deep breath and think: "There is no need to rush. Take it easy. Slow down."

People around me notice a difference. I used to hate supermarket checkouts, regarding them as an affront to my personal crusade for speed and efficiency. Women raking slowly through their purses for the right change were a particular bugbear. Now I find it easy to stand in line without fuming, even when other lines seem to be moving faster. I no longer fret over the "wasted" seconds or minutes. On a recent shopping trip, I actually found myself inviting the man behind me in the lineup to go first since he had fewer items. My wife was stunned. "You really are slowing down," she said, approvingly.

When I set out to write this book, though, the real litmus test for my own deceleration was whether I could take the hurry out of bedtime stories. The news is good. I can now read several books at a sitting without once worrying about the time or feeling the urge to skip a page. And I read slowly, savouring every word, heightening the drama or humour with assumed voices and facial expressions. My son, who is now four, loves it, and story time has become a meeting of minds rather than a war of words. The old "I want more stories!"/"No, that's enough!" sparring is gone.

One evening not long ago, something remarkable happened. I lay down on my son's bed to read him a long fairy tale about a giant. He had lots of questions, and we stopped to answer them all. Then I read an even longer story, this one about a dragon and a farmer's son. As I closed the book on the final page, it suddenly dawned on me that even though I had no idea how long I'd been reading—fifteen minutes, half an hour, maybe more—I was happy to continue. My flirtation with the One-Minute Bedtime Story was now a distant memory. I asked my son if he wanted me to read more. He rubbed his eyes. "Daddy, I think that's enough stories for tonight," he said. "I actually feel quite tired." He kissed me on the cheek and slid under his duvet. I dimmed the bedside lamp before leaving the room. Smiling, I walked slowly down the stairs.

NOTES

Introduction: The Age of Rage

"TIME-SICKNESS": Larry Dossey, *Space, Time and Medicine* (Boston: Shambhala Publications, 1982).

INNER PSYCHOLOGY OF SPEED: From my interview with Guy Claxton in July 2002.

KAMEI SHUJI: Scott North, "Karoshi and Converging Labor Relations in Japan and America," *Labor Center Reporter* 302.

AMPHETAMINES IN THE AMERICAN WORKPLACE: Based on work-place tests carried out by Quest Diagnostics in 2002.

SEVEN PERCENT OF SPANIARDS HAVE SIESTA: Reported in the *Official Journal of the American Academy of Neurology* (June 2002).

FATIGUE AND DISASTERS: Leon Kreitzman, *The 24-Hour Society* (London: Profile Books, 1999), p. 109.

MORE THAN FORTY THOUSAND PEOPLE DIE: Figures from European Commission.

WHAT MUSICIANS CALL TEMPO GIUSTO: Percy A. Scholes, *Oxford Companion to Music* (Oxford: Oxford University Press, 1997), p. 1,018.

Chapter 1: Do Everything Faster

BENEDICTINE MONKS: Jeremy Rifkin, *Time Wars: The Primary Conflict in Human History* (New York: Touchstone, 1987), p. 95.

UVATIARRU: Jay Griffiths, "Boo to Captain Clock," *New Internationalist* 343, March 2002.

COLOGNE CLOCK: Gerhard Dorn-Van Rossum, *History of the Hour: Clocks and Modern Temporal Orders* (Chicago: University of Chicago Press, 1996), pp. 234–35.

LEON ALBERTI: Allen C. Bluedorn, *The Human Organization of Time: Temporal Realities and Experience* (Stanford: Stanford University Press, 2002), p. 227.

CREATION OF GLOBAL STANDARD TIME: Clark Blaise, *Time Lord: The Remarkable Canadian Who Missed His Train, and Changed the World* (Toronto: Knopf, 2000).

PROMOTING PUNCTUALITY AS A CIVIC DUTY: Robert Levine, *A Geography of Time: The Temporal Adventures of a Social Psychologist* (New York: Basic Books, 1997), pp. 67–70.

FREDERICK TAYLOR: Ibid, pp. 71–72.

VELOCITIZATION: Mark Kingwell, "Fast Forward: Our High-Speed Chase to Nowhere," *Harper's Magazine* (May 1998).

FIVE-HUNDRED MILLION NANOSECONDS: Tracy Kidder, *The Soul of a New Machine* (Boston: Little, Brown, 1981), p. 137.

Chapter 2: Slow Is Beautiful

DELETERIOUS EFFECTS OF SPEED: Stephen Kern, *The Culture of Time and Space, 1880–1918* (Cambridge, MA: Harvard University Press, 1983), pp. 125–26.

"BICYCLE FACE": Ibid, p. 111.

Chapter 3: Food: Turning the Tables on Speed

AVERAGE MCDONALD'S MEAL ELEVEN MINUTES: Nicci Gerrard, "The Politics of Thin," *The Observer*, 5 January 2003.

COMMUNAL DINING TOO SLOW: Margaret Visser, *The Rituals of Dinner: The Origins, Evolution, Eccentricities, and Meaning of*

Table Manners (New York: HarperCollins, 1991), p. 354.

PIGS SPED UP: Barbara Adam, *Timescapes of Modernity: The Environment and Invisible Hazards,* Global Environmental Change Series (New York: Routledge, 1998).

SALMON GROW FASTER: James Meek, "Britain Urged To Ban GM Salmon," *Guardian,* 4 September 2002.

TAD'S 30 VARIETIES OF MEALS: Eric Schlosser, *Fast Food Nation: The Dark Side of the All-American Meal* (New York: Penguin, 2001), p. 114.

RÉSTAURATION RAPIDE: Adam Sage, *"Au Revoir* to the Leisurely Lunch," [London] *Times,* 16 October 2002.

E-COLI POISONING FROM HAMBURGERS: Schlosser, *Fast Food Nation,* pp. 196–99.

DWINDLING ARTICHOKE VARIETIES: Figures from Renato Sardo, Director of Slow Food International, quoted by Anna Muoio in "We All Go to the Same Place. Let Us Go There Slowly," *Fast Company,* 5 January 2002.

YACON SUGARS UNMETABOLIZED: National Research Council, *Lost Crops of the Incas: Little-Known Plants of the Andes with Promise for Worldwide Cultivation* (Washington, DC: National Academy Press, 1989), p. 115.

BUSINESS LUNCH LASTS THIRTY-SIX MINUTES: Based on a survey by *Fast Company* magazine.

KWAKIUTL PEOPLE ON FAST EATING: Visser, *Rituals of Dinner,* p. 323.

PATRICK SEROG ON SLOW EATING: Sage, *"Au Revoir."*

ITALIAN CELLPHONE AND FOOD SPENDING: Interview with Carlo Petrini in the *New York Times,* 26 July 2003.

Chapter 4: Cities: Blending Old and New

FIFTEEN HUNDRED PEOPLE FLEE BRITISH CITIES WEEKLY: Based on the 2004 report *Social and Economic Change and Diversity in Rural England* by the Rural Evidence Research Centre.

"URBAN TIME POLICIES": Jean-Yves Boulin and Ulrich Muckenberger, *Times in the City and Quality of Life* (Brussels: European Foundation for the Improvement of Living and Working Conditions, 1999).

WAR ON NOISE IN EUROPE: Emma Daly, "Trying to Quiet Another City That Barely Sleeps," *New York Times,* 7 October 2002.

TRAFFIC AFFECTS COMMUNITY SPIRIT: Donald Appleyard, a professor of Urban Design at the University of California, Berkeley, pioneered research on this subject in 1970.

FLOW TO SUBURBIA SLOWS: Phillip J. Longman, "American Gridlock," *US News and World Report,* 28 May 2001.

PORTLAND MOST LIVEABLE CITY: Charles Siegel, *Slow Is Beautiful: Speed Limits as Political Decisions on Urban Form* (Berkeley: Preservation Institute Policy Study, 1996).

Chapter 5: Mind/Body: Mens Sana in Corpore Sano

RELAXATION A PRECURSOR OF SLOW THINKING: Guy Claxton, *Hare Brain, Tortoise Mind: Why Intelligence Increases When You Think Less* (London: Fourth Estate, 1997), pp. 76–77.

GREATEST THINKERS THINK SLOW: Ibid, p. 4.

TRANSCENDENTAL MEDITATION CUTS HOSPITALIZATION RATES: Results of five-year study of two thousand people across the United States, published in *Psychosomatic Medicine* 49 (1987).

"BEING IN THE ZONE": Robert Levine, *A Geography of Time: The Temporal Adventures of a Social Psychologist* (New York: Basic Books, 1997), pp. 33–34.

FIFTEEN MILLION AMERICANS PRACTISE YOGA: Based on a survey conducted by Harris Interactive Service Bureau for *Yoga Journal* in 2003.

"WALKING TAKES LONGER . . .": Edward Abbey, *The Journey Home: Some Words in Defense of the American West* (New York: Dutton, 1977), p. 205.

SUPERSLOW WORKOUT BOOSTS HDL CHOLESTEROL: Letter submitted to Health101.org by Philip Alexander, M.D., Chief of Medical Staff, College Station Medical Center Faculty, Texas A&M University, College of Medicine.

Chapter 6: Medicine: Doctors and Patience

"BEEPER MEDICINE": James Gleick, *Faster: The Acceleration of Everything* (New York: Random House, 1999), p. 85.

2002 FERTILITY STUDY: Conducted by David Dunson of the National Institute of Environmental Health Sciences in North Carolina, pooling data from seven European cities.

CAM PRACTITIONERS OUTNUMBER GPs: Figures released in 1998 by the British Medical Association.

Chapter 7: Sex: A Lover with a Slow Hand

HALF AN HOUR PER WEEK DEVOTED TO MAKING LOVE: A 1994 study carried out by researchers at the University of Chicago. Cited in James Gleick, *Faster: The Acceleration of Everything* (New York: Random House, 1999), p. 127.

WHAM-BAM-THANK-YOU-MA'AM: See Judith Mackay, *The Penguin Atlas of Human Sexual Behavior* (New York: Penguin Books, 2000), p. 20.

ARVIND AND SHANTA KALE: Quoted in Val Sampson, *Tantra: The Art of Mind-Blowing Sex* (London: Vermillion, 2002), p. 112.

MARITAL PROBLEMS HURT PRODUCTIVITY: Melinda Forthofer, Howard Markman, Martha Cox, Scott Stanley and Ronald Kessler, "Associations Between Marital Distress and Work Loss in a National Sample," *Journal of Marriage and the Family* 58 (August 1996), p. 597.

Chapter 8: Work: The Benefits of Working Less Hard

BENJAMIN FRANKLIN ON SHORTER WORK HOURS: John De Graaf, David Wann and Thomas H. Naylor, *Affluenza: The All-Consuming Epidemic* (San Francisco: Berrett-Koehler, 2001), p. 129.

GEORGE BERNARD SHAW PREDICTED: From a paper delivered by Benjamin Kline Hunnicutt at Symposium on Overwork: Causes and Consequences in Baltimore MA, 11–13 March 1999.

RICHARD NIXON FOUR-DAY WEEK: Dennis Kaplan and Sharon Chelton, "Is It Time to Dump the Forty-Hour Week?," *Conscious Choice,* September 1996.

US SENATE FORECASTS SHORTER WORK HOURS:: De Graaf, *Affluenza,* p. 41.

WHILE AMERICANS WORK AS MUCH: According to figures from the International Labor Organization and the Organization for Economic Cooperation and Development, American working hours rose between 1980 and 2000, then tapered off slightly as the economy slumped.

AVERAGE AMERICAN NOW PUTS IN 350 HOURS MORE: John De Graaf, Take Back Your Time Day website www.timeday.org.

US SUPPLANTED JAPAN IN WORK HOURS: Based on figures from International Labor Organization.

ONE IN FIVE THIRTY-SOMETHING BRITONS: From a national overtime survey commissioned in 2002 by Britain's Department of Trade and Industry and *Management Today* magazine.

MARILYN MACHLOWITZ ON WORKAHOLISM: Matthew Reiss, "American Karoshi," *New Internationalist* 343 (March 2002).

MORE THAN 15% OF CANADIANS ON BRINK OF SUICIDE: Based on an Ipsos-Reid survey carried out in 2002.

BELGIUM, FRANCE AND NORWAY PRODUCTIVITY: Hourly productivity figures based on statistics from the 2003 report from the International Labor Organization.

70% OF PEOPLE WANTED BETTER WORK-LIFE BALANCE: Survey published in 2002 by Andrew Oswald of Warwick University (UK) and David Blanchflower of Dartmouth College (US).

GENERATION FUREETA: Robert Whymant, [London] *Times* magazine, 4 May 2002.

THE AVERAGE GERMAN SPENDS 15% LESS TIME: Based on figures from the International Labor Organization.

LANDMARK POLL ON THIRTY-FIVE-HOUR WEEK: Conducted by CSA (Conseil Sondages Analyses) for *L'Expansion* magazine (September 2003).

JAPAN STUDYING "DUTCH MODEL": Asako Murakami, "Work Sharing Solves Netherlands' Woes," *Japan Times,* 18 May 2002.

PREFER TO WORK FEWER HOURS THAN WIN LOTTERY: From a national overtime survey commissioned in 2002 by Britain's

Department of Trade and Industry and Management Today magazine.

TWICE AS MANY AMERICANS WOULD CHOOSE TIME OFF: Survey conducted by Yankelovich Partners, Inc.

CANADIANS WHO WORKED LESS HAD MORE MONEY: Survey carried out in 1997–98 by Communications, Energy and Paperworkers Union of Canada.

MARRIOTT HOTEL CHAIN'S PILOT PROJECT: Bill Munck, "Changing a Culture of Face Time," *Harvard Business Review* (November 2001).

DONALD HENSRUD: Anne Fisher, "Exhausted All the Time? Still Getting Nowhere?" *Fortune,* 18 March 2002.

A RECENT STUDY BY NASA: Jane E. Brody, "New Respect for the Nap, a Pause That Refreshes," *Science Times,* 4 January 2000.

CHURCHILL ON NAPPING: Walter Graebner, *My Dear Mister Churchill* (London: Michael Joseph, 1965).

Chapter 9: Leisure: The Importance of Being at Rest

PLATO BELIEVED HIGHEST FORM OF LEISURE: Josef Pieper, *Leisure: The Basis of Culture* (South Bend, IN: St. Augustine's Press, 1998), p. 141.

" . . . ROLL IN ECSTASY . . .": Franz Kafka, translator Malcolm Pasley, *The Collected Aphorisms* (London: Syrens, Penguin, 1994), p. 27.

MORE THAN FOUR MILLION AMERICANS: Knitting figures from the Craft Yarn Council of America.

MENTAL EQUIVALENT OF SUPERSLOW EXERCISE: Taken from Cecilia Howard's Cloudwatcher's Journal at www.morelife.org/ cloudwatcher/cloudwatch_112001.html.

LISZT TOOK "PRESQUE UNE HEURE": Grete Wehmeyer, *Prestississimo: The Rediscovery of Slowness in Music* (Hamburg: Rowolth, 1993). (In German.)

MOZART TEMPO TANTRUM: Uwe Kliemt, "On Reasonable Tempi," essay published on the Tempo Giusto website at www.tempogiusto.de.

BEETHOVEN ON VIRTUOSOS: Ibid.

RICHARD ELEN: His review appeared on www.audiorevolution.com.

ORCHESTRAS MUCH LOUDER: Norman Lebrecht, "Turn It Down!," *Evening Standard,* 21 August 2002.

Chapter 10: Children: Raising an Unhurried Child

SLEEP-DEPRIVED KIDS HAVE TROUBLE MAKING FRIENDS: Samantha Levine, "Up Too Late," *US News and World Report,* 9 September 2002.

EAST ASIAN WORK ETHIC BACKFIRING: "Asian Schools Go Back to the Books," *Time,* 9 April 2002.

FINLAND ROUTINELY TOPS WORLD RANKINGS: John Crace, "Heaven and Helsinki," *Guardian,* 16 September 2003.

Conclusion: Finding the Tempo Giusto

WHOLE STRUGGLE OF LIFE: From my interview with Sten Nadolny in 2003.

FUTILITY, AN EERILY PRESCIENT NOVEL: Stephen Kern, *The Culture of Time and Space, 1880–1918* (Cambridge, MA: Harvard University Press, 1983), p. 110.

RESOURCE LIST

I read many books and articles for my research into speed, time and slowness. Below are those that stood out. Though some are academic, most are aimed at the general reader. Farther down is a list of useful websites. These are a good starting point for exploring the benefits of slowness and for connecting with people who are slowing down.

BOOKS

Blaise, Clark. *Time Lord: The Remarkable Canadian Who Missed His Train, and Changed the World.* Toronto: Knopf Canada, 2000.

Bluedorn, Allen C. *The Human Organization of Time: Temporal Realities and Experience.* Stanford: Stanford Business Books, 2002.

Boorstin, Daniel J. *The Discoverers: A History of Man's Search to Know His World and Himself.* New York: Random House, 1983.

Claxton, Guy. *Hare Brain, Tortoise Mind: Why Intelligence Increases When You Think Less.* London: Fourth Estate, 1997.

De Graaf, John, David Wann and Thomas Naylor. *Affluenza: The All-Consuming Epidemic.* San Francisco: Berrett-Koehler, 2001.

Gleick, James. *Faster: The Acceleration of Everything.* New York: Random House, 1999.

Glouberman, Dina. *The Joy of Burnout: How the End of the Road Can Be a New Beginning.* London: Hodder and Stoughton, 2002.

Hirsh-Pasek, Kathy, and Roberta Michnik Golinkoff. *Einstein*

Never Used Flashcards: How Our Children Learn—and Why They Need to Play More and Memorize Less. Emmaus, PA: Rodale, 2003.

Hutton, Will. *The World We're In.* London: Little, Brown, 2002.

James, Matt. *The City Gardener.* London: HarperCollins, 2003.

Kern, Stephen. *The Culture of Time and Space, 1880–1918.* Cambridge, MA: Harvard University Press, 1983.

Kerr, Alex. *Dogs and Demons: The Fall of Modern Japan.* New York: Penguin, 2001.

Kreitzman, Leon. *The 24-Hour Society.* London: Profile Books, 1999.

Kummer, Corby. *The Pleasures of Slow Food: Celebrating Authentic Traditions, Flavors, and Recipes.* San Francisco: Chronicle Books, 2002.

Kundera, Milan. *Slowness.* London: Faber and Faber, 1996.

Levine, Robert. *A Geography of Time: The Temporal Misadventures of a Social Scientist.* New York: Basic Books, 1997.

McDonnell, Kathleen. *Honey, We Lost the Kids: Rethinking Childhood in the Multimedia Age.* Toronto: Second Story Press, 2001.

Meiskins, Peter, and Peter Whalley. *Putting Work In Its Place: A Quiet Revolution.* Ithaca: Cornell University Press, 2002.

Millar, Jeremy, and Michael Schwartz (editors). *Speed: Visions of an Accelerated Age.* London: The Photographers' Gallery, 1998.

Murphy, Bernadette. *Zen and the Art of Knitting: Exploring the Links Between Knitting, Spirituality and Creativity.* Avon: Adams Media Corporation, 2002.

Nadolny, Sten. *The Discovery of Slowness.* Revised edition. Edinburgh: Canongate Books, 2003.

Oiwa, Keibo. *Slow is Beautiful.* Tokyo: Heibon-sha, 2001. (In Japanese only.)

Petrini, Carlo. *Slow Food: Collected Thoughts on Taste, Tradition, and the Honest Pleasures of Food.* White River Jct., VT: Chelsea Green Publishing Co, 2001.

Pieper, Josef. *Leisure: The Basis of Culture.* South Bend, IN: St. Augustine's Press, 1998.

Putnam, Robert D. *Bowling Alone: The Collapse and Revival of American Community.* New York: Simon & Schuster, 2001.

Rifkin, Jeremy. *Time Wars: The Primary Conflict in Human History.* New York: Touchstone, 1987.

Russell, Bertrand. *In Praise of Idleness.* London: Routledge, 2001.

Sampson, Val. *Tantra: The Art of Mind-Blowing Sex.* London: Vermillion, 2002.

Schlosser, Eric. *Fast Food Nation: The Dark Side of the All-American Meal.* New York: Penguin, 2002.

Visser, Margaret. *The Rituals of Dinner: The Origins, Evolution, Eccentricities, and Meaning of Table Manners.* New York: HarperCollins, 1991.

MAGAZINES

Kingwell, Mark. "Fast Forward: Our High-Speed Chase to Nowhere." *Harper's Magazine,* May 1998.

WEBSITES

General

www.zeitverein.com (Society for the Deceleration of Time, Austria)

www.slothclub.org/index02.html (Japan)

www.slow-life.net (Japan)

www.longnow.org (US)

www.simpleliving.net (US)

Food

www.slowfood.com (Italy)

www.farmersmarkets.net (UK)

www.cafecreosote.com/Farmers_Markets/index.php3 (US)

www. marketplace.chef2chef.net/farmer-markets/canada.htm
    (Canada)

Cities

www.matogmer.no/slow_cities__citta_slow.htm
    (Slow Cities, Italy)

www.homezones.org (UK)

www.newurbanism.org (North America)

Mind/Body

www.tm.org (Transcendental Meditation, US)

www.webcom.com/~imcuk/ (International Meditation Centres)

www.qi-flow-golf.com (Chi Kung for golfers, UK)

www.superslow.com (Exercise, US)

Medicine

www.pitt.edu/~cbw/altm.html (Complementary and Alternative
    Medicine, US)

www.haleclinic.com (UK)

www.slowhealing.com (UK)

Sex

www.slowsex.it (Italy)

www.tantra.com (US)

www.diamondlighttantra.com (UK)

Work

www.swt.org (Shorter Work Time Group, US)

www.worktolive.info (US)

www.employersforwork-lifebalance.org.uk (UK)

www.worklessparty.ca (Canada)

www.timeday.org (US)

Leisure

www.tvturnoff.org (US)

www.ausweb.scu.edu.au/aw01/papers/edited/burnett/ (Slow
    Reading, Canada)

www.tempogiusto.de (Germany)

Children

www.pdkintl.org/kappan/k0212hol.htm (Slow Schooling, US)

www.nhen.org (Home Education, US)

www.home-education.org.uk (UK)

www.flora.org/homeschool.ca (Canada)

ACKNOWLEDGMENTS

I could not have written this book without help from many people.

My investigation into the Slow movement began with a series of articles in the *National Post* and I am grateful to my former editor there, John Geiger. With his deft touch, Patrick Walsh, my agent, made writing the book possible. Michael Schellenberg was a superb editor, patient, insightful and meticulous. Louise Dennys and Angelika Glover at Knopf Canada, Gideon Weil at HarperCollins San Francisco and Sue Sumeraj, my copyeditor, also helped to whip the book into shape.

I am indebted to the hundreds of people who took the time to share their stories, views and expertise with me. Only some are named in the book, but every single interview added another piece to the puzzle. A special thanks to Lou Abato; Danira Caleta; Jeff Crump; Diane Dorney; Kyoko Goto; Kathy Hirsh-Pasek; Uwe Kliemt; George Popper; Carlo Petrini and everyone at Slow Food; David Rooney; Val Sampson; Alberto Vitale and Gabriele Wulff.

I would like to thank my parents for their encouragement, and for helping to fine-tune the book. Most of all, I am grateful to my wife, Miranda France, for her unstinting support, her way with words and her knack for seeing the funny side of things.

INDEX

Plus:

Afterword

A few days after *In Praise of Slowness* came out in Spain, my publisher there made a confession. The marketing manager broke the news at the end of a long, languid lunch in Barcelona. "I'm not sure how to tell you this," she said, staring into her empty wineglass. "But we also publish One-Minute Bedtime stories—and they sell like hotcakes."

My first reaction was disbelief. My second was to join in the laughter sweeping round the table: the irony was simply too rich to resist. Later, though, the revelation got me thinking.

In the final chapter of this book, I asked a question: When will the Slow movement turn into a Slow revolution? The enduring popularity of the One-Minute Bedtime series suggests that we still have some way to go.

There is plenty of evidence that the world remains stuck in fast-forward. Not long ago a literary critic announced that he could no longer read poetry because it was "too slow." A few days later, police in California pulled over a woman who was driving down the highway at 70 mph while also typing a letter on her laptop. And just when you think multitasking cannot get any more absurd, it does: a health club near my home in London has introduced speed-dating yoga soirees where time-starved singletons vet potential partners and salute the sun at the same time.

The media still pump out the message that faster is better. On my first book tour of the United States, I saw a magazine peddling sex tips that made a mockery of the Pointer Sisters' plea for a lover with a slow hand. "How To Bring Your Partner to Orgasm In 30 Seconds!" the headline screamed.

The more everyone else bangs on about how fast the world is, the more we assume that slowing down is impossible. Speed becomes a self-fulfilling prophecy.

Thankfully, though, there is another side to the story. Since *In Praise of Slowness* came out, the backlash against the cult of speed has gained momentum.

The book sparked a debate. Since publication I have done hundreds of print, radio and television interviews around the world—and the requests continue to pour in. I also speak at conferences, in classrooms and on the after-dinner circuit. Everybody wants to know more about slowness, and they want to know right now.

Of course, this throws up another irony. What began as a two-week book tour now feels more like a full-time job. Between hikes up e-mail mountain, I zoom around telling everyone how wonderful it is to slow down.

But it seems a small price to pay. Something big is afoot, the first rumblings of a cultural revolution. Everywhere, people are challenging the canard that faster is better and that every moment must be filled with activity—and many are doing so under the Slow banner.

In fall 2004, Canberra, the capital of Australia, held its first Slow Festival, with walks, readings, meditation workshops and long meals, as well as lectures on how slowness has a role to play in everything from education to the workplace. The organizers plan to make it an annual event. Throughout the year, a new group called Slow Downunder runs workshops to help Australians unleash their inner tortoise at work, home, and play.

Poland now has a Voluntary Slowness Movement, complete with a snazzy website

Plus: **Insights, Interviews, and More**

> *"Once you start looking, you notice Americans warming to a slower tempo in all kinds of ways."*

and online chat room where young people swap tips on how to say no to speed. A Canadian group called SlowBiz is making the case for deceleration in the corporate world. Spain is finally rediscovering its passion for the siesta, with hard-nosed companies boosting productivity by encouraging staff to nap during the workday.

Since the book came out, some commentators have tried to paint the Slow movement as a mainly European phenomenon. They could not be more wrong. Life in the US may be faster than anywhere else, but that does not mean Americans are happy about feeling rushed all the time.

Look at the opinion polls, read the letters in the newspaper, sift through the Internet blogs, scan the bestseller lists, eavesdrop round the water cooler, at the playground or in the gym—Americans are fed up with living in roadrunner mode, and eager to relearn the lost art of slowness.

The evidence is everywhere. Slower forms of exercise, from yoga to SuperSlow weight-lifting, continue to win adherents, as do meditation and alternative medicine. New Urbanism marches on. Slow Food now has thirteen thousand members in the US—more than any other country outside Italy.

Even the American appetite for technology is reaching its limits. In early 2005, the Federal Aviation Authority mooted lifting the ban on cell phone use in airplanes. Instead of a surge of public approval—"Now I can call the office or text my partner from 30,000 feet!"—polls show that nearly 70% of travelers want to keep the ban. Why? Because many see the airplane as the last refuge, the one remaining place where they can still sleep, doodle, daydream or read without interruption.

"The plane is the final frontier," one road warrior told me. "It's the only place left where nobody can reach you and you can actually slow down a little. I don't want to lose that."

Once you start looking, you notice Americans warming to a slower tempo in all kinds of ways. Take the remarkable sales of *French Women Don't Get Fat: The Secret of Eating For Pleasure*. Mireille Guiliano's manual preaches the same message as Slow Food: that the way to eat well and stay healthy is to consume modest servings at a leisurely pace. Those slim French women you see swishing through the streets of Paris never eat standing up or in front of their computers. A quick lunch from a drive-thru? Non, merci.

The fight-back against hyperparenting is also gathering steam. In towns across the US, community leaders are pushing for sports leagues that put fun before winning, participation before long hours of practice. The mayor of Minneapolis is spearheading a campaign to encourage families to eat dinner together four nights a week. More and more elite colleges are urging youngsters to stop overloading themselves in pursuit of the perfect resume. The Massachusetts Institute of Technology has even shrunk the section devoted to extracurricular activities on its application form.

The word "slow" is worming its way into the American vernacular as shorthand for a more balanced way of doing things. Woody Tasch, a leading ethical investor, proposes backing companies that think long-term and serve more than just their own bottom line. He calls this the Slow Money approach.

In *Time* magazine, meanwhile, the critic Robert Hughes lamented that much of modern art is as a disposable and nourishing as a Big Mac. "We have had a gutful of fast art and fast food," he thundered. "What we need more of is slow art: art that holds time as a vase holds water: art that . . . (makes) . . . you think and feel; art . . . that doesn't get its

"Most of us, and that includes Americans, have had a gutful of fast food, fast sex, fast exercise, fast relationships, fast work, fast medicine, fast everything."

message across in ten seconds . . . that hooks onto something deep-running in our natures."

Art is just the tip of the iceberg. Most of us, and that includes Americans, have had a gutful of fast food, fast sex, fast exercise, fast relationships, fast work, fast medicine, fast everything. But despite the toll that rusha-holism takes, we still find it hard to slow down. Fear often holds us back—fear of being ridiculed, left behind or just plain bored. The taboo against slowness remains.

Nowhere is that more apparent than in the workplace, especially in the US. Yet even Americans are starting to question their own workaholism. Polls show a growing willing-ness to sacrifice income for more time off, and work-life balance schemes continue to spread. Groups like Take Back Your Time Day are winning more attention in the national media. Meanwhile, leading American com-panies have been forced to dig deeper into their pockets to fight lawsuits from employ-ees claiming they were forced to work unpaid overtime.

When it comes to selling the Slow philos-ophy, corporate America may be the hardest nut to crack, but at least the pressure is mounting.

> *"Despite the setbacks and contradictions, Europe is building an economy where its citizens can work hard without being forced to work too much."*

The picture is mixed in Europe, too. With much of the EU suffering from sluggish economic growth, calls have gone up for Europeans to work longer hours. In 2005, for instance, the French government relaxed the thirty-five-hour limit on the working week.

But rumors of the demise of leisure in Europe have been greatly exaggerated. Many of the continent's economic woes cannot be blamed on shorter working hours, and no serious politician here suggests that Europeans should put in as much time on the job as do Americans. Even the reform of the thirty-five-hour limit in France is more modest than some observers have made out: it simply removed the ban on overtime in the private sector. The French regime was always too rigid for its own good.

Most importantly, though, the EU still supports a forty-eight-hour limit on the working week across the continent. This is even starting to bring relief to some of Europe's most overworked citizens. In Britain, for example, junior doctors have waved goodbye to ninety-hour weeks.

Despite the setbacks and contradictions, Europe is building an economy where its citizens can work hard without being forced to work too much.

I feel more optimistic now than I did when *In Praise of Slowness* was published. One reason is that its message has struck a chord far beyond the industrial world. You might expect that developing countries would have little interest in slowness, that their only priority would be to catch up with the West as quickly as possible. But it turns out that this is not the case. Nations that are racing toward modernity, including behemoths such as India, China and Brazil, are now starting to debate the pros and cons of speed. That means the Slow movement has a global reach.

My spirits are also buoyed by the e-mails that flow into my Web site. They come from around the world, and from people in all walks of life. I hear from mayors, business executives and academics, clerics, social workers and teachers, tech-heads, athletes and teenagers. What unites them all is a desire to live better, and to make the world a better place, by slowing down.

Some of the e-mails are poignant. One woman told me how she realized she needed to slow down when her three-year-old daughter began hiding her laptop. Many recount how a roadrunner lifestyle made them ill or sabotaged their relationships.

Plus: **Insights, Interviews, and More**

One American father wrote to me after he crashed the car with his two children in the back seat. He was doing 10 mph over the speed limit at the time.

"Sitting in the hospital waiting to see if my kids were going to be okay was the darkest moment of my life," he told me. "After that, slowing down was a no-brainer."

Many people love the idea of slowness but question whether we really can put on the brakes, or whether hurry is now hardwired into our DNA. I draw hope from other movements that have brought about social revolutions that seemed impossible in their time.

"Speed still has the upper hand but the pressure for change is building. The tipping point may not be as far away as we think."

Look at feminism. Forty years ago, when a few rebels challenged whether women should be second-class citizens, they were vilified or ignored. The mainstream response was truculent: "Men have always enjoyed higher status and always will. That is the way the world is, and you can't change it." But the feminists refused to take no for an answer—and they ended up changing the world.

Sure, we are a long way from full gender equality, but we have made progress that was once unthinkable. Can you imagine a black woman serving as Secretary of State in

1950? Exactly. The world can change, even when it seems impossible.

I think the Slow movement is at the same point that feminism was in the 1960s. Everywhere, people are waking up to the fact that the cult of speed is a bad thing. And now growing numbers of us are defying convention to embrace slowness. Speed still has the upper hand but the pressure for change is building. The tipping point may not be as far away as we think.

The nineteenth and twentieth centuries were all about speeding up. We now have it within our grasp to roll back the excesses and make slowing down the keynote of the twenty-first century.

Do we want to live in a world where every moment of the day is a race against the clock? Or do we want something better than One-Minute Bedtime stories for our children? The choice is ours. Let's choose to change the world.

—Carl Honoré
London
July 2005